ZANONI

Wildside books by
Edward George Bulwer-Lytton

Fiction

Eugene Aram
Pelham; Or, The Adventures of a Gentleman
Rienzi, the Last of the Roman Tribunes
Vril
The Lady of Lyons
The Last Days of Pompeii
Zanoni

ZANONI

EDWARD GEORGE BULWER-LYTTON

WILDSIDE PRESS
Doylestown, Pennsylvania

Zanoni
A publication of
Wildside Press
P.O. Box 301
Holicong, PA 18928-0301

www.wildsidepress.com

Dedicatory Epistle

First prefixed to the Edition of 1845

To
JOHN GIBSON, R.A., SCULPTOR.

*I*n looking round the wide and luminous circle of our great living Englishmen, to select one to whom I might fitly dedicate this work, — one who, in his life as in his genius, might illustrate the principle I have sought to convey; elevated by the ideal which he exalts, and serenely dwelling in a glorious existence with the images born of his imagination, — in looking round for some such man, my thoughts rested upon you. Afar from our turbulent cabals; from the ignoble jealousy and the sordid strife which degrade and acerbate the ambition of Genius, — in your Roman Home, you have lived amidst all that is loveliest and least perishable in the past, and contributed with the noblest aims, and in the purest spirit, to the mighty heirlooms of the future. Your youth has been devoted to toil, that your manhood may be consecrated to fame: a fame unsullied by one desire of gold. You have escaped the two worst perils that beset the artist in our time and land, — the debasing tendencies of commerce, and the angry rivalries of competition. You have not wrought your marble for the market, — you have not been tempted, by the praises which our vicious criticism has showered upon exaggeration and distortion, to lower your taste to the level of the hour; you have lived, and you have labored, as if you had no rivals but in the dead, — no purchasers, save in judges of what is best. In the divine priesthood of the beautiful, you have sought only to increase her worshippers and enrich her temples. The pupil of Canova, you have inherited his excellences, while you have shunned his errors, — yours his delicacy, not his affectation. Your heart resembles him even more than your genius: you have the same noble enthusiasm for your sublime profession; the same lofty freedom from envy, and the spirit that depreciates; the same generous desire not to war with but to serve artists in your art; aiding, strengthening, advising, elevating the timidity of inexperience, and the vague aspirations of youth. By the intuition of a kindred mind, you have equaled the learning of Winckelman, and the plastic poetry of Goethe, in the intimate comprehension of the antique. Each work of yours, rightly studied, is in itself a *criticism*, illustrating the sublime secrets of the Grecian Art, which, without the servility of plagiarism, you have contributed to revive amongst us; in you we behold its three great and long-undetected principles, — simplicity, calm, and concentration.

But your admiration of the Greeks has not led you to the bigotry of the mere antiquarian, nor made you less sensible of the unappreciated excellence of the mighty modern, worthy to be your countryman, — though till his statue is in the streets of our capital, we show ourselves not worthy of the glory he has shed upon our land. You have not suffered even your gratitude to Canova to blind you to the superiority of Flaxman. When we become sensible of our title deeds to renown in that single name, we may look for an English public capable of real patronage to English Art, — and not till then.

I, artist in words, dedicate, then, to you, artist whose ideas speak in marble, this well-loved work of my matured manhood. I love it not the less because it has been little understood and superficially judged by the common herd: it was not meant for them. I love it not the more because it has found enthusiastic favorers amongst the Few. My affection for my work is rooted in the solemn and pure delight which it gave me to conceive and to perform. If I had graven it on the rocks of a desert, this apparition of my own innermost mind, in its least-clouded moments, would have been to me as dear; and this ought, I believe, to be the sentiment with which he whose Art is born of faith in the truth and beauty of the principles he seeks to illustrate, should regard his work. Your serener existence, uniform and holy, my lot denies, — if my heart covets. But our true nature is in our thoughts, not our deeds: and therefore, in books — which *are* his thoughts — the author's character lies bare to the discerning eye. It is not in the life of cities, — in the turmoil and the crowd; it is in the still, the lonely, and more sacred life, which for some hours, under every sun, the student lives (his stolen retreat from the Agora to the Cave), that I feel there is between us the bond of that secret sympathy, that magnetic chain, which unites the everlasting brotherhood of whose being Zanoni is the type.

E.B.L.
London, May, 1845

Introduction

One of the peculiarities of Bulwer was his passion for occult studies. They had a charm for him early in life, and he pursued them with the earnestness which characterized his pursuit of other studies. He became absorbed in wizard lore; he equipped himself with magical implements, — with rods for transmitting influence, and crystal balls in which to discern coming scenes and persons; and communed with spiritualists and mediums. The fruit of these mystic studies is seen in "Zanoni" and "A strange Story," romances which were a labor of love to the author, and into which he threw all the power he possessed, — power re-enforced by multifarious reading and an instinctive appreciation of Oriental thought. These weird stories, in which the author has formulated his theory of magic, are of a wholly different type from his previous fictions, and, in place of the heroes and villains of everyday life, we have beings that belong in part to another sphere, and that deal with mysterious and occult agencies. Once more the old forgotten lore of the Cabala is unfolded; the furnace of the alchemist, whose fires have been extinct for centuries, is lighted anew, and the lamp of the Rosicrucian re-illumined. No other works of the author, contradictory as have been the opinions of them, have provoked such a diversity of criticism as these. To some persons they represent a temporary aberration of genius rather than any serious thought or definite purpose; while others regard them as surpassing in bold and original speculation, profound analysis of character, and thrilling interest, all of the author's other works. The truth, we believe, lies midway between these extremes. It is questionable whether the introduction into a novel of such subjects as are discussed in these romances be not an offence against good sense and good taste; but it is as unreasonable to deny the vigor and originality of their author's conceptions, as to deny that the execution is imperfect, and, at times, bungling and absurd.

It has been justly said that the present half century has witnessed the rise and triumphs of science, the extent and marvels of which even

Bacon's fancy never conceived, simultaneously with superstitions grosser than any which Bacon's age believed. "The one is, in fact, the natural reaction from the other. The more science seeks to exclude the miraculous, and reduce all nature, animate and inanimate, to an invariable law of sequences, the more does the natural instinct of man rebel, and seek an outlet for those obstinate questionings, those 'blank misgivings of a creature moving about in worlds not realized,' taking refuge in delusions as degrading as any of the so-called Dark Ages." It was the revolt from the chilling materialism of the age which inspired the mystic creations of "Zanoni" and "A Strange Story." Of these works, which support and supplement each other, one is the contemplation of our actual life through a spiritual medium, the other is designed to show that, without some gleams of the supernatural, man is not man, nor nature nature.

In "Zanoni" the author introduces us to two human beings who have achieved immortality: one, Mejnour, void of all passion or feeling, calm, benignant, bloodless, an intellect rather than a man; the other, Zanoni, the pupil of Mejnour, the representative of an ideal life in its utmost perfection, possessing eternal youth, absolute power, and absolute knowledge, and withal the fullest capacity to enjoy and to love, and, as a necessity of that love, to sorrow and despair. By his love for Viola Zanoni is compelled to descend from his exalted state, to lose his eternal calm, and to share in the cares and anxieties of humanity; and this degradation is completed by the birth of a child. Finally, he gives up the life which hangs on that of another, in order to save that other, the loving and beloved wife, who has delivered him from his solitude and isolation. Wife and child are mortal, and to outlive them and his love for them is impossible. But Mejnour, who is the impersonation of thought, — pure intellect without affection, — lives on.

Bulwer has himself justly characterized this work, in the Introduction, as a romance and not a romance, as a truth for those who can comprehend it, and an extravagance for those who cannot. The most careless or matter-of-fact reader must see that the work, like the enigmatical "Faust," deals in types and symbols; that the writer intends to suggest to the mind something more subtle and impalpable than that which is embodied to the senses. What that something is, hardly two persons will agree. The most obvious interpretation of the types is, that in Zanoni the author depicts to us humanity, perfected, sublimed, which lives not for self, but for others; in Mejnour, as we have before said, cold, passionless, self-sufficing intellect; in Glyndon, the young Englishman, the mingled strength and weakness of human nature; in the heartless, selfish artist, Nicot, icy, soulless atheism, believing nothing, hoping nothing, trusting and loving nothing; and in the beautiful, artless Viola, an exquisite creation, pure womanhood, loving, trusting and truthful. As a work of art the romance is one of great power. It is original in its conception, and pervaded by one central idea; but it would have been improved, we think, by a more sparing use of the supernatural. The inevitable effect of so much hackneyed diablerie — of such an accumulation of wonder upon wonder — is to deaden the impression they would naturally make upon us. In Hawthorne's tales we see with what ease a great imaginative artist can produce a deeper thrill by a far slighter use of the weird and the mysterious.

The chief interest of the story for the ordinary reader centers, not in its ghostly characters and improbable machinery, the scenes in Mejnour's chamber in the ruined castle among the Apennines, the colossal and appalling apparitions on Vesuvius, the hideous phantom with its burning eye that haunted Glyndon, but in the loves of Viola and the mysterious Zanoni, the blissful and the fearful scenes through which they pass, and their final destiny, when the hero of the story sacrifices his own "charmed life" to save hers, and the Immortal finds the only true immortality in death. Among the striking passages in the work are the pathetic sketch of the old violinist and composer, Pisani, with his sympathetic "barbiton" which moaned, groaned, growled, and laughed responsive to the feelings of its master; the description of Viola's and her father's triumph, when "The Siren," his masterpiece, is performed at the San Carlo in Naples; Glyndon's adventure at the Carnival in Naples; the death of his sister; the vivid pictures of the Reign of Terror in Paris, closing with the downfall of Robespierre and his satellites; and perhaps, above all, the thrilling scene where Zanoni leaves Viola asleep in prison when his guards call him to execution, and she, unconscious of the terrible sacrifice, but awaking and missing him, has a vision of the procession to the guillotine, with Zanoni there, radiant in youth and beauty, followed by the sudden vanishing of the headsman, — the horror, — and the "Welcome" of her loved one to Heaven in a myriad of melodies from the choral hosts above.

"Zanoni" was originally published by Saunders and Otley, London, in three volumes 12mo., in 1842. A translation into French, made by M. Sheldon under the direction of P. Lorain, was published in Paris in the "Bibliotheque des Meilleurs Romans Etrangers."

W.M.

Preface to the Edition of 1853

As a work of imagination, "Zanoni" ranks, perhaps, amongst the highest of my prose fictions. In the Poem of "King Arthur," published many years afterwards, I have taken up an analogous design, in the contemplation of our positive life through a spiritual medium; and I have enforced, through a far wider development, and, I believe, with more complete and enduring success, that harmony between the external events which are all that the superficial behold on the surface of human affairs, and the subtle and intellectual agencies which in reality influence the conduct of individuals, and shape out the destinies of the world. As man has two lives, — that of action and that of thought, — so I conceive that work to be the truest representation of humanity which faithfully delineates both, and opens some elevating glimpse into the sublimest mysteries of our being, by establishing the inevitable union that exists between the plain things of the day, in which our earthly bodies perform their allotted part, and the latent, often uncultivated, often invisible, affinities of the soul with all the powers that eternally breathe and move throughout the Universe of Spirit.

I refer those who do me the honor to read "Zanoni" with more attention than is given to ordinary romance, to the Poem of "King Arthur," for suggestive conjecture into most of the regions of speculative research, affecting the higher and more important condition of our ultimate being, which have engaged the students of immaterial philosophy in my own age.

Affixed to the "Note" with which this work concludes, and which treats of the distinctions between type and allegory, the reader will find, from the pen of one of our most eminent living writers, an ingenious attempt to explain the interior or typical meanings of the work now before him.

Introduction

*I*t is possible that among my readers there may be a few not unacquainted with an old-book shop, existing some years since in the neighborhood of Covent Garden; I say a few, for certainly there was little enough to attract the many in those precious volumes which the labor of a life had accumulated on the dusty shelves of my old friend D——. There were to be found no popular treatises, no entertaining romances, no histories, no travels, no "Library for the People," no "Amusement for the Million." But there, perhaps, throughout all Europe, the curious might discover the most notable collection, ever amassed by an enthusiast, of the works of alchemist, cabalist, and astrologer. The owner had lavished a fortune in the purchase of unsalable treasures. But old D—— did not desire to sell. It absolutely went to his heart when a customer entered his shop: he watched the movements of the presumptuous intruder with a vindictive glare; he fluttered around him with uneasy vigilance, — he frowned, he groaned, when profane hands dislodged his idols from their niches. If it were one of the favorite sultanas of his wizard harem that attracted you, and the price named were not sufficiently enormous, he would not infrequently double the sum. Demur, and in brisk delight he snatched the venerable charmer from your hands; accede, and he became the picture of despair, — nor infrequently, at the dead of night, would he knock at your door, and entreat you to sell him back, at your own terms, what you had so egregiously bought at his. A believer himself in his Averroes and Paracelsus, he was as loath as the philosophers he studied to communicate to the profane the learning he had collected.

It so chanced that some years ago, in my younger days, whether of authorship or life, I felt a desire to make myself acquainted with the true origin and tenets of the singular sect known by the name of Rosicrucians. Dissatisfied with the scanty and superficial accounts to be found in the works usually referred to on the subject, it struck me as possible that Mr. D——'s collection, which was rich, not only in black-letter, but in manuscripts, might contain some more accurate and authentic records of that famous brotherhood, — written, who knows? by one of their own order, and confirming by authority and detail the pretensions to wisdom and to virtue which Bringaret had arrogated to the successors of the Chaldean and Gymnosophist. Accordingly I repaired to what, doubtless, I ought to be ashamed to confess, was once one of my favorite haunts. But are there no errors and no fallacies, in the chronicles of our own day, as absurd as those of the alchemists of old? Our very newspapers may seem to our posterity as full of delusions as the books of the alchemists do to us; not but what the press is the air we breathe, — and uncommonly foggy the air is too!

On entering the shop, I was struck by the venerable appearance of a customer whom I had never seen there before. I was struck yet more by the respect with which he was treated by the disdainful collector. "Sir," cried the last, emphatically, as I was turning over the leaves of the catalogue, — "sir, you are the only man I have met, in five-and-forty years that I have spent in these researches, who is worthy to be my customer. How — where, in this frivolous age, could you have acquired a knowledge so profound? And this august fraternity, whose doctrines, hinted at by the earliest philosophers, are still a mystery to the latest; tell me if there really exists upon the earth any book, any manuscript, in which their discoveries, their tenets, are to be learned?"

At the words, "august fraternity," I need scarcely say that my attention had been at once aroused, and I listened eagerly for the stranger's reply.

"I do not think," said the old gentleman, "that the masters of the school have ever consigned, except by obscure hint and mystical parable, their real doctrines to the world. And I do not blame them for their discretion."

Here he paused, and seemed about to retire, when I said, somewhat abruptly, to the collector, "I see nothing, Mr. D——, in this catalogue which relates to the Rosicrucians!"

"The Rosicrucians!" repeated the old gentleman, and in his turn he surveyed me with deliberate surprise. "Who but a Rosicrucian could explain the Rosicrucian mysteries! And can you imagine that any members of that sect, the most jealous of all secret societies, would themselves lift the veil that hides the Isis of their wisdom from the world?"

"Aha!" thought I, "this, then, is 'the august fraternity' of which you spoke. Heaven be praised! I certainly have stumbled on one of the brotherhood."

"But," I said aloud, "if not in books, sir, where else am I to obtain information? Nowadays one can hazard nothing in print without authority, and one may scarcely quote Shakespeare without citing chapter and verse. This is the age of facts, — the age of facts, sir."

"Well," said the old gentleman, with a pleasant smile, "if we meet again, perhaps, at least, I may direct your researches to the proper source of intelligence." And with that he buttoned his greatcoat, whistled to his dog, and departed.

It so happened that I did meet again with the old gentleman, exactly four days after our brief conversation in Mr. D——'s book-shop. I was riding leisurely towards Highgate, when, at the foot of its classic hill, I recognized the stranger; he was mounted on a black pony, and before him trotted his dog, which was black also.

If you meet the man whom you wish to know, on horseback, at the commencement of a long hill, where, unless he has borrowed a friend's favorite hack, he cannot, in decent humanity to the brute creation, ride away from you, I apprehend that it is your own fault if you have not gone far in your object before you have gained the top. In short, so well did I succeed, that on reaching Highgate the old gentleman invited me to rest at his house, which was a little apart from the village; and an excellent house it was, — small, but commodious, with a large garden, and commanding from the windows such a prospect as Lucretius would recommend to philosophers: the spires and domes of London, on a clear day, distinctly visible; here the Retreat of the Hermit, and there the Mare Magnum of the world.

The walls of the principal rooms were embellished with pictures of extraordinary merit, and in that high school of art which is so little understood out of Italy. I was surprised to learn that they were all from the hand of the owner. My evident admiration pleased my new friend, and led to talk upon his part, which showed him no less elevated in his theories of art than an adept in the practice. Without fatiguing the reader with irrelevant criticism, it is necessary, perhaps, as elucidating much of the design and character of the work which these prefatory pages introduce, that I should briefly observe, that he insisted as much upon the connection of the arts, as a distinguished author has upon that of the sciences; that he held that in all works of imagination, whether expressed by words or by colors, the artist of the higher schools must make the broadest distinction between the real and the true, — in other words, between the imitation of actual life, and the exaltation of Nature into the Ideal.

"The one," said he, "is the Dutch School, the other is the Greek."

"Sir," said I, "the Dutch is the most in fashion."

"Yes, in painting, perhaps," answered my host, "but in literature —"

"It was of literature I spoke. Our growing poets are all for simplicity and Betty Foy; and our critics hold it the highest praise of a work of imagination, to say that its characters are exact to common life, even in sculpture —"

"In sculpture! No, no! *There* the high ideal must at least be essential!"

"Pardon me; I fear you have not seen Souter Johnny and Tam O'Shanter."

"Ah!" said the old gentleman, shaking his head, "I live very much out of the world, I see. I suppose Shakespeare has ceased to be admired?"

"On the contrary; people make the adoration of Shakespeare the excuse for attacking everybody else. But then our critics have discovered that Shakespeare is so *real!*"

"Real! The poet who has never once drawn a character to be met with in actual life, — who has never once descended to a passion that is false, or a personage who is real!"

I was about to reply very severely to this paradox, when I perceived that my companion was growing a little out of temper. And he who wishes to catch a Rosicrucian, must take care not to disturb the waters. I thought it better, therefore, to turn the conversation.

"Revenons a nos moutons," said I; "you promised to enlighten my ignorance as to the Rosicrucians."

"Well!" quoth he, rather sternly; "but for what purpose? Perhaps you desire only to enter the temple in order to ridicule the rites?"

"What do you take me for! Surely, were I so inclined, the fate of the Abbe de Villars is a sufficient warning to all men not to treat idly of the realms of the Salamander and the Sylph. Everybody knows how mysteriously that ingenious personage was deprived of his life, in revenge for the witty mockeries of his 'Comte de Gabalis.'"

"Salamander and Sylph! I see that you fall into the vulgar error, and translate literally the allegorical language of the mystics."

With that the old gentleman condescended to enter into a very interesting, and, as it seemed to me, a very erudite relation, of the tenets of the Rosicrucians, some of whom, he asserted, still existed, and still prosecuted, in august secrecy, their profound researches into natural science and occult philosophy.

"But this fraternity," said he, "however respectable and virtuous, — virtuous I say, for no monastic order is more severe in the practice of moral precepts, or more ardent in Christian faith, — this fraternity is but a branch of others yet more transcendent in the powers they have obtained, and yet more illustrious in their origin. Are you acquainted with the Platonists?"

"I have occasionally lost my way in their labyrinth," said I. "Faith, they are rather difficult gentlemen to understand."

"Yet their knottiest problems have never yet been published. Their sublimest works are in manuscript, and constitute the initiatory learning, not only of the Rosicrucians, but of the nobler brotherhoods I have referred to. More solemn and sublime still is the knowledge to be gleaned from the elder Pythagoreans, and the immortal masterpieces of Apollonius."

"Apollonius, the imposter of Tyanea! are his writings extant?"

"Imposter!" cried my host; "Apollonius an imposter!"

"I beg your pardon; I did not know he was a friend of yours; and if you vouch for his character, I will believe him to have been a very respectable man, who only spoke the truth when he boasted of his power to be in two places at the same time."

"Is that so difficult?" said the old gentleman; "if so, you have never dreamed!"

Here ended our conversation; but from that time an acquaintance was formed between us which lasted till my venerable friend departed this life. Peace to his ashes! He was a person of singular habits and eccentric opinions; but the chief part of his time was occupied in acts of quiet and unostentatious goodness. He was an enthusiast in the duties of the Samaritan; and as his virtues were softened by the gentlest charity, so his hopes were based upon the devoutest belief. He never conversed upon his own origin and history, nor have I ever been able to penetrate the darkness in which they were concealed. He seemed to have seen much of the world, and to have been an eyewitness of the first French Revolution, a subject upon which he was equally eloquent and instructive. At the same time he did not regard the crimes of that stormy period with the philosophical leniency with which enlightened writers (their heads safe upon their shoulders) are, in the present day, inclined to treat the massacres of the past: he spoke not as a student who had read and reasoned, but as a man who had seen and suffered. The old gentleman seemed alone in the world; nor did I know that he had one relation, till his executor, a distant cousin, residing abroad, informed me of the very handsome legacy which my poor friend had bequeathed me. This consisted, first, of a sum about which I think it best to be guarded, foreseeing the possibility of a new tax upon real and funded property; and, secondly, of certain precious manuscripts, to which the following volumes owe their existence.

I imagine I trace this latter bequest to a visit I paid the Sage, if so I may be permitted to call him, a few weeks before his death.

Although he read little of our modern literature, my friend, with the affable good nature which belonged to him, graciously permitted me to consult him upon various literary undertakings meditated by the desultory ambition of a young and inexperienced student. And at that time I sought his advice upon a work of imagination, intended to depict the effects of enthusiasm upon different modifications of character. He listened to my conception, which was sufficiently trite and prosaic, with his usual patience; and then, thoughtfully turning to his bookshelves, took down an old volume, and read to me, first, in Greek, and secondly, in English, some extracts to the following effect: —

"Plato here expresses four kinds of mania, by which I desire to understand enthusiasm and the inspiration of the gods: Firstly, the musical; secondly, the telestic or mystic; thirdly, the prophetic; and fourthly, that which belongs to love."

The author he quoted, after contending that there is something in the soul above intellect, and stating that there are in our nature distinct energies, — by the one of which we discover and seize, as it were, on sciences and theorems with almost intuitive rapidity, by another, through which high art is accomplished, like the statues of Phidias, — proceeded to state that "enthusiasm, in the true acceptation of the word, is, when that part of the soul which is above intellect is excited to the gods, and thence derives its inspiration."

The author, then pursuing his comment upon Plato, observes, that "one of these manias may suffice (especially that which belongs to love) to lead back the soul to its first divinity and happiness; but that there is an intimate union with them all; and that the ordinary progress through which the soul ascends is, primarily, through the musical; next, through the telestic or mystic; thirdly, through the prophetic; and lastly, through the enthusiasm of love."

While with a bewildered understanding and a reluctant attention I listened to these intricate sublimities, my adviser closed the volume, and said with complacency, "There is the motto for your book, — the thesis for your theme."

"Davus sum, non Oedipus," said I, shaking my head, discontentedly. "All this may be exceedingly fine, but, Heaven forgive me, — I don't understand a word of it. The mysteries of your Rosicrucians, and your fraternities, are mere child's play to the jargon of the Platonists."

"Yet, not till you rightly understand this passage, can you understand the higher theories of the Rosicrucians, or of the still nobler fraternities you speak of with so much levity."

"Oh, if that be the case, I give up in despair. Why not, since you are so well versed in the matter, take the motto for a book of your own?"

"But if I have already composed a book with that thesis for its theme, will you prepare it for the public?"

"With the greatest pleasure," said I, — alas, too rashly!

"I shall hold you to your promise," returned the old gentleman, "and when I am no more, you will receive the manuscripts. From what you say of the prevailing taste in literature, I cannot flatter you with the hope that you will gain much by the undertaking. And I tell you beforehand that you will find it not a little laborious."

"Is your work a romance?"

"It is a romance, and it is not a romance. It is a truth for those who can comprehend it, and an extravagance for those who cannot."

At last there arrived the manuscripts, with a brief note from my deceased friend, reminding me of my imprudent promise.

With mournful interest, and yet with eager impatience, I opened the packet and trimmed my lamp. Conceive my dismay when I found the whole written in an unintelligible cipher. I present the reader with a specimen:

ƎϚ⋔Ӿↄ⅃Ͱ

and so on for nine hundred and forty mortal pages in foolscap. I could scarcely believe my eyes: in fact, I began to think the lamp burned singularly blue; and sundry misgivings as to the unhallowed nature of the characters I had so unwittingly opened upon, coupled with the strange hints and mystical language of the old gentleman, crept through my disordered imagination. Certainly, to say no worse of it, the whole thing looked *uncanny!* I was about, precipitately, to hurry the papers into my desk, with a pious determination to have nothing more to do with them, when my eye fell upon a book, neatly bound in blue morocco, and which, in my eagerness, I had hitherto overlooked. I opened this volume with great precaution, not knowing what might jump out, and — guess my delight — found that it contained a key or dictionary to the hieroglyphics. Not to weary the reader with an account of my labors, I am contented with saying that at last I imagined myself capable of construing the characters, and set to work in good earnest. Still it was no easy task, and two years elapsed before I had made much progress. I then, by way of experiment on the public, obtained the insertion of a few desultory chapters, in a periodical with which, for a few months, I had the honor to be connected. They appeared to excite more curiosity than I had presumed to anticipate; and I renewed, with better heart, my laborious undertaking. But now a new misfortune befell me: I found, as I proceeded, that the author had made two copies of his work, one much more elaborate and detailed than the other; I had stumbled upon the earlier copy, and had my whole task to remodel, and the chapters I had written to retranslate. I may say then, that, exclusive of intervals devoted to more pressing occupations, my unlucky promise cost me the toil of several years before I could bring it to adequate fulfillment. The task was the more difficult, since the style in the original is written in a kind of rhythmical prose, as if the author desired that in some degree his work should be regarded as one of poetical conception and design. To this it was not possible to do justice, and in the attempt

I have doubtless very often need of the reader's indulgent consideration. My natural respect for the old gentleman's vagaries, with a muse of equivocal character, must be my only excuse whenever the language, without luxuriating into verse, borrows flowers scarcely natural to prose. Truth compels me also to confess, that, with all my pains, I am by no means sure that I have invariably given the true meaning of the cipher; nay, that here and there either a gap in the narrative, or the sudden assumption of a new cipher, to which no key was afforded, has obliged me to resort to interpolations of my own, no doubt easily discernible, but which, I flatter myself, are not inharmonious to the general design. This confession leads me to the sentence with which I shall conclude: If, reader, in this book there be anything that pleases you, it is certainly mine; but whenever you come to something you dislike, — lay the blame upon the old gentleman!

London, January, 1842.

N.B. — The notes appended to the text are sometimes by the author, sometimes by the editor. I have occasionally (but not always) marked the distinction; where, however, this is omitted, the ingenuity of the reader will be rarely at fault.

ZANONI

BOOK I

THE MUSICIAN

Due Fontane
Chi di diverso effeto hanno liquore!*

"Ariosto, Orland. Fur." Canto 1.7.

---

* Two Founts
That hold a draught of different effects.

Chapter 1.I.

Vergina era
D' alta belta, ma sua belta non cura:

. . .

Di natura, d' amor, de' cieli amici
Le negligenze sue sono artifici.*

"Gerusal. Lib.," canto ii. xiv.-xviii.

At Naples, in the latter half of the last century, a worthy artist named Gaetano Pisani lived and flourished. He was a musician of great genius, but not of popular reputation; there was in all his compositions something capricious and fantastic which did not please the taste of the Dilettanti of Naples. He was fond of unfamiliar subjects into which he introduced airs and symphonies that excited a kind of terror in those who listened. The names of his pieces will probably suggest their nature. I find, for instance, among his MSS., these titles: "The Feast of the Harpies," "The Witches at Benevento," "The Descent of Orpheus into Hades," "The Evil Eye," "The Eumenides," and many others that evince a powerful imagination delighting in the fearful and supernatural, but often relieved by an airy and delicate fancy with passages of exquisite grace and beauty. It is true that in the selection of his subjects from ancient fable, Gaetano Pisani was much more faithful than his contemporaries to the remote origin and the early genius of Italian Opera.

That descendant, however effeminate, of the ancient union between Song and Drama, when, after long obscurity and dethronement, it regained a punier scepter, though a gaudier purple, by the banks of the Etrurian Arno, or amidst the lagunes of Venice, had chosen all its primary inspirations from the unfamiliar and classic sources of heathen legend; and Pisani's "Descent of Orpheus" was but a bolder, darker, and

---

* She was a virgin of a glorious beauty, but regarded not her beauty . . . Negligence itself is art in those favored by Nature, by love, and by the heavens.

more scientific repetition of the "Euridice" which Jacopi Peri set to music at the august nuptials of Henry of Navarre and Mary of Medicis.* Still, as I have said, the style of the Neapolitan musician was not on the whole pleasing to ears grown nice and euphuistic in the more dulcet melodies of the day; and faults and extravagances easily discernible, and often to appearance willful, served the critics for an excuse for their distaste. Fortunately, or the poor musician might have starved, he was not only a composer, but also an excellent practical performer, especially on the violin, and by that instrument he earned a decent subsistence as one of the orchestra at the Great Theater of San Carlo. Here formal and appointed tasks necessarily kept his eccentric fancies in tolerable check, though it is recorded that no less than five times he had been deposed from his desk for having shocked the cognoscenti, and thrown the whole band into confusion, by impromptu variations of so frantic and startling a nature that one might well have imagined that the harpies or witches who inspired his compositions had clawed hold of his instrument.

The impossibility, however, to find anyone of equal excellence as a performer (that is to say, in his more lucid and orderly moments) had forced his reinstalment, and he had now, for the most part, reconciled himself to the narrow sphere of his appointed adagios or allegros. The audience, too, aware of his propensity, were quick to perceive the least deviation from the text; and if he wandered for a moment, which might also be detected by the eye as well as the ear, in some strange contortion of visage, and some ominous flourish of his bow, a gentle and admonitory murmur recalled the musician from his Elysium or his Tartarus to the sober regions of his desk. Then he would start as if from a dream, cast a hurried, frightened, apologetic glance around, and, with a crestfallen, humbled air, draw his rebellious instrument back to the beaten track of the glib monotony. But at home he would make himself amends for this reluctant drudgery. And there, grasping the unhappy violin with ferocious fingers, he would pour forth, often till the morning rose, strange, wild measures that would startle the early fisherman on the shore below with a superstitious awe, and make him cross himself as if mermaid or sprite had wailed no earthly music in his ear.

This man's appearance was in keeping with the characteristics of his art. The features were noble and striking, but worn and haggard, with black, careless locks tangled into a maze of curls, and a fixed, speculative, dreamy stare in his large and hollow eyes. All his movements were peculiar, sudden, and abrupt, as the impulse seized him; and in gliding

---

* Orpheus was the favorite hero of early Italian Opera, or Lyrical Drama. The Orfeo of Angelo Politiano was produced in 1475. The Orfeo of Monteverde was performed at Venice in 1667.

through the streets, or along the beach, he was heard laughing and talking to himself. Withal, he was a harmless, guileless, gentle creature, and would share his mite with any idle lazzaroni, whom he often paused to contemplate as they lay lazily basking in the sun. Yet was he thoroughly unsocial. He formed no friends, flattered no patrons, resorted to none of the merry-makings so dear to the children of music and the South. He and his art seemed alone suited to each other, — both quaint, primitive, unworldly, irregular. You could not separate the man from his music; it was himself. Without it he was nothing, a mere machine! *with* it, he was king over worlds of his own. Poor man, he had little enough in this! At a manufacturing town in England there is a gravestone on which the epitaph records "one Claudius Phillips, whose absolute contempt for riches, and inimitable performance on the violin, made him the admiration of all that knew him!" Logical conjunction of opposite eulogies! In proportion, O Genius, to thy contempt for riches will be thy performance on thy violin!

Gaetano Pisani's talents as a composer had been chiefly exhibited in music appropriate to this his favorite instrument, of all unquestionably the most various and royal in its resources and power over the passions. As Shakespeare among poets is the Cremona among instruments. Nevertheless, he had composed other pieces of larger ambition and wider accomplishment, and chief of these, his precious, his unpurchased, his unpublished, his unpublishable and imperishable opera of the "Siren." This great work had been the dream of his boyhood, the mistress of his manhood; in advancing age "it stood beside him like his youth." Vainly had he struggled to place it before the world. Even bland, unjealous Paisiello, Maestro di Capella, shook his gentle head when the musician favored him with a specimen of one of his most thrilling scenas. And yet, Paisiello, though that music differs from all Durante taught thee to emulate, there may — but patience, Gaetano Pisani! bide thy time, and keep thy violin in tune!

Strange as it may appear to the fairer reader, this grotesque personage had yet formed those ties which ordinary mortals are apt to consider their especial monopoly, — he was married, and had one child. What is more strange yet, his wife was a daughter of quiet, sober, unfantastic England: she was much younger than himself; she was fair and gentle, with a sweet English face; she had married him from choice, and (will you believe it?) she yet loved him. How she came to marry him, or how this shy, unsocial, wayward creature ever ventured to propose, I can only explain by asking you to look round and explain first to *me* how half the husbands and half the wives you meet ever found a mate! Yet, on reflection, this union was not so extraordinary after all. The girl was a natural child of parents too noble ever to own and claim her. She was brought into Italy to learn the art by which she was to live, for she had taste and voice; she was a dependant and harshly treated, and poor Pisani was her master, and his voice the only one she had heard from her cradle that seemed without one tone that could scorn or chide. And so — well, is the rest natural? Natural or not, they married. This young wife loved her husband; and young and gentle as she was, she might almost be said to be the protector of the two. From how many disgraces with the despots of San Carlo and the Conservatorio had her unknown officious mediation saved him! In how many ailments — for his frame was weak — had she nursed and tended him! Often, in the dark nights, she would wait at the theater with her lantern to light him and her steady arm to lean on; otherwise, in his abstract reveries, who knows but the musician would have walked after his "Siren" into the sea! And then she would so patiently, perhaps (for in true love there is not always the finest taste) so *delightedly*, listen to those storms of eccentric and fitful melody, and steal him — whispering praises all the way — from the unwholesome night watch to rest and sleep!

I said his music was a part of the man, and this gentle creature seemed a part of the music; it was, in fact, when she sat beside him that whatever was tender or fairylike in his motley fantasia crept into the harmony as by stealth. Doubtless her presence acted on the music, and shaped and softened it; but, he, who never examined how or what his inspiration, knew it not. All that he knew was, that he loved and blessed her. He fancied he told her so twenty times a day; but he never did, for he was not of many words, even to his wife. His language was his music, — as hers, her cares! He was more communicative to his barbiton, as the learned Mersennus teaches us to call all the varieties of the great viol family. Certainly barbiton sounds better than fiddle; and barbiton let it be. He would talk to *that* by the hour together, — praise it, scold it, coax it, nay (for such is man, even the most guileless), he had been known to swear at it; but for that excess he was always penitentially remorseful. And the barbiton had a tongue of his own, could take his own part, and when *he* also scolded, had much the best of it. He was a noble fellow, this Violin! — a Tyrolese, the handiwork of the illustrious Steiner. There was something mysterious in his great age. How many hands, now dust, had awakened his strings ere he became the Robin Goodfellow and Familiar of Gaetano Pisani! His very case was venerable, — beautifully painted, it was said, by Caracci. An English collector had offered more for the case than Pisani had ever made by the violin. But Pisani, who cared not if he had inhabited a cabin himself, was proud of a palace for the barbiton. His barbiton, it was his elder child! He had another child, and now we must turn to her.

How shall I describe thee, Viola? Certainly the music had something to answer for in the advent of that young stranger. For both in her form and her character you might have traced a family likeness to that singular and spiritlike life of sound which night after night threw itself in airy and goblin sport over the starry seas. . .Beautiful she was, but of a very uncommon beauty, — a combination, a harmony of opposite attributes. Her hair of a gold richer and purer than that which is seen even in the North; but the eyes, of all the dark, tender, subduing light of more than Italian — almost of Oriental — splendor. The complexion exquisitely fair, but never the same, — vivid in one moment, pale the next. And with the complexion, the expression also varied; nothing now so sad, and nothing now so joyous.

I grieve to say that what we rightly entitle education was much neglected for their daughter by this singular pair. To be sure, neither of them had much knowledge to bestow; and knowledge was not then the fashion, as it is now. But accident or nature favored young Viola. She learned, as of course, her mother's language with her father's. And she contrived soon to read and to write; and her mother, who, by the way, was a Roman Catholic, taught her betimes to pray. But then, to counteract all these acquisitions, the strange habits of Pisani, and the incessant watch and care which he required from his wife, often left the child alone with an old nurse, who, to be sure, loved her dearly, but who was in no way calculated to instruct her.

Dame Gionetta was every inch Italian and Neapolitan. Her youth had been all love, and her age was all superstition. She was garrulous, fond, — a gossip. Now she would prattle to the girl of cavaliers and princes at her feet, and now she would freeze her blood with tales and legends, perhaps as old as Greek or Etrurian fable, of demon and vampire, — of the dances round the great walnut tree at Benevento, and the haunting spell of the Evil Eye. All this helped silently to weave charmed webs over Viola's imagination that afterthought and later years might labor vainly to dispel. And all this especially fitted her to hang, with a fearful joy, upon her father's music. Those visionary strains, ever struggling to translate into wild and broken sounds the language of unearthly beings, breathed around her from her birth. Thus you might have said that her whole mind was full of music; associations, memories, sensations of pleasure or pain, — all were mixed up inexplicably with those sounds that now delighted and now terrified; that greeted her when her eyes opened to the sun, and woke her trembling on her lonely couch in the darkness of the night. The legends and tales of Gionetta only served to make the child better understand the signification of those mysterious tones; they furnished her with words to the music. It was natural that the daughter of such a parent should soon evince some taste in his art. But this developed itself chiefly in the ear and the voice.

She was yet a child when she sang divinely. A great Cardinal — great alike in the State and the Conservatorio — heard of her gifts, and sent for her. From that moment her fate was decided: she was to be the future glory of Naples, the prima donna of San Carlo.

The Cardinal insisted upon the accomplishment of his own predictions, and provided her with the most renowned masters. To inspire her with emulation, his Eminence took her one evening to his own box: it would be something to see the performance, something more to hear the applause lavished upon the glittering signoras she was hereafter to excel! Oh, how gloriously that life of the stage, that fairy world of music and song, dawned upon her! It was the only world that seemed to correspond with her strange childish thoughts. It appeared to her as if, cast hitherto on a foreign shore, she was brought at last to see the forms and hear the language of her native land. Beautiful and true enthusiasm, rich with the promise of genius! Boy or man, thou wilt never be a poet, if thou hast not felt the ideal, the romance, the Calypso's isle that opened to thee when for the first time the magic curtain was drawn aside, and let in the world of poetry on the world of prose!

And now the initiation was begun. She was to read, to study, to depict by a gesture, a look, the passions she was to delineate on the boards; lessons dangerous, in truth, to some, but not to the pure enthusiasm that comes from art; for the mind that rightly conceives art is but a mirror which gives back what is cast on its surface faithfully only — while unsullied. She seized on nature and truth intuitively. Her recitations became full of unconscious power; her voice moved the heart to tears, or warmed it into generous rage. But this arose from that sympathy which genius ever has, even in its earliest innocence, with whatever feels, or aspires, or suffers.

It was no premature woman comprehending the love or the jealousy that the words expressed; her art was one of those strange secrets which the psychologists may unriddle to us if they please, and tell us why children of the simplest minds and the purest hearts are often so acute to distinguish, in the tales you tell them, or the songs you sing, the difference between the true art and the false, passion and jargon, Homer and Racine, — echoing back, from hearts that have not yet felt what they repeat, the melodious accents of the natural pathos. Apart from her studies, Viola was a simple, affectionate, but somewhat wayward child, — wayward, not in temper, for that was sweet and docile; but in her moods, which, as I before hinted, changed from sad to gay and gay to sad without an apparent cause. If cause there were, it must be traced to the early and mysterious influences I have referred to, when seeking to explain the effect produced on her imagination by those restless streams of sound that constantly played around it; for it is noticeable that to those who are much alive to the effects of music, airs and tunes often come back, in the commonest pursuits of life, to vex, as it were, and haunt them. The music, once admitted to the soul, becomes also a sort of spirit, and never dies. It wanders perturbedly through the halls and galleries of the memory, and is often heard again, distinct and living as when it first displaced the wavelets of the air. Now at times, then, these phantoms of sound floated back upon her fancy; if gay, to call a smile from every dimple; if mournful, to throw a shade upon her brow, — to make her cease from her childish mirth, and sit apart and muse.

Rightly, then, in a typical sense, might this fair creature, so airy in her shape, so harmonious in her beauty, so unfamiliar in her ways and thoughts, — rightly might she be called a daughter, less of the musician than the music, a being for whom you could imagine that some fate was reserved, less of actual life than the romance which, to eyes that can see, and hearts that can feel, glides ever along *with* the actual life, stream by stream, to the Dark Ocean.

And therefore it seemed not strange that Viola herself, even in childhood, and yet more as she bloomed into the sweet seriousness of virgin youth, should fancy her life ordained for a lot, whether of bliss or woe, that should accord with the romance and reverie which made the atmosphere she breathed. Frequently she would climb through the thickets that clothed the neighboring grotto of Posilipo, — the mighty work of the old Cimmerians, — and, seated by the haunted Tomb of Virgil, indulge those visions, the subtle vagueness of which no poetry can render palpable and defined; for the Poet that surpasses all who ever sang, is the heart of dreaming youth! Frequently there, too, beside the threshold over which the vine-leaves clung, and facing that dark-blue, waveless sea, she would sit in the autumn noon or summer twilight, and build her castles in the air. Who doth not do the same, — not in youth alone, but with the dimmed hopes of age! It is man's prerogative to dream, the common royalty of peasant and of king. But those daydreams of hers were more habitual, distinct, and solemn than the greater part of us indulge. They seemed like the Orama of the Greeks, — prophets while phantasma.

Chapter I.II.

Fu stupor, fu vaghezza, fu diletto!*

"Gerusal. Lib.," cant. ii. xxi.

Now at last the education is accomplished! Viola is nearly sixteen. The Cardinal declares that the time is come when the new name must be inscribed in the Libro d'Oro, — the Golden Book set apart to the children of Art and Song. Yes, but in what character? — to whose genius is she to give embodiment and form? Ah, there is the secret! Rumors go abroad that the inexhaustible Paisiello, charmed with her performance of his "Nel cor piu non me sento," and his "Io son Lindoro," will produce some new masterpiece to introduce the debutante. Others insist upon it that her forte is the comic, and that Cimarosa is hard at work at another "Matrimonia Segreto." But in the meanwhile there is a check in the diplomacy somewhere. The Cardinal is observed to be out of humor. He has said publicly, — and the words are portentous, — "The silly girl is as mad as her father; what she asks is preposterous!" Conference follows conference; the Cardinal talks to the poor child very solemnly in his closet, — all in vain. Naples is distracted with curiosity and conjecture. The lecture ends in a quarrel, and Viola comes home sullen and pouting: she will not act, — she has renounced the engagement.

Pisani, too inexperienced to be aware of all the dangers of the stage, had been pleased at the notion that one, at least, of his name would add celebrity to his art. The girl's perverseness displeased him. However, he said nothing, — he never scolded in words, but he took up the faithful barbiton. Oh, faithful barbiton, how horribly thou didst scold! It screeched, it gabbled, it moaned, it growled. And Viola's eyes filled with tears, for she understood that language. She stole to her mother, and whispered in her ear; and when Pisani turned from his employment, lo!

---

* "Desire it was, 'twas wonder, 'twas delight."
    Wiffen's Translation.

both mother and daughter were weeping. He looked at them with a wondering stare; and then, as if he felt he had been harsh, he flew again to his Familiar. And now you thought you heard the lullaby which a fairy might sing to some fretful changeling it had adopted and sought to soothe. Liquid, low, silvery, streamed the tones beneath the enchanted bow. The most stubborn grief would have paused to hear; and withal, at times, out came a wild, merry, ringing note, like a laugh, but not mortal laughter. It was one of his most successful airs from his beloved opera, — the Siren in the act of charming the waves and the winds to sleep. Heaven knows what next would have come, but his arm was arrested. Viola had thrown herself on his breast, and kissed him, with happy eyes that smiled through her sunny hair. At that very moment the door opened, — a message from the Cardinal. Viola must go to his Eminence at once. Her mother went with her. All was reconciled and settled; Viola had her way, and selected her own opera. O ye dull nations of the North, with your broils and debates, — your bustling lives of the Pnyx and the Agora! — you cannot guess what a stir throughout musical Naples was occasioned by the rumor of a new opera and a new singer. But whose the opera? No cabinet intrigue ever was so secret. Pisani came back one night from the theater, evidently disturbed and irate. Woe to thine ears hadst thou heard the barbiton that night! They had suspended him from his office, — they feared that the new opera, and the first debut of his daughter as prima donna, would be too much for his nerves. And his variations, his diablerie of sirens and harpies, on such a night, made a hazard not to be contemplated without awe. To be set aside, and on the very night that his child, whose melody was but an emanation of his own, was to perform, — set aside for some new rival: it was too much for a musician's flesh and blood. For the first time he spoke in words upon the subject, and gravely asked — for that question the barbiton, eloquent as it was, could not express distinctly — what was to be the opera, and what the part? And Viola as gravely answered that she was pledged to the Cardinal not to reveal. Pisani said nothing, but disappeared with the violin; and presently they heard the Familiar from the house-top (whither, when thoroughly out of humor, the musician sometimes fled), whining and sighing as if its heart were broken.

The affections of Pisani were little visible on the surface. He was not one of those fond, caressing fathers whose children are ever playing round their knees; his mind and soul were so thoroughly in his art that domestic life glided by him, seemingly as if *that* were a dream, and the heart the substantial form and body of existence. Persons much cultivating an abstract study are often thus; mathematicians proverbially so. When his servant ran to the celebrated French philosopher, shrieking, "The house is on fire, sir!" "Go and tell my wife then, fool!" said the wise man, settling back to his problems; "do *I* ever meddle with domestic affairs?" But what are mathematics to music — music, that not only composes operas, but plays on the barbiton? Do you know what the illustrious Giardini said when the tyro asked how long it would take to learn to play on the violin? Hear, and despair, ye who would bend the bow to which that of Ulysses was a plaything, "Twelve hours a day for twenty years together!" Can a man, then, who plays the barbiton be always playing also with his little ones? No, Pisani; often, with the keen susceptibility of childhood, poor Viola had stolen from the room to weep at the thought that thou didst not love her. And yet, underneath this outward abstraction of the artist, the natural fondness flowed all the same; and as she grew up, the dreamer had understood the dreamer. And now, shut out from all fame himself; to be forbidden to hail even his daughter's fame! — and that daughter herself to be in the conspiracy against him! Sharper than the serpent's tooth was the ingratitude, and sharper than the serpent's tooth was the wail of the pitying barbiton!

The eventful hour is come. Viola is gone to the theater, — her mother with her. The indignant musician remains at home. Gionetta bursts into the room: my Lord Cardinal's carriage is at the door, — the Padrone is sent for. He must lay aside his violin; he must put on his brocade coat and his lace ruffles. Here they are, — quick, quick! And quick rolls the gilded coach, and majestic sits the driver, and statelily prance the steeds. Poor Pisani is lost in a mist of uncomfortable amaze. He arrives at the theater; he descends at the great door; he turns round and round, and looks about him and about: he misses something, — where is the violin? Alas! his soul, his voice, his self of self, is left behind! It is but an automaton that the lackeys conduct up the stairs, through the tier, into the Cardinal's box. But then, what bursts upon him! Does he dream? The first act is over (they did not send for him till success seemed no longer doubtful); the first act has decided all. He feels *that* by the electric sympathy which ever the one heart has at once with a vast audience. He feels it by the breathless stillness of that multitude; he feels it even by the lifted finger of the Cardinal. He sees his Viola on the stage, radiant in her robes and gems, — he hears her voice thrilling through the single heart of the thousands! But the scene, the part, the music! It is his other child, — his immortal child; the spirit-infant of his soul; his darling of many years of patient obscurity and pining genius; his masterpiece; his opera of the Siren!

This, then, was the mystery that had so galled him, — this the cause of the quarrel with the Cardinal; this the secret not to be proclaimed till the success was won, and the daughter had united her father's triumph with her own! And there she stands, as all souls bow before her, — fairer than the very Siren he had called from the deeps of melody.

Oh, long and sweet recompense of toil! Where is on earth the rapture like that which is known to genius when at last it bursts from its hidden cavern into light and fame!

He did not speak, he did not move; he stood transfixed, breathless, the tears rolling down his cheeks; only from time to time his hands still wandered about, — mechanically they sought for the faithful instrument, why was it not there to share his triumph?

At last the curtain fell; but on such a storm and diapason of applause! Up rose the audience as one man, as with one voice that dear name was shouted. She came on, trembling, pale, and in the whole crowd saw but her father's face. The audience followed those moistened eyes; they recognized with a thrill the daughter's impulse and her meaning. The good old Cardinal drew him gently forward. Wild musician, thy daughter has given thee back more than the life thou gavest!

"My poor violin!" said he, wiping his eyes, "they will never hiss thee again now!"

Chapter I.III.

Fra si contrarie tempre in ghiaccio e in foco,
In riso e in pianto, e fra paura e speme
L'ingannatrice Donna* —
                              "Gerusal. Lib.," cant. iv. xciv.

Now notwithstanding the triumph both of the singer and the opera, there had been one moment in the first act, and, consequently, *before* the arrival of Pisani, when the scale seemed more than doubtful. It was in a chorus replete with all the peculiarities of the composer. And when the Maelstrom of Capricci whirled and foamed, and tore ear and sense through every variety of sound, the audience simultaneously

---

* Between such contrarious mixtures of ice and fire, laughter and tears, — fear and hope, the deceiving dame.

recognized the hand of Pisani. A title had been given to the opera which had hitherto prevented all suspicion of its parentage; and the overture and opening, in which the music had been regular and sweet, had led the audience to fancy they detected the genius of their favorite Paisiello. Long accustomed to ridicule and almost to despise the pretensions of Pisani as a composer, they now felt as if they had been unduly cheated into the applause with which they had hailed the overture and the commencing scenas. An ominous buzz circulated round the house: the singers, the orchestra, — electrically sensitive to the impression of the audience, — grew, themselves, agitated and dismayed, and failed in the energy and precision which could alone carry off the grotesqueness of the music.

There are always in every theater many rivals to a new author and a new performer, — a party impotent while all goes well, but a dangerous ambush the instant some accident throws into confusion the march of success. A hiss arose; it was partial, it is true, but the significant silence of all applause seemed to forebode the coming moment when the displeasure would grow contagious. It was the breath that stirred the impending avalanche. At that critical moment Viola, the Siren queen, emerged for the first time from her ocean cave. As she came forward to the lamps, the novelty of her situation, the chilling apathy of the audience, — which even the sight of so singular a beauty did not at the first arouse, — the whispers of the malignant singers on the stage, the glare of the lights, and more — far more than the rest — that recent hiss, which had reached her in her concealment, all froze up her faculties and suspended her voice. And, instead of the grand invocation into which she ought rapidly to have burst, the regal Siren, retransformed into the trembling girl, stood pale and mute before the stern, cold array of those countless eyes.

At that instant, and when consciousness itself seemed about to fail her, as she turned a timid beseeching glance around the still multitude, she perceived, in a box near the stage, a countenance which at once, and like magic, produced on her mind an effect never to be analyzed nor forgotten. It was one that awakened an indistinct, haunting reminiscence, as if she had seen it in those daydreams she had been so wont from infancy to indulge. She could not withdraw her gaze from that face, and as she gazed, the awe and coldness that had before seized her, vanished like a mist from before the sun.

In the dark splendor of the eyes that met her own there was indeed so much of gentle encouragement, of benign and compassionate admiration, — so much that warmed, and animated, and nerved, — that anyone, actor or orator, who has ever observed the effect that a single earnest and kindly look in the crowd that is to be addressed and won, will produce upon his mind, may readily account for the sudden and inspiriting influence which the eye and smile of the stranger exercised on the debutante.

And while yet she gazed, and the glow returned to her heart, the stranger half rose, as if to recall the audience to a sense of the courtesy due to one so fair and young; and the instant his voice gave the signal, the audience followed it by a burst of generous applause. For this stranger himself was a marked personage, and his recent arrival at Naples had divided with the new opera the gossip of the city. And then as the applause ceased, clear, full, and freed from every fetter, like a spirit from the clay, the Siren's voice poured forth its entrancing music. From that time Viola forgot the crowd, the hazard, the whole world, — except the fairy one over with she presided. It seemed that the stranger's presence only served still more to heighten that delusion, in which the artist sees no creation without the circle of his art, she felt as if that serene brow, and those brilliant eyes, inspired her with powers never known before: and, as if searching for a language to express the strange sensations occasioned by his presence, that presence itself whispered to her the melody and the song.

Only when all was over, and she saw her father and felt his joy, did this wild spell vanish before the sweeter one of the household and filial love. Yet again, as she turned from the stage, she looked back involuntarily, and the stranger's calm and half-melancholy smile sank into her heart, — to live there, to be recalled with confused memories, half of pleasure, and half of pain.

Pass over the congratulations of the good Cardinal-Virtuoso, astonished at finding himself and all Naples had been hitherto in the wrong on a subject of taste, — still more astonished at finding himself and all Naples combining to confess it; pass over the whispered ecstasies of admiration which buzzed in the singer's ear, as once more, in her modest veil and quiet dress, she escaped from the crowd of gallants that choked up every avenue behind the scenes; pass over the sweet embrace of father and child, returning through the starlit streets and along the deserted Chiaja in the Cardinal's carriage; never pause now to note the tears and ejaculations of the good, simple-hearted mother, — see them returned; see the well-known room, venimus ad larem nostrum*; see old Gionetta bustling at the supper; and hear Pisani, as he rouses the barbiton from its case, communicating all that has happened to the intelligent Familiar; hark to the mother's merry, low, English laugh. Why, Viola, strange child, sittest thou apart, thy face leaning on thy fair hands, thine eyes fixed on space? Up, rouse thee! Every dimple on the cheek of home must smile tonight.†

* We come to our own house.

And a happy reunion it was round that humble table: a feast Lucullus might have envied in his Hall of Apollo, in the dried grapes, and the dainty sardines, and the luxurious polenta, and the old lacrima a present from the good Cardinal. The barbiton, placed on a chair — a tall, high-backed chair — beside the musician, seemed to take a part in the festive meal. Its honest varnished face glowed in the light of the lamp; and there was an impish, sly demureness in its very silence, as its master, between every mouthful, turned to talk to it of something he had forgotten to relate before. The good wife looked on affectionately, and could not eat for joy; but suddenly she rose, and placed on the artist's temples a laurel wreath, which she had woven beforehand in fond anticipation; and Viola, on the other side her brother, the barbiton, rearranged the chaplet, and, smoothing back her father's hair, whispered, "Caro Padre, you will not let *him* scold me again!"

Then poor Pisani, rather distracted between the two, and excited both by the lacrima and his triumph, turned to the younger child with so naïve and grotesque a pride, "I don't know which to thank the most. You give me so much joy, child, — I am so proud of thee and myself. But he and I, poor fellow, have been so often unhappy together!"

Viola's sleep was broken, — that was natural. The intoxication of vanity and triumph, the happiness in the happiness she had caused, all this was better than sleep. But still from all this, again and again her thoughts flew to those haunting eyes, to that smile with which forever the memory of the triumph, of the happiness, was to be united. Her feelings, like her own character, were strange and peculiar. They were not those of a girl whose heart, for the first time reached through the eye, sighs its natural and native language of first love. It was not so much admiration, though the face that reflected itself on every wave of her restless fancies was of the rarest order of majesty and beauty; nor a pleased and enamored recollection that the sight of this stranger had bequeathed: it was a human sentiment of gratitude and delight, mixed with something more mysterious, of fear and awe. Certainly she had seen before those features; but when and how? Only when her thoughts had sought to shape out her future, and when, in spite of all the attempts to vision forth a fate of flowers and sunshine, a dark and chill foreboding made her recoil back into her deepest self. It was a something found that had long been sought for by a thousand restless yearnings and vague desires, less of the heart than mind; not as when youth discovers the one to be beloved, but rather as when the student, long wandering after the clew to some truth in science, sees it glimmer dimly before him, to beckon, to recede, to allure, and to wane again. She fell at last into unquiet slumber, vexed by deformed, fleeting, shapeless phantoms; and,

---

† "Ridete quidquid est domi cachinnorum." Catull. "ad Sirm. Penin."

waking, as the sun, through a veil of hazy cloud, glinted with a sickly ray across the casement, she heard her father settled back betimes to his one pursuit, and calling forth from his Familiar a low mournful strain, like a dirge over the dead.

"And why," she asked, when she descended to the room below, — "why, my father, was your inspiration so sad, after the joy of last night?"

"I know not, child. I meant to be merry, and compose an air in honor of thee; but he is an obstinate fellow, this, — and he would have it so."

Chapter I.IV.

E cosi i pigri e timidi desiri*

Sprona
"Gerusal. Lib.," cant. iv. lxxxviii.

*I*t was the custom of Pisani, except when the duties of his profession made special demand on his time, to devote a certain portion of the mid-day to sleep, — a habit not so much a luxury as a necessity to a man who slept very little during the night. In fact, whether to compose or to practice, the hours of noon were precisely those in which Pisani could not have been active if he would. His genius resembled those fountains full at dawn and evening, overflowing at night, and perfectly dry at the meridian. During this time, consecrated by her husband to repose, the signora generally stole out to make the purchases necessary for the little household, or to enjoy (as what woman does not?) a little relaxation in gossip with some of her own sex. And the day following this brilliant triumph, how many congratulations would she have to receive!

At these times it was Viola's habit to seat herself without the door of the house, under an awning which sheltered from the sun without obstructing the view; and there now, with the prompt-book on her knee, on which her eye roves listlessly from time to time, you may behold her,

---

* And thus the slow and timid passions urged.

the vine-leaves clustering from their arching trellis over the door behind, and the lazy white-sailed boats skimming along the sea that stretched before.

As she thus sat, rather in reverie than thought, a man coming from the direction of Posilipo, with a slow step and downcast eyes, passed close by the house, and Viola, looking up abruptly, started in a kind of terror as she recognized the stranger. She uttered an involuntary exclamation, and the cavalier turning, saw, and paused.

He stood a moment or two between her and the sunlit ocean, contemplating in a silence too serious and gentle for the boldness of gallantry, the blushing face and the young slight form before him; at length he spoke.

"Are you happy, my child," he said, in almost a paternal tone, "at the career that lies before you? From sixteen to thirty, the music in the breath of applause is sweeter than all the music your voice can utter!"

"I know not," replied Viola, falteringly, but encouraged by the liquid softness of the accents that addressed her, — "I know not whether I am happy now, but I was last night. And I feel, too, Excellency, that I have you to thank, though, perhaps, you scarce know why!"

"You deceive yourself," said the cavalier, with a smile. "I am aware that I assisted to your merited success, and it is you who scarce know how. The *why* I will tell you: because I saw in your heart a nobler ambition than that of the woman's vanity; it was the daughter that interested me. Perhaps you would rather I should have admired the singer?"

"No; oh, no!"

"Well, I believe you. And now, since we have thus met, I will pause to counsel you. When next you go to the theater, you will have at your feet all the young gallants of Naples. Poor infant! the flame that dazzles the eye can scorch the wing. Remember that the only homage that does not sully must be that which these gallants will not give thee. And whatever thy dreams of the future, — and I see, while I speak to thee, how wandering they are, and wild, — may only those be fulfilled which center round the hearth of home."

He paused, as Viola's breast heaved beneath its robe. And with a burst of natural and innocent emotions, scarcely comprehending, though an Italian, the grave nature of his advice, she exclaimed, —

"Ah, Excellency, you cannot know how dear to me that home is already. And my father, — there would be no home, signor, without him!"

A deep and melancholy shade settled over the face of the cavalier. He looked up at the quiet house buried amidst the vine-leaves, and turned again to the vivid, animated face of the young actress.

"It is well," said he. "A simple heart may be its own best guide, and so, go on, and prosper. Adieu, fair singer."

"Adieu, Excellency; but," and something she could not resist — an anxious, sickening feeling of fear and hope, — impelled her to the question, "I shall see you again, shall I not, at San Carlo?"

"Not, at least, for some time. I leave Naples today."

"Indeed!" and Viola's heart sank within her; the poetry of the stage was gone.

"And," said the cavalier, turning back, and gently laying his hand on hers, — "and, perhaps, before we meet, you may have suffered: known the first sharp griefs of human life, — known how little what fame can gain, repays what the heart can lose; but be brave and yield not, — not even to what may seem the piety of sorrow. Observe yon tree in your neighbor's garden. Look how it grows up, crooked and distorted. Some wind scattered the germ from which it sprang, in the clefts of the rock; choked up and walled round by crags and buildings, by Nature and man, its life has been one struggle for the light, — light which makes to that life the necessity and the principle: you see how it has writhed and twisted; how, meeting the barrier in one spot, it has labored and worked, stem and branches, towards the clear skies at last. What has preserved it through each disfavor of birth and circumstances, — why are its leaves as green and fair as those of the vine behind you, which, with all its arms, can embrace the open sunshine? My child, because of the very instinct that impelled the struggle, — because the labor for the light won to the light at length. So with a gallant heart, through every adverse accident of sorrow and of fate to turn to the sun, to strive for the heaven; this it is that gives knowledge to the strong and happiness to the weak. Ere we meet again, you will turn sad and heavy eyes to those quiet boughs, and when you hear the birds sing from them, and see the sunshine come aslant from crag and housetop to be the playfellow of their leaves, learn the lesson that Nature teaches you, and strive through darkness to the light!"

As he spoke he moved on slowly, and left Viola wondering, silent, saddened with his dim prophecy of coming evil, and yet, through sadness, charmed. Involuntarily her eyes followed him, — involuntarily she stretched forth her arms, as if by a gesture to call him back; she would have given worlds to have seen him turn, — to have heard once more his low, calm, silvery voice; to have felt again the light touch of his hand on hers. As moonlight that softens into beauty every angle on which it falls, seemed his presence, — as moonlight vanishes, and things assume their common aspect of the rugged and the mean, he receded from her eyes, and the outward scene was commonplace once more.

The stranger passed on, through that long and lovely road which reaches at last the palaces that face the public gardens, and conducts to the more populous quarters of the city.

A group of young, dissipated courtiers, loitering by the gateway of a house which was open for the favorite pastime of the day, — the resort of the wealthier and more highborn gamesters, — made way for him, as with a courteous inclination he passed them by.

"Per fede," said one, "is not that the rich Zanoni, of whom the town talks?"

"Aye; they say his wealth is incalculable!"

"*They* say, — who are *they*? — what is the authority? He has not been many days at Naples, and I cannot yet find anyone who knows aught of his birthplace, his parentage, or, what is more important, his estates!"

"That is true; but he arrived in a goodly vessel, which *they say* is his own. See, — no, you cannot see it here; but it rides yonder in the bay. The bankers he deals with speak with awe of the sums placed in their hands."

"Whence came he?"

"From some seaport in the East. My valet learned from some of the sailors on the Mole that he had resided many years in the interior of India."

"Ah, I am told that in India men pick up gold like pebbles, and that there are valleys where the birds build their nests with emeralds to attract the moths. Here comes our prince of gamesters, Cetoxa; be sure that he already must have made acquaintance with so wealthy a cavalier; he has that attraction to gold which the magnet has to steel. Well, Cetoxa, what fresh news of the ducats of Signor Zanoni?"

"Oh," said Cetoxa, carelessly, "my friend —"

"Ha! ha! hear him; his friend —"

"Yes; my friend Zanoni is going to Rome for a short time; when he returns, he has promised me to fix a day to sup with me, and I will then introduce him to you, and to the best society of Naples! Diavolo! but he is a most agreeable and witty gentleman!"

"Pray tell us how you came so suddenly to be his friend."

"My dear Belgioso, nothing more natural. He desired a box at San Carlo; but I need not tell you that the expectation of a new opera (ah, how superb it is, — that poor devil, Pisani; who would have thought it?) and a new singer (what a face, — what a voice! — ah!) had engaged every corner of the house. I heard of Zanoni's desire to honor the talent of Naples, and, with my usual courtesy to distinguished strangers, I sent to place my box at his disposal. He accepts it, — I wait on him between the acts; he is most charming; he invites me to supper. Cospetto, what a retinue! We sit late, — I tell him all the news of Naples; we grow bosom friends; he presses on me this diamond before we part, — is a trifle, he tells me: the jewelers value it at 5000 pistoles! — the merriest evening I have passed these ten years."

The cavaliers crowded round to admire the diamond.

"Signor Count Cetoxa," said one grave-looking somber man, who had crossed himself two or three times during the Neapolitan's narrative, "are you not aware of the strange reports about this person; and are you not afraid to receive from him a gift which may carry with it the most fatal consequences? Do you not know that he is said to be a sorcerer; to possess the mal-occhio; to —"

"Prithee, spare us your antiquated superstitions," interrupted Cetoxa, contemptuously. "They are out of fashion; nothing now goes down but skepticism and philosophy. And what, after all, do these rumors, when sifted, amount to? They have no origin but this, — a silly old man of eighty-six, quite in his dotage, solemnly avers that he saw this same Zanoni seventy years ago* at Milan; when this very Zanoni, as you all see, is at least as young as you or I, Belgioso."

"But that," said the grave gentleman, — *"That* is the mystery. Old Avelli declares that Zanoni does not seem a day older than when they met at Milan. He says that even then at Milan — mark this — where, though under another name, this Zanoni appeared in the same splendor, he was attended also by the same mystery. And that an old man *there* remembered to have seen him sixty years before, in Sweden."

"Tush," returned Cetoxa, "the same thing has been said of the quack Cagliostro, — mere fables. I will believe them when I see this diamond turn to a wisp of hay. For the rest," he added gravely, "I consider this illustrious gentleman my friend; and a whisper against his honor and repute will in future be equivalent to an affront to myself."

Cetoxa was a redoubted swordsman, and excelled in a peculiarly awkward maneuver, which he himself had added to the variations of the stoccata. The grave gentleman, however anxious for the spiritual weal of the count, had an equal regard for his own corporeal safety. He contented himself with a look of compassion, and, turning through the gateway, ascended the stairs to the gaming tables.

"Ha, ha!" said Cetoxa, laughing, "our good Loredano is envious of my diamond. Gentlemen, you sup with me tonight. I assure you I never met a more delightful, sociable, entertaining person, than my dear friend the Signor Zanoni."

---

* he himself, the narrator, then a mere boy

Chapter I.V.

Quello Ippogifo, grande e strano augello
Lo porta via.*

"Orlando Furioso," c. vi. xviii.

And now, accompanying this mysterious Zanoni, am I compelled
to bid a short farewell to Naples. Mount behind me, — mount on my
hippogriff, reader; settle yourself at your ease. I bought the pillion the
other day of a poet who loves his comfort; it has been newly stuffed for
your special accommodation. So, so, we ascend! Look as we ride aloft,
— look! — never fear, hippogriffs never stumble; and every hippogriff in
Italy is warranted to carry elderly gentlemen, — look down on the gliding
landscapes! There, near the ruins of the Oscan's old Atella, rises Aversa,
once the stronghold of the Norman; there gleam the columns of Capua,
above the Vulturnian Stream. Hail to ye, cornfields and vineyards
famous for the old Falernian! Hail to ye, golden orange-groves of Mola
di Gaeta! Hail to ye, sweet shrubs and wild flowers, omnis copia narium,
that clothe the mountain-skirts of the silent Lautulae! Shall we rest at
the Volscian Anxur, — the modern Terracina, — where the lofty rock
stands like the giant that guards the last borders of the southern land
of love? Away, away! and hold your breath as we flit above the Pontine
Marshes. Dreary and desolate, their miasma is to the gardens we have
passed what the rank commonplace of life is to the heart when it has
left love behind.

Mournful Campagna, thou openest on us in majestic sadness. Rome,
seven-hilled Rome! receive us as Memory receives the way worn; receive
us in silence, amidst ruins! Where is the traveler we pursue? Turn the
hippogriff loose to graze: he loves the acanthus that wreathes round yon
broken columns. Yes, that is the arch of Titus, the conqueror of Jerusalem, — that the Colosseum! Through one passed the triumph of the
deified invader; in one fell the butchered gladiators. Monuments of

* That hippogriff, great and marvelous bird, bears him away.

murder, how poor the thoughts, how mean the memories ye awaken, compared with those that speak to the heart of man on the heights of Phyle, or by thy lone mound, grey Marathon! We stand amidst weeds and brambles and long waving herbage. Where we stand reigned Nero, — here were his tessellated floors; here,

"Mighty in the heaven, a second heaven,"

hung the vault of his ivory roofs; here, arch upon arch, pillar on pillar, glittered to the world the golden palace of its master, — the Golden House of Nero. How the lizard watches us with his bright, timorous eye! We disturb his reign. Gather that wild flower: the Golden House is vanished, but the wild flower may have kin to those which the stranger's hand scattered over the tyrant's grave; see, over this soil, the grave of Rome, Nature strews the wild flowers still!

In the midst of this desolation is an old building of the Middle Ages. Here dwells a singular recluse. In the season of the malaria the native peasant flies the rank vegetation round; but he, a stranger and a foreigner, no associates, no companions, except books and instruments of science. He is often seen wandering over the grass-grown hills, or sauntering through the streets of the new city, not with the absent brow and incurious air of students, but with observant piercing eyes that seem to dive into the hearts of the passers-by. An old man, but not infirm, — erect and stately, as if in his prime. None know whether he be rich or poor. He asks no charity, and he gives none, — he does no evil, and seems to confer no good. He is a man who appears to have no world beyond himself; but appearances are deceitful, and Science, as well as Benevolence, lives in the Universe. This abode, for the first time since thus occupied, a visitor enters. It is Zanoni.

You observe those two men seated together, conversing earnestly. Years long and many have flown away since they met last, — at least, bodily, and face to face. But if they are sages, thought can meet thought, and spirit spirit, though oceans divide the forms. Death itself divides not the wise. Thou meetest Plato when thine eyes moisten over the Phaedo. May Homer live with all men forever!

They converse; they confess to each other; they conjure up the past, and repeople it; but note how differently do such remembrances affect the two. On Zanoni's face, despite its habitual calm, the emotions change and go. *He* has acted in the past he surveys; but not a trace of the humanity that participates in joy and sorrow can be detected on the passionless visage of his companion; the past, to him, as is now the present, has been but as Nature to the sage, the volume to the student, — a calm and spiritual life, a study, a contemplation.

From the past they turn to the future. Ah! at the close of the last century, the future seemed a thing tangible, — it was woven up in all men's fears and hopes of the present.

At the verge of that hundred years, Man, the ripest born of Time,* stood as at the deathbed of the Old World, and beheld the New Orb, blood red amidst cloud and vapor, — uncertain if a comet or a sun. Behold the icy and profound disdain on the brow of the old man, — the lofty yet touching sadness that darkens the glorious countenance of Zanoni. Is it that one views with contempt the struggle and its issue, and the other with awe or pity? Wisdom contemplating mankind leads but to the two results, — compassion or disdain. He who believes in other worlds can accustom himself to look on this as the naturalist on the revolutions of an anthill, or of a leaf. What is the Earth to Infinity, — what its duration to the Eternal? Oh, how much greater is the soul of one man than the vicissitudes of the whole globe! Child of heaven, and heir of immortality, how from some star hereafter wilt thou look back on the anthill and its commotions, from Clovis to Robespierre, from Noah to the Final Fire. The spirit that can contemplate, that lives only in the intellect, can ascend to its star, even from the midst of the burial-ground called Earth, and while the sarcophagus called Life immures in its clay the everlasting!

But thou, Zanoni, — thou hast refused to live *only* in the intellect; thou hast not mortified the heart; thy pulse still beats with the sweet music of mortal passion; thy kind is to thee still something warmer than an abstraction, — thou wouldst look upon this Revolution in its cradle, which the storms rock; thou wouldst see the world while its elements yet struggle through the chaos!

Go!

Chapter 1. VI.

Precepteurs ignorans de ce faible univers.†

---

* "An des Jahrhunderts Neige,
    Der reifste Sohn der Zeit."
        "Die Kunstler."
† Ignorant teachers of this weak world.

— Voltaire.

Nous etions a table chez un de nos confreres a l'Academie,
Grand Seigneur et homme d'esprit.*

— La Harpe

*O*ne evening, at Paris, several months after the date of our last
chapter, there was a reunion of some of the most eminent wits of the
time, at the house of a personage distinguished alike by noble birth and
liberal accomplishments. Nearly all present were of the views that were
then the mode. For, as came afterwards a time when nothing was so
unpopular as the people, so that was the time when nothing was so
vulgar as aristocracy. The airiest fine gentleman and the haughtiest noble
prated of equality, and lisped enlightenment.

Among the more remarkable guests were Condorcet, then in the
prime of his reputation, the correspondent of the king of Prussia, the
intimate of Voltaire, the member of half the academies of Europe, —
noble by birth, polished in manners, republican in opinions. There, too,
was the venerable Malesherbes, "l'amour et les delices de la Nation."†
There Jean Silvain Bailly, the accomplished scholar, — the aspiring
politician. It was one of those petits soupers for which the capital of all
social pleasures was so renowned. The conversation, as might be expected, was literary and intellectual, enlivened by graceful pleasantry.
Many of the ladies of that ancient and proud noblesse — for the noblesse
yet existed, though its hours were already numbered — added to the
charm of the society; and theirs were the boldest criticisms, and often
the most liberal sentiments.

Vain labor for me — vain labor almost for the grave English language
— to do justice to the sparkling paradoxes that flew from lip to lip. The
favorite theme was the superiority of the moderns to the ancients.
Condorcet on this head was eloquent, and to some, at least, of his
audience, most convincing. That Voltaire was greater than Homer few
there were disposed to deny. Keen was the ridicule lavished on the dull
pedantry which finds everything ancient necessarily sublime.

"Yet," said the graceful Marquis de — , as the champagne danced to
his glass, "more ridiculous still is the superstition that finds everything
incomprehensible holy! But intelligence circulates, Condorcet; like
water, it finds its level. My hairdresser said to me this morning, 'Though
I am but a poor fellow, I believe as little as the finest gentleman!'"
"Unquestionably, the great Revolution draws near to its final comple-

---

* We supped with one of our confreres of the Academy, — a great nobleman and wit.
† The idol and delight of the nation (so-called by his historian, Gaillard).

tion, — a pas de geant, as Montesquieu said of his own immortal work."

Then there rushed from all — wit and noble, courtier and republican — a confused chorus, harmonious only in its anticipation of the brilliant things to which "the great Revolution" was to give birth. Here Condrocet is more eloquent than before.

"Il faut absolument que la Superstition et le Fanatisme fassent place a la Philosophie.* Kings persecute persons, priests opinion. Without kings, men must be safe; and without priests, minds must be free."

"Ah," murmured the marquis, "and as ce cher Diderot has so well sung, —

'Et des boyaux du dernier pretre
Serrez le cou du dernier roi.'"†

"And then," resumed Condorcet, — "then commences the Age of Reason! — equality in instruction, equality in institutions, equality in wealth! The great impediments to knowledge are, first, the want of a common language; and next, the short duration of existence. But as to the first, when all men are brothers, why not a universal language? As to the second, the organic perfectibility of the vegetable world is undisputed, is Nature less powerful in the nobler existence of thinking man? The very destruction of the two most active causes of physical deterioration — here, luxurious wealth; there, abject penury, — must necessarily prolong the general term of life.‡ The art of medicine will then be honored in the place of war, which is the art of murder: the noblest study of the acutest minds will be devoted to the discovery and arrest of the causes of disease. Life, I grant, cannot be made eternal; but it may be prolonged almost indefinitely. And as the meaner animal bequeaths its vigor to its offspring, so man shall transmit his improved organization, mental and physical, to his sons. Oh, yes, to such a consummation does our age approach!"

The venerable Malesherbes sighed. Perhaps he feared the consummation might not come in time for him. The handsome Marquis de — and the ladies, yet handsomer than he, looked conviction and delight.

But two men there were, seated next to each other, who joined not in the general talk: the one a stranger newly arrived in Paris, where his wealth, his person, and his accomplishments, had already made him remarked and courted; the other, an old man, somewhere about seventy, — the witty and virtuous, brave, and still light-hearted Cazotte, the author of "Le Diable Amoureux."

---

* It must necessarily happen that superstition and fanaticism give place to philosophy.
† And throttle the neck of the last king with the string from the bowels of the last priest.
‡ See Condorcet's posthumous work on the Progress of the Human Mind. — Ed.

These two conversed familiarly, and apart from the rest, and only by an occasional smile testified their attention to the general conversation.

"Yes," said the stranger, — "yes, we have met before."

"I thought I could not forget your countenance; yet I task in vain my recollections of the past."

"I will assist you. Recall the time when, led by curiosity, or perhaps the nobler desire of knowledge, you sought initiation into the mysterious order of Martines de Pasqualis."*

"Ah, is it possible! You are one of that theurgic brotherhood?"

"Nay, I attended their ceremonies but to see how vainly they sought to revive the ancient marvels of the cabala."

"Such studies please you? I have shaken off the influence they once had on my own imagination."

"You have not shaken it off," returned the stranger, bravely; "it is on you still, — on you at this hour; it beats in your heart; it kindles in your reason; it will speak in your tongue!"

And then, with a yet lower voice, the stranger continued to address him, to remind him of certain ceremonies and doctrines, — to explain and enforce them by references to the actual experience and history of his listener, which Cazotte thrilled to find so familiar to a stranger.

Gradually the old man's pleasing and benevolent countenance grew overcast, and he turned, from time to time, searching, curious, uneasy glances towards his companion.

The charming Duchesse de G—— archly pointed out to the lively guests the abstracted air and clouded brow of the poet; and Condorcet, who liked no one else to be remarked, when he himself was present, said to Cazotte, "Well, and what do *you* predict of the Revolution, — how, at least, will it affect us?"

At that question Cazotte started; his cheeks grew pale, large drops stood on his forehead; his lips writhed; his gay companions gazed on

---

* It is so recorded of Cazotte. Of Martines de Pasqualis little is known; even the country to which he belonged is matter of conjecture. Equally so the rites, ceremonies, and nature of the cabalistic order he established. St. Martin was a disciple of the school, and that, at least, is in its favor; for in spite of his mysticism, no man more beneficent, generous, pure, and virtuous than St. Martin adorned the last century. Above all, no man more distinguished himself from the herd of skeptical philosophers by the gallantry and fervor with which he combated materialism, and vindicated the necessity of faith amidst a chaos of unbelief. It may also be observed, that Cazotte, whatever else he learned of the brotherhood of Martines, learned nothing that diminished the excellence of his life and the sincerity of his religion. At once gentle and brave, he never ceased to oppose the excesses of the Revolution. To the last, unlike the Liberals of his time, he was a devout and sincere Christian. Before his execution, he demanded a pen and paper to write these words: "Ma femme, mes enfans, ne me pleurez pas; ne m'oubliez pas, mais souvenez-vous surtout de ne jamais offenser Dieu." ("My wife, my children, weep not for me; forget me not, but remember above everything never to offend God.) — Ed.

him in surprise.

"Speak!" whispered the stranger, laying his hand gently upon the arm of the old wit.

At that word Cazotte's face grew locked and rigid, his eyes dwelt vacantly on space, and in a low, hollow voice, he thus answered*, — "You ask how it will affect yourselves, — you, its most learned, and its least selfish agents. I will answer: you, Marquis de Condorcet, will die in prison, but not by the hand of the executioner. In the peaceful happiness of that day, the philosopher will carry about with him not the elixir but the poison."

"My poor Cazotte," said Condorcet, with his gentle smile, "what have prisons, executioners, and poison to do with an age of liberty and brotherhood?"

"It is in the names of Liberty and Brotherhood that the prisons will reek, and the headsman be glutted."

"You are thinking of priestcraft, not philosophy, Cazotte," said Champfort.†

"And what of me?"

"You will open your own veins to escape the fraternity of Cain. Be comforted; the last drops will not follow the razor. For you, venerable Malesherbes; for you, Aimar Nicolai; for you, learned Bailly, — I see them dress the scaffold! And all the while, O great philosophers, your murderers will have no word but philosophy on their lips!"

The hush was complete and universal when the pupil of Voltaire — the prince of the academic skeptics, hot La Harpe — cried with a sarcastic laugh, "Do not flatter me, O prophet, by exemption from the fate of my companions. Shall *I* have no part to play in this drama of your fantasies."

At this question, Cazotte's countenance lost its unnatural expression of awe and sternness; the sardonic humor most common to it came back and played in his brightening eyes.

"Yes, La Harpe, the most wonderful part of all! *You* will become — a Christian!"

---

* The following prophecy (not unfamiliar, perhaps, to some of my readers), with some slight variations, and at greater length, in the text of the authority I am about to cite, is to be found in La Harpe's posthumous works. The MS. is said to exist still in La Harpe's handwriting, and the story is given on M. Petitot's authority, volume i. page 62. It is not for me to enquire if there be doubts of its foundation on fact. — Ed.

† Champfort, one of those men of letters who, though misled by the first fair show of the Revolution, refused to follow the baser men of action into its horrible excesses, lived to express the murderous philanthropy of its agents by the best bon mot of the time. Seeing written on the walls, "Fraternite ou la Mort," he observed that the sentiment should be translated thus, "Sois mon frere, ou je te tue." — "Be my brother, or I kill thee."

This was too much for the audience that a moment before seemed grave and thoughtful, and they burst into an immoderate fit of laughter, while Cazotte, as if exhausted by his predictions, sank back in his chair, and breathed hard and heavily.

"Nay," said Madame de G——, "you who have predicted such grave things concerning us, must prophesy something also about yourself."

A convulsive tremor shook the involuntary prophet, — it passed, and left his countenance elevated by an expression of resignation and calm. "Madame," said he, after a long pause, "during the siege of Jerusalem, we are told by its historian that a man, for seven successive days, went round the ramparts, exclaiming, 'Woe to thee, Jerusalem, — woe to myself!'"

"Well, Cazotte, well?"

"And on the seventh day, while he thus spoke, a stone from the machines of the Romans dashed him into atoms!"

With these words, Cazotte rose; and the guests, awed in spite of themselves, shortly afterwards broke up and retired.

Chapter I.VII.

Qui donc t'a donne la mission s'annoncer au peuple que la divinite n'existe pas? Quel avantage trouves-tu a persuader a l'homme qu'une force aveugle preside a ses destinees et frappe au hasard le crime et la vertu?*
— Robespierre, "Discours," Mai 7, 1794.

*I*t was some time before midnight when the stranger returned home. His apartments were situated in one of those vast abodes which may be called an epitome of Paris itself, — the cellars rented by mechanics,

* Who then invested you with the mission to announce to the people that there is no God? What advantage find you in persuading man that nothing but blind force presides over his destinies, and strikes haphazard both crime and virtue?

scarcely removed a step from paupers, often by outcasts and fugitives from the law, often by some daring writer, who, after scattering amongst the people doctrines the most subversive of order, or the most libelous on the characters of priest, minister, and king, retired amongst the rats, to escape the persecution that attends the virtuous; the ground-floor occupied by shops; the entresol by artists; the principal stories by nobles; and the garrets by journeymen or grisettes.

As the stranger passed up the stairs, a young man of a form and countenance singularly unprepossessing emerged from a door in the entresol, and brushed beside him. His glance was furtive, sinister, savage, and yet timorous; the man's face was of an ashen paleness, and the features worked convulsively. The stranger paused, and observed him with thoughtful looks, as he hurried down the stairs. While he thus stood, he heard a groan from the room which the young man had just quitted; the latter had pulled to the door with hasty vehemence, but some fragment, probably of fuel, had prevented its closing, and it now stood slightly ajar; the stranger pushed it open and entered. He passed a small anteroom, meanly furnished, and stood in a bedchamber of meager and sordid discomfort. Stretched on the bed, and writhing in pain, lay an old man; a single candle lit the room, and threw its feeble ray over the furrowed and deathlike face of the sick person. No attendant was by; he seemed left alone, to breathe his last. "Water," he moaned feebly, — "water: — I parch, — I burn!" The intruder approached the bed, bent over him, and took his hand. "Oh, bless thee, Jean, bless thee!" said the sufferer; "hast thou brought back the physician already? Sir, I am poor, but I can pay you well. I would not die yet, for that young man's sake." And he sat upright in his bed, and fixed his dim eyes anxiously on his visitor.

"What are your symptoms, your disease?"

"Fire, fire, fire in the heart, the entrails: I burn!"

"How long is it since you have taken food?"

"Food! only this broth. There is the basin, all I have taken these six hours. I had scarce drunk it ere these pains began."

The stranger looked at the basin; some portion of the contents was yet left there.

"Who administered this to you?"

"Who? Jean! Who else should? I have no servant, — none! I am poor, very poor, sir. But no! you physicians do not care for the poor. *I am rich!* can you cure me?"

"Yes, if Heaven permit. Wait but a few moments."

The old man was fast sinking under the rapid effects of poison. The stranger repaired to his own apartments, and returned in a few moments with some preparation that had the instant result of an antidote. The pain ceased, the blue and livid color receded from the lips; the old man fell into a profound sleep. The stranger drew the curtains round the bed, took up the light, and inspected the apartment. The walls of both rooms were hung with drawings of masterly excellence. A portfolio was filled with sketches of equal skill, — but these last were mostly subjects that appalled the eye and revolted the taste: they displayed the human figure in every variety of suffering, — the rack, the wheel, the gibbet; all that cruelty has invented to sharpen the pangs of death seemed yet more dreadful from the passionate gusto and earnest force of the designer. And some of the countenances of those thus delineated were sufficiently removed from the ideal to show that they were portraits; in a large, bold, irregular hand was written beneath these drawings, "The Future of the Aristocrats." In a corner of the room, and close by an old bureau, was a small bundle, over which, as if to hide it, a cloak was thrown carelessly. Several shelves were filled with books; these were almost entirely the works of the philosophers of the time, — the philosophers of the material school, especially the Encyclopedistes, whom Robespierre afterwards so singularly attacked when the coward deemed it unsafe to leave his reign without a God.*

A volume lay on a table, — it was one of Voltaire, and the page was opened at his argumentative assertion of the existence of the Supreme Being.† The margin was covered with penciled notes, in the stiff but tremulous hand of old age; all in attempt to refute or to ridicule the logic of the sage of Ferney: Voltaire did not go far enough for the annotator! The clock struck two, when the sound of steps was heard without. The stranger silently seated himself on the farther side of the bed, and its drapery screened him, as he sat, from the eyes of a man who now entered on tiptoe; it was the same person who had passed him on the stairs. The newcomer took up the candle and approached the bed. The old man's face was turned to the pillow; but he lay so still, and his breathing was so inaudible, that his sleep might well, by that hasty, shrinking, guilty glance, be mistaken for the repose of death. The newcomer drew back, and a grim smile passed over his face: he replaced

---

* "Cette secte (les Encyclopedistes) propagea avec beaucoup de zele l'opinion du materialisme, qui prevalut parmi les grands et parmi les beaux esprits; on lui doit en partie cette espece de philosophie pratique qui, reduisant l'Egoisme en systeme regarde la societe humaine comme une guerre de ruse, le succes comme la regle du juste et de l'injuste, la probite comme une affaire de gout, ou de bienseance, le monde comme le patrimoine des fripons adroits." — "Discours de Robespierre," Mai 7, 1794. — This sect (the Encyclopaedists) propagate with much zeal the doctrine of materialism, which prevails among the great and the wits; we owe to it partly that kind of practical philosophy which, reducing Egotism to a system, looks upon society as a war of cunning; success the rule of right and wrong, honesty as an affair of taste or decency: and the world as the patrimony of clever scoundrels.

† "Histoire de Jenni."

the candle on the table, opened the bureau with a key which he took from his pocket, and loaded himself with several rouleaus of gold that he found in the drawers. At this time the old man began to wake. He stirred, he looked up; he turned his eyes towards the light now waning in its socket; he saw the robber at his work; he sat erect for an instant, as if transfixed, more even by astonishment than terror. At last he sprang from his bed.

"Just Heaven! do I dream! Thou — thou — thou, for whom I toiled and starved! — *Thou!*"

The robber started; the gold fell from his hand, and rolled on the floor.

"What!" he said, "art thou not dead yet? Has the poison failed?"

"Poison, boy! Ah!" shrieked the old man, and covered his face with his hands; then, with sudden energy, he exclaimed, "Jean! Jean! recall that word. Rob, plunder me if thou wilt, but do not say thou couldst murder one who only lived for thee! There, there, take the gold; I hoarded it but for thee. Go! go!" and the old man, who in his passion had quitted his bed, fell at the feet of the foiled assassin, and writhed on the ground, — the mental agony more intolerable than that of the body, which he had so lately undergone. The robber looked at him with a hard disdain. "What have I ever done to thee, wretch?" cried the old man, — "what but loved and cherished thee? Thou wert an orphan, — an outcast. I nurtured, nursed, adopted thee as my son. If men call me a miser, it was but that none might despise thee, my heir, because Nature has stunted and deformed thee, when I was no more. Thou wouldst have had all when I was dead. Couldst thou not spare me a few months or days, — nothing to thy youth, all that is left to my age? What have I done to thee?"

"Thou hast continued to live, and thou wouldst make no will."

"Mon Dieu! Mon Dieu!"

"*Ton Dieu!* Thy God! Fool! Hast thou not told me, from my child-hood, that there is *no* God? Hast thou not fed me on philosophy? Hast thou not said, 'Be virtuous, be good, be just, for the sake of mankind: but there is no life after this life'? Mankind! why should I love mankind? Hideous and misshapen, mankind jeer at me as I pass the streets. What hast thou done to me? Thou hast taken away from me, who am the scoff of this world, the hopes of another! Is there no other life? Well, then, I want thy gold, that at least I may hasten to make the best of this!"

"Monster! Curses light on thy ingratitude, thy —"

"And who hears thy curses? Thou knowest there is no God! Mark me; I have prepared all to fly. See, — I have my passport; my horses wait without; relays are ordered. I have thy gold." (And the wretch, as he spoke, continued coldly to load his person with the rouleaus). "And now, if I spare thy life, how shall I be sure that thou wilt not inform against mine?" He advanced with a gloomy scowl and a menacing gesture as he spoke.

The old man's anger changed to fear. He cowered before the savage. "Let me live! let me live! — that — that —"

"That — what?"

"I may pardon thee! Yes, thou hast nothing to fear from me. I swear it!"

"Swear! But by whom and what, old man? I cannot believe thee, if thou believest not in any God! Ha, ha! behold the result of thy lessons."

Another moment and those murderous fingers would have strangled their prey. But between the assassin and his victim rose a form that seemed almost to both a visitor from the world that both denied, — stately with majestic strength, glorious with awful beauty.

The ruffian recoiled, looked, trembled, and then turned and fled from the chamber. The old man fell again to the ground insensible.

Chapter I. VIII.

To know how a bad man will act when in power, reverse all the doctrines he preaches when obscure.

— S. Montague

Antipathies also form a part of magic (falsely) so-called. Man naturally has the same instinct as the animals, which warns them involuntarily against the creatures that are hostile or fatal to their existence. But *he* so often neglects it, that it becomes dormant. Not so the true cultivator of the Great Science, etc.

— Trismegistus the Fourth*

When he again saw the old man the next day, the stranger found

---

* a Rosicrucian

him calm, and surprisingly recovered from the scene and sufferings of the night. He expressed his gratitude to his preserver with tearful fervor, and stated that he had already sent for a relation who would make arrangements for his future safety and mode of life. "For I have money yet left," said the old man; "and henceforth have no motive to be a miser." He proceeded then briefly to relate the origin and circumstances of his connection with his intended murderer.

It seems that in earlier life he had quarreled with his relations, — from a difference in opinions of belief. Rejecting all religion as a fable, he yet cultivated feelings that inclined him — for though his intellect was weak, his dispositions were good — to that false and exaggerated sensibility which its dupes so often mistake for benevolence. He had no children; he resolved to adopt an enfant du peuple. He resolved to educate this boy according to "reason." He selected an orphan of the lowest extraction, whose defects of person and constitution only yet the more moved his pity, and finally engrossed his affection. In this outcast he not only loved a son, he loved a theory! He brought him up most philosophically. Helvetius had proved to him that education can do all; and before he was eight years old, the little Jean's favorite expressions were, "La lumiere et la vertu."* The boy showed talents, especially in art.

The protector sought for a master who was as free from "superstition" as himself, and selected the painter David. That person, as hideous as his pupil, and whose dispositions were as vicious as his professional abilities were undeniable, was certainly as free from "superstition" as the protector could desire. It was reserved for Robespierre hereafter to make the sanguinary painter believe in the Etre Supreme. The boy was early sensible of his ugliness, which was almost preternatural. His benefactor found it in vain to reconcile him to the malice of Nature by his philosophical aphorisms; but when he pointed out to him that in this world money, like charity, covers a multitude of defects, the boy listened eagerly and was consoled. To save money for his protégé, — for the only thing in the world he loved, — this became the patron's passion. Verily, he had met with his reward.

"But I am thankful he has escaped," said the old man, wiping his eyes. "Had he left me a beggar, I could never have accused him."

"No, for you are the author of his crimes."

"How! I, who never ceased to inculcate the beauty of virtue? Explain yourself."

"Alas! if thy pupil did not make this clear to thee last night from his own lips, an angel might come from heaven to preach to thee in vain."

The old man moved uneasily, and was about to reply, when the relative he had sent for — and who, a native of Nancy, happened to be

---

* Light and virtue.

at Paris at the time — entered the room. He was a man somewhat past thirty, and of a dry, saturnine, meager countenance, restless eyes, and compressed lips. He listened, with many ejaculations of horror, to his relation's recital, and sought earnestly, but in vain, to induce him to give information against his protégé.

"Tush, tush, Rene Dumas!" said the old man, "you are a lawyer. You are bred to regard human life with contempt. Let any man break a law, and you shout, 'Execute him!'"

"I!" cried Dumas, lifting up his hands and eyes: "venerable sage, how you misjudge me! I lament more than anyone the severity of our code. I think the state never should take away life, — no, not even the life of a murderer. I agree with that young statesman, — Maximilien Robespierre, — that the executioner is the invention of the tyrant. My very attachment to our advancing revolution is, that it must sweep away this legal butchery."

The lawyer paused, out of breath. The stranger regarded him fixedly and turned pale.

"You change countenance, sir," said Dumas; "you do not agree with me."

"Pardon me, I was at that moment repressing a vague fear which seemed prophetic."

"And that —"

"Was that we should meet again, when your opinions on Death and the philosophy of Revolutions might be different."

"Never!"

"You enchant me, Cousin Rene," said the old man, who had listened to his relation with delight. "Ah, I see you have proper sentiments of justice and philanthropy. Why did I not seek to know you before? You admire the Revolution; — you, equally with me, detest the barbarity of kings and the fraud of priests?"

"Detest! How could I love mankind if I did not?"

"And," said the old man, hesitatingly, "you do not think, with this noble gentleman, that I erred in the precepts I instilled into that wretched man?"

"Erred! Was Socrates to blame if Alcibiades was an adulterer and a traitor?"

"You hear him, you hear him! But Socrates had also a Plato; henceforth you shall be a Plato to me. You hear him?" exclaimed the old man, turning to the stranger.

But the latter was at the threshold. Who shall argue with the most stubborn of all bigotries, — the fanaticism of unbelief?

"Are you going?" exclaimed Dumas, "and before I have thanked you, blessed you, for the life of this dear and venerable man? Oh, if ever I

can repay you, — if ever you want the heart's blood of Rene Dumas!"
Thus volubly delivering himself, he followed the stranger to the threshold of the second chamber, and there, gently detaining him, and after
looking over his shoulder, to be sure that he was not heard by the owner,
he whispered, "I ought to return to Nancy. One would not lose one's
time, — you don't think, sir, that that scoundrel took away *all* the old
fool's money?"

"Was it thus Plato spoke of Socrates, Monsieur Dumas?"

"Ha, ha! — you are caustic. Well, you have a right. Sir, we shall meet
again."

"*Again!*" muttered the stranger, and his brow darkened. He hastened
to his chamber; he passed the day and the night alone, and in studies,
no matter of what nature, — they served to increase his gloom.

What could ever connect his fate with Rene Dumas, or the fugitive
assassin? Why did the buoyant air of Paris seem to him heavy with the
steams of blood; why did an instinct urge him to fly from those
sparkling circles, from that focus of the world's awakened hopes, warning him from return? — he, whose lofty existence defied — but away these
dreams and omens! He leaves France behind. Back, O Italy, to thy
majestic wrecks! On the Alps his soul breathes the free air once more.
Free air! Alas! let the world-healers exhaust their chemistry; man never
shall be as free in the marketplace as on the mountain. But we, reader,
we too escape from these scenes of false wisdom clothing godless crime.
Away, once more

> "In den heitern Regionen
> Wo die reinen Formen wohnen."

Away, to the loftier realm where the pure dwellers are. Unpolluted by
the Actual, the Ideal lives only with Art and Beauty. Sweet Viola, by the
shores of the blue Parthenope, by Virgil's tomb, and the Cimmerian
cavern, we return to thee once more.

Chapter I.IX.

Che non vuol che 'l destrier piu vada in alto,
Poi lo lega nel margine marino
A un verde mirto in mezzo un lauro *e un pino.**
                                    "Orlando Furioso," c. vi. xxiii.

*O*Musician! art thou happy now? Thou art reinstalled at thy stately desk, — thy faithful barbiton has its share in the triumph. It is thy masterpiece which fills thy ear; it is thy daughter who fills the scene, — the music, the actress, so united, that applause to one is applause to both. They make way for thee, at the orchestra, — they no longer jeer and wink, when, with a fierce fondness, thou dost caress thy Familiar, that plains, and wails, and chides, and growls, under thy remorseless hand. They understand now how irregular is ever the symmetry of real genius. The inequalities in its surface make the moon luminous to man. Giovanni Paisiello, Maestro di Capella, if thy gentle soul could know envy, thou must sicken to see thy Elfrida and thy Pirro laid aside, and all Naples turned fanatic to the Siren, at whose measures shook querulously thy gentle head! But thou, Paisiello, calm in the long prosperity of fame, knowest that the New will have its day, and comfortest thyself that the Elfrida and the Pirro will live forever. Perhaps a mistake, but it is by such mistakes that true genius conquers envy. "To be immortal," says Schiller, "live in the whole." To be superior to the hour, live in thy self-esteem. The audience now would give their ears for those variations and flights they were once wont to hiss. No! — Pisani has been two-thirds of a life at silent work on his masterpiece: there is nothing he can add to *that,* however he might have sought to improve on the masterpieces of others. Is not this common? The least little critic, in reviewing some work of art, will say, "pity this, and pity that;" "this should have been

---

* As he did not wish that his charger (the hippogriff) should take any further excursions into the higher regions for the present, he bound him at the seashore to a green myrtle between a laurel and a pine.

altered, — that omitted." Yea, with his wiry fiddle string will he creak
out his accursed variations. But let him sit down and compose himself.
He sees no improvement in variations *then!* Every man can control his
fiddle when it is his own work with which its vagaries would play the
devil.

And Viola is the idol, the theme of Naples. She is the spoiled sultana
of the boards. To spoil her acting may be easy enough, — shall they spoil
her nature? No, I think not. There, at home, she is still good and simple;
and there, under the awning by the doorway, — there she still sits,
divinely musing. How often, crook-trunked tree, she looks to thy green
boughs; how often, like thee, in her dreams, and fancies, does she
struggle for the light, — not the light of the stage-lamps. Pooh, child! be
contented with the lamps, even with the rush-lights. A farthing candle
is more convenient for household purposes than the stars.

Weeks passed, and the stranger did not reappear; months had passed,
and his prophecy of sorrow was not yet fulfilled. One evening Pisani
was taken ill. His success had brought on the long-neglected composer
pressing applications for concerti and sonata, adapted to his more
peculiar science on the violin. He had been employed for some weeks,
day and night, on a piece in which he hoped to excel himself. He took,
as usual, one of those seemingly impracticable subjects which it was his
pride to subject to the expressive powers of his art, — the terrible legend
connected with the transformation of Philomel. The pantomime of
sound opened with the gay merriment of a feast. The monarch of Thrace
is at his banquet; a sudden discord brays through the joyous notes, —
the string seems to screech with horror. The king learns the murder of
his son by the hands of the avenging sisters. Swift rage the chords,
through the passions of fear, of horror, of fury, and dismay. The father
pursues the sisters. Hark! what changes the dread — the discord — into
that long, silvery, mournful music? The transformation is completed;
and Philomel, now the nightingale, pours from the myrtle-bough the
full, liquid, subduing notes that are to tell evermore to the world the
history of her woes and wrongs. Now, it was in the midst of this
complicated and difficult attempt that the health of the overtasked
musician, excited alike by past triumph and new ambition, suddenly
gave way. He was taken ill at night. The next morning the doctor
pronounced that his disease was a malignant and infectious fever. His
wife and Viola shared in their tender watch; but soon that task was left
to the last alone. The Signora Pisani caught the infection, and in a few
hours was even in a state more alarming than that of her husband. The
Neapolitans, in common with the inhabitants of all warm climates, are
apt to become selfish and brutal in their dread of infectious disorders.
Gionetta herself pretended to be ill, to avoid the sick-chamber. The

whole labor of love and sorrow fell on Viola. It was a terrible trial, — I am willing to hurry over the details. The wife died first!

One day, a little before sunset, Pisani woke partially recovered from the delirium which had preyed upon him, with few intervals, since the second day of the disease; and casting about him his dizzy and feeble eyes, he recognized Viola, and smiled. He faltered her name as he rose and stretched his arms. She fell upon his breast, and strove to suppress her tears.

"Thy mother?" he said. "Does she sleep?"

"She sleeps, — ah, yes!" and the tears gushed forth.

"I thought — eh! I know not *what* I have thought. But do not weep: I shall be well now, — quite well. She will come to me when she wakes, — will she?"

Viola could not speak; but she busied herself in pouring forth an anodyne, which she had been directed to give the sufferer as soon as the delirium should cease. The doctor had told her, too, to send for him the instant so important a change should occur.

She went to the door and called to the woman who, during Gionetta's pretended illness, had been induced to supply her place; but the hireling answered not. She flew through the chambers to search for her in vain, — the hireling had caught Gionetta's fears, and vanished. What was to be done? The case was urgent, — the doctor had declared not a moment should be lost in obtaining his attendance; she must leave her father, — she must go herself! She crept back into the room, — the anodyne seemed already to have taken benign effect; the patient's eyes were closed, and he breathed regularly, as in sleep. She stole away, threw her veil over her face, and hurried from the house.

Now the anodyne had not produced the effect which it appeared to have done; instead of healthful sleep, it had brought on a kind of lightheaded somnolence, in which the mind, preternaturally restless, wandered about its accustomed haunts, waking up its old familiar instincts and inclinations. It was not sleep, — it was not delirium; it was the dream-wakefulness which opium sometimes induces, when every nerve grows tremulously alive, and creates a corresponding activity in the frame, to which it gives a false and hectic vigor. Pisani missed something, — what, he scarcely knew; it was a combination of the two wants most essential to his mental life, — the voice of his wife, the touch of his Familiar. He rose, — he left his bed, he leisurely put on his old dressing-robe, in which he had been wont to compose. He smiled complacently as the associations connected with the garment came over his memory; he walked tremulously across the room, and entered the small cabinet next to his chamber, in which his wife had been accustomed more often to watch than sleep, when illness separated her from his side. The room was desolate and void. He looked round wistfully, and muttered to himself, and then proceeded regularly, and with a noiseless step, through the chambers of the silent house, one by one.

He came at last to that in which old Gionetta — faithful to her own safety, if nothing else — nursed herself, in the remotest corner of the house, from the danger of infection. As he glided in, — wan, emaciated, with an uneasy, anxious, searching look in his haggard eyes, — the old woman shrieked aloud, and fell at his feet. He bent over her, passed his thin hands along her averted face, shook his head, and said in a hollow voice, —

"I cannot find them; where are they?"

"Who, dear master? Oh, have compassion on yourself; they are not here. Blessed saints! this is terrible; he has touched me; I am dead!"

"Dead! who is dead? Is anyone dead?"

"Ah! don't talk so; you must know it well: my poor mistress, — she caught the fever from you; it is infectious enough to kill a whole city. San Gennaro protect me! My poor mistress, she is dead, — buried, too; and I, your faithful Gionetta, woe is me! Go, go — to — to bed again, dearest master, — go!"

The poor musician stood for one moment mute and unmoving, then a slight shiver ran through his frame; he turned and glided back, silent and specterlike, as he had entered. He came into the room where he had been accustomed to compose, — where his wife, in her sweet patience, had so often sat by his side, and praised and flattered when the world had but jeered and scorned. In one corner he found the laurel-wreath she had placed on his brows that happy night of fame and triumph; and near it, half hid by her mantilla, lay in its case the neglected instrument.

Viola was not long gone: she had found the physician; she returned with him; and as they gained the threshold, they heard a strain of music from within, — a strain of piercing, heart-rending anguish. It was not like some senseless instrument, mechanical in its obedience to a human hand, — it was as some spirit calling, in wail and agony from the forlorn shades, to the angels it beheld afar beyond the Eternal Gulf. They exchanged glances of dismay. They hurried into the house; they hastened into the room. Pisani turned, and his look, full of ghastly intelligence and stern command, awed them back. The black mantilla, the faded laurel-leaf, lay there before him. Viola's heart guessed all at a single glance; she sprung to his knees; she clasped them, — "Father, father, *I* am left thee still!"

The wail ceased, — the note changed; with a confused association — half of the man, half of the artist — the anguish, still a melody, was connected with sweeter sounds and thoughts. The nightingale had escaped the pursuit, — soft, airy, birdlike, thrilled the delicious notes a moment, and then died away. The instrument fell to the floor, and its chords snapped. You heard that sound through the silence. The artist looked on his kneeling child, and then on the broken chords . . . "Bury me by her side," he said, in a very calm, low voice; "and *that* by mine." And with these words his whole frame became rigid, as if turned to stone. The last change passed over his face. He fell to the ground, sudden and heavy. The chords *there*, too, — the chords of the human instrument were snapped asunder. As he fell, his robe brushed the laurel-wreath, and that fell also, near but not in reach of the dead man's nerveless hand.

Broken instrument, broken heart, withered laurel-wreath! — the setting sun through the vine-clad lattice streamed on all! So smiles the eternal Nature on the wrecks of all that make life glorious! And not a sun that sets not somewhere on the silenced music, — on the faded laurel!

Chapter I.X.

Che difesa miglior ch' usbergo e scudo,
E la santa innocenza al petto ignudo!*

"Ger. Lib.," c. viii. xli.

*A*nd they buried the musician and his barbiton together, in the same coffin. That famous Steiner — primeval Titan of the great Tyrolese race — often hast thou sought to scale the heavens, and therefore must thou, like the meaner children of men, descend to the dismal Hades! Harder fate for thee than thy mortal master. For *thy* soul sleeps with thee in the coffin. And the music that belongs to *his*, separate from the instrument, ascends on high, to be heard often by a daughter's pious ears when the heaven is serene and the earth sad. For there is a sense of hearing that the vulgar know not. And the voices of the dead breathe soft and frequent to those who can unite the memory with the faith.

* Better defense than shield or breastplate is holy innocence to the naked breast.

And now Viola is alone in the world, — alone in the home where loneliness had seemed from the cradle a thing that was not of nature. And at first the solitude and the stillness were insupportable. Have you, ye mourners, to whom these sibyl leaves, weird with many a dark enigma, shall be borne, have you not felt that when the death of some best-loved one has made the hearth desolate, — have you not felt as if the gloom of the altered home was too heavy for thought to bear? — you would leave it, though a palace, even for a cabin. And yet, — sad to say, — when you obey the impulse, when you fly from the walls, when in the strange place in which you seek your refuge nothing speaks to you of the lost, have ye not felt again a yearning for that very food to memory which was just before but bitterness and gall? Is it not almost impious and profane to abandon that dear hearth to strangers? And the desertion of the home where your parents dwelt, and blessed you, upbraids your conscience as if you had sold their tombs.

Beautiful was the Etruscan superstition that the ancestors become the household gods. Deaf is the heart to which the Lares call from the desolate floors in vain. At first Viola had, in her intolerable anguish, gratefully welcomed the refuge which the house and family of a kindly neighbor, much attached to her father, and who was one of the orchestra that Pisani shall perplex no more, had proffered to the orphan. But the company of the unfamiliar in our grief, the consolation of the stranger, how it irritates the wound! And then, to hear elsewhere the name of father, mother, child, — as if death came alone to you, — to see elsewhere the calm regularity of those lives united in love and order, keeping account of happy hours, the unbroken timepiece of home, as if nowhere else the wheels were arrested, the chain shattered, the hands motionless, the chime still! No, the grave itself does not remind us of our loss like the company of those who have no loss to mourn. Go back to thy solitude, young orphan, — go back to thy home: the sorrow that meets thee on the threshold can greet thee, even in its sadness, like the smile upon the face of the dead. And there, from thy casement, and there, from without thy door, thou seest still the tree, solitary as thyself, and springing from the clefts of the rock, but forcing its way to light, — as, through all sorrow, while the seasons yet can renew the verdure and bloom of youth, strives the instinct of the human heart! Only when the sap is dried up, only when age comes on, does the sun shine in vain for man and for the tree.

Weeks and months — months sad and many — again passed, and Naples will not longer suffer its idol to seclude itself from homage. The world ever plucks us back from ourselves with a thousand arms. And again Viola's voice is heard upon the stage, which, mystically faithful to life, is in naught more faithful than this, that it is the appearances that fill the scene; and we pause not to ask of what realities they are the proxies. When the actor of Athens moved all hearts as he clasped the burial urn, and burst into broken sobs; how few, there, knew that it held the ashes of his son! Gold, as well as fame, was showered upon the young actress; but she still kept to her simple mode of life, to her lowly home, to the one servant whose faults, selfish as they were, Viola was too inexperienced to perceive. And it was Gionetta who had placed her when first born in her father's arms! She was surrounded by every snare, wooed by every solicitation that could beset her unguarded beauty and her dangerous calling. But her modest virtue passed unsullied through them all. It is true that she had been taught by lips now mute the maiden duties enjoined by honor and religion. And all love that spoke not of the altar only shocked and repelled her. But besides that, as grief and solitude ripened her heart, and made her tremble at times to think how deeply it could feel, her vague and early visions shaped themselves into an ideal of love. And till the ideal is found, how the shadow that it throws before it chills us to the actual! With that ideal, ever and ever, unconsciously, and with a certain awe and shrinking, came the shape and voice of the warning stranger. Nearly two years had passed since he had appeared at Naples. Nothing had been heard of him, save that his vessel had been directed, some months after his departure, to sail for Leghorn. By the gossips of Naples, his existence, supposed so extraordinary, was well nigh forgotten; but the heart of Viola was more faithful. Often he glided through her dreams, and when the wind sighed through that fantastic tree, associated with his remembrance, she started with a tremor and a blush, as if she had heard him speak.

But amongst the train of her suitors was one to whom she listened more gently than to the rest; partly because, perhaps, he spoke in her mother's native tongue; partly because in his diffidence there was little to alarm and displease; partly because his rank, nearer to her own than that of lordlier wooers, prevented his admiration from appearing insult; partly because he himself, eloquent and a dreamer, often uttered thoughts that were kindred to those buried deepest in her mind. She began to like, perhaps to love him, but as a sister loves; a sort of privileged familiarity sprung up between them. If in the Englishman's breast arose wild and unworthy hopes, he had not yet expressed them. Is there danger to thee here, lone Viola, or is the danger greater in thy unfound ideal?

And now, as the overture to some strange and wizard spectacle, closes this opening prelude. Wilt thou hear more? Come with thy faith prepared. I ask not the blinded eyes, but the awakened sense. As the enchanted Isle, remote from the homes of men, —

"Ove alcun legno
Rado, o non mai va dalle nostre sponde,"*

— "Ger.Lib.," cant. xiv. 69

is the space in the weary ocean of actual life to which the Muse or Sibyl (ancient in years, but ever young in aspect), offers thee no unhallowed sail, —

"Quinci ella in cima a una montagna ascende
Disabitata, e d' ombre oscura e bruna;
E par incanto a lei nevose rende
Le spalle e i fianchi; e sensa neve alcuna
Gli lascia il capo verdeggiante e vago;
E vi fonda un palagio appresso un lago."†

---

* Where ship seldom or never comes from our coasts.
† There, she a mountain's lofty peak ascends,
   Unpeopled, shady, shagg'd with forests brown,
   Whose sides, by power of magic, half-way down
   She heaps with slippery ice and frost and snow,
   But sunshiny and verdant leaves the crown
   With orange-woods and myrtles, — speaks, and lo!
   Rich from the bordering lake a palace rises slow.
        Wiffin's "Translation."

BOOK II

ART, LOVE, AND WONDER

Diversi aspetti in un confusi e misti.*

"Ger. Lib," cant. iv. 7.

---

* Different appearances, confused and mixt in one.

Chapter 2.I.

Centauri, e Sfingi, e pallide Gorgoni.*

"Ger. Lib.," c. iv. v.

One moonlit night, in the Gardens at Naples, some four or five gentleman were seated under a tree, drinking their sherbet, and listening, in the intervals of conversation, to the music which enlivened that gay and favorite resort of an indolent population. One of this little party was a young Englishman, who had been the life of the whole group, but who, for the last few moments, had sunk into a gloomy and abstracted reverie. One of his countrymen observed this sudden gloom, and, tapping him on the back, said, "What ails you, Glyndon? Are you ill? You have grown quite pale, — you tremble. Is it a sudden chill? You had better go home: these Italian nights are often dangerous to our English constitutions."

"No, I am well now; it was a passing shudder. I cannot account for it myself."

A man, apparently of about thirty years of age, and of a mien and countenance strikingly superior to those around him, turned abruptly, and looked steadfastly at Glyndon.

"I think I understand what you mean," said he; "and perhaps," he added, with a grave smile, "I could explain it better than yourself." Here, turning to the others, he added, "You must often have felt, gentlemen, each and all of you, especially when sitting alone at night, a strange and unaccountable sensation of coldness and awe creep over you; your blood curdles, and the heart stands still; the limbs shiver; the hair bristles; you are afraid to look up, to turn your eyes to the darker corners of the room; you have a horrible fancy that something unearthly is at hand; presently the whole spell, if I may so call it, passes away, and you are ready to laugh at your own weakness. Have you not often felt what I

---

* Centaurs and Sphinxes and pallid Gorgons.

have thus imperfectly described? — if so, you can understand what our young friend has just experienced, even amidst the delights of this magical scene, and amidst the balmy whispers of a July night."

"Sir," replied Glyndon, evidently much surprised, "you have defined exactly the nature of that shudder which came over me. But how could my manner be so faithful an index to my impressions?"

"I know the signs of the visitation," returned the stranger, gravely; "they are not to be mistaken by one of my experience."

All the gentleman present then declared that they could comprehend, and had felt, what the stranger had described.

"According to one of our national superstitions," said Mervale, the Englishman who had first addressed Glyndon, "the moment you so feel your blood creep, and your hair stand on end, some one is walking over the spot which shall be your grave."

"There are in all lands different superstitions to account for so common an occurrence," replied the stranger: "one sect among the Arabians holds that at that instant God is deciding the hour either of your death, or of some one dear to you. The African savage, whose imagination is darkened by the hideous rites of his gloomy idolatry, believes that the Evil Spirit is pulling you towards him by the hair: so do the Grotesque and the Terrible mingle with each other."

"It is evidently a mere physical accident, — a derangement of the stomach, a chill of the blood," said a young Neapolitan, with whom Glyndon had formed a slight acquaintance.

"Then why is it always coupled in all nations with some superstitious presentiment or terror, — some connection between the material frame and the supposed world without us? For my part, I think —"

"Aye, what do you think, sir?" asked Glyndon, curiously.

"I think," continued the stranger, "that it is the repugnance and horror with which our more human elements recoil from something, indeed, invisible, but antipathetic to our own nature; and from a knowledge of which we are happily secured by the imperfection of our senses."

"You are a believer in spirits, then?" said Mervale, with an incredulous smile.

"Nay, it was not precisely of spirits that I spoke; but there may be forms of matter as invisible and impalpable to us as the animalculae in the air we breathe, — in the water that plays in yonder basin. Such beings may have passions and powers like our own — as the animalculae to which I have compared them. The monster that lives and dies in a drop of water — carnivorous, insatiable, subsisting on the creatures minuter than himself — is not less deadly in his wrath, less ferocious in his nature, than the tiger of the desert. There may be things around us that would be dangerous and hostile to men, if Providence had not placed a wall between them and us, merely by different modifications of matter."

"And think you that wall never can be removed?" asked young Glyndon, abruptly. "Are the traditions of sorcerer and wizard, universal and immemorial as they are, merely fables?"

"Perhaps yes, — perhaps no," answered the stranger, indifferently. "But who, in an age in which the reason has chosen its proper bounds, would be mad enough to break the partition that divides him from the boa and the lion, — to repine at and rebel against the law which confines the shark to the great deep? Enough of these idle speculations."

Here the stranger rose, summoned the attendant, paid for his sherbet, and, bowing slightly to the company, soon disappeared among the trees.

"Who is that gentleman?" asked Glyndon, eagerly.

The rest looked at each other, without replying, for some moments.

"I never saw him before," said Mervale, at last.

"Nor I."

"Nor I."

"I know him well," said the Neapolitan, who was, indeed, the Count Cetoxa. "If you remember, it was as my companion that he joined you. He visited Naples about two years ago, and has recently returned; he is very rich, — indeed, enormously so. A most agreeable person. I am sorry to hear him talk so strangely tonight; it serves to encourage the various foolish reports that are circulated concerning him."

"And surely," said another Neapolitan, "the circumstance that occurred but the other day, so well known to yourself, Cetoxa, justifies the reports you pretend to deprecate."

"Myself and my countryman," said Glyndon, "mix so little in Neapolitan society, that we lose much that appears well worthy of lively interest. May I enquire what are the reports, and what is the circumstance you refer to?"

"As to the reports, gentlemen," said Cetoxa, courteously, addressing himself to the two Englishmen, "it may suffice to observe, that they attribute to the Signor Zanoni certain qualities which everybody desires for himself, but damns anyone else for possessing. The incident Signor Belgioso alludes to, illustrates these qualities, and is, I must own, somewhat startling. You probably play, gentlemen?" (Here Cetoxa paused; and as both Englishmen had occasionally staked a few scudi at the public gaming-tables, they bowed assent to the conjecture.) Cetoxa continued. "Well, then, not many days since, and on the very day that Zanoni returned to Naples, it so happened that I had been playing pretty high, and had lost considerably. I rose from the table, resolved no longer to tempt fortune, when I suddenly perceived Zanoni, whose acquaintance I had before made (and who, I may say, was under some slight

obligation to me), standing by, a spectator. Ere I could express my
gratification at this unexpected recognition, he laid his hand on my
arm. 'You have lost much,' said he; 'more than you can afford. For my
part, I dislike play; yet I wish to have some interest in what is going on.
Will you play this sum for me? the risk is mine, — the half profits yours.'
I was startled, as you may suppose, at such an address; but Zanoni had
an air and tone with him it was impossible to resist; besides, I was
burning to recover my losses, and should not have risen had I had any
money left about me. I told him I would accept his offer, provided we
shared the risk as well as profits. 'As you will,' said he, smiling; 'we need
have no scruple, for you will be sure to win.' I sat down; Zanoni stood
behind me; my luck rose, — I invariably won. In fact, I rose from the
table a rich man."

"There can be no foul play at the public tables, especially when foul
play would make against the bank?" This question was put by Glyndon.

"Certainly not," replied the count. "But our good fortune was,
indeed, marvelous, — so extraordinary that a Sicilian (the Sicilians are
all ill-bred, bad-tempered fellows) grew angry and insolent. 'Sir,' said he,
turning to my new friend, 'you have no business to stand so near to the
table. I do not understand this; you have not acted fairly.' Zanoni
replied, with great composure, that he had done nothing against the
rules, — that he was very sorry that one man could not win without
another man losing; and that he could not act unfairly, even if disposed
to do so. The Sicilian took the stranger's mildness for apprehension,
and blustered more loudly. In fact, he rose from the table, and confronted Zanoni in a manner that, to say the least of it, was provoking
to any gentleman who has some quickness of temper, or some skill with
the small-sword."

"And," interrupted Belgioso, "the most singular part of the whole to
me was, that this Zanoni, who stood opposite to where I sat, and whose
face I distinctly saw, made no remark, showed no resentment. He fixed
his eyes steadfastly on the Sicilian; never shall I forget that look! it is
impossible to describe it, — it froze the blood in my veins. The Sicilian
staggered back as if struck. I saw him tremble; he sank on the bench.
And then —"

"Yes, then," said Cetoxa, "to my infinite surprise, our gentleman, thus
disarmed by a look from Zanoni, turned his whole anger upon me, *the*
— but perhaps you do not know, gentlemen, that I have some repute
with my weapon?"

"The best swordsman in Italy," said Belgioso.

"Before I could guess why or wherefore," resumed Cetoxa, "I found
myself in the garden behind the house, with Ughelli (that was the
Sicilian's name) facing me, and five or six gentlemen, the witnesses of

the duel about to take place, around. Zanoni beckoned me aside. 'This man will fall,' said he. 'When he is on the ground, go to him, and ask whether he will be buried by the side of his father in the church of San Gennaro?' 'Do you then know his family?' I asked with great surprise. Zanoni made me no answer, and the next moment I was engaged with the Sicilian. To do him justice, his imbrogliato was magnificent, and a swifter lounger never crossed a sword; nevertheless," added Cetoxa, with a pleasing modesty, "he was run through the body. I went up to him; he could scarcely speak. 'Have you any request to make, — any affairs to settle?' He shook his head. 'Where would you wish to be interred?' He pointed towards the Sicilian coast. 'What!' said I, in surprise, 'Not by the side of your father, in the church of San Gennaro?' As I spoke, his face altered terribly; he uttered a piercing shriek, — the blood gushed from his mouth, and he fell dead. The most strange part of the story is to come. We buried him in the church of San Gennaro. In doing so, we took up his father's coffin; the lid came off in moving it, and the skeleton was visible. In the hollow of the skull we found a very slender wire of sharp steel; this caused surprise and inquiry. The father, who was rich and a miser, had died suddenly, and been buried in haste, owing, it was said, to the heat of the weather. Suspicion once awakened, the examination became minute. The old man's servant was questioned, and at last confessed that the son had murdered the sire. The contrivance was ingenious: the wire was so slender that it pierced to the brain, and drew but one drop of blood, which the grey hairs concealed. The accomplice will be executed."

"And Zanoni, — did he give evidence, did he account for —"

"No," interrupted the count: "he declared that he had by accident visited the church that morning; that he had observed the tombstone of the Count Ughelli; that his guide had told him the count's son was in Naples, — a spendthrift and a gambler. While we were at play, he had heard the count mentioned by name at the table; and when the challenge was given and accepted, it had occurred to him to name the place of burial, by an instinct which he either could not or would not account for."

"A very lame story," said Mervale.

"Yes! but we Italians are superstitious, — the alleged instinct was regarded by many as the whisper of Providence. The next day the stranger became an object of universal interest and curiosity. His wealth, his manner of living, his extraordinary personal beauty, have assisted also to make him the rage; besides, I have had the pleasure in introducing so eminent a person to our gayest cavaliers and our fairest ladies."

"A most interesting narrative," said Mervale, rising. "Come, Glyndon; shall we seek our hotel? It is almost daylight. Adieu, signor!"

"What think you of this story?" said Glyndon, as the young men walked homeward.

"Why, it is very clear that this Zanoni is some imposter, — some clever rogue; and the Neapolitan shares the booty, and puffs him off with all the hackneyed charlatanism of the marvelous. An unknown adventurer gets into society by being made an object of awe and curiosity; he is more than ordinarily handsome, and the women are quite content to receive him without any other recommendation than his own face and Cetoxa's fables."

"I cannot agree with you. Cetoxa, though a gambler and a rake, is a nobleman of birth and high repute for courage and honor. Besides, this stranger, with his noble presence and lofty air, — so calm, so unobtrusive, — has nothing in common with the forward garrulity of an imposter."

"My dear Glyndon, pardon me; but you have not yet acquired any knowledge of the world! The stranger makes the best of a fine person, and his grand air is but a trick of the trade. But to change the subject, — how advances the love affair?"

"Oh, Viola could not see me today."

"You must not marry her. What would they all say at home?"

"Let us enjoy the present," said Glyndon, with vivacity; "we are young, rich, good-looking; let us not think of tomorrow."

"Bravo, Glyndon! Here we are at the hotel. Sleep sound, and don't dream of Signor Zanoni."

Chapter 2.II.

Prende, giovine audace e impaziente,
L'occasione offerta avidamente.*

"Ger. Lib.," c. vi. xxix.

*C*larence Glyndon was a young man of fortune, not large, but easy

---

* Take, youth, bold and impatient, the offered occasion eagerly.

and independent. His parents were dead, and his nearest relation was an only sister, left in England under the care of her aunt, and many years younger than himself. Early in life he had evinced considerable promise in the art of painting, and rather from enthusiasm than any pecuniary necessity for a profession, he determined to devote himself to a career in which the English artist generally commences with rapture and historical composition, to conclude with avaricious calculation and portraits of Alderman Simpkins. Glyndon was supposed by his friends to possess no inconsiderable genius; but it was of a rash and presumptuous order. He was averse from continuous and steady labor, and his ambition rather sought to gather the fruit than to plant the tree. In common with many artists in their youth, he was fond of pleasure and excitement, yielding with little forethought to whatever impressed his fancy or appealed to his passions. He had traveled through the more celebrated cities of Europe, with the avowed purpose and sincere resolution of studying the divine masterpieces of his art. But in each, pleasure had too often allured him from ambition, and living beauty distracted his worship from the senseless canvas. Brave, adventurous, vain, restless, inquisitive, he was ever involved in wild projects and pleasant dangers, — the creature of impulse and the slave of imagination.

It was then the period when a feverish spirit of change was working its way to that hideous mockery of human aspirations, the Revolution of France; and from the chaos into which were already jarring the sanctities of the World's Venerable Belief, arose many shapeless and unformed chimeras. Need I remind the reader that, while that was the day for polished skepticism and affected wisdom, it was the day also for the most egregious credulity and the most mystical superstitions, — the day in which magnetism and magic found converts amongst the disciples of Diderot; when prophecies were current in every mouth; when the salon of a philosophical deist was converted into an Heraclea, in which necromancy professed to conjure up the shadows of the dead; when the Crosier and the Book were ridiculed, and Mesmer and Cagliostro were believed. In that Heliacal Rising, heralding the new sun before which all vapors were to vanish, stalked from their graves in the feudal ages all the phantoms that had flitted before the eyes of Paracelsus and Agrippa. Dazzled by the dawn of the Revolution, Glyndon was yet more attracted by its strange accompaniments; and natural it was with him, as with others, that the fancy which ran riot amidst the hopes of a social Utopia, should grasp with avidity all that promised, out of the dusty tracks of the beaten science, the bold discoveries of some marvelous Elysium.

In his travels he had listened with vivid interest, at least, if not with implicit belief, to the wonders told of each more renowned Ghost-seer, and his mind was therefore prepared for the impression which the mysterious Zanoni at first sight had produced upon it.

There might be another cause for this disposition to credulity. A remote ancestor of Glyndon's on the mother's side, had achieved no inconsiderable reputation as a philosopher and alchemist. Strange stories were afloat concerning this wise progenitor. He was said to have lived to an age far exceeding the allotted boundaries of mortal existence, and to have preserved to the last the appearance of middle life. He had died at length, it was supposed, of grief for the sudden death of a great-grandchild, the only creature he had ever appeared to love. The works of this philosopher, though rare, were extant, and found in the library of Glyndon's home. Their Platonic mysticism, their bold assertions, the high promises that might be detected through their figurative and typical phraseology, had early made a deep impression on the young imagination of Clarence Glyndon. His parents, not alive to the consequences of encouraging fancies which the very enlightenment of the age appeared to them sufficient to prevent or dispel, were fond, in the long winter nights, of conversing on the traditional history of this distinguished progenitor. And Clarence thrilled with a fearful pleasure when his mother playfully detected a striking likeness between the features of the young heir and the faded portrait of the alchemist that overhung their mantelpiece, and was the boast of their household and the admiration of their friends, — the child is, indeed, more often than we think for, "the father of the man."

I have said that Glyndon was fond of pleasure. Facile, as genius ever must be, to cheerful impression, his careless artist-life, ere artist-life settles down to labor, had wandered from flower to flower. He had enjoyed, almost to the reaction of satiety, the gay revelries of Naples, when he fell in love with the face and voice of Viola Pisani. But his love, like his ambition, was vague and desultory. It did not satisfy his whole heart and fill up his whole nature; not from want of strong and noble passions, but because his mind was not yet matured and settled enough for their development. As there is one season for the blossom, another for the fruit; so it is not till the bloom of fancy begins to fade, that the heart ripens to the passions that the bloom precedes and foretells. Joyous alike at his lonely easel or amidst his boon companions, he had not yet known enough of sorrow to love deeply. For man must be disappointed with the lesser things of life before he can comprehend the full value of the greatest. It is the shallow sensualists of France, who, in their salon-language, call love "a folly," — love, better understood, is wisdom. Besides, the world was too much with Clarence Glyndon. His ambition of art was associated with the applause and estimation of that miserable minority of the surface that we call the Public.

Like those who deceive, he was ever fearful of being himself the dupe. He distrusted the sweet innocence of Viola. He could not venture the hazard of seriously proposing marriage to an Italian actress; but the modest dignity of the girl, and something good and generous in his own nature, had hitherto made him shrink from anymore worldly but less honorable designs. Thus the familiarity between them seemed rather that of kindness and regard than passion. He attended the theater; he stole behind the scenes to converse with her; he filled his portfolio with countless sketches of a beauty that charmed him as an artist as well as lover; and day after day he floated on through a changing sea of doubt and irresolution, of affection and distrust. The last, indeed, constantly sustained against his better reason by the sober admonitions of Mervale, a matter-of-fact man!

The day following that eve on which this section of my story opens, Glyndon was riding alone by the shores of the Neapolitan sea, on the other side of the Cavern of Posilipo. It was past noon; the sun had lost its early fervor, and a cool breeze sprung up voluptuously from the sparkling sea. Bending over a fragment of stone near the roadside, he perceived the form of a man; and when he approached, he recognized Zanoni.

The Englishman saluted him courteously. "Have you discovered some antique?" said he, with a smile; "they are common as pebbles on this road."

"No," replied Zanoni; "it was but one of those antiques that have their date, indeed, from the beginning of the world, but which Nature eternally withers and renews." So saying, he showed Glyndon a small herb with a pale-blue flower, and then placed it carefully in his bosom.

"You are an herbalist?"

"I am."

"It is, I am told, a study full of interest."

"To those who understand it, doubtless."

"Is the knowledge, then, so rare?"

"Rare! The deeper knowledge is perhaps rather, among the arts, *lost* to the modern philosophy of commonplace and surface! Do you imagine there was no foundation for those traditions which come dimly down from remoter ages, — as shells now found on the mountaintops inform us where the seas have been? What was the old Colchian magic, but the minute study of Nature in her lowliest works? What the fable of Medea, but a proof of the powers that may be extracted from the germ and leaf? The most gifted of all the Priestcrafts, the mysterious sisterhoods of Cuth, concerning whose incantations Learning vainly bewilders itself amidst the maze of legends, sought in the meanest herbs what, perhaps, the Babylonian Sages explored in vain amidst the loftiest stars. Tradition yet tells you that there existed a race* who could slay their enemies from afar, without weapon, without movement. The herb that ye tread on may have deadlier powers than your engineers can give to their mightiest instruments of war. Can you guess that to these Italian shores, to the old Circaean Promontory, came the Wise from the farthest East, to search for plants and simples which your Pharmacists of the Counter would fling from them as weeds? The first herbalists — the master chemists of the world — were the tribe that the ancient reverence called by the name of Titans.† I remember once, by the Hebrus, in the reign of — But this talk," said Zanoni, checking himself abruptly, and with a cold smile, "serves only to waste your time and my own." He paused, looked steadily at Glyndon, and continued, "Young man, think you that vague curiosity will supply the place of earnest labor? I read your heart. You wish to know me, and not this humble herb: but pass on; your desire cannot be satisfied."

"You have not the politeness of your countrymen," said Glyndon, somewhat discomposed. "Suppose I were desirous to cultivate your acquaintance, why should you reject my advances?"

"I reject no man's advances," answered Zanoni; "I must know them if they so desire; but *me*, in return, they can never comprehend. If you ask my acquaintance, it is yours; but I would warn you to shun me."

"And why are you, then, so dangerous?"

"On this earth, men are often, without their own agency, fated to be dangerous to others. If I were to predict your fortune by the vain calculations of the astrologer, I should tell you, in their despicable jargon, that my planet sat darkly in your house of life. Cross me not, if you can avoid it. I warn you now for the first time and last."

"You despise the astrologers, yet you utter a jargon as mysterious as theirs. I neither gamble nor quarrel; why, then, should I fear you?"

"As you will; I have done."

"Let me speak frankly, — your conversation last night interested and perplexed me."

"I know it: minds like yours are attracted by mystery."

Glyndon was piqued at these words, though in the tone in which they were spoken there was no contempt.

"I see you do not consider me worthy of your friendship. Be it so. Good-day!"

Zanoni coldly replied to the salutation; and as the Englishman rode on, returned to his botanical employment.

The same night, Glyndon went, as usual, to the theater. He was standing behind the scenes watching Viola, who was on the stage in one

---

* 'Plut. Symp.' l. 5. c. 7.
† Syncellus, page 14. — "Chemistry the Invention of the Giants."

of her most brilliant parts. The house resounded with applause. Glyndon was transported with a young man's passion and a young man's pride: "This glorious creature," thought he, "may yet be mine."

He felt, while thus wrapped in delicious reverie, a slight touch upon his shoulder; he turned, and beheld Zanoni. "You are in danger," said the latter. "Do not walk home tonight; or if you do, go not alone."

Before Glyndon recovered from his surprise, Zanoni disappeared; and when the Englishman saw him again, he was in the box of one of the Neapolitan nobles, where Glyndon could not follow him.

Viola now left the stage, and Glyndon accosted her with an unaccustomed warmth of gallantry. But Viola, contrary to her gentle habit, turned with an evident impatience from the address of her lover. Taking aside Gionetta, who was her constant attendant at the theater, she said, in an earnest whisper, —

"Oh, Gionetta! He is here again! — the stranger of whom I spoke to thee! — and again, he alone, of the whole theater, withholds from me his applause."

"Which is he, my darling?" said the old woman, with fondness in her voice. "He must indeed be dull — not worth a thought."

The actress drew Gionetta nearer to the stage, and pointed out to her a man in one of the boxes, conspicuous amongst all else by the simplicity of his dress, and the extraordinary beauty of his features.

"Not worth a thought, Gionetta!" repeated Viola, — "Not worth a thought! Alas, not to think of him, seems the absence of thought itself!"

The prompter summoned the Signora Pisani. "Find out his name, Gionetta," said she, moving slowly to the stage, and passing by Glyndon, who gazed at her with a look of sorrowful reproach.

The scene on which the actress now entered was that of the final catastrophe, wherein all her remarkable powers of voice and art were pre-eminently called forth. The house hung on every word with breathless worship; but the eyes of Viola sought only those of one calm and unmoved spectator; she exerted herself as if inspired. Zanoni listened, and observed her with an attentive gaze, but no approval escaped his lips; no emotion changed the expression of his cold and half-disdainful aspect. Viola, who was in the character of one who loved, but without return, never felt so acutely the part she played. Her tears were truthful; her passion that of nature: it was almost too terrible to behold. She was borne from the stage exhausted and insensible, amidst such a tempest of admiring rapture as Continental audiences alone can raise. The crowd stood up, handkerchiefs waved, garlands and flowers were thrown on the stage, — men wiped their eyes, and women sobbed aloud.

"By heavens!" said a Neapolitan of great rank, "She has fired me beyond endurance. Tonight — this very night — she shall be mine! You have arranged all, Mascari?"

"All, signor. And the young Englishman?"

"The presuming barbarian! As I before told thee, let him bleed for his folly. I will have no rival."

"But an Englishman! There is always a search after the bodies of the English."

"Fool! is not the sea deep enough, or the earth secret enough, to hide one dead man? Our ruffians are silent as the grave itself; and I! — who would dare to suspect, to arraign the Prince di ——? See to it, — this night. I trust him to you. Robbers murder him, you understand, — the country swarms with them; plunder and strip him, the better to favor such report. Take three men; the rest shall be my escort."

Mascari shrugged his shoulders, and bowed submissively.

The streets of Naples were not then so safe as now, and carriages were both less expensive and more necessary. The vehicle which was regularly engaged by the young actress was not to be found. Gionetta, too aware of the beauty of her mistress and the number of her admirers to contemplate without alarm the idea of their return on foot, communicated her distress to Glyndon, and he besought Viola, who recovered but slowly, to accept his own carriage. Perhaps before that night she would not have rejected so slight a service. Now, for some reason or other, she refused. Glyndon, offended, was retiring sullenly, when Gionetta stopped him. "Stay, signor," said she, coaxingly: "the dear signora is not well, — do not be angry with her; I will make her accept your offer."

Glyndon stayed, and after a few moments spent in expostulation on the part of Gionetta, and resistance on that of Viola, the offer was accepted. Gionetta and her charge entered the carriage, and Glyndon was left at the door of the theater to return home on foot. The mysterious warning of Zanoni then suddenly occurred to him; he had forgotten it in the interest of his lover's quarrel with Viola. He thought it now advisable to guard against danger foretold by lips so mysterious. He looked round for some one he knew: the theater was disgorging its crowds; they hustled, and jostled, and pressed upon him; but he recognized no familiar countenance. While pausing irresolute, he heard Mervale's voice calling on him, and, to his great relief, discovered his friend making his way through the throng.

"I have secured you," said he, "a place in the Count Cetoxa's carriage. Come along, he is waiting for us."

"How kind in you! how did you find me out?"

"I met Zanoni in the passage, — 'Your friend is at the door of the theater,' said he; 'do not let him go home on foot tonight; the streets of Naples are not always safe.' I immediately remembered that some of the Calabrian bravos had been busy within the city the last few weeks, and suddenly meeting Cetoxa — but here he is."

Further explanation was forbidden, for they now joined the count. As Glyndon entered the carriage and drew up the glass, he saw four men standing apart by the pavement, who seemed to eye him with attention.

"Cospetto!" cried one; "that is the Englishman!" Glyndon imperfectly heard the exclamation as the carriage drove on. He reached home in safety.

The familiar and endearing intimacy which always exists in Italy between the nurse and the child she has reared, and which the "Romeo and Juliet" of Shakespeare in no way exaggerates, could not but be drawn yet closer than usual, in a situation so friendless as that of the orphan-actress. In all that concerned the weaknesses of the heart, Gionetta had large experience; and when, three nights before, Viola, on returning from the theater, had wept bitterly, the nurse had succeeded in extracting from her a confession that she had seen one, — not seen for two weary and eventful years, — but never forgotten, and who, alas! had not evinced the slightest recognition of herself. Gionetta could not comprehend all the vague and innocent emotions that swelled this sorrow; but she resolved them all, with her plain, blunt understanding, to the one sentiment of love. And here, she was well fitted to sympathize and console. Confidante to Viola's entire and deep heart she never could be, — for that heart never could have words for all its secrets. But such confidence as she could obtain, she was ready to repay by the most unreproving pity and the most ready service.

"Have you discovered who he is?" asked Viola, as she was now alone in the carriage with Gionetta.

"Yes; he is the celebrated Signor Zanoni, about whom all the great ladies have gone mad. They say he is so rich! — oh! so much richer than any of the Inglesi! — not but what the Signor Glyndon —"

"Cease!" interrupted the young actress. "Zanoni! Speak of the Englishman no more."

The carriage was now entering that more lonely and remote part of the city in which Viola's house was situated, when it suddenly stopped.

Gionetta, in alarm, thrust her head out of the window, and perceived, by the pale light of the moon, that the driver, torn from his seat, was already pinioned in the arms of two men; the next moment the door was opened violently, and a tall figure, masked and mantled, appeared.

"Fear not, fairest Pisani," said he, gently; "no ill shall befall you." As he spoke, he wound his arm round the form of the fair actress, and endeavored to lift her from the carriage. But Gionetta was no ordinary ally, — she thrust back the assailant with a force that astonished him, and followed the shock by a volley of the most energetic reprobation.

The mask drew back, and composed his disordered mantle.

"By the body of Bacchus!" said he, half laughing, "she is well protected. Here, Luigi, Giovanni! seize the hag! — quick! — why loiter ye?"

The mask retired from the door, and another and yet taller form presented itself. "Be calm, Viola Pisani," said he, in a low voice; "with me you are indeed safe!" He lifted his mask as he spoke, and showed the noble features of Zanoni.

"Be calm, be hushed, — I can save you." He vanished, leaving Viola lost in surprise, agitation, and delight. There were, in all, nine masks: two were engaged with the driver; one stood at the head of the carriage-horses; a fourth guarded the well-trained steeds of the party; three others (besides Zanoni and the one who had first accosted Viola) stood apart by a carriage drawn to the side of the road. To these three Zanoni motioned; they advanced; he pointed towards the first mask, who was in fact the Prince di ——, and to his unspeakable astonishment the prince was suddenly seized from behind.

"Treason!" he cried. "Treason among my own men! What means this?"

"Place him in his carriage! If he resist, his blood be on his own head!" said Zanoni, calmly.

He approached the men who had detained the coachman.

"You are outnumbered and outwitted," said he; "join your lord; you are three men, — we six, armed to the teeth. Thank our mercy that we spare your lives. Go!"

The men gave way, dismayed. The driver remounted.

"Cut the traces of their carriage and the bridles of their horses," said Zanoni, as he entered the vehicle containing Viola, which now drove on rapidly, leaving the discomfited ravisher in a state of rage and stupor impossible to describe.

"Allow me to explain this mystery to you," said Zanoni. "I discovered the plot against you, — no matter how; I frustrated it thus: The head of this design is a nobleman, who has long persecuted you in vain. He and two of his creatures watched you from the entrance of the theater, having directed six others to await him on the spot where you were attacked; myself and five of my servants supplied their place, and were mistaken for his own followers. I had previously ridden alone to the spot where the men were waiting, and informed them that their master would not require their services that night. They believed me, and accordingly dispersed. I then joined my own band, whom I had left in the rear; you know all. We are at your door."

Chapter 2.III.

When most I wink, then do mine eyes best see,
For all the day they view things unrespected;
But when I sleep, in dreams they look on thee,
And, darkly bright, are bright in dark directed.

Shakespeare

Zanoni followed the young Neapolitan into her house; Gionetta vanished, — they were left alone.

Alone, in that room so often filled, in the old happy days, with the wild melodies of Pisani; and now, as she saw this mysterious, haunting, yet beautiful and stately stranger, standing on the very spot where she had sat at her father's feet, thrilled and spellbound, — she almost thought, in her fantastic way of personifying her own airy notions, that that spiritual Music had taken shape and life, and stood before her glorious in the image it assumed. She was unconscious all the while of her own loveliness. She had thrown aside her hood and veil; her hair, somewhat disordered, fell over the ivory neck which the dress partially displayed; and as her dark eyes swam with grateful tears, and her cheek flushed with its late excitement, the god of light and music himself never, amidst his Arcadian valleys, wooed, in his mortal guise, maiden or nymph more fair.

Zanoni gazed at her with a look in which admiration seemed not unmingled with compassion. He muttered a few words to himself, and then addressed her aloud.

"Viola, I have saved you from a great peril; not from dishonor only, but perhaps from death. The Prince di ——, under a weak despot and a venal administration, is a man above the law. He is capable of every crime; but amongst his passions he has such prudence as belongs to ambition; if you were not to reconcile yourself to your shame, you would never enter the world again to tell your tale. The ravisher has no heart for repentance, but he has a hand that can murder. I have saved you,

Viola. Perhaps you would ask me wherefore?" Zanoni paused, and smiled mournfully, as he added, "You will not wrong me by the thought that he who has preserved is not less selfish than he who would have injured. Orphan, I do not speak to you in the language of your wooers; enough that I know pity, and am not ungrateful for affection. Why blush, why tremble at the word? I read your heart while I speak, and I see not one thought that should give you shame. I say not that you love me yet; happily, the fancy may be roused long before the heart is touched. But it has been my fate to fascinate your eye, to influence your imagination. It is to warn you against what could bring you but sorrow, as I warned you once to prepare for sorrow itself, that I am now your guest. The Englishman, Glyndon, loves thee well, — better, perhaps, than I can ever love; if not worthy of thee, yet, he has but to know thee more to deserve thee better. He may wed thee, he may bear thee to his own free and happy land, — the land of thy mother's kin. Forget me; teach thyself to return and deserve his love; and I tell thee that thou wilt be honored and be happy."

Viola listened with silent, inexpressible emotion, and burning blushes, to this strange address, and when he had concluded, she covered her face with her hands, and wept. And yet, much as his words were calculated to humble or irritate, to produce indignation or excite shame, those were not the feelings with which her eyes streamed and her heart swelled. The woman at that moment was lost in the child; and *as* a child, with all its exacting, craving, yet innocent desire to be loved, weeps in unrebuking sadness when its affection is thrown austerely back upon itself, — so, without anger and without shame, wept Viola.

Zanoni contemplated her thus, as her graceful head, shadowed by its redundant tresses, bent before him; and after a moment's pause he drew near to her, and said, in a voice of the most soothing sweetness, and with a half smile upon his lip, —

"Do you remember, when I told you to struggle for the light, that I pointed for example to the resolute and earnest tree? I did not tell you, fair child, to take example by the moth, that would soar to the star, but falls scorched beside the lamp. Come, I will talk to thee. This Englishman —"

Viola drew herself away, and wept yet more passionately.

"This Englishman is of thine own years, not far above thine own rank. Thou mayst share his thoughts in life, — thou mayst sleep beside him in the same grave in death! And I — but *that* view of the future should concern us not. Look into thy heart, and thou wilt see that till again my shadow crossed thy path, there had grown up for this thine equal a pure and calm affection that would have ripened into love. Hast thou never pictured to thyself a home in which thy partner was thy young wooer?"

"Never!" said Viola, with sudden energy, — "never but to feel that such was not the fate ordained me. And, oh!" she continued, rising suddenly, and, putting aside the tresses that veiled her face, she fixed her eyes upon the questioner, — "and, oh! whoever thou art that thus wouldst read my soul and shape my future, do not mistake the sentiment that, that —" she faltered an instant, and went on with downcast eyes, — "that has fascinated my thoughts to thee. Do not think that I could nourish a love unsought and unreturned. It is not love that I feel for thee, stranger. Why should I? Thou hast never spoken to me but to admonish, — and now, to wound!" Again she paused, again her voice faltered; the tears trembled on her eyelids; she brushed them away and resumed. "No, not love, — if that be love which I have heard and read of, and sought to simulate on the stage, — but a more solemn, fearful, and, it seems to me, almost preternatural attraction, which makes me associate thee, waking or dreaming, with images that at once charm and awe. Thinkest thou, if it were love, that I could speak to thee thus; that," she raised her looks suddenly to his, "mine eyes could thus search and confront thine own? Stranger, I ask but at times to see, to hear thee! Stranger, talk not to me of others. Forewarn, rebuke, bruise my heart, reject the not unworthy gratitude it offers thee, if thou wilt, but come not always to me as an omen of grief and trouble. Sometimes have I seen thee in my dreams surrounded by shapes of glory and light; thy looks radiant with a celestial joy which they wear not now. Stranger, thou hast saved me, and I thank and bless thee! Is that also a homage thou wouldst reject?" With these words, she crossed her arms meekly on her bosom, and inclined lowlily before him. Nor did her humility seem unwomanly or abject, nor that of mistress to lover, of slave to master, but rather of a child to its guardian, of a neophyte of the old religion to her priest. Zanoni's brow was melancholy and thoughtful. He looked at her with a strange expression of kindness, of sorrow, yet of tender affection, in his eyes; but his lips were stern, and his voice cold, as he replied, —

"Do you know what you ask, Viola? Do you guess the danger to yourself — perhaps to both of us — which you court? Do you know that my life, separated from the turbulent herd of men, is one worship of the Beautiful, from which I seek to banish what the Beautiful inspires in most? As a calamity, I shun what to man seems the fairest fate, — the love of the daughters of earth. At present I can warn and save thee from many evils; if I saw more of thee, would the power still be mine? You understand me not. What I am about to add, it will be easier to comprehend. I bid thee banish from thy heart all thought of me, but as one whom the Future cries aloud to thee to avoid. Glyndon, if thou acceptest his homage, will love thee till the tomb closes upon both. I, too," he added with emotion, — "I, too, might love thee!"

"You!" cried Viola, with the vehemence of a sudden impulse of delight, of rapture, which she could not suppress; but the instant after, she would have given worlds to recall the exclamation.

"Yes, Viola, I might love thee; but in that love what sorrow and what change! The flower gives perfume to the rock on whose heart it grows. A little while, and the flower is dead; but the rock still endures, — the snow at its breast, the sunshine on its summit. Pause, — think well. Danger besets thee yet. For some days thou shalt be safe from thy remorseless persecutor; but the hour soon comes when thy only security will be in flight. If the Englishman love thee worthily, thy honor will be dear to him as his own; if not, there are yet other lands where love will be truer, and virtue less in danger from fraud and force. Farewell; my own destiny I cannot foresee except through cloud and shadow. I know, at least, that we shall meet again; but learn ere then, sweet flower, that there are more genial resting-places than the rock."

He turned as he spoke, and gained the outer door where Gionetta discreetly stood. Zanoni lightly laid his hand on her arm. With the gay accent of a jesting cavalier, he said, —

"The Signor Glyndon woos your mistress; he may wed her. I know your love for her. Disabuse her of any caprice for me. I am a bird ever on the wing."

He dropped a purse into Gionetta's hand as he spoke, and was gone.

Chapter 2.IV.

Les Intelligences Celestes se font voir, et see communiquent plus volontiers, dans le silence et dans la tranquillite de la soli-tude. On aura donc une petite chambre ou un cabinet secret, etc.*

---

* The Celestial Intelligences exhibit and explain themselves most freely in silence and the tranquillity of solitude. One will have then a little chamber, or a secret cabinet, etc.

"Les Clavicules de Rabbi Salomon," chapter 3;
traduites exactement du texte Hebreu par M. Pierre Moris-
soneau, Professeur des Langues Orientales, et Sectateur de la Philosophie des Sages Cabalistes.*

*T*he palace retained by Zanoni was in one of the less frequented quarters of the city. It still stands, now ruined and dismantled, a monument of the splendor of a chivalry long since vanished from Naples, with the lordly races of the Norman and the Spaniard.

As he entered the rooms reserved for his private hours, two Indians, in the dress of their country, received him at the threshold with the grave salutations of the East. They had accompanied him from the far lands in which, according to rumor, he had for many years fixed his home. But they could communicate nothing to gratify curiosity or justify suspicion. They spoke no language but their own. With the exception of these two his princely retinue was composed of the native hirelings of the city, whom his lavish but imperious generosity made the implicit creatures of his will. In his house, and in his habits, so far as they were seen, there was nothing to account for the rumors which were circulated abroad. He was not, as we are told of Albertus Magnus or the great Leonardo da Vinci, served by airy forms; and no brazen image, the invention of magic mechanism, communicated to him the influences of the stars. None of the apparatus of the alchemist — the crucible and the metals — gave solemnity to his chambers, or accounted for his wealth; nor did he even seem to interest himself in those serener studies which might be supposed to color his peculiar conversation with abstract notions, and often with recondite learning. No books spoke to him in his solitude; and if ever he had drawn from them his knowledge, it seemed now that the only page he read was the wide one of Nature, and that a capacious and startling memory supplied the rest. Yet was there one exception to what in all else seemed customary and common-place, and which, according to the authority we have prefixed to this chapter, might indicate the follower of the occult sciences. Whether at Rome or Naples, or, in fact, wherever his abode, he selected one room remote from the rest of the house, which was fastened by a lock scarcely larger than the seal of a ring, yet which sufficed to baffle the most cunning instruments of the locksmith: at least, one of his servants, prompted by irresistible curiosity, had made the attempt in vain; and though he had fancied it was tried in the most favorable time for secrecy, — not a soul near, in the dead of night, Zanoni himself absent from

---

* Manuscript Translation.

home, — yet his superstition, or his conscience, told him the reason why
the next day the Major Domo quietly dismissed him. He compensated
himself for this misfortune by spreading his own story, with a thousand
amusing exaggerations. He declared that, as he approached the door,
invisible hands seemed to pluck him away; and that when he touched
the lock, he was struck, as by a palsy, to the ground. One surgeon, who
heard the tale, observed, to the distaste of the wonder-mongers, that
possibly Zanoni made a dexterous use of electricity. Howbeit, this room,
once so secured, was never entered save by Zanoni himself.

The solemn voice of Time, from the neighboring church at last
aroused the lord of the palace from the deep and motionless reverie,
rather resembling a trance than thought, in which his mind was absorbed.

"It is one more sand out of the mighty hour-glass," said he, murmur-
ingly, "and yet time neither adds to, nor steals from, an atom in the
Infinite! Soul of mine, the luminous, the Augoeides*, why descendest
thou from thy sphere, — why from the eternal, starlike, and passionless
Serene, shrinkest thou back to the mists of the dark sarcophagus? How
long, too austerely taught that companionship with the things that die
brings with it but sorrow in its sweetness, hast thou dwelt contented
with thy majestic solitude?"

As he thus murmured, one of the earliest birds that salute the dawn
broke into sudden song from amidst the orange trees in the garden
below his casement; and as suddenly, song answered song; the mate,
awakened at the note, gave back its happy answer to the bird. He listened;
and not the soul he had questioned, but the heart replied. He rose, and
with restless strides paced the narrow floor. "Away from this world!" he
exclaimed at length, with an impatient tone. "Can no time loosen its
fatal ties? As the attraction that holds the earth in space, is the attraction
that fixes the soul to earth. Away from the dark grey planet! Break, ye
fetters: arise, ye wings!"

He passed through the silent galleries, and up the lofty stairs, and
entered the secret chamber.

---

* Augoeides, — a word favored by the mystical Platonists, sphaira psuches augoeides,
otan mete ekteinetai epi ti, mete eso suntreche mete sunizane, alla photi lampetai,
o ten aletheian opa ten panton, kai ten en aute. — Marc. Ant., lib. 2. — The sense
of which beautiful sentence of the old philosophy, which, as Bayle well observes,
in his article on Cornelius Agrippa, the modern Quietists have (however impotently)
sought to imitate, is to the effect that 'the sphere of the soul is luminous when
nothing external has contact with the soul itself; but when lit by its own light, it
sees the truth of all things and the truth centered in itself.'

Chapter 2.V.

I and my fellows
Are ministers of Fate.

"The Tempest."

*T*he next day Glyndon bent his steps towards Zanoni's palace. The young man's imagination, naturally inflammable, was singularly excited by the little he had seen and heard of this strange being, — a spell, he could neither master nor account for, attracted him towards the stranger. Zanoni's power seemed mysterious and great, his motives kindly and benevolent, yet his manners chilling and repellent. Why at one moment reject Glyndon's acquaintance, at another save him from danger? How had Zanoni thus acquired the knowledge of enemies unknown to Glyndon himself? His interest was deeply roused, his gratitude appealed to; he resolved to make another effort to conciliate the ungracious herbalist.

The signor was at home, and Glyndon was admitted into a lofty saloon, where in a few moments Zanoni joined him.

"I am come to thank you for your warning last night," said he, "and to entreat you to complete my obligation by informing me of the quarter to which I may look for enmity and peril."

"You are a gallant," said Zanoni, with a smile, and in the English language, "and do you know so little of the South as not to be aware that gallants have always rivals?"

"Are you serious?" said Glyndon, coloring.

"Most serious. You love Viola Pisani; you have for rival one of the most powerful and relentless of the Neapolitan princes. Your danger is indeed great."

"But pardon me! — how came it known to you?"

"I give no account of myself to mortal man," replied Zanoni, haughtily; "and to me it matters nothing whether you regard or scorn my warning."

"Well, if I may not question you, be it so; but at least advise me what to do."

"Would you follow my advice?"

"Why not?"

"Because you are constitutionally brave; you are fond of excitement and mystery; you like to be the hero of a romance. Were I to advise you to leave Naples, would you do so while Naples contains a foe to confront or a mistress to pursue?"

"You are right," said the young Englishman, with energy. "No! and you cannot reproach me for such a resolution."

"But there is another course left to you: do you love Viola Pisani truly and fervently? — if so, marry her, and take a bride to your native land."

"Nay," answered Glyndon, embarrassed; "Viola is not of my rank. Her profession, too, is — in short, I am enslaved by her beauty, but I cannot wed her."

Zanoni frowned.

"Your love, then, is but selfish lust, and I advise you to your own happiness no more. Young man, Destiny is less inexorable than it appears. The resources of the great Ruler of the Universe are not so scanty and so stern as to deny to men the divine privilege of Free Will; all of us can carve out our own way, and God can make our very contradictions harmonize with His solemn ends. You have before you an option. Honorable and generous love may even now work out your happiness, and effect your escape; a frantic and selfish passion will but lead you to misery and doom."

"Do you pretend, then, to read the future?"

"I have said all that it pleases me to utter."

"While you assume the moralist to me, Signor Zanoni," said Glyndon, with a smile, "are you yourself so indifferent to youth and beauty as to act the stoic to its allurements?"

"If it were necessary that practice square with precept," said Zanoni, with a bitter smile, "our monitors would be but few. The conduct of the individual can affect but a small circle beyond himself; the permanent good or evil that he works to others lies rather in the sentiments he can diffuse. His acts are limited and momentary; his sentiments may pervade the universe, and inspire generations till the day of doom. All our virtues, all our laws, are drawn from books and maxims, which *are* sentiments, not from deeds. In conduct, Julian had the virtues of a Christian, and Constantine the vices of a Pagan. The sentiments of Julian reconverted thousands to Paganism; those of Constantine helped, under Heaven's will, to bow to Christianity the nations of the earth. In conduct, the humblest fisherman on yonder sea, who believes in the miracles of San Gennaro, may be a better man than Luther; to the sentiments of Luther the mind of modern Europe is indebted for the noblest revolution it has known. Our opinions, young Englishman, are the angel part of us; our acts, the earthly."

"You have reflected deeply for an Italian," said Glyndon.

"Who told you that I was an Italian?"

"Are you not? And yet, when I hear you speak my own language as a native, I —"

"Tush!" interrupted Zanoni, impatiently turning away. Then, after a pause, he resumed in a mild voice, "Glyndon, do you renounce Viola Pisani? Will you take some days to consider what I have said?"

"Renounce her, — never!"

"Then you will marry her?"

"Impossible!"

"Be it so; she will then renounce you. I tell you that you have rivals."

"Yes; the Prince di ——; but I do not fear him."

"You have another whom you will fear more."

"And who is he?"

"Myself."

Glyndon turned pale, and started from his seat.

"You, Signor Zanoni! — you, — and you dare to tell me so?"

"Dare! Alas! there are times when I wish that I could fear."

These arrogant words were not uttered arrogantly, but in a tone of the most mournful dejection. Glyndon was enraged, confounded, and yet awed. However, he had a brave English heart within his breast, and he recovered himself quickly.

"Signor," said he, calmly, "I am not to be duped by these solemn phrases and these mystical assumptions. You may have powers which I cannot comprehend or emulate, or you may be but a keen imposter."

"Well, proceed!"

"I mean, then," continued Glyndon, resolutely, though somewhat disconcerted, — "I mean you to understand, that, though I am not to be persuaded or compelled by a stranger to marry Viola Pisani, I am not the less determined never tamely to yield her to another."

Zanoni looked gravely at the young man, whose sparkling eyes and heightened color testified the spirit to support his words, and replied, "So bold! well; it becomes you. But take my advice; wait yet nine days, and tell me then if you will marry the fairest and the purest creature that ever crossed your path."

"But if you love her, why — why —"

"Why am I anxious that she should wed another? — to save her from myself! Listen to me. That girl, humble and uneducated though she be, has in her the seeds of the most lofty qualities and virtues. She can be all to the man she loves, — all that man can desire in wife. Her soul, developed by affection, will elevate your own; it will influence your fortunes, exalt your destiny; you will become a great and a prosperous man. If, on the contrary, she fall to me, I know not what may be her lot; but I know that there is an ordeal which few can pass, and which hitherto no woman has survived."

As Zanoni spoke, his face became colorless, and there was something in his voice that froze the warm blood of the listener.

"What is this mystery which surrounds you?" exclaimed Glyndon, unable to repress his emotion. "Are you, in truth, different from other men? Have you passed the boundary of lawful knowledge? Are you, as some declare, a sorcerer, or only a —"

"Hush!" interrupted Zanoni, gently, and with a smile of singular but melancholy sweetness; "have you earned the right to ask me these questions? Though Italy still boast an Inquisition, its power is rivelled as a leaf which the first wind shall scatter. The days of torture and persecution are over; and a man may live as he pleases, and talk as it suits him, without fear of the stake and the rack. Since I can defy persecution, pardon me if I do not yield to curiosity."

Glyndon blushed, and rose. In spite of his love for Viola, and his natural terror of such a rival, he felt himself irresistibly drawn towards the very man he had most cause to suspect and dread. He held out his hand to Zanoni, saying, "Well, then, if we are to be rivals, our swords must settle our rights; till then I would fain be friends."

"Friends! You know not what you ask."

"Enigmas again!"

"Enigmas!" cried Zanoni, passionately; "aye! can you dare to solve them? Not till then could I give you my right hand, and call you friend."

"I could dare everything and all things for the attainment of super-human wisdom," said Glyndon, and his countenance was lighted up with wild and intense enthusiasm.

Zanoni observed him in thoughtful silence.

"The seeds of the ancestor live in the son," he muttered; "he may — yet —" He broke off abruptly; then, speaking aloud, "Go, Glyndon," said he; "we shall meet again, but I will not ask your answer till the hour presses for decision."

Chapter 2. VI.

'Tis certain that this man has an estate of fifty thousand livres, and seems to be a person of very great accomplishments. But, then, if he's a wizard, are wizards so devoutly given as this man seems to be? In short, I could make neither head nor tail on't.
— The Count de Gabalis,
Translation affixed to the second edition
of the "Rape of the Lock."

*O*f all the weaknesses which little men rail against, there is none that they are more apt to ridicule than the tendency to believe. And of all the signs of a corrupt heart and a feeble head, the tendency of incredulity is the surest.

Real philosophy seeks rather to solve than to deny. While we hear, every day, the small pretenders to science talk of the absurdities of alchemy and the dream of the Philosopher's Stone, a more erudite knowledge is aware that by alchemists the greatest discoveries in science have been made, and much which still seems abstruse, had we the key to the mystic phraseology they were compelled to adopt, might open the way to yet more noble acquisitions. The Philosopher's Stone itself has seemed no visionary chimera to some of the soundest chemists that even the present century has produced.* Man cannot contradict the Laws of Nature. But are all the laws of Nature yet discovered?

"Give me a proof of your art," says the rational inquirer. "When I have seen the effect, I will endeavor, with you, to ascertain the causes."

Somewhat to the above effect were the first thoughts of Clarence Glyndon on quitting Zanoni. But Clarence Glyndon was no "rational inquirer." The more vague and mysterious the language of Zanoni, the

---

* Mr. Disraeli, in his "Curiosities of Literature" (article "Alchem"), after quoting the sanguine judgments of modern chemists as to the transmutation of metals, observes of one yet greater and more recent than those to which Glyndon's thoughts could have referred, "Sir Humphry Davy told me that he did not consider this undiscovered art as impossible; but should it ever be discovered, it would certainly be useless."

more it imposed upon him. A proof would have been something tangible, with which he would have sought to grapple. And it would have only disappointed his curiosity to find the supernatural reduced to Nature. He endeavored in vain, at some moments rousing himself from credulity to the skepticism he deprecated, to reconcile what he had heard with the probable motives and designs of an imposter. Unlike Mesmer and Cagliostro, Zanoni, whatever his pretensions, did not make them a source of profit; nor was Glyndon's position or rank in life sufficient to render any influence obtained over his mind, subservient to schemes, whether of avarice or ambition. Yet, ever and anon, with the suspicion of worldly knowledge, he strove to persuade himself that Zanoni had at least some sinister object in inducing him to what his English pride and manner of thought considered a derogatory marriage with the poor actress. Might not Viola and the Mystic be in league with each other? Might not all this jargon of prophecy and menace be but artifices to dupe him?

He felt an unjust resentment towards Viola at having secured such an ally. But with that resentment was mingled a natural jealousy. Zanoni threatened him with rivalry. Zanoni, who, whatever his character or his arts, possessed at least all the external attributes that dazzle and command. Impatient of his own doubts, he plunged into the society of such acquaintances as he had made at Naples — chiefly artists, like himself, men of letters, and the rich commercialists, who were already vying with the splendor, though debarred from the privileges, of the nobles. From these he heard much of Zanoni, already with them, as with the idler classes, an object of curiosity and speculation.

He had noticed, as a thing remarkable, that Zanoni had conversed with him in English, and with a command of the language so complete that he might have passed for a native. On the other hand, in Italian, Zanoni was equally at ease. Glyndon found that it was the same in languages less usually learned by foreigners. A painter from Sweden, who had conversed with him, was positive that he was a Swede; and a merchant from Constantinople, who had sold some of his goods to Zanoni, professed his conviction that none but a Turk, or at least a native of the East, could have so thoroughly mastered the soft Oriental intonations. Yet in all these languages, when they came to compare their several recollections, there was a slight, scarce perceptible distinction, not in pronunciation, nor even accent, but in the key and chime, as it were, of the voice, between himself and a native. This faculty was one which Glyndon called to mind, that sect, whose tenets and powers have never been more than most partially explored, the Rosicrucians, especially arrogated. He remembered to have heard in Germany of the work of John Bringeret*, asserting that all the languages of the earth were known to the genuine Brotherhood of the Rosy Cross. Did Zanoni belong to this mystical Fraternity, who, in an earlier age, boasted of secrets of which the Philosopher's Stone was but the least; who considered themselves the heirs of all that the Chaldeans, the Magi, the Gymnosophists, and the Platonists had taught; and who differed from all the darker Sons of Magic in the virtue of their lives, the purity of their doctrines, and their insisting, as the foundation of all wisdom, on the subjugation of the senses, and the intensity of Religious Faith? — a glorious sect, if they lied not! And, in truth, if Zanoni had powers beyond the race of worldly sages, they seemed not unworthily exercised. The little known of his life was in his favor. Some acts, not of indiscriminate, but judicious generosity and beneficence, were recorded; in repeating which, still, however, the narrators shook their heads, and expressed surprise how a stranger should have possessed so minute a knowledge of the quiet and obscure distresses he had relieved. Two or three sick persons, when abandoned by their physicians, he had visited, and conferred with alone. They had recovered: they ascribed to him their recovery; yet they could not tell by what medicines they had been healed. They could only depose that he came, conversed with them, and they were cured; it usually, however, happened that a deep sleep had preceded the recovery.

Another circumstance was also beginning to be remarked, and spoke yet more in his commendation. Those with whom he principally associated — the gay, the dissipated, the thoughtless, the sinners and publicans of the more polished world — all appeared rapidly, yet insensibly to themselves, to awaken to purer thoughts and more regulated lives. Even Cetoxa, the prince of gallants, duelists, and gamesters, was no longer the same man since the night of the singular events which he had related to Glyndon. The first trace of his reform was in his retirement from the gaming-houses; the next was his reconciliation with an hereditary enemy of his house, whom it had been his constant object for the last six years to entangle in such a quarrel as might call forth his inimitable maneuver of the stoccata. Nor when Cetoxa and his young companions were heard to speak of Zanoni, did it seem that this change had been brought about by any sober lectures or admonitions. They all described Zanoni as a man keenly alive to enjoyment: of manners the reverse of formal, — not precisely gay, but equable, serene, and cheerful; ever ready to listen to the talk of others, however idle, or to charm all ears with an inexhaustible fund of brilliant anecdote and worldly experience. All manners, all nations, all grades of men, seemed familiar to him. He was reserved only if allusion were ever ventured to his birth or history.

§ Printed in 1615.

The more general opinion of his origin certainly seemed the more plausible. His riches, his familiarity with the languages of the East, his residence in India, a certain gravity which never deserted his most cheerful and familiar hours, the lustrous darkness of his eyes and hair, and even the peculiarities of his shape, in the delicate smallness of the hands, and the Arablike turn of the stately head, appeared to fix him as belonging to one at least of the Oriental races. And a dabbler in the Eastern tongues even sought to reduce the simple name of Zanoni, which a century before had been borne by an inoffensive naturalist of Bologna*, to the radicals of the extinct language. Zan was unquestionably the Chaldean appellation for the sun. Even the Greeks, who mutilated every Oriental name, had retained the right one in this case, as the Cretan inscription on the tomb of Zeus† significantly showed. As to the rest, the Zan, or Zaun, was, with the Sidonians, no uncommon prefix to On. Adonis was but another name for Zanonas, whose worship in Sidon Hesychius records. To this profound and unanswerable derivation Mervale listened with great attention, and observed that he now ventured to announce an erudite discovery he himself had long since made, — namely, that the numerous family of Smiths in England were undoubtedly the ancient priests of the Phrygian Apollo. "For," said he, "was not Apollo's surname, in Phrygia, Smintheus? How clear all the ensuing corruptions of the august name, — Smintheus, Smitheus, Smithe, Smith! And even now, I may remark that the more ancient branches of that illustrious family, unconsciously anxious to approximate at least by a letter nearer to the true title, take a pious pleasure in writing their names Smith*e!*"

The philologist was much struck with this discovery, and begged Mervale's permission to note it down as an illustration suitable to a work he was about to publish on the origin of languages, to be called "Babel," and published in three quartos by subscription.

---

* The author of two works on botany and rare plants.
† Ode megas keitai Zan. — "Cyril contra Julian." (Here lies great Jove.)

Chapter 2.VII.

Learn to be poor in spirit, my son, if you would penetrate that
sacred night which environs truth. Learn of the Sages to allow
to the Devils no power in Nature, since the fatal stone has shut
'em up in the depth of the abyss. Learn of the Philosophers always to look for natural causes in all extraordinary events; and
when such natural causes are wanting, recur to God.
— The Count de Gabalis

*A*ll these additions to his knowledge of Zanoni, picked up in the
various lounging-places and resorts that he frequented, were unsatisfac-
tory to Glyndon. That night Viola did not perform at the theater; and
the next day, still disturbed by bewildered fancies, and averse to the
sober and sarcastic companionship of Mervale, Glyndon sauntered
musingly into the public gardens, and paused under the very tree under
which he had first heard the voice that had exercised upon his mind so
singular an influence. The gardens were deserted. He threw himself on
one of the seats placed beneath the shade; and again, in the midst of
his reverie, the same cold shudder came over him which Zanoni had so
distinctly defined, and to which he had ascribed so extraordinary a
cause.

He roused himself with a sudden effort, and started to see, seated
next him, a figure hideous enough to have personated one of the
malignant beings of whom Zanoni had spoken. It was a small man,
dressed in a fashion strikingly at variance with the elaborate costume
of the day: an affectation of homeliness and poverty approaching to
squalor, in the loose trousers, coarse as a ship's sail; in the rough jacket,
which appeared rent willfully into holes; and the black, ragged, tangled
locks that streamed from their confinement under a woolen cap, accorded but ill with other details which spoke of comparative wealth.
The shirt, open at the throat, was fastened by a brooch of gaudy stones;
and two pendent massive gold chains announced the foppery of two

watches.

The man's figure, if not absolutely deformed, was yet marvelously ill-favored; his shoulders high and square; his chest flattened, as if crushed in; his gloveless hands were knotted at the joints, and, large, bony, and muscular, dangled from lean, emaciated wrists, as if not belonging to them. His features had the painful distortion sometimes seen in the countenance of a cripple, — large, exaggerated, with the nose nearly touching the chin; the eyes small, but glowing with a cunning fire as they dwelt on Glyndon; and the mouth was twisted into a grin that displayed rows of jagged, black, broken teeth. Yet over this frightful face there still played a kind of disagreeable intelligence, an expression at once astute and bold; and as Glyndon, recovering from the first impression, looked again at his neighbor, he blushed at his own dismay, and recognized a French artist, with whom he had formed an acquaintance, and who was possessed of no inconsiderable talents in his calling.

Indeed, it was to be remarked that this creature, whose externals were so deserted by the Graces, particularly delighted in designs aspiring to majesty and grandeur. Though his coloring was hard and shallow, as was that generally of the French school at the time, his *drawings* were admirable for symmetry, simple elegance, and classic vigor; at the same time they unquestionably wanted ideal grace. He was fond of selecting subjects from Roman history, rather than from the copious world of Grecian beauty, or those still more sublime stories of scriptural record from which Raphael and Michael Angelo borrowed their inspirations. His grandeur was that not of gods and saints, but mortals. His delineation of beauty was that which the eye cannot blame and the soul does not acknowledge. In a word, as it was said of Dionysus, he was an Anthropographos, or Painter of Men. It was also a notable contradiction in this person, who was addicted to the most extravagant excesses in every passion, whether of hate or love, implacable in revenge, and insatiable in debauch, that he was in the habit of uttering the most beautiful sentiments of exalted purity and genial philanthropy. The world was not good enough for him; he was, to use the expressive German phrase, *A world-betterer!* Nevertheless, his sarcastic lip often seemed to mock the sentiments he uttered, as if it sought to insinuate that he was above even the world he would construct.

Finally, this painter was in close correspondence with the Republicans of Paris, and was held to be one of those missionaries whom, from the earliest period of the Revolution, the regenerators of mankind were pleased to dispatch to the various states yet shackled, whether by actual tyranny or wholesome laws. Certainly, as the historian of Italy* has observed, there was no city in Italy where these new doctrines would be

---

* Botta.

received with greater favor than Naples, partly from the lively temper of the people, principally because the most hateful feudal privileges, however partially curtailed some years before by the great minister, Tanuccini, still presented so many daily and practical evils as to make change wear a more substantial charm than the mere and meretricious bloom on the cheek of the harlot, Novelty. This man, whom I will call Jean Nicot, was, therefore, an oracle among the younger and bolder spirits of Naples; and before Glyndon had met Zanoni, the former had not been among the least dazzled by the eloquent aspirations of the hideous philanthropist.

"It is so long since we have met, cher confrere," said Nicot, drawing his seat nearer to Glyndon's, "that you cannot be surprised that I see you with delight, and even take the liberty to intrude on your meditations.

"They were of no agreeable nature," said Glyndon; "and never was intrusion more welcome."

"You will be charmed to hear," said Nicot, drawing several letters from his bosom, "that the good work proceeds with marvelous rapidity. Mirabeau, indeed, is no more; but, mort Diable! the French people are now a Mirabeau themselves." With this remark, Monsieur Nicot proceeded to read and to comment upon several animated and interesting passages in his correspondence, in which the word virtue was introduced twenty-seven times, and God not once. And then, warmed by the cheering prospects thus opened to him, he began to indulge in those anticipations of the future, the outline of which we have already seen in the eloquent extravagance of Condorcet. All the old virtues were dethroned for a new Pantheon: patriotism was a narrow sentiment; philanthropy was to be its successor. No love that did not embrace all mankind, as warm for Indus and the Pole as for the hearth of home, was worthy the breast of a generous man. Opinion was to be free as air; and in order to make it so, it was necessary to exterminate all those whose opinions were not the same as Mons. Jean Nicot's. Much of this amused, much revolted Glyndon; but when the painter turned to dwell upon a science that all should comprehend, and the results of which all should enjoy, — a science that, springing from the soil of equal institutions and equal mental cultivation, should give to all the races of men wealth without labor, and a life longer than the Patriarchs', without care, — then Glyndon listened with interest and admiration, not unmixed with awe. "Observe," said Nicot, "how much that we now cherish as a virtue will then be rejected as meanness. Our oppressors, for instance, preach to us of the excellence of gratitude. Gratitude, the confession of inferiority! What so hateful to a noble spirit as the humiliating sense of obligation? But where there is equality there can be no means for power thus to enslave merit. The benefactor and the client will alike cease, and —"

"And in the meantime," said a low voice, at hand, — "in the meantime, Jean Nicot?"

The two artists started, and Glyndon recognized Zanoni.

He gazed with a brow of unusual sternness on Nicot, who, lumped together as he sat, looked up at him askew, and with an expression of fear and dismay upon his distorted countenance.

Ho, ho! Messire Jean Nicot, thou who fearest neither God nor Devil, why fearest thou the eye of a man?

"It is not the first time I have been a witness to your opinions on the infirmity of gratitude," said Zanoni.

Nicot suppressed an exclamation, and, after gloomily surveying Zanoni with an eye villainous and sinister, but full of hate impotent and unutterable, said, "I know you not, — what would you of me?"

"Your absence. Leave us!"

Nicot sprang forward a step, with hands clenched, and showing his teeth from ear to ear, like a wild beast incensed. Zanoni stood motionless, and smiled at him in scorn. Nicot halted abruptly, as if fixed and fascinated by the look, shivered from head to foot, and sullenly, and with a visible effort, as if impelled by a power not his own, turned away.

Glyndon's eyes followed him in surprise.

"And what know you of this man?" said Zanoni.

"I know him as one like myself, — a follower of art."

"Of *Art!* Do not so profane that glorious word. What Nature is to God, art should be to man, — a sublime, beneficent, genial, and warm creation. That wretch may be a *Painter,* not an *Artist.*"

"And pardon me if I ask what *you* know of one you thus disparage?"

"I know thus much, that you are beneath my care if it be necessary to warn you against him; his own lips show the hideousness of his heart. Why should I tell you of the crimes he has committed? He *speaks* crime!"

"You do not seem, Signor Zanoni, to be one of the admirers of the dawning Revolution. Perhaps you are prejudiced against the man because you dislike the opinions?"

"What opinions?"

Glyndon paused, somewhat puzzled to define; but at length he said, "Nay, I must wrong you; for you, of all men, I suppose, cannot discredit the doctrine that preaches the infinite improvement of the human species."

"You are right; the few in every age improve the many; the many now may be as wise as the few were; but improvement is at a standstill, if you tell me that the many now are as wise as the few *are.*"

"I comprehend you; you will not allow the law of universal equality!"

"Law! If the whole world conspired to enforce the falsehood they could not make it *law*. Level all conditions today, and you only smooth away all obstacles to tyranny tomorrow. A nation that aspires to *equality* is unfit for *freedom*. Throughout all creation, from the archangel to the worm, from Olympus to the pebble, from the radiant and completed planet to the nebula that hardens through ages of mist and slime into the habitable world, the first law of Nature is inequality."

"Harsh doctrine, if applied to states. Are the cruel disparities of life never to be removed?"

"Disparities of the *physical* life? Oh, let us hope so. But disparities of the *intellectual* and the *moral,* never! Universal equality of intelligence, of mind, of genius, of virtue! — no teacher left to the world! no men wiser, better than others, — were it not an impossible condition, *what a hopeless prospect for humanity!* No, while the world lasts, the sun will gild the mountaintop before it shines upon the plain. Diffuse all the knowledge the earth contains equally over all mankind today, and some men will be wiser than the rest tomorrow. And *this* is not a harsh, but a loving law, — the *real* law of improvement; the wiser the few in one generation, the wiser will be the multitude the next!"

As Zanoni thus spoke, they moved on through the smiling gardens, and the beautiful bay lay sparkling in the noontide. A gentle breeze just cooled the sunbeam, and stirred the ocean; and in the inexpressible clearness of the atmosphere there was something that rejoiced the senses. The very soul seemed to grow lighter and purer in that lucid air.

"And these men, to commence their era of improvement and equality, are jealous even of the Creator. They would deny an intelligence, — a God!" said Zanoni, as if involuntarily. "Are you an artist, and, looking on the world, can you listen to such a dogma? Between God and genius there is a necessary link, — there is almost a correspondent language. Well said the Pythagorean*, 'A good intellect is the chorus of divinity.'"

Struck and touched with these sentiments, which he little expected to fall from one to whom he ascribed those powers which the superstitions of childhood ascribe to the darker agencies, Glyndon said: "And yet you have confessed that your life, separated from that of others, is one that man should dread to share. Is there, then, a connection between magic and religion?"

"Magic! And what is magic! When the traveler beholds in Persia the ruins of palaces and temples, the ignorant inhabitants inform him they were the work of magicians. What is beyond their own power, the vulgar cannot comprehend to be lawfully in the power of others. But if by magic you mean a perpetual research amongst all that is more latent and obscure in Nature, I answer, I profess that magic, and that he who

---

* Sextus, the Pythagorean.

does so comes but nearer to the fountain of all belief. Knowest thou not that magic was taught in the schools of old? But how, and by whom? As the last and most solemn lesson, by the Priests who ministered to the Temple.* And you, who would be a painter, is not there a magic also in that art you would advance? Must you not, after long study of the Beautiful that has been, seize upon new and airy combinations of a beauty that is to be? See you not that the grander art, whether of poet or of painter, ever seeking for the *true,* abhors the *real*; that you must seize Nature as her master, not lackey her as her slave?

"You demand mastery over the past, a conception of the future. Has not the art that is truly noble for its domain the future and the past? You would conjure the invisible beings to your charm; and what is painting but the fixing into substance the Invisible? Are you discontented with this world? This world was never meant for genius! To exist, it must create another. What magician can do more; nay, what science can do as much? There are two avenues from the little passions and the drear calamities of earth; both lead to heaven and away from hell, — art and science. But art is more godlike than science; science discovers, art creates. You have faculties that may command art; be contented with your lot. The astronomer who catalogues the stars cannot add one atom to the universe; the poet can call a universe from the atom; the chemist may heal with his drugs the infirmities of the human form; the painter, or the sculptor, fixes into everlasting youth forms divine, which no disease can ravage, and no years impair. Renounce those wandering fancies that lead you now to myself, and now to yon orator of the human race; to us two, who are the antipodes of each other! Your pencil is your wand; your canvas may raise Utopias fairer than Condorcet dreams of. I press not yet for your decision; but what man of genius ever asked more to cheer his path to the grave than love and glory?"

"But," said Glyndon, fixing his eyes earnestly on Zanoni, "if there be a power to baffle the grave itself —"

Zanoni's brow darkened. "And were this so," he said, after a pause, "would it be so sweet a lot to outlive all you loved, and to recoil from every human tie? Perhaps the fairest immortality on earth is that of a noble name."

"You do not answer me, — you equivocate. I have read of the long lives far beyond the date common experience assigns to man," persisted Glyndon, "which some of the alchemists enjoyed. Is the golden elixir but a fable?"

"If not, and these men discovered it, they died, because they refused to live! There may be a mournful warning in your conjecture. Turn once more to the easel and the canvas!"

---

* Psellus de Daemon (MS.)

So saying, Zanoni waved his hand, and, with downcast eyes and a slow step, bent his way back into the city.

Chapter 2. VIII.

The Goddess Wisdom
To some she is the goddess great;
To some the milch cow of the field;
Their care is but to calculate
What butter she will yield.

From Schiller

*T*his last conversation with Zanoni left upon the mind of Glyndon a tranquilizing and salutary effect.

From the confused mists of his fancy glittered forth again those happy, golden schemes which part from the young ambition of art, to play in the air, to illumine the space like rays that kindle from the sun. And with these projects mingled also the vision of a love purer and serener than his life yet had known. His mind went back into that fair childhood of genius, when the forbidden fruit is not yet tasted, and we know of no land beyond the Eden which is gladdened by an Eve. Insensibly before him there rose the scenes of a home, with his art sufficing for all excitement, and Viola's love circling occupation with happiness and content; and in the midst of these fantasies of a future that might be at his command, he was recalled to the present by the clear, strong voice of Mervale, the man of common-sense.

Whoever has studied the lives of persons in whom the imagination is stronger than the will, who suspect their own knowledge of actual life, and are aware of their facility to impressions, will have observed the influence which a homely, vigorous, worldly understanding obtains over such natures. It was thus with Glyndon. His friend had often extricated him from danger, and saved him from the consequences of imprudence; and there was something in Mervale's voice alone that damped his enthusiasm, and often made him yet more ashamed of noble impulses than weak conduct. For Mervale, though a downright honest man, could not sympathize with the extravagance of generosity anymore than with that of presumption and credulity. He walked the straight line of life, and felt an equal contempt for the man who wandered up the hillsides, no matter whether to chase a butterfly, or to catch a prospect of the ocean.

"I will tell you your thoughts, Clarence," said Mervale, laughing, "though I am no Zanoni. I know them by the moisture of your eyes, and the half-smile on your lips. You are musing upon that fair perdition, — the little singer of San Carlo."

The little singer of San Carlo! Glyndon colored as he answered, —

"Would you speak thus of her if she were my wife?"

"No! for then any contempt I might venture to feel would be for yourself. One may dislike the duper, but it is the dupe that one despises."

"Are you sure that I should be the dupe in such a union? Where can I find one so lovely and so innocent, — where one whose virtue has been tried by such temptation? Does even a single breath of slander sully the name of Viola Pisani?"

"I know not all the gossip of Naples, and therefore cannot answer; but I know this, that in England no one would believe that a young Englishman, of good fortune and respectable birth, who marries a singer from the theater of Naples, has not been lamentably taken in. I would save you from a fall of position so irretrievable. Think how many mortifications you will be subjected to; how many young men will visit at your house, — and how many young wives will as carefully avoid it."

"I can choose my own career, to which commonplace society is not essential. I can owe the respect of the world to my art, and not to the accidents of birth and fortune."

"That is, you still persist in your second folly, — the absurd ambition of daubing canvas. Heaven forbid I should say anything against the laudable industry of one who follows such a profession for the sake of subsistence; but with means and connections that will raise you in life, why voluntarily sink into a mere artist? As an accomplishment in leisure moments, it is all very well in its way; but as the occupation of existence, it is a frenzy."

"Artists have been the friends of princes."

"Very rarely so, I fancy, in sober England. There in the great center of political aristocracy, what men respect is the practical, not the ideal. Just suffer me to draw two pictures of my own. Clarence Glyndon returns to England; he marries a lady of fortune equal to his own, of friends and parentage that advance rational ambition. Clarence Glyndon, thus a wealthy and respectable man, of good talents, of bustling energies then concentrated, enters into practical life. He has a house at which he can receive those whose acquaintance is both advantage and honor; he has leisure which he can devote to useful studies; his reputation, built on a solid base, grows in men's mouths. He attaches himself to a party; he enters political life; and new connections serve to promote his objects. At the age of five-and-forty, what, in all probability, may Clarence Glyndon be? Since you are ambitious I leave that question for you to decide! Now turn to the other picture. Clarence Glyndon returns to England with a wife who can bring him no money, unless he lets her out on the stage; so handsome, that everyone asks who she is, and everyone hears, — the celebrated singer, Pisani. Clarence Glyndon shuts himself up to grind colors and paint pictures in the grand historical school, which nobody buys. There is even a prejudice against him, as not having studied in the Academy, — as being an amateur. Who is Mr. Clarence Glyndon? Oh, the celebrated Pisani's husband! What else? Oh, he exhibits those large pictures! Poor man! they have merit in their way; but Teniers and Watteau are more convenient, and almost as cheap. Clarence Glyndon, with an easy fortune while single, has a large family which his fortune, unaided by marriage, can just rear up to callings more plebeian than his own. He retires into the country, to save and to paint; he grows slovenly and discontented; 'the world does not appreciate him,' he says, and he runs away from the world. At the age of forty-five what will be Clarence Glyndon? Your ambition shall decide that question also!"

"If all men were as worldly as you," said Glyndon, rising, "there would never have been an artist or a poet!"

"Perhaps we should do just as well without them," answered Mervale. "Is it not time to think of dinner? The mullets here are remarkably fine!"

Chapter 2.IX.

Wollt ihr hoch auf ihren Flugeln schweben,
Werft die Angst des Irdischen von euch!

Fliehet aus dem engen dumpfen Leben
In des Ideales Reich!

"Das Ideal und das Leben"

Wouldst thou soar heavenward on its joyous wing?
Cast off the earthly burden of the Real;
High from this cramped and dungeoned being, spring
Into the realm of the Ideal.

*A*s some injudicious master lowers and vitiates the taste of the student by fixing his attention to what he falsely calls the Natural, but which, in reality, is the Commonplace, and understands not that beauty in art is created by what Raphael so well describes, — namely, *the idea of beauty in the painter's own mind;* and that in every art, whether its plastic expression be found in words or marble, colors or sounds, the servile imitation of Nature is the work of journeymen and tyros, — so in conduct the man of the world vitiates and lowers the bold enthusiasm of loftier natures by the perpetual reduction of whatever is generous and trustful to all that is trite and coarse. A great German poet has well defined the distinction between discretion and the larger wisdom. In the last there is a certain rashness which the first disdains, —

"The purblind see but the receding shore, Not that to which the bold wave wafts them o'er."

Yet in this logic of the prudent and the worldly there is often a reasoning unanswerable of its kind.

You must have a feeling, — a faith in whatever is self-sacrificing and divine, whether in religion or in art, in glory or in love; or Common-sense will reason you out of the sacrifice, and a syllogism will debase the Divine to an article in the market.

Every true critic in art, from Aristotle and Pliny, from Winkelman and Vasari to Reynolds and Fuseli, has sought to instruct the painter that Nature is not to be copied, but *exalted*; that the loftiest order of art, selecting only the loftiest combinations, is the perpetual struggle of Humanity to approach the gods. The great painter, as the great author, embodies what is *possible* to *man,* it is true, but what is not *common* to *mankind.* There is truth in Hamlet; in Macbeth, and his witches; in Desdemona; in Othello; in Prospero, and in Caliban; there is truth in the cartoons of Raphael; there is truth in the Apollo, the Antinous, and the Laocoon. But you do not meet the originals of the words, the cartoons, or the marble, in Oxford Street or St. James's. All these, to return to Raphael, are the creatures of the idea in the artist's mind. This idea is not inborn, it has come from an intense study. But that study has been of the ideal that can be raised from the positive and the actual into grandeur and beauty. The commonest model becomes full of exquisite suggestions to him who has formed this idea; a Venus of flesh and blood would be vulgarized by the imitation of him who has not.

When asked where he got his models, Guido summoned a common porter from his calling, and drew from a mean original a head of surpassing beauty. It resembled the porter, but idealized the porter to the hero. It was true, but it was not real. There are critics who will tell you that the Boor of Teniers is more true to Nature than the Porter of Guido! The commonplace public scarcely understand the idealizing principle, even in art; for high art is an acquired taste.

But to come to my comparison. Still less is the kindred principle comprehended in conduct. And the advice of worldly prudence would as often deter from the risks of virtue as from the punishments of vice; yet in conduct, as in art, there is an idea of the great and beautiful, by which men should exalt the hackneyed and the trite of life. Now Glyndon felt the sober prudence of Mervale's reasonings; he recoiled from the probable picture placed before him, in his devotion to the one master-talent he possessed, and the one master-passion that, rightly directed, might purify his whole being as a strong wind purifies the air.

But though he could not bring himself to decide in the teeth of so rational a judgment, neither could he resolve at once to abandon the pursuit of Viola. Fearful of being influenced by Zanoni's counsels and his own heart, he had for the last two days shunned an interview with the young actress. But after a night following his last conversation with Zanoni, and that we have just recorded with Mervale, — a night colored by dreams so distinct as to seem prophetic, dreams that appeared so to shape his future according to the hints of Zanoni that he could have fancied Zanoni himself had sent them from the house of sleep to haunt his pillow, — he resolved once more to seek Viola; and though without a definite or distinct object, he yielded himself up to the impulse of his heart.

Chapter 2.X.

O sollecito dubbio e fredda tema
Che pensando l'accresci.*

Tasso, Canzone vi.

She was seated outside her door, — the young actress! The sea before her in that heavenly bay seemed literally to sleep in the arms of the shore; while, to the right, not far off, rose the dark and tangled crags to which the traveler of today is duly brought to gaze on the tomb of Virgil, or compare with the cavern of Posilipo the archway of Highgate Hill. There were a few fisherman loitering by the cliffs, on which their nets were hung to dry; and at a distance the sound of some rustic pipe (more common at that day than at this), mingled now and then with the bells of the lazy mules, broke the voluptuous silence, — the silence of declining noon on the shores of Naples; never, till you have enjoyed it, never, till you have felt its enervating but delicious charm, believe that you can comprehend all the meaning of the Dolce far niente†; and when that luxury has been known, when you have breathed that atmosphere of fairy-land, then you will no longer wonder why the heart ripens into fruit so sudden and so rich beneath the rosy skies and the glorious sunshine of the South.

The eyes of the actress were fixed on the broad blue deep beyond. In the unwonted negligence of her dress might be traced the abstraction of her mind. Her beautiful hair was gathered up loosely, and partially bandaged by a kerchief whose purple color served to deepen the golden hue of her tresses. A stray curl escaped and fell down the graceful neck. A loose morning-robe, girded by a sash, left the breeze. That came ever and anon from the sea, to die upon the bust half disclosed; and the tiny slipper, that Cinderella might have worn, seemed a world too wide for the tiny foot which it scarcely covered. It might be the heat of the day

---

* O anxious doubt and chilling fear that grows by thinking.
† The pleasure of doing nothing.

that deepened the soft bloom of the cheeks, and gave an unwonted languor to the large, dark eyes. In all the pomp of her stage attire, — in all the flush of excitement before the intoxicating lamps, — never had Viola looked so lovely.

By the side of the actress, and filling up the threshold, — stood Gionetta, with her arms thrust to the elbow in two huge pockets on either side of her gown.

"But I assure you," said the nurse, in that sharp, quick, ear-splitting tone in which the old women of the South are more than a match for those of the North, — "but I assure you, my darling, that there is not a finer cavalier in all Naples, nor a more beautiful, than this Inglese; and I am told that all these Inglesi are much richer than they seem. Though they have no trees in their country, poor people! and instead of twenty-four they have only twelve hours to the day, yet I hear that they shoe their horses with scudi; and since they cannot (the poor heretics!) turn grapes into wine, for they have no grapes, they turn gold into physic, and take a glass or two of pistoles whenever they are troubled with the colic. But you don't hear me, little pupil of my eyes, — you don't hear me!"

"And these things are whispered of Zanoni!" said Viola, half to herself, and unheeding Gionetta's eulogies on Glyndon and the English.

"Blessed Maria! do not talk of this terrible Zanoni. You may be sure that his beautiful face, like his yet more beautiful pistoles, is only witchcraft. I look at the money he gave me the other night, every quarter of an hour, to see whether it has not turned into pebbles."

"Do you then really believe," said Viola, with timid earnestness, "that sorcery still exists?"

"Believe! Do I believe in the blessed San Gennaro? How do you think he cured old Filippo the fisherman, when the doctor gave him up? How do you think he has managed himself to live at least these three hundred years? How do you think he fascinates everyone to his bidding with a look, as the vampires do?"

"Ah, is this only witchcraft? It is like it, — it must be!" murmured Viola, turning very pale. Gionetta herself was scarcely more superstitious than the daughter of the musician. And her very innocence, chilled at the strangeness of virgin passion, might well ascribe to magic what hearts more experienced would have resolved to love.

"And then, why has this great Prince di —— been so terrified by him? Why has he ceased to persecute us? Why has he been so quiet and still? Is there no sorcery in all that?"

"Think you, then," said Viola, with sweet inconsistency, "that I owe that happiness and safety to his protection? Oh, let me so believe! Be silent, Gionetta! Why have I only thee and my own terrors to consult?

O beautiful sun!" and the girl pressed her hand to her heart with wild energy; "thou lightest every spot but this. Go, Gionetta! leave me alone, — leave me!"

"And indeed it is time I should leave you; for the polenta will be spoiled, and you have eat nothing all day. If you don't eat you will lose your beauty, my darling, and then nobody will care for you. Nobody cares for us when we grow ugly, — I know that; and then you must, like old Gionetta, get some Viola of your own to spoil. I'll go and see to the polenta."

"Since I have known this man," said the girl, half aloud, — "since his dark eyes have haunted me, I am no longer the same. I long to escape from myself, — to glide with the sunbeam over the hill-tops; to become something that is not of earth. Phantoms float before me at night; and a fluttering, like the wing of a bird, within my heart, seems as if the spirit were terrified, and would break its cage."

While murmuring these incoherent rhapsodies, a step that she did not hear approached the actress, and a light hand touched her arm.

"Viola! — bellissima! — Viola!"

She turned, and saw Glyndon. The sight of his fair young face calmed her at once. His presence gave her pleasure.

"Viola," said the Englishman, taking her hand, and drawing her again to the bench from which she had risen, as he seated himself beside her, "you shall hear me speak! You must know already that I love thee! It has not been pity or admiration alone that has led me ever and ever to thy dear side; reasons there may have been why I have not spoken, save by my eyes, before; but this day — I know not how it is — I feel a more sustained and settled courage to address thee, and learn the happiest or the worst. I have rivals, I know, — rivals who are more powerful than the poor artist; are they also more favored?"

Viola blushed faintly; but her countenance was grave and distressed. Looking down, and marking some hieroglyphical figures in the dust with the point of her slipper, she said, with some hesitation, and a vain attempt to be gay, "Signor, whoever wastes his thoughts on an actress must submit to have rivals. It is our unhappy destiny not to be sacred even to ourselves."

"But you do not love this destiny, glittering though it seem; your heart is not in the vocation which your gifts adorn."

"Ah, no!" said the actress, her eyes filling with tears. "Once I loved to be the priestess of song and music; now I feel only that it is a miserable lot to be slave to a multitude."

"Fly, then, with me," said the artist, passionately; "quit forever the calling that divides that heart I would have all my own. Share my fate now and forever, — my pride, my delight, my ideal! Thou shalt inspire my canvas and my song; thy beauty shall be made at once holy and renowned. In the galleries of princes, crowds shall gather round the effigy of a Venus or a Saint, and a whisper shall break forth, 'It is Viola Pisani!' Ah! Viola, I adore thee; tell me that I do not worship in vain."

"Thou art good and fair," said Viola, gazing on her lover, as he pressed nearer to her, and clasped her hand in his; "but what should I give thee in return?"

"Love, love, — only love!"

"A sister's love?"

"Ah, speak not with such cruel coldness!"

"It is all I have for thee. Listen to me, signor: when I look on your face, when I hear your voice, a certain serene and tranquil calm creeps over and lulls thoughts, — oh, how feverish, how wild! When thou art gone, the day seems a shade more dark; but the shadow soon flies. I miss thee not; I think not of thee: no, I love thee not; and I will give myself only where I love."

"But I would teach thee to love me; fear it not. Nay, such love as thou describest, in our tranquil climates, is the love of innocence and youth."

"Of innocence!" said Viola. "Is it so? Perhaps —" She paused, and added, with an effort, "Foreigner! and wouldst thou wed the orphan? Ah, *thou* at least art generous! It is not the innocence thou wouldst destroy!"

Glyndon drew back, conscience-stricken.

"No, it may not be!" she said, rising, but not conscious of the thoughts, half of shame, half suspicion, that passed through the mind of her lover. "Leave me, and forget me. You do not understand, you could not comprehend, the nature of her whom you think to love. From my childhood upward, I have felt as if I were marked out for some strange and preternatural doom; as if I were singled from my kind. This feeling (and, oh! at times it is one of delirious and vague delight, at others of the darkest gloom) deepens within me day by day. It is like the shadow of twilight, spreading slowly and solemnly around. My hour approaches: a little while, and it will be night!"

As she spoke, Glyndon listened with visible emotion and perturbation. "Viola!" he exclaimed, as she ceased, "your words more than ever enchain me to you. As you feel, I feel. I, too, have been ever haunted with a chill and unearthly foreboding. Amidst the crowds of men I have felt alone. In all my pleasures, my toils, my pursuits, a warning voice has murmured in my ear, 'Time has a dark mystery in store for thy manhood.' When you spoke, it was as the voice of my own soul."

Viola gazed upon him in wonder and fear. Her countenance was as white as marble; and those features, so divine in their rare symmetry, might have served the Greek with a study for the Pythoness, when, from the mystic cavern and the bubbling spring, she first hears the voice of the inspiring god. Gradually the rigor and tension of that wonderful face relaxed, the color returned, the pulse beat: the heart animated the frame.

"Tell me," she said, turning partially aside, — "tell me, have you seen — do you know — a stranger in this city, — one of whom wild stories are afloat?"

"You speak of Zanoni? I have seen him: I know him, — and you? Ah, he, too, would be my rival! — he, too, would bear thee from me!"

"You err," said Viola, hastily, and with a deep sigh; "he pleads for you: he informed me of your love; he besought me not — not to reject it."

"Strange being! incomprehensible enigma! Why did you name him?"

"Why! ah, I would have asked whether, when you first saw him, the foreboding, the instinct, of which you spoke, came on you more fearfully, more intelligibly than before; whether you felt at once repelled from him, yet attracted towards him; whether you felt," and the actress spoke with hurried animation, "that with *him* was connected the secret of your life?"

"All this I felt," answered Glyndon, in a trembling voice, "the first time I was in his presence. Though all around me was gay, — music, amidst lamp-lit trees, light converse near, and heaven without a cloud above, — my knees knocked together, my hair bristled, and my blood curdled like ice. Since then he has divided my thoughts with thee."

"No more, no more!" said Viola, in a stifled tone; "there must be the hand of fate in this. I can speak to you no more now. Farewell!" She sprung past him into the house, and closed the door. Glyndon did not follow her, nor, strange as it may seem, was he so inclined. The thought and recollection of that moonlit hour in the gardens, of the strange address of Zanoni, froze up all human passion. Viola herself, if not forgotten, shrunk back like a shadow into the recesses of his breast. He shivered as he stepped into the sunlight, and musingly retraced his steps into the more populous parts of that liveliest of Italian cities.

BOOK III

THEURGIA

— i cavalier sen vanno
dove il pino fatal gli attende in porto.*

Gerus. Lib., cant. xv†

---

* The knights came where the fatal bark
   Awaited them in the port.
† Argomento.

Chapter 3.I.

But that which especially distinguishes the brotherhood is their
marvelous knowledge of all the resources of medical art. They
work not by charms, but simples.
  — "MS. Account of the Origin and Attributes of the true Rosicrucians," by J. Von D——.

*A*t this time it chanced that Viola had the opportunity to return
the kindness shown to her by the friendly musician whose house had
received and sheltered her when first left an orphan on the world. Old
Bernardi had brought up three sons to the same profession as himself,
and they had lately left Naples to seek their fortunes in the wealthier
cities of Northern Europe, where the musical market was less over-
stocked. There was only left to glad the household of his aged wife and
himself, a lively, prattling, dark-eyed girl of some eight years old, the
child of his second son, whose mother had died in giving her birth. It
so happened that, about a month previous to the date on which our
story has now entered, a paralytic affection had disabled Bernardi from
the duties of his calling. He had been always a social, harmless, improvi-
dent, generous fellow — living on his gains from day to day, as if the
day of sickness and old age never was to arrive. Though he received a
small allowance for his past services, it ill sufficed for his wants,; neither
was he free from debt. Poverty stood at his hearth, — when Viola's
grateful smile and liberal hand came to chase the grim fiend away. But
it is not enough to a heart truly kind to send and give; more charitable
is it to visit and console. "Forget not thy father's friend." So almost
daily went the bright idol of Naples to the house of Bernardi. Suddenly
a heavier affliction than either poverty or the palsy befell the old
musician. His grandchild, his little Beatrice, fell ill, suddenly and
dangerously ill, of one of those rapid fevers common to the South; and
Viola was summoned from her strange and fearful reveries of love or

fancy, to the sick-bed of the young sufferer.

The child was exceedingly fond of Viola, and the old people thought that her mere presence would bring healing; but when Viola arrived, Beatrice was insensible. Fortunately there was no performance that evening at San Carlo, and she resolved to stay the night and partake its fearful cares and dangerous vigil.

But during the night the child grew worse, the physician (the leech-craft has never been very skillful at Naples) shook his powdered head, kept his aromatics at his nostrils, administered his palliatives, and departed. Old Bernardi seated himself by the bedside in stern silence; here was the last tie that bound him to life. Well, let the anchor break and the battered ship go down! It was an iron resolve, more fearful than sorrow. An old man, with one foot in the grave, watching by the couch of a dying child, is one of the most awful spectacles in human calamities. The wife was more active, more bustling, more hopeful, and more tearful. Viola took heed of all three. But towards dawn, Beatrice's state became so obviously alarming, that Viola herself began to despair. At this time she saw the old woman suddenly rise from before the image of the saint at which she had been kneeling, wrap herself in her cloak and hood, and quietly quit the chamber. Viola stole after her.

"It is cold for thee, good mother, to brave the air; let me go for the physician?"

"Child, I am not going to him. I have heard of one in the city who has been tender to the poor, and who, they say, has cured the sick when physicians failed. I will go and say to him, 'Signor, we are beggars in all else, but yesterday we were rich in love. We are at the close of life, but we lived in our grandchild's childhood. Give us back our wealth, — give us back our youth. Let us die blessing God that the thing we love survives us.'"

She was gone. Why did thy heart beat, Viola? The infant's sharp cry of pain called her back to the couch; and there still sat the old man, unconscious of his wife's movements, not stirring, his eyes glazing fast as they watched the agonies of that slight frame. By degrees the wail of pain died into a low moan, — the convulsions grew feebler, but more frequent; the glow of fever faded into the blue, pale tinge that settles into the last bloodless marble.

The daylight came broader and clearer through the casement; steps were heard on the stairs, — the old woman entered hastily; she rushed to the bed, cast a glance on the patient, "She lives yet, signor, she lives!"

Viola raised her eyes, — the child's head was pillowed on her bosom, — and she beheld Zanoni. He smiled on her with a tender and soft approval, and took the infant from her arms. Yet even then, as she saw him bending silently over that pale face, a superstitious fear mingled with her hopes. "Was it by lawful — by holy art that —" her self-questioning ceased abruptly; for his dark eye turned to her as if he read her soul, and his aspect accused her conscience for its suspicion, for it spoke reproach not unmingled with disdain.

"Be comforted," he said, gently turning to the old man, "the danger is not beyond the reach of human skill;" and, taking from his bosom a small crystal vase, he mingled a few drops with water. No sooner did this medicine moisten the infant's lips, than it seemed to produce an astonishing effect. The color revived rapidly on the lips and cheeks; in a few moments the sufferer slept calmly, and with the regular breathing of painless sleep. And then the old man rose, rigidly, as a corpse might rise, — looked down, listened, and creeping gently away, stole to the corner of the room, and wept, and thanked Heaven!

Now, old Bernardi had been, hitherto, but a cold believer; sorrow had never before led him aloft from earth. Old as he was, he had never before thought as the old should think of death, — that endangered life of the young had wakened up the careless soul of age. Zanoni whispered to the wife, and she drew the old man quietly from the room.

"Dost thou fear to leave me an hour with thy charge, Viola? Thinkest thou still that this knowledge is of the Fiend?"

"Ah," said Viola, humbled and yet rejoiced, "forgive me, forgive me, signor. Thou biddest the young live and the old pray. My thoughts never shall wrong thee more!"

Before the sun rose, Beatrice was out of danger; at noon Zanoni escaped from the blessings of the aged pair, and as he closed the door of the house, he found Viola awaiting him without.

She stood before him timidly, her hands crossed meekly on her bosom, her downcast eyes swimming with tears.

"Do not let me be the only one you leave unhappy!"

"And what cure can the herbs and anodynes effect for thee? If thou canst so readily believe ill of those who have aided and yet would serve thee, thy disease is of the heart; and — nay, weep not! nurse of the sick, and comforter of the sad, I should rather approve than chide thee. Forgive thee! Life, that ever needs forgiveness, has, for its first duty, to forgive."

"No, do not forgive me yet. I do not deserve a pardon; for even now, while I feel how ungrateful I was to believe, suspect, aught injurious and false to my preserver, my tears flow from happiness, not remorse. Oh!" she continued, with a simple fervor, unconscious, in her innocence and her generous emotions, of all the secrets she betrayed, — "thou knowest not how bitter it was to believe thee not more good, more pure, more sacred than all the world. And when I saw thee, — the wealthy, the noble, coming from thy palace to minister to the sufferings of the hovel, —

when I heard those blessings of the poor breathed upon thy parting footsteps, I felt my very self exalted, — good in thy goodness, noble at least in those thoughts that did *not* wrong thee."

"And thinkest thou, Viola, that in a mere act of science there is so much virtue? The commonest leech will tend the sick for his fee. Are prayers and blessings a less reward than gold?"

"And mine, then, are not worthless? Thou wilt accept of mine?"

"Ah, Viola!" exclaimed Zanoni, with a sudden passion, that covered her face with blushes, "thou only, methinks, on all the earth, hast the power to wound or delight me!" He checked himself, and his face became grave and sad. "And this," he added, in an altered tone, "because, if thou wouldst heed my counsels, methinks I could guide a guileless heart to a happy fate."

"Thy counsels! I will obey them all. Mould me to what thou wilt. In thine absence, I am as a child that fears every shadow in the dark; in thy presence, my soul expands, and the whole world seems calm with a celestial noonday. Do not deny to me that presence. I am fatherless and ignorant and alone!"

Zanoni averted his face, and, after a moment's silence, replied calmly, —

"Be it so. Sister, I will visit thee again!"

Chapter 3.II.

Gilding pale streams with heavenly alchemy.

Shakespeare

W ho so happy as Viola now! A dark load was lifted from her heart: her step seemed to tread on air; she would have sung for very delight as she went gaily home. It is such happiness to the pure to love, — but oh, such more than happiness to believe in the worth of the one beloved. Between them there might be human obstacles, — wealth, rank, man's little world. But there was no longer that dark gulf which the imagination recoils to dwell on, and which separates forever soul from soul. He did not love her in return. Love her! But did she ask for love? Did she herself love? No; or she would never have been at once so humble and so bold. How merrily the ocean murmured in her ear; how radiant an aspect the commonest passer-by seemed to wear! She gained her home, — she looked upon the tree, glancing, with fantastic branches, in the sun. "Yes, brother mine!" she said, laughing in her joy, "like thee, I *have* struggled to the light!"

She had never hitherto, like the more instructed Daughters of the North, accustomed herself to that delicious Confessional, the transfusion of thought to writing. Now, suddenly, her heart felt an impulse; a newborn instinct, that bade it commune with itself, bade it disentangle its web of golden fancies, — made her wish to look upon her inmost self as in a glass. Upsprung from the embrace of Love and Soul — the Eros and the Psyche — their beautiful offspring, Genius! She blushed, she sighed, she trembled as she wrote. And from the fresh world that she had built for herself, she was awakened to prepare for the glittering stage. How dull became the music, how dim the scene, so exquisite and so bright of old. Stage, thou art the Fairy Land to the vision of the worldly. Fancy, whose music is not heard by men, whose scenes shift not by mortal hand, as the stage to the present world, art thou to the future and the past!

Chapter 3.III.

In faith, I do not love thee with mine eyes.

Shakespeare

*T*he next day, at noon, Zanoni visited Viola; and the next day and the next and again the next, — days that to her seemed like a special time set apart from the rest of life. And yet he never spoke to her in the language of flattery, and almost of adoration, to which she had been accustomed. Perhaps his very coldness, so gentle as it was, assisted to this mysterious charm. He talked to her much of her past life, and she was scarcely surprised (she now never thought of *terror*) to perceive how much of that past seemed known to him.

He made her speak to him of her father; he made her recall some of the airs of Pisani's wild music. And those airs seemed to charm and lull him into reverie.

"As music was to the musician," said he, "may science be to the wise. Your father looked abroad in the world; all was discord to the fine sympathies that he felt with the harmonies that daily and nightly float to the throne of Heaven. Life, with its noisy ambition and its mean passions, is so poor and base! Out of his soul he created the life and the world for which his soul was fitted. Viola, thou art the daughter of that life, and wilt be the denizen of that world."

In his earlier visits he did not speak of Glyndon. The day soon came on which he renewed the subject. And so trustful, obedient, and entire was the allegiance that Viola now owned to his dominion, that, unwelcome as that subject was, she restrained her heart, and listened to him in silence.

At last he said, "Thou hast promised thou wilt obey my counsels, and if, Viola, I should ask thee, nay adjure, to accept this stranger's hand, and share his fate, should he offer to thee such a lot, — wouldst thou refuse?"

And then she pressed back the tears that gushed to her eyes; and with a strange pleasure in the midst of pain, — the pleasure of one who sacrifices heart itself to the one who commands that heart, — she answered falteringly, "If thou *canst* ordain it, why —"

"Speak on."

"Dispose of me as thou wilt!"

Zanoni stood in silence for some moments: he saw the struggle which the girl thought she concealed so well; he made an involuntary movement towards her, and pressed her hand to his lips; it was the first time he had ever departed even so far from a certain austerity which perhaps made her fear him and her own thoughts the less.

"Viola," said he, and his voice trembled, "the danger that I can avert no more, if thou linger still in Naples, comes hourly near and near to thee! On the third day from this thy fate must be decided. I accept thy promise. Before the last hour of that day, come what may, I shall see thee again, *here,* at thine own house. Till then, farewell!"

Chapter 3.IV.

Between two worlds life hovers like a star
'Twixt night and morn.

Byron

When Glyndon left Viola, as recorded in the concluding chapter of the second division of this work, he was absorbed again in those mystical desires and conjectures which the haunting recollection of Zanoni always served to create. And as he wandered through the streets, he was scarcely conscious of his own movements till, in the mechanism of custom, he found himself in the midst of one of the noble collections of pictures which form the boast of those Italian cities whose glory is in the past. Thither he had been wont, almost daily, to repair, for the gallery contained some of the finest specimens of a master especially the object of his enthusiasm and study. There, before the works of Salvator, he had often paused in deep and earnest reverence. The striking characteristic of that artist is the "Vigor of Will;" void of the elevated idea of abstract beauty, which furnishes a model and archetype to the genius of more illustrious order, the singular energy of the man hews out of the rock a dignity of his own. His images have the majesty, not of the god, but the savage; utterly free, like the sublimer schools, from the commonplace of imitation, — apart, with them, from the conventional littleness of the Real, — he grasps the imagination, and compels it to follow him, not to the heaven, but through all that is most wild and fantastic upon earth; a sorcery, not of the starry magian, but of the gloomy wizard, — a man of romance whose heart beat strongly, griping art with a hand of iron, and forcing it to idealize the scenes of his actual life. Before this powerful will, Glyndon drew back more awed and admiring than before the calmer beauty which rose from the soul of Raphael, like Venus from the deep.

And now, as awaking from his reverie, he stood opposite to that wild and magnificent gloom of Nature which frowned on him from the canvas, the very leaves on those gnomelike, distorted trees seemed to rustle sibylline secrets in his ear. Those rugged and somber Apennines, the cataract that dashed between, suited, more than the actual scenes would have done, the mood and temper of his mind. The stern, uncouth forms at rest on the crags below, and dwarfed by the giant size of the Matter that reigned around them, impressed him with the might of Nature and the littleness of Man. As in genius of the more spiritual cast, the living man, and the soul that lives in him, are studiously made the prominent image; and the mere accessories of scene kept down, and cast back, as if to show that the exile from paradise is yet the monarch of the outward world, — so, in the landscapes of Salvator, the tree, the mountain, the waterfall, become the principal, and man himself dwindles to the accessory. The Matter seems to reign supreme, and its true lord to creep beneath its stupendous shadow. Inert matter giving interest to the immortal man, not the immortal man to the inert matter. A terrible philosophy in art!

While something of these thoughts passed through the mind of the painter, he felt his arm touched, and saw Nicot by his side.

"A great master," said Nicot, "but I do not love the school."

"I do not love, but I am awed by it. We love the beautiful and serene, but we have a feeling as deep as love for the terrible and dark."

"True," said Nicot, thoughtfully. "And yet that feeling is only a superstition. The nursery, with its tales of ghosts and goblins, is the cradle of many of our impressions in the world. But art should not seek to pander to our ignorance; art should represent only truths. I confess that Raphael pleases me less, because I have no sympathy with his subjects. His saints and virgins are to me only men and women."

"And from what source should painting, then, take its themes?"

"From history, without doubt," returned Nicot, pragmatically, — "those great Roman actions which inspire men with sentiments of liberty and valor, with the virtues of a republic. I wish the cartoons of Raphael had illustrated the story of the Horatii; but it remains for France and her Republic to give to posterity the new and the true school, which could never have arisen in a country of priestcraft and delusion."

"And the saints and virgins of Raphael are to you only men and women?" repeated Glyndon, going back to Nicot's candid confession in amaze, and scarcely hearing the deductions the Frenchman drew from his proposition.

"Assuredly. Ha, ha!" and Nicot laughed hideously, "do you ask me to believe in the calendar, or what?"

"But the ideal?"

"The ideal!" interrupted Nicot. "Stuff! The Italian critics, and your English Reynolds, have turned your head. They are so fond of their

'gusto grande,' and their 'ideal beauty that speaks to the soul!' — soul!
— *is* there a soul? I understand a man when he talks of composing for
a refined taste, — for an educated and intelligent reason; for a sense that
comprehends truths. But as for the soul, — bah! — we are but modifications of matter, and painting is modification of matter also."

Glyndon turned his eyes from the picture before him to Nicot, and
from Nicot to the picture. The dogmatist gave a voice to the thoughts
which the sight of the picture had awakened. He shook his head without
reply.

"Tell me," said Nicot, abruptly, "that imposter, — Zanoni! — oh! I
have now learned his name and quackeries, forsooth, — what did he say
to thee of me?"

"Of thee? Nothing; but to warn me against thy doctrines."

"Aha! was that all?" said Nicot. "He is a notable inventor, and since,
when we met last, I unmasked his delusions, I thought he might retaliate
by some tale of slander."

"Unmasked his delusions! — how?"

"A dull and long story: he wished to teach an old doting friend of
mine his secrets of prolonged life and philosophical alchemy. I advise
thee to renounce so discreditable an acquaintance."

With that Nicot nodded significantly, and, not wishing to be further
questioned, went his way.

Glyndon's mind at that moment had escaped to his art, and the
comments and presence of Nicot had been no welcome interruption.
He turned from the landscape of Salvator, and his eye falling on a
Nativity by Coreggio, the contrast between the two ranks of genius
struck him as a discovery. That exquisite repose, that perfect sense of
beauty, that strength without effort, that breathing moral of high art,
which speaks to the mind through the eye, and raises the thoughts, by
the aid of tenderness and love, to the regions of awe and wonder, — aye!
That was the true school. He quitted the gallery with reluctant steps and
inspired ideas; he sought his own home. Here, pleased not to find the
sober Mervale, he leaned his face on his hands, and endeavored to recall
the words of Zanoni in their last meeting. Yes, he felt Nicot's talk even
on art was crime; it debased the imagination itself to mechanism. Could
he, who saw nothing in the soul but a combination of matter, prate of
schools that should excel a Raphael? Yes, art was magic; and as he owned
the truth of the aphorism, he could comprehend that in magic there
may be religion, for religion is an essential to art. His old ambition,
freeing itself from the frigid prudence with which Mervale sought to
desecrate all images less substantial than the golden calf of the world,
revived, and stirred, and kindled. The subtle detection of what he
conceived to be an error in the school he had hitherto adopted, made

more manifest to him by the grinning commentary of Nicot, seemed
to open to him a new world of invention. He seized the happy moment,
— he placed before him the colors and the canvas. Lost in his conceptions of a fresh ideal, his mind was lifted aloft into the airy realms of
beauty; dark thoughts, unhallowed desires, vanished. Zanoni was right:
the material world shrunk from his gaze; he viewed Nature as from a
mountaintop afar; and as the waves of his unquiet heart became calm
and still, again the angel eyes of Viola beamed on them as a holy star.

Locking himself in his chamber, he refused even the visits of Mervale.
Intoxicated with the pure air of his fresh existence, he remained for three
days, and almost nights, absorbed in his employment; but on the fourth
morning came that reaction to which all labor is exposed. He woke
listless and fatigued; and as he cast his eyes on the canvas, the glory
seemed to have gone from it. Humiliating recollections of the great
masters he aspired to rival forced themselves upon him; defects before
unseen magnified themselves to deformities in his languid and discontented eyes. He touched and retouched, but his hand failed him; he
threw down his instruments in despair; he opened his casement: the day
without was bright and lovely; the street was crowded with that life which
is ever so joyous and affluent in the animated population of Naples.
He saw the lover, as he passed, conversing with his mistress by those
mute gestures which have survived all changes of languages, the same
now as when the Etruscan painted yon vases in the Museo Borbonico.
Light from without beckoned his youth to its mirth and its pleasures;
and the dull walls within, lately large enough to comprise heaven and
earth, seemed now cabined and confined as a felon's prison. He welcomed the step of Mervale at his threshold, and unbarred the door.

"And is that all you have done?" said Mervale, glancing disdainfully
at the canvas. "Is it for this that you have shut yourself out from the
sunny days and moonlit nights of Naples?"

"While the fit was on me, I basked in a brighter sun, and imbibed
the voluptuous luxury of a softer moon."

"You own that the fit is over. Well, that is some sign of returning
sense. After all, it is better to daub canvas for three days than make a
fool of yourself for life. This little siren?"

"Be dumb! I hate to hear you name her."

Mervale drew his chair nearer to Glyndon's, thrust his hands deep in
his breeches-pockets, stretched his legs, and was about to begin a serious
strain of expostulation, when a knock was heard at the door, and Nicot,
without waiting for leave, obtruded his ugly head.

"Good-day, mon cher confrere. I wished to speak to you. Hein! you
have been at work, I see. This is well, — very well! A bold outline, — great
freedom in that right hand. But, hold! is the composition good? You

have not got the great pyramidal form. Don't you think, too, that you have lost the advantage of contrast in this figure; since the right leg is put forward, surely the right arm should be put back? Peste! but that little finger is very fine!"

Mervale detested Nicot. For all speculators, Utopians, alterers of the world, and wanderers from the high road, were equally hateful to him; but he could have hugged the Frenchman at that moment. He saw in Glyndon's expressive countenance all the weariness and disgust he endured. After so wrapped a study, to be prated to about pyramidal forms and right arms and right legs, the accidence of the art, the whole conception to be overlooked, and the criticism to end in approval of the little finger!

"Oh," said Glyndon, peevishly, throwing the cloth over his design, "enough of my poor performance. What is it you have to say to me?"

"In the first place," said Nicot, huddling himself together upon a stool, — "in the first place, this Signor Zanoni, — this second Cagliostro, — who disputes my doctrines! (no doubt a spy of the man Capet) I am not vindictive; as Helvetius says, 'our errors arise from our passions.' I keep mine in order; but it is virtuous to hate in the cause of mankind; I would I had the denouncing and the judging of Signor Zanoni at Paris." And Nicot's small eyes shot fire, and he gnashed his teeth.

"Have you any new cause to hate him?"

"Yes," said Nicot, fiercely. "Yes, I hear he is courting the girl I mean to marry."

"You! Whom do you speak of?"

"The celebrated Pisani! She is divinely handsome. She would make my fortune in a republic. And a republic we shall have before the year is out."

Mervale rubbed his hands, and chuckled. Glyndon colored with rage and shame.

"Do you know the Signora Pisani? Have you ever spoken to her?"

"Not yet. But when I make up my mind to anything, it is soon done. I am about to return to Paris. They write me word that a handsome wife advances the career of a patriot. The age of prejudice is over. The sublimer virtues begin to be understood. I shall take back the handsomest wife in Europe."

"Be quiet! What are you about?" said Mervale, seizing Glyndon as he saw him advance towards the Frenchman, his eyes sparkling, and his hands clenched.

"Sir!" said Glyndon, between his teeth, "you know not of whom you thus speak. Do you affect to suppose that Viola Pisani would accept *you?*"

"Not if she could get a better offer," said Mervale, looking up to the ceiling.

"A better offer? You don't understand me," said Nicot. "I, Jean Nicot, propose to marry the girl; marry her! Others may make her more liberal offers, but no one, I apprehend, would make one so honorable. I alone have pity on her friendless situation. Besides, according to the dawning state of things, one will always, in France, be able to get rid of a wife whenever one wishes. We shall have new laws of divorce. Do you imagine that an Italian girl — and in no country in the world are maidens, it seems, more chaste (though wives may console themselves with virtues more philosophical) — would refuse the hand of an artist for the settlements of a prince? No; I think better of the Pisani than you do. I shall hasten to introduce myself to her."

"I wish you all success, Monsieur Nicot," said Mervale, rising, and shaking him heartily by the hand.

Glyndon cast at them both a disdainful glance.

"Perhaps, Monsieur Nicot," said he, at length, constraining his lips into a bitter smile, — "perhaps you may have rivals."

"So much the better," replied Monsieur Nicot, carelessly, kicking his heels together, and appearing absorbed in admiration at the size of his large feet.

"I myself admire Viola Pisani."

"Every painter must!"

"I may offer her marriage as well as yourself."

"That would be folly in you, though wisdom in me. You would not know how to draw profit from the speculation! Cher confrere, you have prejudices."

"You do not dare to say you would make profit from your own wife?"

"The virtuous Cato lent his wife to a friend. I love virtue, and I cannot do better than imitate Cato. But to be serious, — I do not fear you as a rival. You are good-looking, and I am ugly. But you are irresolute, and I decisive. While you are uttering fine phrases, I shall say, simply, 'I have a bon etat. Will you marry me?' So do your worst, cher confrere. Au revoir, behind the scenes!"

So saying, Nicot rose, stretched his long arms and short legs, yawned till he showed all his ragged teeth from ear to ear, pressed down his cap on his shaggy head with an air of defiance, and casting over his left shoulder a glance of triumph and malice at the indignant Glyndon, sauntered out of the room.

Mervale burst into a violent fit of laughter. "See how your Viola is estimated by your friend. A fine victory, to carry her off from the ugliest dog between Lapland and the Calmucks."

Glyndon was yet too indignant to answer, when a new visitor arrived. It was Zanoni himself. Mervale, on whom the appearance and aspect of this personage imposed a kind of reluctant deference, which he was unwilling to acknowledge, and still more to betray, nodded to Glyndon, and saying, simply, "More when I see you again," left the painter and his unexpected visitor.

"I see," said Zanoni, lifting the cloth from the canvas, "that you have not slighted the advice I gave you. Courage, young artist; this is an escape from the schools: this is full of the bold self-confidence of real genius. You had no Nicot — no Mervale — at your elbow when this image of true beauty was conceived!"

Charmed back to his art by this unlooked-for praise, Glyndon replied modestly, "I thought well of my design till this morning; and then I was disenchanted of my happy persuasion."

"Say, rather, that, unaccustomed to continuous labor, you were fatigued with your employment."

"That is true. Shall I confess it? I began to miss the world without. It seemed to me as if, while I lavished my heart and my youth upon visions of beauty, I was losing the beautiful realities of actual life. And I envied the merry fisherman, singing as he passed below my casement, and the lover conversing with his mistress."

"And," said Zanoni, with an encouraging smile, "do you blame yourself for the natural and necessary return to earth, in which even the most habitual visitor of the Heavens of Invention seeks his relaxation and repose? Man's genius is a bird that cannot be always on the wing; when the craving for the actual world is felt, it is a hunger that must be appeased. They who command best the ideal, enjoy ever most the real. See the true artist, when abroad in men's thoroughfares, ever observant, ever diving into the heart, ever alive to the least as to the greatest of the complicated truths of existence; descending to what pedants would call the trivial and the frivolous. From every mesh in the social web, he can disentangle a grace. And for him each airy gossamer floats in the gold of the sunlight. Know you not that around the animalcule that sports in the water there shines a halo, as around the star* that revolves in bright pastime through the space? True art finds beauty everywhere. In the street, in the marketplace, in the hovel, it gathers food for the hive of its thoughts. In the mire of politics, Dante and Milton selected pearls for the wreath of song.

"Who ever told you that Raphael did not enjoy the life without, carrying everywhere with him the one inward idea of beauty which attracted and imbedded in its own amber every straw that the feet of the dull man trampled into mud? As some lord of the forest wanders abroad for its prey, and scents and follows it over plain and hill, through

---

* The monas mica, found in the purest pools, is encompassed with a halo. And this is frequent amongst many other species of animalcule.

brake and jungle, but, seizing it at last, bears the quarry to its unwitnessed cave, — so Genius searches through wood and waste, untiringly and eagerly, every sense awake, every nerve strained to speed and strength, for the scattered and flying images of matter, that it seizes at last with its mighty talons, and bears away with it into solitudes no footstep can invade. Go, seek the world without; it is for art the inexhaustible pasture-ground and harvest to the world within!"

"You comfort me," said Glyndon, brightening. "I had imagined my weariness a proof of my deficiency! But not now would I speak to you of these labors. Pardon me, if I pass from the toil to the reward. You have uttered dim prophecies of my future, if I wed one who, in the judgment of the sober world, would only darken its prospects and obstruct its ambition. Do you speak from the wisdom which is experience, or that which aspires to prediction?"

"Are they not allied? Is it not he best accustomed to calculation who can solve at a glance any new problem in the arithmetic of chances?"

"You evade my question."

"No; but I will adapt my answer the better to your comprehension, for it is upon this very point that I have sought you. Listen to me!" Zanoni fixed his eyes earnestly on his listener, and continued: "For the accomplishment of whatever is great and lofty, the clear perception of truths is the first requisite, — truths adapted to the object desired. The warrior thus reduces the chances of battle to combinations almost of mathematics. He can predict a result, if he can but depend upon the materials he is forced to employ. At such a loss he can cross that bridge; in such a time he can reduce that fort. Still more accurately, for he depends less on material causes than ideas at his command, can the commander of the purer science or diviner art, if he once perceive the truths that are in him and around, foretell what he can achieve, and in what he is condemned to fail. But this perception of truths is disturbed by many causes, — vanity, passion, fear, indolence in himself, ignorance of the fitting means without to accomplish what he designs. He may miscalculate his own forces; he may have no chart of the country he would invade. It is only in a peculiar state of the mind that it is capable of perceiving truth; and that state is profound serenity. Your mind is fevered by a desire for truth: you would compel it to your embraces; you would ask me to impart to you, without ordeal or preparation, the grandest secrets that exist in Nature. But truth can no more be seen by the mind unprepared for it, than the sun can dawn upon the midst of night. Such a mind receives truth only to pollute it: to use the simile of one who has wandered near to the secret of the sublime Goetia*, 'He who pours water into the muddy well, does but disturb the mud.'"†

* or the magic that lies within Nature, as electricity within the cloud

"What do you tend to?"

"This: that you have faculties that may attain to surpassing power, that may rank you among those enchanters who, greater than the magian, leave behind them an enduring influence, worshipped wherever beauty is comprehended, wherever the soul is sensible of a higher world than that in which matter struggles for crude and incomplete existence.

"But to make available those faculties, need I be a prophet to tell you that you must learn to concenter upon great objects all your desires? The heart must rest, that the mind may be active. At present you wander from aim to aim. As the ballast to the ship, so to the spirit are faith and love. With your whole heart, affections, humanity, centered in one object, your mind and aspirations will become equally steadfast and in earnest. Viola is a child as yet; you do not perceive the high nature the trials of life will develop. Pardon me, if I say that her soul, purer and loftier than your own, will bear it upward, as a secret hymn carries aloft the spirits of the world. Your nature wants the harmony, the music which, as the Pythagoreans wisely taught, at once elevates and soothes. I offer you that music in her love."

"But am I sure that she does love me?"

"Artist, no; she loves you not at present; her affections are full of another. But if I could transfer to you, as the loadstone transfers its attraction to the magnet, the love that she has now for me, — if I could cause her to see in you the ideal of her dreams —"

"Is such a gift in the power of man?"

"I offer it to you, if your love be lawful, if your faith in virtue and yourself be deep and loyal; if not, think you that I would disenchant her with truth to make her adore a falsehood?"

"But if," persisted Glyndon, — "if she be all that you tell me, and if she love you, how can you rob yourself of so priceless a treasure?"

"Oh, shallow and mean heart of man!" exclaimed Zanoni, with unaccustomed passion and vehemence, "dost thou conceive so little of love as not to know that it sacrifices all — love itself — for the happiness of the thing it loves? Hear me!" And Zanoni's face grew pale. "Hear me! I press this upon you, because I love her, and because I fear that with me her fate will be less fair than with yourself. Why, — ask not, for I will not tell you. Enough! Time presses now for your answer; it cannot long be delayed. Before the night of the third day from this, all choice will be forbid you!"

"But," said Glyndon, still doubting and suspicious, — "but why this haste?"

"Man, you are not worthy of her when you ask me. All I can tell you here, you should have known yourself. This ravisher, this man of will,

---

** "Iamb. de Vit. Pythag."

this son of the old Visconti, unlike you, — steadfast, resolute, earnest even in his crimes, — never relinquishes an object. But one passion controls his lust, — it is his avarice. The day after his attempt on Viola, his uncle, the Cardinal — , from whom he has large expectations of land and gold, sent for him, and forbade him, on pain of forfeiting all the possessions which his schemes already had parceled out, to pursue with dishonorable designs one whom the Cardinal had heeded and loved from childhood. This is the cause of his present pause from his pursuit. While we speak, the cause expires. Before the hand of the clock reaches the hour of noon, the Cardinal — will be no more. At this very moment thy friend, Jean Nicot, is with the Prince di ——."

"He! wherefore?"

"To ask what dower shall go with Viola Pisani, the morning that she leaves the palace of the prince."

"And how do you know all this?"

"Fool! I tell thee again, because a lover is a watcher by night and day; because love never sleeps when danger menaces the beloved one!"

"And you it was that informed the Cardinal — ?"

"Yes; and what has been my task might as easily have been thine. Speak, — thine answer!"

"You shall have it on the third day from this."

"Be it so. Put off, poor waverer, thy happiness to the last hour. On the third day from this, I will ask thee thy resolve."

"And where shall we meet?"

"Before midnight, where you may least expect me. You cannot shun me, though you may seek to do so!"

"Stay one moment! You condemn me as doubtful, irresolute, suspicious. Have I no cause? Can I yield without a struggle to the strange fascination you exert upon my mind? What interest can you have in me, a stranger, that you should thus dictate to me the gravest action in the life of man? Do you suppose that anyone in his senses would not pause, and deliberate, and ask himself, 'Why should this stranger care thus for me?'"

"And yet," said Zanoni, "if I told thee that I could initiate thee into the secrets of that magic which the philosophy of the whole existing world treats as a chimera, or imposture; if I promised to show thee how to command the beings of air and ocean, how to accumulate wealth more easily than a child can gather pebbles on the shore, to place in thy hands the essence of the herbs which prolong life from age to age, the mystery of that attraction by which to awe all danger and disarm all violence and subdue man as the serpent charms the bird, — if I told thee that all these it was mine to possess and to communicate, thou wouldst listen to me then, and obey me without a doubt!"

"It is true; and I can account for this only by the imperfect associations of my childhood, — by traditions in our house of —"

"Your forefather, who, in the revival of science, sought the secrets of Apollonius and Paracelsus."

"What!" said Glyndon, amazed, "are you so well acquainted with the annals of an obscure lineage?"

"To the man who aspires to know, no man who has been the meanest student of knowledge should be unknown. You ask me why I have shown this interest in your fate? There is one reason which I have not yet told you. There is a fraternity as to whose laws and whose mysteries the most inquisitive schoolmen are in the dark. By those laws all are pledged to warn, to aid, and to guide even the remotest descendants of men who have toiled, though vainly, like your ancestor, in the mysteries of the Order. We are bound to advise them to their welfare; nay, more, — if they command us to it, we must accept them as our pupils. I am a survivor of that most ancient and immemorial union. This it was that bound me to thee at the first; this, perhaps, attracted thyself unconsciously, Son of our Brotherhood, to me."

"If this be so, I command thee, in the name of the laws thou obeyest, to receive me as thy pupil!"

"What do you ask?" said Zanoni, passionately. "Learn, first, the conditions. No neophyte must have, at his initiation, one affection or desire that chains him to the world. He must be pure from the love of woman, free from avarice and ambition, free from the dreams even of art, or the hope of earthly fame. The first sacrifice thou must make is — Viola herself. And for what? For an ordeal that the most daring courage only can encounter, the most ethereal natures alone survive! Thou art unfit for the science that has made me and others what we are or have been; for thy whole nature is one fear!"

"Fear!" cried Glyndon, coloring with resentment, and rising to the full height of his stature.

"Fear! and the worst fear, — fear of the world's opinion; fear of the Nicots and the Mervales; fear of thine own impulses when most generous; fear of thine own powers when thy genius is most bold; fear that virtue is not eternal; fear that God does not live in heaven to keep watch on earth; fear, the fear of little men; and that fear is never known to the great."

With these words Zanoni abruptly left the artist, humbled, bewildered, and not convinced. He remained alone with his thoughts till he was aroused by the striking of the clock; he then suddenly remembered Zanoni's prediction of the Cardinal's death; and, seized with an intense desire to learn its truth, he hurried into the streets, — he gained the Cardinal's palace. Five minutes before noon his Eminence had expired, after an illness of less than an hour. Zanoni's visit had occupied more time than the illness of the Cardinal. Awed and perplexed, he turned from the palace, and as he walked through the Chiaja, he saw Jean Nicot emerge from the portals of the Prince di ——.

Chapter 3. V.

Two loves I have of comfort and despair,
Which like two spirits do suggest me still.

Shakespeare

Venerable Brotherhood, so sacred and so little known, from whose secret and precious archives the materials for this history have been drawn; ye who have retained, from century to century, all that time has spared of the august and venerable science, — thanks to you, if now, for the first time, some record of the thoughts and actions of no false and self-styled luminary of your Order be given, however imperfectly, to the world. Many have called themselves of your band; many spurious pretenders have been so-called by the learned ignorance which still, baffled and perplexed, is driven to confess that it knows nothing of your origin, your ceremonies or doctrines, nor even if you still have local habitation on the earth. Thanks to you if I, the only one of my country, in this age, admitted, with a profane footstep, into your mysterious Academe*, have been by you empowered and instructed to adapt to the comprehension of the uninitiated, some few of the starry truths which shone on the great Shemaia of the Chaldean Lore, and gleamed dimly through the darkened knowledge of latter disciples, laboring, like Psellus and Iamblichus, to revive the embers of the fire which burned in the Hamarin of the East. Though not to us of an aged and hoary world is vouchsafed the *name* which, so say the earliest oracles of the earth,

---

* The reader will have the goodness to remember that this is said by the author of the original MS., not by the editor.

"rushes into the infinite worlds," yet is it ours to trace the reviving truths, through each new discovery of the philosopher and chemist. The laws of attraction, of electricity, and of the yet more mysterious agency of that great principal of life, which, if drawn from the universe, would leave the universe a grave, were but the code in which the Theurgy of old sought the guides that led it to a legislation and science of its own. To rebuild on words the fragments of this history, it seems to me as if, in a solemn trance, I was led through the ruins of a city whose only remains were tombs. From the sarcophagus and the urn I awake the genius* of the extinguished Torch, and so closely does its shape resemble Eros, that at moments I scarcely know which of ye dictates to me, — O Love! O Death!

And it stirred in the virgin's heart, — this new, unfathomable, and divine emotion! Was it only the ordinary affection of the pulse and the fancy, of the eye to the Beautiful, of the ear to the Eloquent, or did it not justify the notion she herself conceived of it, — that it was born not of the senses, that it was less of earthly and human love than the effect of some wondrous but not unholy charm? I said that, from that day in which, no longer with awe and trembling, she surrendered herself to the influence of Zanoni, she had sought to put her thoughts into words. Let the thoughts attest their own nature.

The Self Confessional.

"Is it the daylight that shines on me, or the memory of thy presence? Wherever I look, the world seems full of thee; in every ray that trembles on the water, that smiles upon the leaves, I behold but a likeness to thine eyes. What is this change, that alters not only myself, but the face of the whole universe?

. . .

How instantaneously leaped into life the power with which thou swayest my heart in its ebb and flow. Thousands were around me, and I saw but thee. That was the night in which I first entered upon the world which crowds life into a drama, and has no language but music. How strangely and how suddenly with thee became that world evermore connected! What the delusion of the stage was to others, thy presence was to me. My life, too, seemed to center into those short hours, and from thy lips I heard a music, mute to all ears but mine. I sit in the room where my father dwelt. Here, on that happy night, forgetting why *they* were so happy, I shrunk into the shadow, and sought to guess what thou wert to me; and my mother's low voice woke me, and I crept to my father's side, close — close, from fear of my own thoughts.

---

* The Greek Genius of Death.

"Ah! sweet and sad was the morrow to that night, when thy lips warned me of the future. An orphan now, — what is there that lives for me to think of, to dream upon, to revere, but thou!

"How tenderly thou hast rebuked me for the grievous wrong that my thoughts did thee! Why should I have shuddered to feel thee glancing upon my thoughts like the beam on the solitary tree, to which thou didst once liken me so well? It was — it was, that, like the tree, I struggled for the light, and the light came. They tell me of love, and my very life of the stage breathes the language of love into my lips. No; again and again, I know *that* is not the love that I feel for thee! — it is not a passion, it is a thought! I ask not to be loved again. I murmur not that thy words are stern and thy looks are cold. I ask not if I have rivals; I sigh not to be fair in thine eyes. It is my *spirit* that would blend itself with thine. I would give worlds, though we were apart, though oceans rolled between us, to know the hour in which thy gaze was lifted to the stars, — in which thy heart poured itself in prayer. They tell me thou art more beautiful than the marble images that are fairer than all human forms; but I have never dared to gaze steadfastly on thy face, that memory might compare thee with the rest. Only thine eyes and thy soft, calm smile haunt me; as when I look upon the moon, all that passes into my heart is her silent light.

. . .

"Often, when the air is calm, I have thought that I hear the strains of my father's music; often, though long stilled in the grave, have they waked me from the dreams of the solemn night. Methinks, ere thou comest to me that I hear them herald thy approach. Methinks I hear them wail and moan, when I sink back into myself on seeing thee depart. Thou art *of* that music, — its spirit, its genius. My father must have guessed at thee and thy native regions, when the winds hushed to listen to his tones, and the world deemed him mad! I hear where I sit, the far murmur of the sea. Murmur on, ye blessed waters! The waves are the pulses of the shore. They beat with the gladness of the morning wind, — so beats my heart in the freshness and light that make up the thoughts of thee!

. . .

"Often in my childhood I have mused and asked for what I was born; and my soul answered my heart and said, *'Thou wert born to worship!'* Yes; I know why the real world has ever seemed to me so false and cold. I know why the world of the stage charmed and dazzled me. I know why it was so sweet to sit apart and gaze my whole being into the distant heavens. My nature is not formed for this life, happy though that life seem to others. It is its very want to have ever before it some image loftier than itself! Stranger, in what realm above, when the grave is past, shall my soul, hour after hour, worship at the same source as thine?

. . .

"In the gardens of my neighbor there is a small fountain. I stood by it this morning after sunrise. How it sprung up, with its eager spray, to the sunbeams! And then I thought that I should see thee again this day, and so sprung my heart to the new morning which thou bringest me from the skies.

. . .

"I *have* seen, I have *listened* to thee again. How bold I have become! I ran on with my childlike thoughts and stories, my recollections of the past, as if I had known thee from an infant. Suddenly the idea of my presumption struck me. I stopped, and timidly sought thine eyes.

"'Well, and when you found that the nightingale refused to sing?' —

"'Ah!' I said, 'what to thee this history of the heart of a child?'

"'Viola,' didst thou answer, with that voice, so inexpressibly calm and earnest! — 'Viola, the darkness of a child's heart is often but the shadow of a star. Speak on! And thy nightingale, when they caught and caged it, refused to sing?'

"'And I placed the cage yonder, amidst the vine-leaves, and took up my lute, and spoke to it on the strings; for I thought that all music was its native language, and it would understand that I sought to comfort it.'

"'Yes,' saidst thou. 'And at last it answered thee, but not with song, — in a sharp, brief cry; so mournful, that thy hands let fall the lute, and the tears gushed from thine eyes. So softly didst thou unbar the cage, and the nightingale flew into yonder thicket; and thou heardst the foliage rustle, and, looking through the moonlight, thine eyes saw that it had found its mate. It sang to thee then from the boughs a long, loud, joyous jubilee. And musing, thou didst feel that it was not the vine-leaves or the moonlight that made the bird give melody to night, and that the secret of its music was the presence of a thing beloved.'

"How didst thou know my thoughts in that childlike time better than I knew myself! How is the humble life of my past years, with its mean events, so mysteriously familiar to thee, bright stranger! I wonder, — but I do not again dare to fear thee!

. . .

"Once the thought of him oppressed and weighed me down. As

an infant that longs for the moon, my being was one vague desire for something never to be attained. Now I feel rather as if to think of thee sufficed to remove every fetter from my spirit. I float in the still seas of light, and nothing seems too high for my wings, too glorious for my eyes. It was mine ignorance that made me fear thee. A knowledge that is not in books seems to breathe around thee as an atmosphere. How little have I read! — how little have I learned! Yet when thou art by my side, it seems as if the veil were lifted from all wisdom and all Nature. I startle when I look even at the words I have written; they seem not to come from myself, but are the signs of another language which thou hast taught my heart, and which my hand traces rapidly, as at thy dictation. Sometimes, while I write or muse, I could fancy that I heard light wings hovering around me, and saw dim shapes of beauty floating round, and vanishing as they smiled upon me. No unquiet and fearful dream ever comes to me now in sleep, yet sleep and waking are alike but as one dream. In sleep I wander with thee, not through the paths of earth, but through impalpable air — an air which seems a music — upward and upward, as the soul mounts on the tones of a lyre! Till I knew thee, I was as a slave to the earth. Thou hast given to me the liberty of the universe! Before, it was life; it seems to me now as if I had commenced eternity!

. . .

"Formerly, when I was to appear upon the stage, my heart beat more loudly. I trembled to encounter the audience, whose breath gave shame or renown; and now I have no fear of them. I see them, heed them, hear them not! I know that there will be music in my voice, for it is a hymn that I pour to thee. Thou never comest to the theater; and that no longer grieves me. Thou art become too sacred to appear a part of the common world, and I feel glad that thou art not by when crowds have a right to judge me.

. . .

"And he spoke to me of *another*: to another he would consign me! No, it is not love that I feel for thee, Zanoni; or why did I hear thee without anger, why did thy command seem to me not a thing impossible? As the strings of the instrument obey the hand of the master, thy look modulates the wildest chords of my heart to thy will. If it please thee, — yes, let it be so. Thou art lord of my destinies; they cannot rebel against thee! I almost think I could love him, whoever it be, on whom thou wouldst shed the rays that circumfuse thyself. Whatever thou hast touched, I love; whatever thou speakest of, I love. Thy hand played with these vine leaves; I wear them in my bosom. Thou seemest to me the source of all love; too high and too bright to be loved thyself, but darting light into other objects, on which the eye can gaze less dazzled. No, no; it is not love that I feel for thee, and therefore it is that I do not blush to nourish and confess it. Shame on me if I loved, knowing myself so worthless a thing to thee!

. . .

"*Another!* — my memory echoes back that word. Another! Dost thou mean that I shall see thee no more? It is not sadness, — it is not despair that seizes me. I cannot weep. It is an utter sense of desolation. I am plunged back into the common life; and I shudder coldly at the solitude. But I will obey thee, if thou wilt. Shall I not see thee again beyond the grave? O how sweet it were to die!

"Why do I not struggle from the web in which my will is thus entangled? Hast thou a right to dispose of me thus? Give me back — give me back the life I knew before I gave life itself away to thee. Give me back the careless dreams of my youth, — my liberty of heart that sung aloud as it walked the earth. Thou hast disenchanted me of everything that is not of thyself. Where was the sin, at least, to think of thee, — to see thee? Thy kiss still glows upon my hand; is that hand mine to bestow? Thy kiss claimed and hallowed it to thyself. Stranger, I will *not* obey thee.

. . .

"Another day, — one day of the fatal three is gone! It is strange to me that since the sleep of the last night, a deep calm has settled upon my breast. I feel so assured that my very being is become a part of thee, that I cannot believe that my life can be separated from thine; and in this conviction I repose, and smile even at thy words and my own fears. Thou art fond of one maxim, which thou repeatest in a thousand forms, — that the beauty of the soul is faith; that as ideal loveliness to the sculptor, faith is to the heart; that faith, rightly understood, extends over all the works of the Creator, whom we can know but through belief; that it embraces a tranquil confidence in ourselves, and a serene repose as to our future; that it is the moonlight that sways the tides of the human sea. That faith I comprehend now. I reject all doubt, all fear. I know that I have inextricably linked the whole that makes the inner life to thee; and thou canst not tear me from thee, if thou wouldst! And this change from struggle into calm came to me with sleep, — a sleep without a dream; but when I woke, it was with a mysterious sense of happiness, — an indistinct memory of something blessed, — as if thou hadst cast from afar off a smile upon my slumber. At night I was so sad; not a blossom that had not closed itself up, as if never more to open to the sun; and the night itself, in the heart as on the earth, has ripened the blossoms into flowers. The world is beautiful once more, but beautiful in repose, — not a breeze stirs thy tree, not a doubt my soul!"

Chapter 3. VI.

Tu vegga o per violenzia o per inganno
Patire o disonore o mortal danno.*
                    "Orlando Furioso," Cant. xlii. i.

*I*t was a small cabinet; the walls were covered with pictures, one of which was worth more than the whole lineage of the owner of the palace. Oh, yes! Zanoni was right. The painter *is* a magician; the gold he at least wrings from his crucible is no delusion. A Venetian noble might be a fribble, or an assassin, — a scoundrel, or a dolt; worthless, or worse than worthless, yet he might have sat to Titian, and his portrait may be inestimable, — a few inches of painted canvas a thousand times more valuable than a man with his veins and muscles, brain, will, heart, and intellect!

In this cabinet sat a man of about three-and-forty, — dark-eyed, sallow, with short, prominent features, a massive conformation of jaw, and thick, sensual, but resolute lips; this man was the Prince di ——. His form, above the middle height, and rather inclined to corpulence, was clad in a loose dressing-robe of rich brocade. On a table before him lay an old-fashioned sword and hat, a mask, dice and dice-box, a portfolio, and an inkstand of silver curiously carved.

"Well, Mascari," said the prince, looking up towards his parasite, who stood by the embrasure of the deep-set barricadoed window, — "well! the Cardinal sleeps with his fathers. I require comfort for the loss of so excellent a relation; and where a more dulcet voice than Viola Pisani's?"

---

* Thou art about, either through violence or artifice, to suffer either dishonor or mortal loss.

"Is your Excellency serious? So soon after the death of his Eminence?"

"It will be the less talked of, and I the less suspected. Hast thou ascertained the name of the insolent who baffled us that night, and advised the Cardinal the next day?"

"Not yet."

"Sapient Mascari! I will inform thee. It was the strange Unknown."

"The Signor Zanoni! Are you sure, my prince?"

"Mascari, yes. There is a tone in that man's voice that I never can mistake; so clear, and so commanding, when I hear it I almost fancy there is such a thing as conscience. However, we must rid ourselves of an impertinent. Mascari, Signor Zanoni hath not yet honored our poor house with his presence. He is a distinguished stranger, — we must give a banquet in his honor."

"Ah, and the Cyprus wine! The cypress is a proper emblem of the grave."

"But this anon. I am superstitious; there are strange stories of Zanoni's power and foresight; remember the death of Ughelli. No matter, though the Fiend were his ally, he should not rob me of my prize; no, nor my revenge."

"Your Excellency is infatuated; the actress has bewitched you."

"Mascari," said the prince, with a haughty smile, "through these veins rolls the blood of the old Visconti — of those who boasted that no woman ever escaped their lust, and no man their resentment. The crown of my fathers has shrunk into a gewgaw and a toy, — their ambition and their spirit are undecayed! My honor is now enlisted in this pursuit, — Viola must be mine!"

"Another ambuscade?" said Mascari, inquiringly.

"Nay, why not enter the house itself? — the situation is lonely, and the door is not made of iron."

"But what if, on her return home, she tell the tale of our violence? A house forced, — a virgin stolen! Reflect; though the feudal privileges are not destroyed, even a Visconti is not now above the law."

"Is he not, Mascari? Fool! in what age of the world, even if the Madmen of France succeed in their chimeras, will the iron of law not bend itself, like an osier twig, to the strong hand of power and gold? But look not so pale, Mascari; I have foreplanned all things. The day that she leaves this palace, she will leave it for France, with Monsieur Jean Nicot."

Before Mascari could reply, the gentleman of the chamber announced the Signor Zanoni.

The prince involuntarily laid his hand upon the sword placed on the table, then with a smile at his own impulse, rose, and met his visitor at the threshold, with all the profuse and respectful courtesy of Italian simulation.

"This is an honor highly prized," said the prince. "I have long desired to clasp the hand of one so distinguished."

"And I give it in the spirit with which you seek it," replied Zanoni.

The Neapolitan bowed over the hand he pressed; but as he touched it a shiver came over him, and his heart stood still. Zanoni bent on him his dark, smiling eyes, and then seated himself with a familiar air.

"Thus it is signed and sealed; I mean our friendship, noble prince. And now I will tell you the object of my visit. I find, Excellency, that, unconsciously perhaps, we are rivals. Can we not accommodate out pretensions!"

"Ah!" said the prince, carelessly, "you, then, were the cavalier who robbed me of the reward of my chase. All stratagems fair in love, as in war. Reconcile our pretensions! Well, here is the dice-box; let us throw for her. He who casts the lowest shall resign his claim."

"Is this a decision by which you will promise to be bound?"

"Yes, on my faith."

"And for him who breaks his word so plighted, what shall be the forfeit?"

"The sword lies next to the dice-box, Signor Zanoni. Let him who stands not by his honor fall by the sword."

"And you invoke that sentence if either of us fail his word? Be it so; let Signor Mascari cast for us."

"Well said! — Mascari, the dice!"

The prince threw himself back in his chair; and, world-hardened as he was, could not suppress the glow of triumph and satisfaction that spread itself over his features. Mascari took up the three dice, and rattled them noisily in the box. Zanoni, leaning his cheek on his hand, and bending over the table, fixed his eyes steadfastly on the parasite; Mascari in vain struggled to extricate from that searching gaze; he grew pale, and trembled, he put down the box.

"I give the first throw to your Excellency. Signor Mascari, be pleased to terminate our suspense."

Again Mascari took up the box; again his hand shook so that the dice rattled within. He threw; the numbers were sixteen.

"It is a high throw," said Zanoni, calmly; "nevertheless, Signor Mascari, I do not despond."

Mascari gathered up the dice, shook the box, and rolled the contents once more on the table: the number was the highest that can be thrown, — eighteen.

The prince darted a glance of fire at his minion, who stood with gaping mouth, staring at the dice, and trembling from head to foot.

"I have won, you see," said Zanoni; "may we be friends still?"

"Signor," said the prince, obviously struggling with anger and confusion, "the victory is yours. But pardon me, you have spoken lightly of this young girl, — will anything tempt you to yield your claim?"

"Ah, do not think so ill of my gallantry; and," resumed Zanoni, with a stern meaning in his voice, "forget not the forfeit your own lips have named."

The prince knit his brow, but constrained the haughty answer that was his first impulse.

"Enough!" he said, forcing a smile; "I yield. Let me prove that I do not yield ungraciously; will you favor me with your presence at a little feast I propose to give in honor," he added, with a sardonic mockery, "of the elevation of my kinsman, the late Cardinal, of pious memory, to the true seat of St. Peter?"

"It is, indeed, a happiness to hear one command of yours I can obey."

Zanoni then turned the conversation, talked lightly and gaily, and soon afterwards departed.

"Villain!" then exclaimed the prince, grasping Mascari by the collar, "you betrayed me!"

"I assure your Excellency that the dice were properly arranged; he should have thrown twelve; but he is the Devil, and that's the end of it."

"There is no time to be lost," said the prince, quitting his hold of his parasite, who quietly resettled his cravat.

"My blood is up, — I will win this girl, if I die for it! What noise is that?"

"It is but the sword of your illustrious ancestor that has fallen from the table."

Chapter 3.VII.

Il ne faut appeler aucun ordre si ce n'est en tems clair et serein.*
                        "Les Clavicules du Rabbi Salomon."

---

* No order of spirits must be invoked unless the weather be clear and serene.

Letter from Zanoni to Mejnour.

My art is already dim and troubled. I have lost the tranquility which is power. I cannot influence the decisions of those whom I would most guide to the shore; I see them wander farther and deeper into the infinite ocean where our barks sail evermore to the horizon that flies before us! Amazed and awed to find that I can only warn where I would control, I have looked into my own soul. It is true that the desires of earth chain me to the present, and shut me from the solemn secrets which Intellect, purified from all the dross of the clay, alone can examine and survey. The stern condition on which we hold our nobler and diviner gifts darkens our vision towards the future of those for whom we know the human infirmities of jealousy or hate or love. Mejnour, all around me is mist and haze; I have gone back in our sublime existence; and from the bosom of the imperishable youth that blooms only in the spirit, springs up the dark poison-flower of human love.

This man is not worthy of her, — I know that truth; yet in his nature are the seeds of good and greatness, if the tares and weeds of worldly vanities and fears would suffer them to grow. If she were his, and I had thus transplanted to another soil the passion that obscures my gaze and disarms my power, unseen, unheard, unrecognized, I could watch over his fate, and secretly prompt his deeds, and minister to her welfare through his own. But time rushes on! Through the shadows that encircle me, I see, gathering round her, the darkest dangers. No choice but flight, — no escape save with him or me. With me! — the rapturous thought, — the terrible conviction! With me! Mejnour, canst thou wonder that I would save her from myself? A moment in the life of ages, — a bubble on the shoreless sea. What else to me can be human love? And in this exquisite nature of hers, — more pure, more spiritual, even in its young affections than ever heretofore the countless volumes of the heart, race after race, have given to my gaze: there is yet a deep-buried feeling that warns me of inevitable woe. Thou austere and remorseless Hierophant, — thou who hast sought to convert to our brotherhood every spirit that seemed to thee most high and bold, — even thou knowest, by horrible experience, how vain the hope to banish *fear* from the heart of woman.

My life would be to her one marvel. Even if, on the other hand, I sought to guide her path through the realms of terror to the light, think of the Haunter of the Threshold, and shudder with me at the awful hazard! I have endeavored to fill the Englishman's ambition with the true glory of his art; but the restless spirit of his ancestor still seems to whisper in him, and to attract to the spheres in which it lost its own wandering way. There is a mystery in man's inheritance from his fathers. Peculiarities of the mind, as diseases of the body, rest dormant for generations, to revive in some distant descendant, baffle all treatment and elude all skill. Come to me from thy solitude amidst the wrecks of Rome! I pant for a living confidant, — for one who in the old time has himself known jealousy and love. I have sought commune with Adon-Ai; but his presence, that once inspired such heavenly content with knowledge, and so serene a confidence in destiny, now only troubles and perplexes me. From the height from which I strive to search into the shadows of things to come, I see confused specters of menace and wrath. Methinks I behold a ghastly limit to the wondrous existence I have held, — methinks that, after ages of the Ideal Life, I see my course merge into the most stormy whirlpool of the Real. Where the stars opened to me their gates, there looms a scaffold, — thick steams of blood rise as from a shambles. What is more strange to me, a creature here, a very type of the false ideal of common men, — body and mind, a hideous mockery of the art that shapes the Beautiful, and the desires that seek the Perfect, ever haunts my vision amidst these perturbed and broken clouds of the fate to be. By that shadowy scaffold it stands and gibbers at me, with lips dropping slime and gore. Come, O friend of the far-time; for me, at least, thy wisdom has not purged away thy human affections. According to the bonds of our solemn order, reduced now to thee and myself, lone survivors of so many haughty and glorious aspirants, thou art pledged, too, to warn the descendant of those whom thy counsels sought to initiate into the great secret in a former age. The last of that bold Visconti who was once thy pupil is the relentless persecutor of this fair child. With thoughts of lust and murder, he is digging his own grave; thou mayest yet daunt him from his doom. And I also mysteriously, by the same bond, am pledged to obey, if he so command, a less guilty descendant of a baffled but nobler student. If he reject my counsel, and insist upon the pledge, Mejnour, thou wilt have another neophyte. Beware of another victim! Come to me! This will reach thee with all speed. Answer it by the pressure of one hand that I can dare to clasp!

Chapter 3. VIII.

Il lupo
Ferito, credo, mi conobbe e 'ncontro
Mi venne con la bocca sanguinosa.*

"Aminta," At. iv. Sc. i.

At Naples, the tomb of Virgil, beetling over the cave of Posilipo, is reverenced, not with the feelings that should hallow the memory of the poet, but the awe that wraps the memory of the magician. To his charms they ascribe the hollowing of that mountain passage; and tradition yet guards his tomb by the spirits he had raised to construct the cavern. This spot, in the immediate vicinity of Viola's home, had often attracted her solitary footsteps. She had loved the dim and solemn fancies that beset her as she looked into the lengthened gloom of the grotto, or, ascending to the tomb, gazed from the rock on the dwarfed figures of the busy crowd that seemed to creep like insects along the windings of the soil below; and now, at noon, she bent thither her thoughtful way. She threaded the narrow path, she passed the gloomy vineyard that clambers up the rock, and gained the lofty spot, green with moss and luxuriant foliage, where the dust of him who yet soothes and elevates the minds of men is believed to rest. From afar rose the huge fortress of St. Elmo, frowning darkly amidst spires and domes that glittered in the sun. Lulled in its azure splendor lay the Siren's sea; and the grey smoke of Vesuvius, in the clear distance, soared like a moving pillar into the lucid sky. Motionless on the brink of the precipice, Viola looked upon the lovely and living world that stretched below; and the sullen vapor of Vesuvius fascinated her eye yet more than the scattered gardens, or the gleaming Caprea, smiling amidst the smiles of the sea. She heard not a step that had followed her on her path and started to hear a voice at hand. So sudden was the apparition of the form that stood by her side, emerging from the bushes that clad the crags, and so singularly did

---

* The wounded wolf, I think, knew me, and came to meet me with its bloody mouth.

it harmonize in its uncouth ugliness with the wild nature of the scene immediately around her, and the wizard traditions of the place, that the color left her cheek, and a faint cry broke from her lips.

"Tush, pretty trembler! — do not be frightened at my face," said the man, with a bitter smile. "After three months' marriage, there is no different between ugliness and beauty. Custom is a great leveler. I was coming to your house when I saw you leave it; so, as I have matters of importance to communicate, I ventured to follow your footsteps. My name is Jean Nicot, a name already favorably known as a French artist. The art of painting and the art of music are nearly connected, and the stage is an altar that unites the two."

There was something frank and unembarrassed in the man's address that served to dispel the fear his appearance had occasioned. He seated himself, as he spoke, on a crag beside her, and, looking up steadily into her face, continued: —

"You are very beautiful, Viola Pisani, and I am not surprised at the number of your admirers. If I presume to place myself in the list, it is because I am the only one who loves thee honestly, and woos thee fairly. Nay, look not so indignant! Listen to me. Has the Prince di —— ever spoken to thee of marriage; or the beautiful imposter Zanoni, or the young blue-eyed Englishman, Clarence Glyndon? It is marriage, — it is a home, it is safety, it is reputation, that I offer to thee; and these last when the straight form grows crooked, and the bright eyes dim. What say you?" and he attempted to seize her hand.

Viola shrunk from him, and silently turned to depart. He rose abruptly and placed himself on her path.

"Actress, you must hear me! Do you know what this calling of the stage is in the eyes of prejudice, — that is, of the common opinion of mankind? It is to be a princess before the lamps, and a Pariah before the day. No man believes in your virtue, no man credits your vows; you are the puppet that they consent to trick out with tinsel for their amusement, not an idol for their worship. Are you so enamored of this career that you scorn even to think of security and honor? Perhaps you are different from what you seem. Perhaps you laugh at the prejudice that would degrade you, and would wisely turn it to advantage. Speak frankly to me; I have no prejudice either. Sweet one, I am sure we should agree. Now, this Prince di ——, I have a message from him. Shall I deliver it?"

Never had Viola felt as she felt then, never had she so thoroughly seen all the perils of her forlorn condition and her fearful renown. Nicot continued: —

"Zanoni would but amuse himself with thy vanity; Glyndon would despise himself, if he offered thee his name, and thee, if thou wouldst accept it; but the Prince di —— is in earnest, and he is wealthy. Listen!"

And Nicot approached his lips to her, and hissed a sentence which she did not suffer him to complete. She darted from him with one glance of unutterable disdain. As he strove to regain his hold of her arm, he lost his footing, and fell down the sides of the rock till, bruised and lacerated, a pine-branch saved him from the yawning abyss below. She heard his exclamation of rage and pain as she bounded down the path, and, without once turning to look behind, regained her home. By the porch stood Glyndon, conversing with Gionetta. She passed him abruptly, entered the house, and, sinking on the floor, wept loud and passionately.

Glyndon, who had followed her in surprise, vainly sought to soothe and calm her. She would not reply to his questions; she did not seem to listen to his protestations of love, till suddenly, as Nicot's terrible picture of the world's judgment of that profession which to her younger thoughts had seemed the service of Song and the Beautiful, forced itself upon her, she raised her face from her hands, and, looking steadily upon the Englishman, said, "False one, dost thou talk of me of love?"

"By my honor, words fail to tell thee how I love!"

"Wilt thou give me thy home, thy name? Dost thou woo me as thy wife?" And at that moment, had Glyndon answered as his better angel would have counseled, perhaps, in that revolution of her whole mind which the words of Nicot had effected, which made her despise her very self, sicken of her lofty dreams, despair of the future, and distrust her whole ideal, — perhaps, I say, in restoring her self-esteem, — he would have won her confidence, and ultimately secured her love. But against the prompting of his nobler nature rose up at that sudden question all those doubts which, as Zanoni had so well implied, made the true enemies of his soul. Was he thus suddenly to be entangled into a snare laid for his credulity by deceivers? Was she not instructed to seize the moment to force him into an avowal which prudence must repent? Was not the great actress rehearsing a premeditated part? He turned round, as these thoughts, the children of the world, passed across him, for he literally fancied that he heard the sarcastic laugh of Mervale without. Nor was he deceived. Mervale was passing by the threshold, and Gionetta had told him his friend was within. Who does not know the effect of the world's laugh? Mervale was the personation of the world. The whole world seemed to shout derision in those ringing tones. He drew back, — he recoiled. Viola followed him with her earnest, impatient eyes. At last, he faltered forth, "Do all of thy profession, beautiful Viola, exact marriage as the sole condition of love?" Oh, bitter question! Oh, poisoned taunt! He repented it the moment after. He was seized with remorse of reason, of feeling, and of conscience. He saw her form shrink, as it were, at his cruel words. He saw the color come and go, to leave the writing lips like marble; and then, with a sad, gentle look of self-pity, rather than reproach, she pressed her hands tightly to her bosom, and said, —

"He was right! Pardon me, Englishman; I see now, indeed, that I am the Pariah and the outcast."

"Hear me. I retract. Viola, Viola! it is for you to forgive!"

But Viola waved him from her, and, smiling mournfully as she passed him by, glided from the chamber; and he did not dare to detain her.

Chapter 3.IX.

Dafne: Ma, chi lung' e d'Amor?
Tirsi: Chi teme e fugge.
Dafne: E che giova fuggir da lui ch' ha l' ali?
Tirsi: *Amor nascente ha corte l' ali!*

"Aminta," At. ii. Sc. ii.

When Glyndon found himself without Viola's house, Mervale, still loitering at the door, seized his arm. Glyndon shook him off abruptly.

"Thou and thy counsels," said he, bitterly, "have made me a coward and a wretch. But I will go home, — I will write to her. I will pour out my whole soul; she will forgive me yet."

Mervale, who was a man of imperturbable temper, arranged his ruffles, which his friend's angry gesture had a little discomposed, and not till Glyndon had exhausted himself awhile by passionate exclamations and reproaches, did the experienced angler begin to tighten the

---

* Dafne: But, who is far from Love?
   Tirsi: He who fears and flies.
   Dafne: What use to flee from one who has wings?
   Tirsi: The wings of Love, while he yet grows, are short.

line. He then drew from Glyndon the explanation of what had passed, and artfully sought not to irritate, but soothe him. Mervale, indeed, was by no means a bad man; he had stronger moral notions than are common amongst the young. He sincerely reproved his friend for harboring dishonorable intentions with regard to the actress. "Because I would not have her thy wife, I never dreamed that thou shouldst degrade her to thy mistress. Better of the two an imprudent match than an illicit connection. But pause yet, do not act on the impulse of the moment."

"But there is no time to lose. I have promised to Zanoni to give him my answer by tomorrow night. Later than that time, all option ceases."

"Ah!" said Mervale, "this seems suspicious. Explain yourself."

And Glyndon, in the earnestness of his passion, told his friend what had passed between himself and Zanoni, — suppressing only, he scarce knew why, the reference to his ancestor and the mysterious brotherhood.

This recital gave to Mervale all the advantage he could desire. Heavens! with what sound, shrewd common-sense he talked. How evidently some charlatanic coalition between the actress, and perhaps, — who knows? — her clandestine protector, sated with possession! How equivocal the character of one, — the position of the other! What cunning in the question of the actress! How profoundly had Glyndon, at the first suggestion of his sober reason, seen through the snare. What! was he to be thus mystically cajoled and hurried into a rash marriage, because Zanoni, a mere stranger, told him with a grave face that he must decide before the clock struck a certain hour?

"Do this at least," said Mervale, reasonably enough, — "wait till the time expires; it is but another day. Baffle Zanoni. He tells thee that he will meet thee before midnight tomorrow, and defies thee to avoid him. Pooh! let us quit Naples for some neighboring place, where, unless he be indeed the Devil, he cannot possibly find us. Show him that you will not be led blindfold even into an act that you meditate yourself. Defer to write to her, or to see her, till after tomorrow. This is all I ask. Then visit her, and decide for yourself."

Glyndon was staggered. He could not combat the reasonings of his friend; he was not convinced, but he hesitated; and at that moment Nicot passed them. He turned round, and stopped, as he saw Glyndon.

"Well, and do you think still of the Pisani?"

"Yes; and you —"

"Have seen and conversed with her. She shall be Madame Nicot before this day week! I am going to the café, in the Toledo; and hark ye, when next you meet your friend Signor Zanoni, tell him that he has twice crossed my path. Jean Nicot, though a painter, is a plain, honest man, and always pays his debts."

"It is a good doctrine in money matters," said Mervale; "as to revenge, it is not so moral, and certainly not so wise. But is it in your love that Zanoni has crossed your path? How that, if your suit prosper so well?"

"Ask Viola Pisani that question. Bah! Glyndon, she is a prude only to thee. But I have no prejudices. Once more, farewell."

"Rouse thyself, man!" said Mervale, slapping Glyndon on the shoulder. "What think you of your fair one now?"

"This man must lie."

"Will you write to her at once?"

"No; if she be really playing a game, I could renounce her without a sigh. I will watch her closely; and, at all events, Zanoni shall not be the master of my fate. Let us, as you advise, leave Naples at daybreak tomorrow."

Chapter 3.X.

O chiunque tu sia, che fuor d'ogni uso
Pieghi Natura ad opre altere e strane,
E, spiando i segreti, entri al piu chiuso
Spazi' a tua voglia delle menti umane —
Deh, Dimmi!*

                     "Gerus. Lib.," Cant. x. xviii.

*E*arly the next morning the young Englishmen mounted their horses, and took the road towards Baiae. Glyndon left word at his hotel, that if Signor Zanoni sought him, it was in the neighborhood of that once celebrated watering-place of the ancients that he should be found.

They passed by Viola's house, but Glyndon resisted the temptation

---

* O thou, whoever thou art, who through every use bendest Nature
to works foreign and strange; and by spying into her secrets,
enterest at thy will into the closest recesses of the human
mind, — O speak! O tell me!

of pausing there; and after threading the grotto of Posilipo, they wound by a circuitous route back into the suburbs of the city, and took the opposite road, which conducts to Portici and Pompeii. It was late at noon when they arrived at the former of these places. Here they halted to dine; for Mervale had heard much of the excellence of the macaroni at Portici, and Mervale was a bon vivant.

They put up at an inn of very humble pretensions, and dined under an awning. Mervale was more than usually gay; he pressed the lacrima upon his friend, and conversed gaily.

"Well, my dear friend, we have foiled Signor Zanoni in one of his predictions at least. You will have no faith in him hereafter."

"The ides are come, not gone."

"Tush! If he be the soothsayer, you are not the Caesar. It is your vanity that makes you credulous. Thank Heaven, I do not think myself of such importance that the operations of Nature should be changed in order to frighten me."

"But why should the operations of Nature be changed? There may be a deeper philosophy than we dream of, — a philosophy that discovers the secrets of Nature, but does not alter, by penetrating, its courses."

"Ah, you relapse into your heretical credulity; you seriously suppose Zanoni to be a prophet, — a reader of the future; perhaps an associate of genii and spirits!"

Here the landlord, a little, fat, oily fellow, came up with a fresh bottle of lacrima. He hoped their Excellencies were pleased. He was most touched — touched to the heart, that they liked the macaroni. Were their Excellencies going to Vesuvius? There was a slight eruption; they could not see it where they were, but it was pretty, and would be prettier still after sunset.

"A capital idea!" cried Mervale. "What say you, Glyndon?"

"I have not yet seen an eruption; I should like it much."

"But is there no danger?" asked the prudent Mervale.

"Oh, not at all; the mountain is very civil at present. It only plays a little, just to amuse their Excellencies the English."

"Well, order the horses, and bring the bill; we will go before it is dark. Clarence, my friend, — nunc est bibendum; but take care of the pede libero, which will scarce do for walking on lava!"

The bottle was finished, the bill paid; the gentlemen mounted, the landlord bowed, and they bent their way, in the cool of the delightful evening, towards Resina.

The wine, perhaps the excitement of his thoughts, animated Glyndon, whose unequal spirits were, at times, high and brilliant as those of a schoolboy released; and the laughter of the Northern tourists sounded oft and merrily along the melancholy domains of buried cities.

Hesperus had lighted his lamp amidst the rosy skies as they arrived at Resina. Here they quitted their horses, and took mules and a guide. As the sky grew darker and more dark, the mountain fire burned with an intense luster. In various streaks and streamlets, the fountain of flame rolled down the dark summit, and the Englishmen began to feel increase upon them, as they ascended, that sensation of solemnity and awe which makes the very atmosphere that surrounds the Giant of the Plains of the Antique Hades.

It was night, when, leaving the mules, they ascended on foot, accompanied by their guide, and a peasant who bore a rude torch. The guide was a conversable, garrulous fellow, like most of his country and his calling; and Mervale, who possessed a sociable temper, loved to amuse or to instruct himself on every incidental occasion.

"Ah, Excellency," said the guide, "your countrymen have a strong passion for the volcano. Long life to them, they bring us plenty of money! If our fortunes depended on the Neapolitans, we should starve."

"True, they have no curiosity," said Mervale. "Do you remember, Glyndon, the contempt with which that old count said to us, 'You will go to Vesuvius, I suppose? I have never been; why should I go? You have cold, you have hunger, you have fatigue, you have danger, and all for nothing but to see fire, which looks just as well in a brazier as on a mountain.' Ha! ha! the old fellow was right."

"But, Excellency," said the guide, "that is not all: some cavaliers think to ascend the mountain without our help. I am sure they deserve to tumble into the crater."

"They must be bold fellows to go alone; you don't often find such."

"Sometimes among the French, signor. But the other night — I never was so frightened — I had been with an English party, and a lady had left a pocketbook on the mountain, where she had been sketching. She offered me a handsome sum to return for it, and bring it to her at Naples. So I went in the evening. I found it, sure enough, and was about to return, when I saw a figure that seemed to emerge from the crater itself. The air there was so pestiferous that I could not have conceived a human creature could breathe it, and live. I was so astounded that I stood still as a stone, till the figure came over the hot ashes, and stood before me, face to face. Santa Maria, what a head!"

"What! hideous?"

"No; so beautiful, but so terrible. It had nothing human in its aspect."

"And what said the salamander?"

"Nothing! It did not even seem to perceive me, though I was near as I am to you; but its eyes seemed to emerge prying into the air. It passed by me quickly, and, walking across a stream of burning lava, soon vanished on the other side of the mountain. I was curious and foolhardy, and resolved to see if I could bear the atmosphere which this visitor had left; but though I did not advance within thirty yards of the spot at which he had first appeared, I was driven back by a vapor that well-nigh stifled me. Cospetto! I have spat blood ever since."

"Now will I lay a wager that you fancy this fire-king must be Zanoni," whispered Mervale, laughing.

The little party had now arrived nearly at the summit of the mountain; and unspeakably grand was the spectacle on which they gazed. From the crater arose a vapor, intensely dark, that overspread the whole background of the heavens; in the center whereof rose a flame that assumed a form singularly beautiful. It might have been compared to a crest of gigantic feathers, the diadem of the mountain, high-arched, and drooping downward, with the hues delicately shaded off, and the whole shifting and tremulous as the plumage on a warrior's helmet.

The glare of the flame spread, luminous and crimson, over the dark and rugged ground on which they stood, and drew an innumerable variety of shadows from crag and hollow. An oppressive and sulfurous exhalation served to increase the gloomy and sublime terror of the place. But on turning from the mountain, and towards the distant and unseen ocean, the contrast was wonderfully great; the heavens serene and blue, the stars still and calm as the eyes of Divine Love. It was as if the realms of the opposing principles of Evil and of Good were brought in one view before the gaze of man! Glyndon — once more the enthusiast, the artist — was enchained and entranced by emotions vague and undefinable, half of delight and half of pain. Leaning on the shoulder of his friend, he gazed around him, and heard with deepening awe the rumbling of the earth below, the wheels and voices of the Ministry of Nature in her darkest and most inscrutable recess. Suddenly, as a bomb from a shell, a huge stone was flung hundreds of yards up from the jaws of the crater, and falling with a mighty crash upon the rock below, split into ten thousand fragments, which bounded down the sides of the mountain, sparkling and groaning as they went. One of these, the largest fragment, struck the narrow space of soil between the Englishmen and the guide, not three feet from the spot where the former stood. Mervale uttered an exclamation of terror, and Glyndon held his breath, and shuddered.

"Diavolo!" cried the guide. "Descend, Excellencies, — descend! we have not a moment to lose; follow me close!"

So saying, the guide and the peasant fled with as much swiftness as they were able to bring to bear. Mervale, ever more prompt and ready than his friend, imitated their example; and Glyndon, more confused than alarmed, followed close. But they had not gone many yards, before, with a rushing and sudden blast, came from the crater an enormous volume of vapor. It pursued, — it overtook, it overspread them. It swept the light from the heavens. All was abrupt and utter darkness; and through the gloom was heard the shout of the guide, already distant, and lost in an instant amidst the sound of the rushing gust and the groans of the earth beneath. Glyndon paused. He was separated from his friend, from the guide. He was alone, — with the Darkness and the Terror. The vapor rolled sullenly away; the form of the plumed fire was again dimly visible, and its struggling and perturbed reflection again shed a glow over the horrors of the path. Glyndon recovered himself, and sped onward. Below, he heard the voice of Mervale calling on him, though he no longer saw his form. The sound served as a guide. Dizzy and breathless, he bounded forward; when — hark! — a sullen, slow rolling sounded in his ear! He halted, — and turned back to gaze. The fire had overflowed its course; it had opened itself a channel amidst the furrows of the mountain. The stream pursued him fast — fast; and the hot breath of the chasing and preternatural foe came closer and closer upon his cheek! He turned aside; he climbed desperately with hands and feet upon a crag that, to the right, broke the scathed and blasted level of the soil. The stream rolled beside and beneath him, and then taking a sudden wind round the spot on which he stood, interposed its liquid fire, — a broad and impassable barrier between his resting-place and escape. There he stood, cut off from descent, and with no alternative but to retrace his steps towards the crater, and thence seek, without guide or clew, some other pathway.

For a moment his courage left him; he cried in despair, and in that overstrained pitch of voice which is never heard afar off, to the guide, to Mervale, to return to aid him.

No answer came; and the Englishman, thus abandoned solely to his own resources, felt his spirit and energy rise against the danger. He turned back, and ventured as far towards the crater as the noxious exhalation would permit; then, gazing below, carefully and deliberately he chalked out for himself a path by which he trusted to shun the direction the fire-stream had taken, and trod firmly and quickly over the crumbling and heated strata.

He had proceeded about fifty yards, when he halted abruptly; an unspeakable and unaccountable horror, not hitherto experienced amidst all his peril, came over him. He shook in every limb; his muscles refused his will, — he felt, as it were, palsied and death-stricken. The horror, I say, was unaccountable, for the path seemed clear and safe. The fire, above and behind, burned clear and far; and beyond, the stars lent him their cheering guidance. No obstacle was visible, — no danger seemed at hand. As thus, spellbound, and panic-stricken, he stood chained to the soil, — his breast heaving, large drops rolling down his brow, and his eyes starting wildly from their sockets, — he saw before him, at some distance, gradually shaping itself more and more distinctly to his gaze, a colossal shadow; a shadow that seemed partially borrowed from the human shape, but immeasurably above the human stature; vague, dark, almost formless; and differing, he could not tell where or why, not only from the proportions, but also from the limbs and outline of man.

The glare of the volcano, that seemed to shrink and collapse from this gigantic and appalling apparition, nevertheless threw its light, redly and steadily, upon another shape that stood beside, quiet and motionless; and it was, perhaps, the contrast of these two things — the Being and the Shadow — that impressed the beholder with the difference between them, — the Man and the Superhuman. It was but for a moment — nay, for the tenth part of a moment — that this sight was permitted to the wanderer. A second eddy of sulfurous vapors from the volcano, yet more rapidly, yet more densely than its predecessor, rolled over the mountain; and either the nature of the exhalation, or the excess of his own dread, was such, that Glyndon, after one wild gasp for breath, fell senseless on the earth.

Chapter 3.XI.

Was hab'ich,
Wenn ich nicht Alles habe? — sprach der Jungling.*
                              "Das Verschleierte Bild zu Sais."

*M*ervale and the Italians arrived in safety at the spot where they had left the mules; and not till they had recovered their own alarm and breath did they think of Glyndon. But then, as the minutes passed, and he appeared not, Mervale, whose heart was as good at least as human hearts are in general, grew seriously alarmed. He insisted on returning

* "What have I, if I possess not All?" said the youth.

to search for his friend; and by dint of prodigal promises prevailed at last on the guide to accompany him. The lower part of the mountain lay calm and white in the starlight; and the guide's practiced eye could discern all objects on the surface at a considerable distance. They had not, however, gone very far, before they perceived two forms slowly approaching them.

As they came near, Mervale recognized the form of his friend. "Thank Heaven, he is safe!" he cried, turning to the guide.

"Holy angels befriend us!" said the Italian, trembling, — "behold the very being that crossed me last Friday night. It is he, but his face is human now!"

"Signor Inglese," said the voice of Zanoni, as Glyndon — pale, wan, and silent — returned passively the joyous greeting of Mervale, — "Signor Inglese, I told your friend that we should meet tonight. You see you have *not* foiled my prediction."

"But how? — but where?" stammered Mervale, in great confusion and surprise.

"I found your friend stretched on the ground, overpowered by the mephitic exhalation of the crater. I bore him to a purer atmosphere; and as I know the mountain well, I have conducted him safely to you. This is all our history. You see, sir, that were it not for that prophecy which you desired to frustrate, your friend would ere this time have been a corpse; one minute more, and the vapor had done its work. Adieu; goodnight, and pleasant dreams."

"But, my preserver, you will not leave us?" said Glyndon, anxiously, and speaking for the first time. "Will you not return with us?"

Zanoni paused, and drew Glyndon aside. "Young man," said he, gravely, "it is necessary that we should again meet tonight. It is necessary that you should, ere the first hour of morning, decide on your own fate. I know that you have insulted her whom you profess to love. It is not too late to repent. Consult not your friend: he is sensible and wise; but not now is his wisdom needed. There are times in life when, from the imagination, and not the reason, should wisdom come, — this, for you, is one of them. I ask not your answer now. Collect your thoughts, — recover your jaded and scattered spirits. It wants two hours of midnight. Before midnight I will be with you."

"Incomprehensible being!" replied the Englishman, "I would leave the life you have preserved in your own hands; but what I have seen this night has swept even Viola from my thoughts. A fiercer desire than that of love burns in my veins, — the desire not to resemble but to surpass my kind; the desire to penetrate and to share the secret of your own existence — the desire of a preternatural knowledge and unearthly power. I make my choice. In my ancestor's name, I adjure and remind thee of thy pledge. Instruct me; school me; make me thine; and I surrender to thee at once, and without a murmur, the woman whom, till I saw thee, I would have defied a world to obtain."

"I bid thee consider well: on the one hand, Viola, a tranquil home, a happy and serene life; on the other hand, all is darkness, — darkness, that even these eyes cannot penetrate."

"But thou hast told me, that if I wed Viola, I must be contented with the common existence, — if I refuse, it is to aspire to thy knowledge and thy power."

"Vain man, knowledge and power are not happiness."

"But they are better than happiness. Say! — if I marry Viola, wilt thou be my master, — my guide? Say this, and I am resolved.

"It were impossible."

"Then I renounce her? I renounce love. I renounce happiness. Welcome solitude, — welcome despair; if they are the entrances to thy dark and sublime secret."

"I will not take thy answer now. Before the last hour of night thou shalt give it in one word, — aye or no! Farewell till then."

Zanoni waved his hand, and, descending rapidly, was seen no more.

Glyndon rejoined his impatient and wondering friend; but Mervale, gazing on his face, saw that a great change had passed there. The flexile and dubious expression of youth was forever gone. The features were locked, rigid, and stern; and so faded was the natural bloom, that an hour seemed to have done the work of years.

Chapter 3.XII.

Was ist's
Das hinter diesem Schleier sich verbirgt?*
                              "Das Verschleierte Bild zu Sais."

---

* What is it that conceals itself behind this veil?

On returning from Vesuvius or Pompeii, you enter Naples through its most animated, its most Neapolitan quarter, — through that quarter in which modern life most closely resembles the ancient; and in which, when, on a fair-day, the thoroughfare swarms alike with Indolence and Trade, you are impressed at once with the recollection of that restless, lively race from which the population of Naples derives its origin; so that in one day you may see at Pompeii the habitations of a remote age; and on the Mole, at Naples, you may imagine you behold the very beings with whom those habitations had been peopled.

But now, as the Englishmen rode slowly through the deserted streets, lighted but by the lamps of heaven, all the gayety of day was hushed and breathless. Here and there, stretched under a portico or a dingy booth, were sleeping groups of houseless Lazzaroni, — a tribe now merging its indolent individuality amidst an energetic and active population.

The Englishman rode on in silence; for Glyndon neither appeared to heed nor hear the questions and comments of Mervale, and Mervale himself was almost as weary as the jaded animal he bestrode.

Suddenly the silence of earth and ocean was broken by the sound of a distant clock that proclaimed the quarter preceding the last hour of night. Glyndon started from his reverie, and looked anxiously round. As the final stroke died, the noise of hoofs rung on the broad stones of the pavement, and from a narrow street to the right emerged the form of a solitary horseman. He neared the Englishmen, and Glyndon recognized the features and mien of Zanoni.

"What! do we meet again, signor?" said Mervale, in a vexed but drowsy tone.

"Your friend and I have business together," replied Zanoni, as he wheeled his steed to the side of Glyndon. "But it will be soon transacted. Perhaps you, sir, will ride on to your hotel."

"Alone!"

"There is no danger!" returned Zanoni, with a slight expression of disdain in his voice.

"None to me; but to Glyndon?"

"Danger from me! Ah, perhaps you are right."

"Go on, my dear Mervale," said Glyndon; "I will join you before you reach the hotel."

Mervale nodded, whistled, and pushed his horse into a kind of amble.

"Now your answer, — quick?"

"I have decided. The love of Viola has vanished from my heart. The pursuit is over."

"You have decided?"

"I have; and now my reward."

"Thy reward! Well; ere this hour tomorrow it shall await thee."

Zanoni gave the rein to his horse; it sprang forward with a bound: the sparks flew from its hoofs, and horse and rider disappeared amidst the shadows of the street whence they had emerged.

Mervale was surprised to see his friend by his side, a minute after they had parted.

"What has passed between you and Zanoni?"

"Mervale, do not ask me tonight! I am in a dream."

"I do not wonder at it, for even I am in a sleep. Let us push on."

In the retirement of his chamber, Glyndon sought to recollect his thoughts. He sat down on the foot of his bed, and pressed his hands tightly to his throbbing temples. The events of the last few hours; the apparition of the gigantic and shadowy Companion of the Mystic, amidst the fires and clouds of Vesuvius; the strange encounter with Zanoni himself, on a spot in which he could never, by ordinary reasoning, have calculated on finding Glyndon, filled his mind with emotions, in which terror and awe the least prevailed. A fire, the train of which had been long laid, was lighted at his heart, — the asbestos-fire that, once lit, is never to be quenched. All his early aspirations — his young ambition, his longings for the laurel — were merged in one passionate yearning to surpass the bounds of the common knowledge of man, and reach that solemn spot, between two worlds, on which the mysterious stranger appeared to have fixed his home.

Far from recalling with renewed affright the remembrance of the apparition that had so appalled him, the recollection only served to kindle and concentrate his curiosity into a burning focus. He had said aright, — *love had vanished from his heart*; there was no longer a serene space amidst its disordered elements for human affection to move and breathe. The enthusiast was rapt from this earth; and he would have surrendered all that mortal beauty ever promised, that mortal hope ever whispered, for one hour with Zanoni beyond the portals of the visible world.

He rose, oppressed and fevered with the new thoughts that raged within him, and threw open his casement for air. The ocean lay suffused in the starry light, and the stillness of the heavens never more eloquently preached the morality of repose to the madness of earthly passions. But such was Glyndon's mood that their very hush only served to deepen the wild desires that preyed upon his soul; and the solemn stars, that are mysteries in themselves, seemed, by a kindred sympathy, to agitate the wings of the spirit no longer contented with its cage. As he gazed, a star shot from its brethren, and vanished from the depth of space!

Chapter 3.XIII.

O, be gone!
By Heaven, I love thee better than myself,
For I came hither armed against myself.

"Romeo and Juliet"

*T*he young actress and Gionetta had returned from the theater; and
Viola fatigued and exhausted, had thrown herself on a sofa, while
Gionetta busied herself with the long tresses which, released from the
fillet that bound them, half-concealed the form of the actress, like a veil
of threads of gold. As she smoothed the luxuriant locks, the old nurse
ran gossiping on about the little events of the night, the scandal and
politics of the scenes and the tireroom. Gionetta was a worthy soul.
Almanzor, in Dryden's tragedy of "Almahide," did not change sides
with more gallant indifference than the exemplary nurse. She was at last
grieved and scandalized that Viola had not selected one chosen cavalier.
But the choice she left wholly to her fair charge. Zegri or Abencerrage,
Glyndon or Zanoni, it had been the same to her, except that the rumors
she had collected respecting the latter, combined with his own recom-
mendations of his rival, had given her preference to the Englishman.
She interpreted ill the impatient and heavy sigh with which Viola greeted
her praises of Glyndon, and her wonder that he had of late so neglected
his attentions behind the scenes, and she exhausted all her powers of
panegyric upon the supposed object of the sigh. "And then, too," she
said, "if nothing else were to be said against the other signor, it is enough
that he is about to leave Naples."

"Leave Naples! — Zanoni?"

"Yes, darling! In passing by the Mole today, there was a crowd round
some outlandish-looking sailors. His ship arrived this morning, and
anchors in the bay. The sailors say that they are to be prepared to sail
with the first wind; they were taking in fresh stores. They —"

"Leave me, Gionetta! Leave me!"

The time had already passed when the girl could confide in Gionetta. Her thoughts had advanced to that point when the heart recoils from all confidence, and feels that it cannot be comprehended. Alone now, in the principal apartment of the house, she paced its narrow boundaries with tremulous and agitated steps: she recalled the frightful suit of Nicot, — the injurious taunt of Glyndon; and she sickened at the remembrance of the hollow applauses which, bestowed on the actress, not the woman, only subjected her to contumely and insult. In that room the recollection of her father's death, the withered laurel and the broken chords, rose chillingly before her. Hers, she felt, was a yet gloomier fate, — the chords may break while the laurel is yet green. The lamp, waning in its socket, burned pale and dim, and her eyes instinctively turned from the darker corner of the room. Orphan, by the hearth of thy parent, dost thou fear the presence of the dead!

And was Zanoni indeed about to quit Naples? Should she see him no more? Oh, fool, to think that there was grief in any other thought! The past! — that was gone! The future! — there was no future to her, Zanoni absent! But this was the night of the third day on which Zanoni had told her that, come what might, he would visit her again. It was, then, if she might believe him, some appointed crisis in her fate; and how should she tell him of Glyndon's hateful words? The pure and the proud mind can never confide its wrongs to another, only its triumphs and its happiness. But at that late hour would Zanoni visit her, — could she receive him? Midnight was at hand. Still in undefined suspense, in intense anxiety, she lingered in the room. The quarter before midnight sounded, dull and distant. All was still, and she was about to pass to her sleeping-room, when she heard the hoofs of a horse at full speed; the sound ceased, there was a knock at the door. Her heart beat violently; but fear gave way to another sentiment when she heard a voice, too well known, calling on her name. She paused, and then, with the fearlessness of innocence, descended and unbarred the door.

Zanoni entered with a light and hasty step. His horseman's cloak fitted tightly to his noble form, and his broad hat threw a gloomy shade over his commanding features.

The girl followed him into the room she had just left, trembling and blushing deeply, and stood before him with the lamp she held shining upward on her cheek and the long hair that fell like a shower of light over the half-clad shoulders and heaving bust.

"Viola," said Zanoni, in a voice that spoke deep emotion, "I am by thy side once more to save thee. Not a moment is to be lost. Thou must fly with me, or remain the victim of the Prince di ——. I would have made the charge I now undertake another's; thou knowest I would, — thou knowest it! — but he is not worthy of thee, the cold Englishman!

I throw myself at thy feet; have trust in me, and fly."

He grasped her hand passionately as he dropped on his knee, and looked up into her face with his bright, beseeching eyes.

"Fly with thee!" said Viola, scarce believing her senses.

"With me. Name, fame, honor, — all will be sacrificed if thou dost not."

"Then — then," said the wild girl, falteringly, and turning aside her face, — "then I am not indifferent to thee; thou wouldst not give me to another?"

Zanoni was silent; but his breast heaved, his cheeks flushed, his eyes darted dark and impassioned fire.

"Speak!" exclaimed Viola, in jealous suspicion of his silence.

"Indifferent to me! No; but I dare not yet say that I love thee."

"Then what matters my fate?" said Viola, turning pale, and shrinking from his side; "leave me, — I fear no danger. My life, and therefore my honor, is in mine own hands."

"Be not so mad," said Zanoni. "Hark! do you hear the neigh of my steed? — it is an alarm that warns us of the approaching peril. Haste, or you are lost!"

"Why dost thou care for me?" said the girl, bitterly. "Thou hast read my heart; thou knowest that thou art become the lord of my destiny. But to be bound beneath the weight of a cold obligation; to be the beggar on the eyes of indifference; to cast myself on one who loves me not, — *that* were indeed the vilest sin of my sex. Ah, Zanoni, rather let me die!"

She had thrown back her clustering hair from her face while she spoke; and as she now stood, with her arms drooping mournfully, and her hands clasped together with the proud bitterness of her wayward spirit, giving new zest and charm to her singular beauty, it was impossible to conceive a sight more irresistible to the eye and the heart.

"Tempt me not to thine own danger, — perhaps destruction!" exclaimed Zanoni, in faltering accents. "Thou canst not dream of what thou wouldst demand, — come!" and, advancing, he wound his arm round her waist. "Come, Viola; believe at least in my friendship, my honor, my protection —"

"And not thy love," said the Italian, turning on him her reproachful eyes. Those eyes met his, and he could not withdraw from the charm of their gaze. He felt her heart throbbing beneath his own; her breath came warm upon his cheek. He trembled, — *he!* the lofty, the mysterious Zanoni, who seemed to stand aloof from his race. With a deep and burning sigh, he murmured, "Viola, I love thee! Oh!" he continued passionately, and, releasing his hold, he threw himself abruptly at her feet, "I no more command, — as woman should be wooed, I woo thee.

From the first glance of those eyes, from the first sound of thy voice, thou becamest too fatally dear to me. Thou speakest of fascination, — it lives and it breathes in thee! I fled from Naples to fly from thy presence, — it pursued me. Months, years passed, and thy sweet face still shone upon my heart. I returned, because I pictured thee alone and sorrowful in the world, and knew that dangers, from which I might save thee, were gathering near thee and around. Beautiful Soul! whose leaves I have read with reverence, it was for thy sake, thine alone, that I would have given thee to one who might make thee happier on earth than I can. Viola! Viola! thou knowest not — never canst thou know — how dear thou art to me!"

It is in vain to seek for words to describe the delight — the proud, the full, the complete, and the entire delight — that filled the heart of the Neapolitan. He whom she had considered too lofty even for love, — more humble to her than those she had half-despised! She was silent, but her eyes spoke to him; and then slowly, as aware, at last, that the human love had advanced on the ideal, she shrank into the terrors of a modest and virtuous nature. She did not dare, — she did not dream to ask him the question she had so fearlessly made to Glyndon; but she felt a sudden coldness, — a sense that a barrier was yet between love and love. "Oh, Zanoni!" she murmured, with downcast eyes, "ask me not to fly with thee; tempt me not to my shame. Thou wouldst protect me from others. Oh, protect me from thyself!"

"Poor orphan!" said he, tenderly, "and canst thou think that I ask from thee one sacrifice, — still less the greatest that woman can give to love? As my wife I woo thee, and by every tie, and by every vow that can hallow and endear affection. Alas! they have belied love to thee indeed, if thou dost not know the religion that belongs to it! They who truly love would seek, for the treasure they obtain, every bond that can make it lasting and secure. Viola, weep not, unless thou givest me the holy right to kiss away thy tears!"

And that beautiful face, no more averted, drooped upon his bosom; and as he bent down, his lips sought the rosy mouth: a long and burning kiss, — danger, life, the world was forgotten! Suddenly Zanoni tore himself from her.

"Hearest thou the wind that sighs, and dies away? As that wind, my power to preserve thee, to guard thee, to foresee the storm in thy skies, is gone. No matter. Haste, haste; and may love supply the loss of all that it has dared to sacrifice! Come."

Viola hesitated no more. She threw her mantle over her shoulders, and gathered up her disheveled hair; a moment, and she was prepared, when a sudden crash was heard below.

"Too late! — fool that I was, too late!" cried Zanoni, in a sharp tone of agony, as he hurried to the door. He opened it, only to be borne back by the press of armed men. The room literally swarmed with the followers of the ravisher, masked, and armed to the teeth.

Viola was already in the grasp of two of the myrmidons. Her shriek smote the ear of Zanoni. He sprang forward; and Viola heard his wild cry in a foreign tongue. She saw the blades of the ruffians pointed at his breast! She lost her senses; and when she recovered, she found herself gagged, and in a carriage that was driven rapidly, by the side of a masked and motionless figure. The carriage stopped at the portals of a gloomy mansion. The gates opened noiselessly; a broad flight of steps, brilliantly illumined, was before her. She was in the palace of the Prince di ——.

Chapter 3.XIV.

Ma lasciamo, per Dio, Signore, ormai
Di parlar d' ira, e di cantar di morte.*
"Orlando Furioso," Canto xvii. xvii.

*T*he young actress was led to, and left alone in a chamber adorned with all the luxurious and half-Eastern taste that at one time characterized the palaces of the great seigneurs of Italy. Her first thought was for Zanoni. Was he yet living? Had he escaped unscathed the blades of the foe, — her new treasure, the new light of her life, her lord, at last her lover?

She had short time for reflection. She heard steps approaching the chamber; she drew back, but trembled not. A courage not of herself, never known before, sparkled in her eyes, and dilated her stature. Living or dead, she would be faithful still to Zanoni! There was a new motive to the preservation of honor. The door opened, and the prince entered in the gorgeous and gaudy custume still worn at that time in Naples.

---

* But leave me, I solemnly conjure thee, signor, to speak of wrath, and to sing of death.

"Fair and cruel one," said he, advancing with a half-sneer upon his lip, "thou wilt not too harshly blame the violence of love." He attempted to take her hand as he spoke.

"Nay," said he, as she recoiled, "reflect that thou art now in the power of one that never faltered in the pursuit of an object less dear to him than thou art. Thy lover, presumptuous though he be, is not by to save thee. Mine thou art; but instead of thy master, suffer me to be thy slave."

"Prince," said Viola, with a stern gravity, "your boast is in vain. Your power! I am *not* in your power. Life and death are in my own hands. I will not defy; but I do not fear you. I feel — and in some feelings," added Viola, with a solemnity almost thrilling, "there is all the strength, and all the divinity of knowledge — I feel that I am safe even here; but you — you, Prince di ——, have brought danger to your home and hearth!"

The Neapolitan seemed startled by an earnestness and boldness he was but little prepared for. He was not, however, a man easily intimidated or deterred from any purpose he had formed; and, approaching Viola, he was about to reply with much warmth, real or affected, when a knock was heard at the door of the chamber. The sound was repeated, and the prince, chafed at the interruption, opened the door and demanded impatiently who had ventured to disobey his orders, and invade his leisure. Mascari presented himself, pale and agitated: "My lord," said he, in a whisper, "pardon me; but a stranger is below, who insists on seeing you; and, from some words he let fall, I judged it advisable even to infringe your commands."

"A stranger! — And at this hour! What business can he pretend? Why was he even admitted?"

"He asserts that your life is in imminent danger. The source whence it proceeds he will relate to your Excellency alone."

The prince frowned; but his color changed. He mused a moment, and then, reentering the chamber and advancing towards Viola, he said, —

"Believe me, fair creature, I have no wish to take advantage of my power. I would fain trust alone to the gentler authorities of affection. Hold yourself queen within these walls more absolutely than you have ever enacted that part on the stage. Tonight, farewell! May your sleep be calm, and your dreams propitious to my hopes."

With these words he retired, and in a few moments Viola was surrounded by officious attendants, whom she at length, with some difficulty, dismissed; and, refusing to retire to rest, she spent the night in examining the chamber, which she found was secured, and in thoughts of Zanoni, in whose power she felt an almost preternatural confidence.

Meanwhile the prince descended the stairs and sought the room into which the stranger had been shown.

He found the visitor wrapped from head to foot in a long robe, half-gown, half-mantle, such as was sometimes worn by ecclesiastics. The face of this stranger was remarkable. So sunburned and swarthy were his hues, that he must, apparently, have derived his origin amongst the races of the farthest East. His forehead was lofty, and his eyes so penetrating yet so calm in their gaze that the prince shrank from them as we shrink from a questioner who is drawing forth the guiltiest secret of our hearts.

"What would you with me?" asked the prince, motioning his visitor to a seat.

"Prince of ——," said the stranger, in a voice deep and sweet, but foreign in its accent, — "son of the most energetic and masculine race that ever applied godlike genius to the service of Human Will, with its winding wickedness and its stubborn grandeur; descendant of the great Visconti in whose chronicles lies the history of Italy in her palmy day, and in whose rise was the development of the mightiest intellect, ripened by the most restless ambition, — I come to gaze upon the last star in a darkening firmament. By this hour tomorrow space shall know it not. Man, unless thy whole nature change, thy days are numbered!"

"What means this jargon?" said the prince, in visible astonishment and secret awe. "Comest thou to menace me in my own halls, or wouldst thou warn me of a danger? Art thou some itinerant mountebank, or some unguessed-of friend? Speak out, and plainly. What danger threatens me?"

"Zanoni and thy ancestor's sword," replied the stranger.

"Ha! Ha!" said the prince, laughing scornfully; "I half-suspected thee from the first. Thou art then the accomplice or the tool of that most dexterous, but, at present, defeated charlatan? And I suppose thou wilt tell me that if I were to release a certain captive I have made, the danger would vanish, and the hand of the dial would be put back?"

"Judge of me as thou wilt, Prince di ——. I confess my knowledge of Zanoni. Thou, too, wilt know his power, but not till it consume thee. I would save, therefore I warn thee. Dost thou ask me why? I will tell thee. Canst thou remember to have heard wild tales of thy grandsire; of his desire for a knowledge that passes that of the schools and cloisters; of a strange man from the East who was his familiar and master in lore against which the Vatican has, from age to age, launched its mimic thunder? Dost thou call to mind the fortunes of thy ancestor? — How he succeeded in youth to little but a name; how, after a career wild and dissolute as thine, he disappeared from Milan, a pauper, and a self-exile; how, after years spent, none knew in what climes or in what pursuits, he again revisited the city where his progenitors had reigned; how with him came the wise man of the East, the mystic Mejnour; how they who beheld him, beheld with amaze and fear that time had ploughed no furrow on his brow; that youth seemed fixed, as by a spell, upon his face and form? Dost thou not know that from that hour his fortunes rose? Kinsmen the most remote died; estate upon estate fell into the hands of the ruined noble. He became the guide of princes, the first magnate of Italy. He founded anew the house of which thou art the last lineal upholder, and transferred his splendor from Milan to the Sicilian realms. Visions of high ambition were then present with him nightly and daily. Had he lived, Italy would have known a new dynasty, and the Visconti would have reigned over Magna-Graecia. He was a man such as the world rarely sees; but his ends, too earthly, were at war with the means he sought. Had his ambition been more or less, he had been worthy of a realm mightier than the Caesars swayed; worthy of our solemn order; worthy of the fellowship of Mejnour, whom you now behold before you."

The prince, who had listened with deep and breathless attention to the words of his singular guest, started from his seat at his last words. "Imposter!" he cried, "can you dare thus to play with my credulity? Sixty years have flown since my grandsire died; were he living, he had passed his hundred and twentieth year; and you, whose old age is erect and vigorous, have the assurance to pretend to have been his contemporary! But you have imperfectly learned your tale. You know not, it seems, that my grandsire, wise and illustrious indeed, in all save his faith in a charlatan, was found dead in his bed, in the very hour when his colossal plans were ripe for execution, and that Mejnour was guilty of his murder."

"Alas!" answered the stranger, in a voice of great sadness, "had he but listened to Mejnour, — had he but delayed the last and most perilous ordeal of daring wisdom until the requisite training and initiation had been completed, — your ancestor would have stood with me upon an eminence which the waters of Death itself wash everlastingly, but cannot overflow. Your grandsire resisted my fervent prayers, disobeyed my most absolute commands, and in the sublime rashness of a soul that panted for secrets, which he who desires orbs and scepters never can obtain, perished, the victim of his own frenzy."

"He was poisoned, and Mejnour fled."

"Mejnour fled not," answered the stranger, proudly — "Mejnour could not fly from danger; for to him danger is a thing long left behind. It was the day before the duke took the fatal draft which he believed was to confer on the mortal the immortal boon, that, finding my power over him was gone, I abandoned him to his doom. But a truce with this: I loved your grandsire! I would save the last of his race. Oppose not thyself to Zanoni. Yield not thy soul to thine evil passions. Draw back from the precipice while there is yet time. In thy front, and in thine eyes, I detect some of that diviner glory which belonged to thy race. Thou hast in thee some germs of their hereditary genius, but they are choked up by worse than thy hereditary vices. Recollect that by genius thy house rose; by vice it ever failed to perpetuate its power. In the laws which regulate the universe, it is decreed that nothing wicked can long endure. Be wise, and let history warn thee. Thou standest on the verge of two worlds, the past and the future; and voices from either shriek omen in thy ear. I have done. I bid thee farewell!"

"Not so; thou shalt not quit these walls. I will make experiment of thy boasted power. What, ho there! — ho!"

The prince shouted; the room was filled with his minions.

"Seize that man!" he cried, pointing to the spot which had been filled by the form of Mejnour. To his inconceivable amaze and horror, the spot was vacant. The mysterious stranger had vanished like a dream; but a thin and fragrant mist undulated, in pale volumes, round the walls of the chamber. "Look to my lord," cried Mascari. The prince had fallen to the floor insensible. For many hours he seemed in a kind of trance. When he recovered, he dismissed his attendants, and his step was heard in his chamber, pacing to and fro, with heavy and disordered strides. Not till an hour before his banquet the next day did he seem restored to his wonted self.

Chapter 3.XV.

Oime! come poss' io
Altri trovar, se me trovar non posso.*

"Amint.," At. i. Sc. ii.

*T*he sleep of Glyndon, the night after his last interview with Zanoni, was unusually profound; and the sun streamed full upon his eyes as he opened them to the day. He rose refreshed, and with a strange sentiment

---

* Alas! how can I find another when I cannot find myself?

of calmness that seemed more the result of resolution than exhaustion. The incidents and emotions of the past night had settled into distinct and clear impressions. He thought of them but slightly, — he thought rather of the future. He was as one of the initiated in the old Egyptian mysteries who have crossed the gate only to long more ardently for the penetralia.

He dressed himself, and was relieved to find that Mervale had joined a party of his countrymen on an excursion to Ischia. He spent the heat of noon in thoughtful solitude, and gradually the image of Viola returned to his heart. It was a holy — for it was a *human* — image. He had resigned her; and though he repented not, he was troubled at the thought that repentance would have come too late.

He started impatiently from his seat, and strode with rapid steps to the humble abode of the actress.

The distance was considerable, and the air oppressive. Glyndon arrived at the door breathless and heated. He knocked; no answer came. He lifted the latch and entered. He ascended the stairs; no sound, no sight of life met his ear and eye. In the front chamber, on a table, lay the guitar of the actress, and some manuscript parts in the favorite operas. He paused, and, summoning courage, tapped at the door which seemed to lead into the inner apartment. The door was ajar; and, hearing no sound within, he pushed it open. It was the sleeping-chamber of the young actress, that holiest ground to a lover; and well did the place become the presiding deity: none of the tawdry finery of the profession was visible, on the one hand; none of the slovenly disorder common to the humbler classes of the South, on the other. All was pure and simple; even the ornaments were those of an innocent refinement, — a few books, placed carefully on shelves, a few half-faded flowers in an earthen vase, which was modeled and painted in the Etruscan fashion. The sunlight streamed over the snowy draperies of the bed, and a few articles of clothing on the chair beside it. Viola was not there; but the nurse! — was she gone also? He made the house resound with the name of Gionetta, but there was not even an echo to reply. At last, as he reluctantly quitted the desolate abode, he perceived Gionetta coming towards him from the street.

The poor old woman uttered an exclamation of joy on seeing him; but, to their mutual disappointment, neither had any cheerful tidings or satisfactory explanation to afford the other. Gionetta had been aroused from her slumber the night before by the noise in the rooms below; but ere she could muster courage to descend, Viola was gone! She found the marks of violence on the door without; and all she had since been able to learn in the neighborhood was, that a Lazzarone, from his nocturnal resting-place on the Chiaja, had seen by the moonlight a carriage, which he recognized as belonging to the Prince di ——, pass and repass that road about the first hour of morning. Glyndon, on gathering from the confused words and broken sobs of the old nurse the heads of this account, abruptly left her, and repaired to the palace of Zanoni. There he was informed that the signor was gone to the banquet of the Prince di ——, and would not return till late. Glyndon stood motionless with perplexity and dismay; he knew not what to believe, or how to act. Even Mervale was not at hand to advise him. His conscience smote him bitterly. He had had the power to save the woman he had loved, and had foregone that power; but how was it that in this Zanoni himself had failed? How was it that he was gone to the very banquet of the ravisher? Could Zanoni be aware of what had passed? If not, should he lose a moment in apprising him? Though mentally irresolute, no man was more physically brave. He would repair at once to the palace of the prince himself; and if Zanoni failed in the trust he had half-appeared to arrogate, he, the humble foreigner, would demand the captive of fraud and force, in the very halls and before the assembled guests of the Prince di ——.

Chapter 3.XVI.

Ardua vallatur duris sapientia scrupis.*
Hadr. Jun., "Emblem." xxxvii.

We must go back some hours in the progress of this narrative. It was the first faint and gradual break of the summer dawn; and two men stood in a balcony overhanging a garden fragrant with the scents of the awakening flowers. The stars had not yet left the sky, — the birds were yet silent on the boughs: all was still, hushed, and tranquil; but how different the tranquility of reviving day from the solemn repose of night! In the music of silence there are a thousand variations. These men, who

---

* Lofty wisdom is circled round with rugged rocks.

alone seemed awake in Naples, were Zanoni and the mysterious stranger who had but an hour or two ago startled the Prince di —— in his voluptuous palace.

"No," said the latter; "hadst thou delayed the acceptance of the Arch-gift until thou hadst attained to the years, and passed through all the desolate bereavements that chilled and seared myself ere my researches had made it mine, thou wouldst have escaped the curse of which thou complainest now, — thou wouldst not have mourned over the brevity of human affection as compared to the duration of thine own existence; for thou wouldst have survived the very desire and dream of the love of woman. Brightest, and, but for that error, perhaps the loftiest, of the secret and solemn race that fills up the interval in creation between mankind and the children of the Empyreal, age after age wilt thou rue the splendid folly which made thee ask to carry the beauty and the passions of youth into the dreary grandeur of earthly immortality."

"I do not repent, nor shall I," answered Zanoni. "The transport and the sorrow, so wildly blended, which have at intervals diversified my doom, are better than the calm and bloodless tenor of thy solitary way — thou, who lovest nothing, hatest nothing, feelest nothing, and walkest the world with the noiseless and joyless footsteps of a dream!"

"You mistake," replied he who had owned the name of Mejnour, — "though I care not for love, and am dead to every *passion* that agitates the sons of clay, I am not dead to their more serene enjoyments. I carry down the stream of the countless years, not the turbulent desires of youth, but the calm and spiritual delights of age. Wisely and deliberately I abandoned youth forever when I separated my lot from men. Let us not envy or reproach each other. I would have saved this Neapolitan, Zanoni (since so it now pleases thee to be called), partly because his grandsire was but divided by the last airy barrier from our own brotherhood, partly because I know that in the man himself lurk the elements of ancestral courage and power, which in earlier life would have fitted him for one of us. Earth holds but few to whom Nature has given the qualities that can bear the ordeal. But time and excess, that have quickened his grosser senses, have blunted his imagination. I relinquish him to his doom."

"And still, then, Mejnour, you cherish the desire to revive our order, limited now to ourselves alone, by new converts and allies. Surely — surely — thy experience might have taught thee, that scarcely once in a thousand years is born the being who can pass through the horrible gates that lead into the worlds without! Is not thy path already strewed with thy victims? Do not their ghastly faces of agony and fear — the blood-stained suicide, the raving maniac — rise before thee, and warn what is yet left to thee of human sympathy from thy insane ambition?"

"Nay," answered Mejnour; "have I not had success to counterbalance failure? And can I forego this lofty and august hope, worthy alone of our high condition, — the hope to form a mighty and numerous race with a force and power sufficient to permit them to acknowledge to mankind their majestic conquests and dominion, to become the true lords of this planet, invaders, perchance, of others, masters of the inimical and malignant tribes by which at this moment we are surrounded: a race that may proceed, in their deathless destinies, from stage to stage of celestial glory, and rank at last amongst the nearest ministrants and agents gathered round the Throne of Thrones? What matter a thousand victims for one convert to our band? And you, Zanoni," continued Mejnour, after a pause, — "you, even you, should this affection for a mortal beauty that you have dared, despite yourself, to cherish, be more than a passing fancy; should it, once admitted into your inmost nature, partake of its bright and enduring essence, — even you may brave all things to raise the beloved one into your equal. Nay, interrupt me not. Can you see sickness menace her; danger hover around; years creep on; the eyes grow dim; the beauty fade, while the heart, youthful still, clings and fastens round your own, — can you see this, and know it is yours to —"

"Cease!" cried Zanoni, fiercely. "What is all other fate as compared to the death of terror? What, when the coldest sage, the most heated enthusiast, the hardiest warrior with his nerves of iron, have been found dead in their beds, with straining eyeballs and horrent hair, at the first step of the Dread Progress, — thinkest thou that this weak woman — from whose cheek a sound at the window, the screech of the night-owl, the sight of a drop of blood on a man's sword, would start the color — could brave one glance of — Away! the very thought of such sights for her makes even myself a coward!"

"When you told her you loved her, — when you clasped her to your breast, you renounced all power to foresee her future lot, or protect her from harm. Henceforth to her you are human, and human only. How know you, then, to what you may be tempted; how know you what her curiosity may learn and her courage brave? But enough of this, — you are bent on your pursuit?"

"The fiat has gone forth."

"And tomorrow?"

"Tomorrow, at this hour, our bark will be bounding over yonder ocean, and the weight of ages will have fallen from my heart! I compassionate thee, O foolish sage, — *thou* hast given up *thy* youth!"

Chapter 3.XVII.

Alch: Thou always speakest riddles. Tell me if thou art that fountain of which Bernard Lord Trevizan writ?
Merc: I am not that fountain, but I am the water. The fountain compasseth me about.

Sandivogius, "New Light of Alchymy"

*T*he Prince di —— was not a man whom Naples could suppose to be addicted to superstitious fancies. Still, in the South of Italy, there was then, and there still lingers a certain spirit of credulity, which may, ever and anon, be visible amidst the boldest dogmas of their philosophers and skeptics. In his childhood, the prince had learned strange tales of the ambition, the genius, and the career of his grandsire, — and secretly, perhaps influenced by ancestral example, in earlier youth he himself had followed science, not only through her legitimate course, but her antiquated and erratic windings. I have, indeed, been shown in Naples a little volume, blazoned with the arms of the Visconti, and ascribed to the nobleman I refer to, which treats of alchemy in a spirit half-mocking and half-reverential.

Pleasure soon distracted him from such speculations, and his talents, which were unquestionably great, were wholly perverted to extravagant intrigues, or to the embellishment of a gorgeous ostentation with something of classic grace. His immense wealth, his imperious pride, his unscrupulous and daring character, made him an object of no inconsiderable fear to a feeble and timid court; and the ministers of the indolent government willingly connived at excesses which allured him at least from ambition. The strange visit and yet more strange departure of Mejnour filled the breast of the Neapolitan with awe and wonder, against which all the haughty arrogance and learned skepticism of his maturer manhood combated in vain. The apparition of Mejnour served, indeed, to invest Zanoni with a character in which the prince had not hitherto regarded him. He felt a strange alarm at the rival he had braved,

— at the foe he had provoked. When, a little before his banquet, he had resumed his self-possession, it was with a fell and gloomy resolution that he brooded over the perfidious schemes he had previously formed. He felt as if the death of the mysterious Zanoni were necessary for the preservation of his own life; and if at an earlier period of their rivalry he had determined on the fate of Zanoni, the warnings of Mejnour only served to confirm his resolve.

"We will try if his magic can invent an antidote to the bane," said he, half-aloud, and with a stern smile, as he summoned Mascari to his presence. The poison which the prince, with his own hands, mixed into the wine intended for his guest, was compounded from materials, the secret of which had been one of the proudest heirlooms of that able and evil race which gave to Italy her wisest and guiltiest tyrants. Its operation was quick yet not sudden: it produced no pain, — it left on the form no grim convulsion, on the skin no purpling spot, to arouse suspicion; you might have cut and carved every membrane and fiber of the corpse, but the sharpest eyes of the leech would not have detected the presence of the subtle life-queller. For twelve hours the victim felt nothing save a joyous and elated exhilaration of the blood; a delicious languor followed, the sure forerunner of apoplexy. No lancet then could save! Apoplexy had run much in the families of the enemies of the Visconti!

The hour of the feast arrived, — the guests assembled. There were the flower of the Neapolitan seignorie, the descendants of the Norman, the Teuton, the Goth; for Naples had then a nobility, but derived it from the North, which has indeed been the Nutrix Leonum, — the nurse of the lion-hearted chivalry of the world.

Last of the guests came Zanoni; and the crowd gave way as the dazzling foreigner moved along to the lord of the palace. The prince greeted him with a meaning smile, to which Zanoni answered by a whisper, "He who plays with loaded dice does not always win."

The prince bit his lip, and Zanoni, passing on, seemed deep in conversation with the fawning Mascari.

"Who is the prince's heir?" asked the guest.

"A distant relation on the mother's side; with his Excellency dies the male line."

"Is the heir present at our host's banquet?"

"No; they are not friends."

"No matter; he will be here tomorrow."

Mascari stared in surprise; but the signal for the banquet was given, and the guests were marshaled to the board. As was the custom then, the feast took place not long after mid-day. It was a long, oval hall, the whole of one side opening by a marble colonnade upon a court or garden, in which the eye rested gratefully upon cool fountains and

statues of whitest marble, half-sheltered by orange trees. Every art that
luxury could invent to give freshness and coolness to the languid and
breezeless heat of the day without (a day on which the breath of the
sirocco was abroad) had been called into existence. Artificial currents of
air through invisible tubes, silken blinds waving to and fro, as if to cheat
the senses into the belief of an April wind, and miniature jets d'eau in
each corner of the apartment, gave to the Italians the same sense of
exhilaration and *comfort* (if I may use the word) which the well-drawn
curtains and the blazing hearth afford to the children of colder climes.

The conversation was somewhat more lively and intellectual than is
common amongst the languid pleasure-hunters of the South; for the
prince, himself accomplished, sought his acquaintance not only
amongst the beaux esprits of his own country, but amongst the gay
foreigners who adorned and relieved the monotony of the Neapolitan
circles. There were present two or three of the brilliant Frenchmen of
the old regime, who had already emigrated from the advancing Revolution; and their peculiar turn of thought and wit was well calculated for
the meridian of a society that made the dolce far niente at once its
philosophy and its faith. The prince, however, was more silent than
usual; and when he sought to rouse himself, his spirits were forced and
exaggerated. To the manners of his host, those of Zanoni afforded a
striking contrast. The bearing of this singular person was at all times
characterized by a calm and polished ease, which was attributed by the
courtiers to the long habit of society. He could scarcely be called gay;
yet few persons more tended to animate the general spirits of a convivial
circle. He seemed, by a kind of intuition, to elicit from each companion
the qualities in which he most excelled; and if occasionally a certain
tone of latent mockery characterized his remarks upon the topics on
which the conversation fell, it appeared to men who took nothing in
earnest to be the language both of wit and wisdom. To the Frenchmen,
in particular, there was something startling in his intimate knowledge
of the minutest events in their own capital and country, and his
profound penetration (evinced but in epigrams and sarcasms) into the
eminent characters who were then playing a part upon the great stage
of continental intrigue.

It was while this conversation grew animated, and the feast was at its
height, that Glyndon arrived at the palace. The porter, perceiving by his
dress that he was not one of the invited guests, told him that his
Excellency was engaged, and on no account could be disturbed; and
Glyndon then, for the first time, became aware how strange and embar-
rassing was the duty he had taken on himself. To force an entrance into
the banquet-hall of a great and powerful noble, surrounded by the rank
of Naples, and to arraign him for what to his boon-companions would

appear but an act of gallantry, was an exploit that could not fail to be at once ludicrous and impotent. He mused a moment, and, slipping a piece of gold into the porter's hand, said that he was commissioned to seek the Signor Zanoni upon an errand of life and death, and easily won his way across the court, and into the interior building. He passed up the broad staircase, and the voices and merriment of the revelers smote his ear at a distance. At the entrance of the reception-rooms he found a page, whom he dispatched with a message to Zanoni. The page did the errand; and Zanoni, on hearing the whispered name of Glyndon, turned to his host.

"Pardon me, my lord; an English friend of mine, the Signor Glyndon (not unknown by name to your Excellency) waits without, — the business must indeed be urgent on which he has sought me in such an hour. You will forgive my momentary absence."

"Nay, signor," answered the prince, courteously, but with a sinister smile on his countenance, "would it not be better for your friend to join us? An Englishman is welcome everywhere; and even were he a Dutchman, your friendship would invest his presence with attraction. Pray his attendance; we would not spare you even for a moment."

Zanoni bowed; the page was dispatched with all flattering messages to Glyndon, — a seat next to Zanoni was placed for him, and the young Englishman entered.

"You are most welcome, sir. I trust your business to our illustrious guest is of good omen and pleasant import. If you bring evil news, defer it, I pray you."

Glyndon's brow was sullen; and he was about to startle the guests by his reply, when Zanoni, touching his arm significantly, whispered in English, "I know why you have sought me. Be silent, and witness what ensues."

"You know then that Viola, whom you boasted you had the power to save from danger —"

"Is in this house! — yes. I know also that Murder sits at the right hand of our host. But his fate is now separated from hers forever; and the mirror which glasses it to my eye is clear through the streams of blood. Be still, and learn the fate that awaits the wicked!"

"My lord," said Zanoni, speaking aloud, "the Signor Glyndon has indeed brought me tidings not wholly unexpected. I am compelled to leave Naples, — an additional motive to make the most of the present hour."

"And what, if I may venture to ask, may be the cause that brings such affliction on the fair dames of Naples?"

"It is the approaching death of one who honored me with most loyal friendship," replied Zanoni, gravely. "Let us not speak of it; grief cannot put back the dial. As we supply by new flowers those that fade in our vases, so it is the secret of worldly wisdom to replace by fresh friendships those that fade from our path."

"True philosophy!" exclaimed the prince. "'Not to admire,' was the Roman's maxim; 'Never to mourn,' is mine. There is nothing in life to grieve for, save, indeed, Signor Zanoni, when some young beauty, on whom we have set our hearts, slips from our grasp. In such a moment we have need of all our wisdom, not to succumb to despair, and shake hands with death. What say you, signor? You smile! Such never could be your lot. Pledge me in a sentiment, 'Long life to the fortunate lover, — a quick release to the baffled suitor'?"

"I pledge you," said Zanoni; and, as the fatal wine was poured into his glass, he repeated, fixing his eyes on the prince, "I pledge you even in this wine!"

He lifted the glass to his lips. The prince seemed ghastly pale, while the gaze of his guest bent upon him, with an intent and stern brightness, beneath which the conscience-stricken host cowered and quailed. Not till he had drained his draft, and replaced the glass upon the board, did Zanoni turn his eyes from the prince; and he then said, "Your wine has been kept too long; it has lost its virtues. It might disagree with many, but do not fear: it will not harm me, prince, Signor Mascari, you are a judge of the grape; will you favor us with your opinion?"

"Nay," answered Mascari, with well-affected composure, "I like not the wines of Cyprus; they are heating. Perhaps Signor Glyndon may not have the same distaste? The English are said to love their potations warm and pungent."

"Do you wish my friend also to taste the wine, prince?" said Zanoni. "Recollect, all cannot drink it with the same impunity as myself."

"No," said the prince, hastily; "if you do not recommend the wine, Heaven forbid that we should constrain our guests! My lord duke," turning to one of the Frenchmen, "yours is the true soil of Bacchus. What think you of this cask from Burgundy? Has it borne the journey?"

"Ah," said Zanoni, "let us change both the wine and the theme."

With that, Zanoni grew yet more animated and brilliant. Never did wit more sparkling, airy, exhilarating, flash from the lips of reveler. His spirits fascinated all present — even the prince himself, even Glyndon — with a strange and wild contagion. The former, indeed, whom the words and gaze of Zanoni, when he drained the poison, had filled with fearful misgivings, now hailed in the brilliant eloquence of his wit a certain sign of the operation of the bane. The wine circulated fast; but none seemed conscious of its effects. One by one the rest of the party fell into a charmed and spellbound silence, as Zanoni continued to pour forth sally upon sally, tale upon tale. They hung on his words, they almost held their breath to listen. Yet, how bitter was his mirth; how full of contempt for the triflers present, and for the trifles which made their life!

Night came on; the room grew dim, and the feast had lasted several hours longer than was the customary duration of similar entertainments at that day. Still the guests stirred not, and still Zanoni continued, with glittering eye and mocking lip, to lavish his stores of intellect and anecdote; when suddenly the moon rose, and shed its rays over the flowers and fountains in the court without, leaving the room itself half in shadow, and half tinged by a quiet and ghostly light.

It was then that Zanoni rose. "Well, gentlemen," said he, "we have not yet wearied our host, I hope; and his garden offers a new temptation to protract our stay. Have you no musicians among your train, prince, that might regale our ears while we inhale the fragrance of your orange trees?"

"An excellent thought!" said the prince. "Mascari, see to the music."

The party rose simultaneously to adjourn to the garden; and then, for the first time, the effect of the wine they had drunk seemed to make itself felt.

With flushed cheeks and unsteady steps they came into the open air, which tended yet more to stimulate that glowing fever of the grape. As if to make up for the silence with which the guests had hitherto listened to Zanoni, every tongue was now loosened, — every man talked, no man listened. There was something wild and fearful in the contrast between the calm beauty of the night and scene, and the hubbub and clamor of these disorderly roisters. One of the Frenchmen, in especial, the young Duc de R——, a nobleman of the highest rank, and of all the quick, vivacious, and irascible temperament of his countrymen, was particularly noisy and excited. And as circumstances, the remembrance of which is still preserved among certain circles of Naples, rendered it afterwards necessary that the duc should himself give evidence of what occurred, I will here translate the short account he drew up, and which was kindly submitted to me some few years ago by my accomplished and lively friend, Il Cavaliere di B——.

"I never remember," writes the duc, "to have felt my spirits so excited as on that evening; we were like so many boys released from school, jostling each other as we reeled or ran down the flight of seven or eight stairs that led from the colonnade into the garden, — some laughing, some whooping, some scolding, some babbling. The wine had brought out, as it were, each man's inmost character. Some were loud and quarrelsome, others sentimental and whining; some, whom we had hitherto thought dull, most mirthful; some, whom we had ever regarded as discreet and taciturn, most garrulous and uproarious. I remember that in the midst of our clamorous gayety, my eye fell upon the cavalier Signor Zanoni, whose conversation had so enchanted us all; and I felt a certain chill come over me to perceive that he wore the same calm and unsympathizing smile upon his countenance which had characterized it in his singular and curious stories of the court of Louis XIV. I felt, indeed, half-inclined to seek a quarrel with one whose composure was almost an insult to our disorder. Nor was such an effect of this irritating and mocking tranquility confined to myself alone. Several of the party have told me since, that on looking at Zanoni they felt their blood yet more heated, and gayety change to resentment. There seemed in his icy smile a very charm to wound vanity and provoke rage. It was at this moment that the prince came up to me, and, passing his arm into mine, led me a little apart from the rest. He had certainly indulged in the same excess as ourselves, but it did not produce the same effect of noisy excitement. There was, on the contrary, a certain cold arrogance and supercilious scorn in his bearing and language, which, even while affecting so much caressing courtesy towards me, roused my self-love against him. He seemed as if Zanoni had infected him; and in imitating the manner of his guest, he surpassed the original. He rallied me on some court gossip, which had honored my name by associating it with a certain beautiful and distinguished Sicilian lady, and affected to treat with contempt that which, had it been true, I should have regarded as a boast. He spoke, indeed, as if he himself had gathered all the flowers of Naples, and left us foreigners only the gleanings he had scorned. At this my natural and national gallantry was piqued, and I retorted by some sarcasms that I should certainly have spared had my blood been cooler. He laughed heartily, and left me in a strange fit of resentment and anger. Perhaps (I must own the truth) the wine had produced in me a wild disposition to take offence and provoke quarrel. As the prince left me, I turned, and saw Zanoni at my side.

"'The prince is a braggart,' said he, with the same smile that displeased me before. 'He would monopolize all fortune and all love. Let us take our revenge.'

"'And how?'

"'He has at this moment, in his house, the most enchanting singer in Naples, — the celebrated Viola Pisani. She is here, it is true, not by her own choice; he carried her hither by force, but he will pretend that she adores him. Let us insist on his producing this secret treasure, and when she enters, the Duc de R—— can have no doubt that his flatteries and attentions will charm the lady, and provoke all the jealous fears of our host. It would be a fair revenge upon his imperious self-conceit.'

"This suggestion delighted me. I hastened to the prince. At that instant the musicians had just commenced; I waved my hand, ordered the music to stop, and, addressing the prince, who was standing in the center of one of the gayest groups, complained of his want of hospitality in affording to us such poor proficients in the art, while he reserved for his own solace the lute and voice of the first performer in Naples. I demanded, half-laughingly, half-seriously, that he should produce the Pisani. My demand was received with shouts of applause by the rest. We drowned the replies of our host with uproar, and would hear no denial. 'Gentlemen,' at last said the prince, when he could obtain an audience, 'even were I to assent to your proposal, I could not induce the signora to present herself before an assemblage as riotous as they are noble. You have too much chivalry to use compulsion with her, though the Duc de R—— forgets himself sufficiently to administer it to me.'

"I was stung by this taunt, however well deserved. 'Prince,' said I, 'I have for the indelicacy of compulsion so illustrious an example that I cannot hesitate to pursue the path honored by your own footsteps. All Naples knows that the Pisani despises at once your gold and your love; that force alone could have brought her under your roof; and that you refuse to produce her, because you fear her complaints, and know enough of the chivalry your vanity sneers at to feel assured that the gentlemen of France are not more disposed to worship beauty than to defend it from wrong.'

"'You speak well, sir,' said Zanoni, gravely. 'The prince dares not produce his prize!'

"The prince remained speechless for a few moments, as if with indignation. At last he broke out into expressions the most injurious and insulting against Signor Zanoni and myself. Zanoni replied not; I was more hot and hasty. The guests appeared to delight in our dispute. None, except Mascari, whom we pushed aside and disdained to hear, strove to conciliate; some took one side, some another. The issue may be well foreseen. Swords were called for and procured. Two were offered me by one of the party. I was about to choose one, when Zanoni placed in my hand the other, which, from its hilt, appeared of antiquated workmanship. At the same moment, looking towards the prince, he said, smilingly, 'The duc takes your grandsire's sword. Prince, you are too brave a man for superstition; you have forgot the forfeit!' Our host seemed to me to recoil and turn pale at those words; nevertheless, he returned Zanoni's smile with a look of defiance. The next moment all was broil and disorder. There might be some six or eight persons engaged in a strange and confused kind of melee, but the prince and myself only sought each other. The noise around us, the confusion of the guests, the cries of the musicians, the clash of our own swords, only served to stimulate our unhappy fury. We feared to be interrupted by the atten-dants, and fought like madmen, without skill or method. I thrust and parried mechanically, blind and frantic, as if a demon had entered into me, till I saw the prince stretched at my feet, bathed in his blood, and Zanoni bending over him, and whispering in his ear. That sight cooled us all. The strife ceased; we gathered, in shame, remorse, and horror, round our ill-fated host; but it was too late, — his eyes rolled fearfully in his head. I have seen many men die, but never one who wore such horror on his countenance. At last all was over! Zanoni rose from the corpse, and, taking, with great composure, the sword from my hand, said calmly, 'Ye are witnesses, gentlemen, that the prince brought his fate upon himself. The last of that illustrious house has perished in a brawl.'

"I saw no more of Zanoni. I hastened to our envoy to narrate the event, and abide the issue. I am grateful to the Neapolitan government, and to the illustrious heir of the unfortunate nobleman, for the lenient and generous, yet just, interpretation put upon a misfortune the memory of which will afflict me to the last hour of my life.

(Signed) "Louis Victor, Duc de R."

In the above memorial, the reader will find the most exact and minute account yet given of an event which created the most lively sensation at Naples in that day.

Glyndon had taken no part in the affray, neither had he participated largely in the excesses of the revel. For his exemption from both he was perhaps indebted to the whispered exhortations of Zanoni. When the last rose from the corpse, and withdrew from that scene of confusion, Glyndon remarked that in passing the crowd he touched Mascari on the shoulder, and said something which the Englishman did not overhear. Glyndon followed Zanoni into the banquet room, which, save where the moonlight slept on the marble floor, was wrapped in the sad and gloomy shadows of the advancing night.

"How could you foretell this fearful event? He fell not by your arm!" said Glyndon, in a tremulous and hollow tone.

"The general who calculates on the victory does not fight in person," answered Zanoni; "let the past sleep with the dead. Meet me at midnight by the seashore, half a mile to the left of your hotel. You will know the spot by a rude pillar — the only one near — to which a broken chain is attached. There and then, if thou wouldst learn our lore, thou shalt find the master. Go; I have business here yet. Remember, Viola is still in the house of the dead man!"

Here Mascari approached, and Zanoni, turning to the Italian, and waving his hand to Glyndon, drew the former aside. Glyndon slowly departed.

"Mascari," said Zanoni, "your patron is no more; your services will be valueless to his heir, — a sober man whom poverty has preserved from vice. For yourself, thank me that I do not give you up to the executioner; recollect the wine of Cyprus. Well, never tremble, man; it could not act on me, though it might react on others; in that it is a common type of crime. I forgive you; and if the wine should kill me, I promise you that my ghost shall not haunt so worshipful a penitent. Enough of this; conduct me to the chamber of Viola Pisani. You have no further need of her. The death of the jailer opens the cell of the captive. Be quick; I would be gone."

Mascari muttered some inaudible words, bowed low, and led the way to the chamber in which Viola was confined.

Chapter 3.XVIII.

Merc: Tell me, therefore, what thou seekest after, and what thou wilt have. What dost thou desire to make?
Alch: The Philosopher's Stone.

Sandivogius

*I*t wanted several minutes of midnight, and Glyndon repaired to the appointed spot. The mysterious empire which Zanoni had acquired over him, was still more solemnly confirmed by the events of the last few hours; the sudden fate of the prince, so deliberately foreshadowed, and yet so seemingly accidental, brought out by causes the most commonplace, and yet associated with words the most prophetic, impressed him with the deepest sentiments of admiration and awe. It was as if this dark and wondrous being could convert the most ordinary events and the meanest instruments into the agencies of his inscrutable will; yet, if so, why have permitted the capture of Viola? Why not have prevented the crime rather than punish the criminal? And did Zanoni really feel love for Viola? Love, and yet offer to resign her to himself, — to a rival whom his arts could not have failed to baffle. He no longer reverted to the belief that Zanoni or Viola had sought to dupe him into marriage. His fear and reverence for the former now forbade the notion of so poor an imposture. Did he any longer love Viola himself? No; when that morning he had heard of her danger, he had, it is true, returned to the sympathies and the fears of affection; but with the death of the prince her image faded from his heart, and he felt no jealous pang at the thought that she had been saved by Zanoni, — that at that moment she was perhaps beneath his roof. Whoever has, in the course of his life, indulged the absorbing passion of the gamester, will remember how all other pursuits and objects vanished from his mind; how solely he was wrapped in the one wild delusion; with what a scepter of magic power the despot-demon ruled every feeling and every thought. Far more intense than the passion of the gamester was the frantic yet sublime desire that mastered the breast of Glyndon. He would be the rival of Zanoni, not in human and perishable affections, but in preternatural and eternal lore. He would have laid down life with content — nay, rapture — as the price of learning those solemn secrets which separated the stranger from mankind. Enamored of the goddess of goddesses, he stretched forth his arms — the wild Ixion — and embraced a cloud!

The night was most lovely and serene, and the waves scarcely rippled at his feet as the Englishman glided on by the cool and starry beach. At length he arrived at the spot, and there, leaning against the broken pillar, he beheld a man wrapped in a long mantle, and in an attitude of profound repose. He approached, and uttered the name of Zanoni. The figure turned, and he saw the face of a stranger: a face not stamped by the glorious beauty of Zanoni, but equally majestic in its aspect, and perhaps still more impressive from the mature age and the passionless depth of thought that characterized the expanded forehead, and deep-set but piercing eyes.

"You seek Zanoni," said the stranger; "he will be here anon; but, perhaps, he whom you see before you is more connected with your destiny, and more disposed to realize your dreams."

"Hath the earth, then, another Zanoni?"

"If not," replied the stranger, "why do you cherish the hope and the wild faith to be yourself a Zanoni? Think you that none others have burned with the same godlike dream? Who, indeed in his first youth, — youth when the soul is nearer to the heaven from which it sprang, and its divine and primal longings are not all effaced by the sordid passions and petty cares that are begot in time, — who is there in youth that has not nourished the belief that the universe has secrets not known to the common herd, and panted, as the hart for the water-springs, for the fountains that lie hid and far away amidst the broad wilderness of trackless science? The music of the fountain is heard in the soul *within,* till the steps, deceived and erring, rove away from its waters, and the wanderer dies in the mighty desert. Think you that none who have cherished the hope have found the truth, or that the yearning after the Ineffable Knowledge was given to us utterly in vain? No! Every desire in human hearts is but a glimpse of things that exist, alike distant and divine. No! in the world there have been from age to age some brighter and happier spirits who have attained to the air in which the beings above mankind move and breathe. Zanoni, great though he be, stands not alone. He has had his predecessors, and long lines of successors may be yet to come."

"And will you tell me," said Glyndon, "that in yourself I behold one of that mighty few over whom Zanoni has no superiority in power and wisdom?"

"In me," answered the stranger, "you see one from whom Zanoni himself learned some of his loftiest secrets. On these shores, on this spot, have I stood in ages that your chroniclers but feebly reach. The Phoenician, the Greek, the Oscan, the Roman, the Lombard, I have seen them all! — leaves gay and glittering on the trunk of the universal life, scattered in due season and again renewed; till, indeed, the same race that gave its glory to the ancient world bestowed a second youth upon the new. For the pure Greeks, the Hellenes, whose origin has bewildered your dreaming scholars, were of the same great family as the Norman tribe, born to be the lords of the universe, and in no land on earth destined to become the hewers of wood. Even the dim traditions of the learned, which bring the sons of Hellas from the vast and undetermined territories of Northern Thrace, to be the victors of the pastoral Pelasgi, and the founders of the line of demigods; which assign to a population bronzed beneath the suns of the West, the blue-eyed Minerva and the yellow-haired Achilles (physical characteristics of the North); which introduce, amongst a pastoral people, warlike aristocracies and limited monarchies, the feudalism of the classic time, — even these might serve you to trace back the primeval settlements of the Hellenes to the same region whence, in later times, the Norman warriors broke on the dull and savage hordes of the Celt, and became the Greeks of the Christian world. But this interests you not, and you are wise in your indifference. Not in the knowledge of things without, but in the perfection of the soul within, lies the empire of man aspiring to be more than man."

"And what books contain that science; from what laboratory is it wrought?"

"Nature supplies the materials; they are around you in your daily walks. In the herbs that the beast devours and the chemist disdains to cull; in the elements from which matter in its meanest and its mightiest shapes is deduced; in the wide bosom of the air; in the black abysses of the earth; everywhere are given to mortals the resources and libraries of immortal lore. But as the simplest problems in the simplest of all studies are obscure to one who braces not his mind to their comprehension; as the rower in yonder vessel cannot tell you why two circles can touch each other only in one point, — so though all earth were carved over and inscribed with the letters of diviner knowledge, the characters would be valueless to him who does not pause to inquire the language and meditate the truth. Young man, if thy imagination is vivid, if thy heart is daring, if thy curiosity is insatiate, I will accept thee as my pupil. But the first lessons are stern and dread."

"If thou hast mastered them, why not I?" answered Glyndon, boldly. "I have felt from my boyhood that strange mysteries were reserved for my career; and from the proudest ends of ordinary ambition I have carried my gaze into the cloud and darkness that stretch beyond. The instant I beheld Zanoni, I felt as if I had discovered the guide and the tutor for which my youth had idly languished and vainly burned."

"And to me his duty is transferred," replied the stranger. "Yonder lies, anchored in the bay, the vessel in which Zanoni seeks a fairer home; a little while and the breeze will rise, the sail will swell; and the stranger will have passed, like a wind, away. Still, like the wind, he leaves in thy heart the seeds that may bear the blossom and the fruit. Zanoni hath performed his task, — he is wanted no more; the perfecter of his work is at thy side. He comes! I hear the dash of the oar. You will have your choice submitted to you. According as you decide we shall meet again." With these words the stranger moved slowly away, and disappeared beneath the shadow of the cliffs. A boat glided rapidly across the waters: it touched land; a man leaped on shore, and Glyndon recognized Zanoni.

"I give thee, Glyndon, — I give thee no more the option of happy love and serene enjoyment. That hour is past, and fate has linked the hand that might have been thine own to mine. But I have ample gifts to bestow upon thee, if thou wilt abandon the hope that gnaws thy heart, and the realization of which even *I* have not the power to foresee. Be thine ambition human, and I can gratify it to the full. Men desire four things in life, — love, wealth, fame, power. The first I cannot give thee, the rest are at my disposal. Select which of them thou wilt, and let us part in peace."

"Such are not the gifts I covet. I choose knowledge; that knowledge must be thine own. For this, and for this alone, I surrendered the love of Viola; this, and this alone, must be my recompense."

"I cannot gain say thee, though I can warn. The desire to learn does not always contain the faculty to acquire. I can give thee, it is true, the teacher, — the rest must depend on thee. Be wise in time, and take that which I can assure to thee."

"Answer me but these questions, and according to your answer I will decide. Is it in the power of man to attain intercourse with the beings of other worlds? Is it in the power of man to influence the elements, and to insure life against the sword and against disease?"

"All this may be possible," answered Zanoni, evasively, "to the few; but for one who attains such secrets, millions may perish in the attempt."

"One question more. Thou —"

"Beware! Of myself, as I have said before, I render no account."

"Well, then, the stranger I have met this night, — are his boasts to be believed? Is he in truth one of the chosen seers whom you allow to have mastered the mysteries I yearn to fathom?"

"Rash man," said Zanoni, in a tone of compassion, "thy crisis is past, and thy choice made! I can only bid thee be bold and prosper; yes, I resign thee to a master who *has* the power and the will to open to thee the gates of an awful world. Thy weal or woe are as naught in the eyes of his relentless wisdom. I would bid him spare thee, but he will heed me not. Mejnour, receive thy pupil!" Glyndon turned, and his heart beat when he perceived that the stranger, whose footsteps he had not heard upon the pebbles, whose approach he had not beheld in the moonlight, was once more by his side.

"Farewell," resumed Zanoni; "thy trial commences. When next we meet, thou wilt be the victim or the victor."

Glyndon's eyes followed the receding form of the mysterious stranger. He saw him enter the boat, and he then for the first time noticed that besides the rowers there was a female, who stood up as Zanoni gained the boat. Even at the distance he recognized the once-adored form of Viola. She waved her hand to him, and across the still and shining air came her voice, mournfully and sweetly, in her mother's tongue, "Farewell, Clarence, — I forgive thee! — farewell, farewell!"

He strove to answer; but the voice touched a chord at his heart, and the words failed him. Viola was then lost forever, gone with this dread stranger; darkness was round her lot! And he himself had decided her fate and his own! The boat bounded on, the soft waves flashed and sparkled beneath the oars, and it was along one sapphire track of moonlight that the frail vessel bore away the lovers. Farther and farther from his gaze sped the boat, till at last the speck, scarcely visible, touched the side of the ship that lay lifeless in the glorious bay. At that instant, as if by magic, up sprang, with a glad murmur, the playful and freshening wind: and Glyndon turned to Mejnour and broke the silence.

"Tell me — if thou canst read the future — tell me that *her* lot will be fair, and that *her* choice at least is wise?"

"My pupil!" answered Mejnour, in a voice the calmness of which well accorded with the chilling words, "thy first task must be to withdraw all thought, feeling, sympathy from others. The elementary stage of knowledge is to make self, and self alone, thy study and thy world. Thou hast decided thine own career; thou hast renounced love; thou hast rejected wealth, fame, and the vulgar pomps of power. What, then, are all mankind to thee? To perfect thy faculties, and concentrate thy emotions, is henceforth thy only aim!"

"And will happiness be the end?"

"If happiness exist," answered Mejnour, "it must be centered in a *self* to which all passion is unknown. But happiness is the last state of being; and as yet thou art on the threshold of the first."

As Mejnour spoke, the distant vessel spread its sails to the wind, and moved slowly along the deep. Glyndon sighed, and the pupil and the master retraced their steps towards the city.

BOOK IV

THE DWELLER
OF THE THRESHOLD

Bey hinter ihm was will! Ich heb ihn auf.*
                              "Das Verschleierte Bildzu Sais"

---

*   Be behind what there may, – I raise the veil.

Chapter 4.I.

Come vittima io vengo all' ara.*

"Metast.," At. ii. Sc. 7.

*I*t was about a month after the date of Zanoni's departure and Glyndon's introduction to Mejnour, when two Englishmen were walking, arm-in-arm, through the Toledo.

"I tell you," said one (who spoke warmly), "that if you have a particle of common-sense left in you, you will accompany me to England. This Mejnour is an imposter more dangerous, because more in earnest, than Zanoni. After all, what do his promises amount to? You allow that nothing can be more equivocal. You say that he has left Naples, — that he has selected a retreat more congenial than the crowded thoroughfares of men to the studies in which he is to initiate you; and this retreat is among the haunts of the fiercest bandits of Italy, — haunts which justice itself dares not penetrate. Fitting hermitage for a sage! I tremble for you. What if this stranger — of whom nothing is known — be leagued with the robbers; and these lures for your credulity bait but the traps for your property, — perhaps your life? You might come off cheaply by a ransom of half your fortune. You smile indignantly! Well, put common sense out of the question; take your own view of the matter. You are to undergo an ordeal which Mejnour himself does not profess to describe as a very tempting one. It may, or it may not, succeed: if it does not, you are menaced with the darkest evils; and if it does, you cannot be better off than the dull and joyless mystic whom you have taken for a master. Away with this folly; enjoy youth while it is left to you; return with me to England; forget these dreams; enter your proper career; form affections more respectable than those which lured you awhile to an Italian adventuress. Attend to your fortune, make money, and become a happy and distinguished man. This is the advice of sober friendship; yet the

---

* As a victim I go to the altar.

promises I hold out to you are fairer than those of Mejnour."

"Mervale," said Glyndon, doggedly, "I cannot, if I would, yield to your wishes. A power that is above me urges me on; I cannot resist its influence. I will proceed to the last in the strange career I have commenced. Think of me no more. Follow yourself the advice you give to me, and be happy."

"This is madness," said Mervale; "your health is already failing; you are so changed I should scarcely know you. Come; I have already had your name entered in my passport; in another hour I shall be gone, and you, boy that you are, will be left, without a friend, to the deceits of your own fancy and the machinations of this relentless mountebank."

"Enough," said Glyndon, coldly; "you cease to be an effective counselor when you suffer your prejudices to be thus evident. I have already had ample proof," added the Englishman, and his pale cheek grew more pale, "of the power of this man, — if man he be, which I sometimes doubt, — and, come life, come death, I will not shrink from the paths that allure me. Farewell, Mervale; if we never meet again, — if you hear, amidst our old and cheerful haunts, that Clarence Glyndon sleeps the last sleep by the shores of Naples, or amidst yon distant hills, say to the friends of our youth, 'He died worthily, as thousands of martyr-students have died before him, in the pursuit of knowledge.'"

He wrung Mervale's hand as he spoke, darted from his side, and disappeared amidst the crowd.

By the corner of the Toledo he was arrested by Nicot.

"Ah, Glyndon! I have not seen you this month. Where have you hid yourself? Have you been absorbed in your studies?"

"Yes."

"I am about to leave Naples for Paris. Will you accompany me? Talent of all order is eagerly sought for there, and will be sure to rise."

"I thank you; I have other schemes for the present."

"So laconic! — what ails you? Do you grieve for the loss of the Pisani? Take example by me. I have already consoled myself with Bianca Sacchini, — a handsome woman, enlightened, no prejudices. A valuable creature I shall find her, no doubt. But as for this Zanoni!"

"What of him?"

"If ever I paint an allegorical subject, I will take his likeness as Satan. Ha, ha! a true painter's revenge, — eh? And the way of the world, too! When we can do nothing else against a man whom we hate, we can at least paint his effigies as the Devil's. Seriously, though: I abhor that man."

"Wherefore?'

"Wherefore! Has he not carried off the wife and the dowry I had marked for myself! Yet, after all," added Nicot, musingly, "had he served instead of injured me, I should have hated him all the same. His very form, and his very face, made me at once envy and detest him. I felt that there is something antipathetic in our natures. I feel, too, that we shall meet again, when Jean Nicot's hate may be less impotent. We, too, cher confrere, — we, too, may meet again! Vive la Republique! I to my new world!"

"And I to mine. Farewell!"

That day Mervale left Naples; the next morning Glyndon also quitted the City of Delight alone, and on horseback. He bent his way into those picturesque but dangerous parts of the country which at that time were infested by banditti, and which few travelers dared to pass, even in broad daylight, without a strong escort. A road more lonely cannot well be conceived than that on which the hoofs of his steed, striking upon the fragments of rock that encumbered the neglected way, woke a dull and melancholy echo. Large tracts of wasteland, varied by the rank and profuse foliage of the South, lay before him; occasionally a wild goat peeped down from some rocky crag, or the discordant cry of a bird of prey, startled in its somber haunt, was heard above the hills. These were the only signs of life; not a human being was met, — not a hut was visible. Wrapped in his own ardent and solemn thoughts, the young man continued his way, till the sun had spent its noonday heat, and a breeze that announced the approach of eve sprung up from the unseen ocean which lay far distant to his right. It was then that a turn in the road brought before him one of those long, desolate, gloomy villages which are found in the interior of the Neapolitan dominions: and now he came upon a small chapel on one side the road, with a gaudily painted image of the Virgin in the open shrine. Around this spot, which, in the heart of a Christian land, retained the vestige of the old idolatry (for just such were the chapels that in the pagan age were dedicated to the demon-saints of mythology), gathered six or seven miserable and squalid wretches, whom the curse of the leper had cut off from mankind. They set up a shrill cry as they turned their ghastly visages towards the horseman; and, without stirring from the spot, stretched out their gaunt arms, and implored charity in the name of the Merciful Mother! Glyndon hastily threw them some small coins, and, turning away his face, clapped spurs to his horse, and relaxed not his speed till he entered the village. On either side the narrow and miry street, fierce and haggard forms — some leaning against the ruined walls of blackened huts, some seated at the threshold, some lying at full length in the mud — presented groups that at once invoked pity and aroused alarm: pity for their squalor, alarm for the ferocity imprinted on their savage aspects. They gazed at him, grim and sullen, as he rode slowly up the rugged street; sometimes whispering significantly to each other, but without attempting to stop his way. Even the children hushed their babble, and ragged urchins, devouring him with sparkling eyes, muttered to their mothers; "We shall feast well tomorrow!" It was, indeed, one of those hamlets in which Law sets not its sober step, in which Violence and Murder house secure, — hamlets common then in the wilder parts of Italy, in which the peasant was but the gentler name for the robber.

Glyndon's heart somewhat failed him as he looked around, and the question he desired to ask died upon his lips. At length from one of the dismal cabins emerged a form superior to the rest. Instead of the patched and ragged overall, which made the only garment of the men he had hitherto seen, the dress of this person was characterized by all the trappings of the national bravery. Upon his raven hair, the glossy curls of which made a notable contrast to the matted and elfin locks of the savages around, was placed a cloth cap, with a gold tassel that hung down to his shoulder; his mustaches were trimmed with care, and a silk kerchief of gay hues was twisted round a well-shaped but sinewy throat; a short jacket of rough cloth was decorated with several rows of gilt filigree buttons; his nether garments fitted tight to his limbs, and were curiously braided; while in a broad parti-colored sash were placed two silver-hilted pistols, and the sheathed knife, usually worn by Italians of the lower order, mounted in ivory elaborately carved. A small carbine of handsome workmanship was slung across his shoulder and completed his costume. The man himself was of middle size, athletic yet slender, with straight and regular features, sunburned, but not swarthy; and an expression of countenance which, though reckless and bold, had in it frankness rather than ferocity, and, if defying, was not altogether un-prepossessing.

Glyndon, after eyeing this figure for some moments with great attention, checked his rein, and asked the way to the "Castle of the Mountain."

The man lifted his cap as he heard the question, and, approaching Glyndon, laid his hand upon the neck of the horse, and said, in a low voice, "Then you are the cavalier whom our patron the signor expected. He bade me wait for you here, and lead you to the castle. And indeed, signor, it might have been unfortunate if I had neglected to obey the command."

The man then, drawing a little aside, called out to the bystanders in a loud voice, "Ho, ho! my friends, pay henceforth and forever all respect to this worshipful cavalier. He is the expected guest of our blessed patron of the Castle of the Mountain. Long life to him! May he, like his host, be safe by day and by night; on the hill and in the waste; against the dagger and the bullet, — in limb and in life! Cursed be he who touches a hair of his head, or a baioccho in his pouch. Now and forever we will protect and honor him, — for the law or against the law; with the faith and to the death. Amen! Amen!"

"Amen!" responded, in wild chorus, a hundred voices; and the scattered and straggling groups pressed up the street, nearer and nearer to the horseman.

"And that he may be known," continued the Englishman's strange protector, "to the eye and to the ear, I place around him the white sash, and I give him the sacred watchword, 'Peace to the Brave.' Signor, when you wear this sash, the proudest in these parts will bare the head and bend the knee. Signor, when you utter this watchword, the bravest hearts will be bound to your bidding. Desire you safety, or ask you revenge — to gain a beauty, or to lose a foe, — speak but the word, and we are yours: we are yours! Is it not so, comrades?"

And again the hoarse voices shouted, "Amen, Amen!"

"Now, signor," whispered the bravo, "if you have a few coins to spare, scatter them amongst the crowd, and let us be gone."

Glyndon, not displeased at the concluding sentence, emptied his purse in the streets; and while, with mingled oaths, blessings, shrieks, and yells, men, women, and children scrambled for the money, the bravo, taking the rein of the horse, led it a few paces through the village at a brisk trot, and then, turning up a narrow lane to the left, in a few minutes neither houses nor men were visible, and the mountains closed their path on either side. It was then that, releasing the bridle and slackening his pace, the guide turned his dark eyes on Glyndon with an arch expression, and said, —

"Your Excellency was not, perhaps, prepared for the hearty welcome we have given you."

"Why, in truth, I *ought* to have been prepared for it, since the signor, to whose house I am bound, did not disguise from me the character of the neighborhood. And your name, my friend, if I may so call you?"

"Oh, no ceremonies with me, Excellency. In the village I am generally called Maestro Paolo. I had a surname once, though a very equivocal one; and I have forgotten *that* since I retired from the world."

"And was it from disgust, from poverty, or from some — some ebullition of passion which entailed punishment, that you betook yourself to the mountains?"

"Why, signor," said the bravo, with a gay laugh, "hermits of my class seldom love the confessional. However, I have no secrets while my step is in these defiles, my whistle in my pouch, and my carbine at my back." With that the robber, as if he loved permission to talk at his will, hemmed thrice, and began with much humor; though, as his tale proceeded, the memories it roused seemed to carry him farther than he at first intended, and reckless and light-hearted ease gave way to that fierce and varied play of countenance and passion of gesture which characterize the emotions of his countrymen.

"I was born at Terracina, — a fair spot, is it not? My father was a learned monk of high birth; my mother — Heaven rest her! — an innkeeper's pretty daughter. Of course there could be no marriage in the case; and when I was born, the monk gravely declared my appearance to be miraculous. I was dedicated from my cradle to the altar; and my head was universally declared to be the orthodox shape for a cowl. As I grew up, the monk took great pains with my education; and I learned Latin and psalmody as soon as less miraculous infants learn crowing. Nor did the holy man's care stint itself to my interior accomplishments. Although vowed to poverty, he always contrived that my mother should have her pockets full; and between her pockets and mine there was soon established a clandestine communication; accordingly, at fourteen, I wore my cap on one side, stuck pistols in my belt, and assumed the swagger of a cavalier and a gallant. At that age my poor mother died; and about the same period my father, having written a History of the Pontifical Bulls, in forty volumes, and being, as I said, of high birth, obtained a cardinal's hat. From that time he thought fit to disown your humble servant. He bound me over to an honest notary at Naples, and gave me two hundred crowns by way of provision. Well, signor, I saw enough of the law to convince me that I should never be rogue enough to shine in the profession. So, instead of spoiling parchment, I made love to the notary's daughter. My master discovered our innocent amusement, and turned me out of doors; that was disagreeable. But my Ninetta loved me, and took care that I should not lie out in the streets with the Lazzaroni. Little jade! I think I see her now with her bare feet, and her finger to her lips, opening the door in the summer nights, and bidding me creep softly into the kitchen, where, praised be the saints! a flask and a manchet always awaited the hungry amoroso. At last, however, Ninetta grew cold. It is the way of the sex, signor. Her father found her an excellent marriage in the person of a withered old picture-dealer. She took the spouse, and very properly clapped the door in the face of the lover. I was not disheartened, Excellency; no, not I. Women are plentiful while we are young. So, without a ducat in my pocket or a crust for my teeth, I set out to seek my fortune on board of a Spanish merchantman. That was duller work than I expected; but luckily we were attacked by a pirate, — half the crew were butchered, the rest captured. I was one of the last: always in luck, you see, signor, — monks' sons have a knack that way! The captain of the pirates took a fancy to me. 'Serve with us?' said he. 'Too happy,' said I. Behold me, then, a pirate! O jolly life! how I blessed the old notary for turning me out of doors! What feasting, what fighting, what wooing, what quarreling! Sometimes we ran ashore and enjoyed ourselves like princes; sometimes we lay in a calm for days together on the loveliest sea that man ever traversed. And then, if the breeze rose and a sail came in sight, who so merry as we? I passed three years in that charming profession, and then, signor, I grew ambitious. I caballed against the captain; I wanted his post. One still night we struck the blow. The ship was like a log in the sea, no land to be seen from the masthead, the waves like glass, and the moon at its full. Up we rose, thirty of us and more. Up we rose with a shout; we poured into the captain's cabin, I at the head. The brave old boy had caught the alarm, and there he stood at the doorway, a pistol in each hand; and his one eye (he had only one) worse to meet than the pistols were.

"'Yield!' cried I; 'your life shall be safe.'

"'Take that,' said he, and whiz went the pistol; but the saints took care of their own, and the ball passed by my cheek, and shot the boatswain behind me. I closed with the captain, and the other pistol went off without mischief in the struggle. Such a fellow he was, — six feet four without his shoes! Over we went, rolling each on the other. Santa Maria! no time to get hold of one's knife. Meanwhile all the crew were up, some for the captain, some for me, — clashing and firing, and swearing and groaning, and now and then a heavy splash in the sea. Fine supper for the sharks that night! At last old Bilboa got uppermost; out flashed his knife; down it came, but not in my heart. No! I gave my left arm as a shield; and the blade went through to the hilt, with the blood spurting up like the rain from a whale's nostril! With the weight of the blow the stout fellow came down so that his face touched mine; with my right hand I caught him by the throat, turned him over like a lamb, signor, and faith it was soon all up with him: the boatswain's brother, a fat Dutchman, ran him through with a pike.

"'Old fellow,' said I, as he turned his terrible eye to me, 'I bear you no malice, but we must try to get on in the world, you know.' The captain grinned and gave up the ghost. I went upon deck, — what a sight! Twenty bold fellows stark and cold, and the moon sparkling on the puddles of blood as calmly as if it were water. Well, signor, the victory was ours, and the ship mine; I ruled merrily enough for six months. We then attacked a French ship twice our size; what sport it was! And we had not had a good fight so long, we were quite like virgins at it! We got the best of it, and won ship and cargo. They wanted to pistol the captain, but that was against my laws: so we gagged him, for he scolded as loud as if we were married to him; left him and the rest of his crew on board our own vessel, which was terribly battered; clapped our black flag on the Frenchman's, and set off merrily, with a brisk wind in our favor. But luck deserted us on forsaking our own dear old ship. A storm came on, a plank struck; several of us escaped in a boat; we had lots of gold with us, but no water. For two days and two nights we suffered horribly; but at last we ran ashore near a French seaport. Our sorry plight moved compassion, and as we had money, we were not suspected, – people only suspect the poor. Here we soon recovered our fatigues, rigged ourselves out gaily, and your humble servant was considered as noble a captain as ever walked deck. But now, alas! my fate would have it that I should fall in love with a silk-mercer's daughter. Ah, how I loved her! – the pretty Clara! Yes, I loved her so well that I was seized with horror at my past life! I resolved to repent, to marry her, and settle down into an honest man. Accordingly, I summoned my messmates, told them my resolution, resigned my command, and persuaded them to depart. They were good fellows, engaged with a Dutchman, against whom I heard afterwards they made a successful mutiny, but I never saw them more. I had two thousand crowns still left; with this sum I obtained the consent of the silk-mercer, and it was agreed that I should become a partner in the firm. I need not say that no one suspected that I had been so great a man, and I passed for a Neapolitan goldsmith's son instead of a cardinal's. I was very happy then, signor, very, – I could not have harmed a fly! Had I married Clara, I had been as gentle a mercer as ever handled a measure."

The bravo paused a moment, and it was easy to see that he felt more than his words and tone betokened. "Well, well, we must not look back at the past too earnestly, – the sunlight upon it makes one's eyes water. The day was fixed for our wedding, – it approached. On the evening before the appointed day, Clara, her mother, her little sister, and myself, were walking by the port; and as we looked on the sea, I was telling them old gossip-tales of mermaids and sea-serpents, when a red-faced, bottle-nosed Frenchman clapped himself right before me, and, placing his spectacles very deliberately astride his proboscis, echoed out, 'Sacre, mille tonnerres! this is the damned pirate who boarded the "Niobe!"'

"'None of your jests,' said I, mildly. 'Ho, ho!' said he; 'I can't be mistaken; help there!' and he griped me by the collar. I replied, as you may suppose, by laying him in the kennel; but it would not do. The French captain had a French lieutenant at his back, whose memory was as good as his chief's. A crowd assembled; other sailors came up: the odds were against me. I slept that night in prison; and in a few weeks afterwards I was sent to the galleys. They spared my life, because the old Frenchman politely averred that I had made my crew spare his. You may believe that the oar and the chain were not to my taste. I and two others escaped; they took to the road, and have, no doubt, been long since broken on the wheel. I, soft soul, would not commit another crime to gain my bread, for Clara was still at my heart with her sweet eyes; so, limiting my rogueries to the theft of a beggar's rags, which I compensated by leaving him my galley attire instead, I begged my way to the town where I left Clara. It was a clear winter's day when I approached the outskirts of the town. I had no fear of detection, for my beard and hair were as good as a mask. Oh, Mother of Mercy! there came across my way a funeral procession! There, now you know it; I can tell you no more. She had died, perhaps of love, more likely of shame. Can you guess how I spent that night? — I stole a pickaxe from a mason's shed, and all alone and unseen, under the frosty heavens, I dug the fresh mould from the grave; I lifted the coffin, I wrenched the lid, I saw her again — again! Decay had not touched her. She was always pale in life! I could have sworn she lived! It was a blessed thing to see her once more, and all alone too! But then, at dawn, to give her back to the earth, — to close the lid, to throw down the mould, to hear the pebbles rattle on the coffin: that was dreadful! Signor, I never knew before, and I don't wish to think now, how valuable a thing human life is. At sunrise I was again a wanderer; but now that Clara was gone, my scruples vanished, and again I was at war with my betters. I contrived at last, at O——, to get taken on board a vessel bound to Leghorn, working out my passage. From Leghorn I went to Rome, and stationed myself at the door of the cardinal's palace. Out he came, his gilded coach at the gate.

"'Ho, father!' said I; 'don't you know me?'

"'Who are you?'

"'Your son,' said I, in a whisper.

"The cardinal drew back, looked at me earnestly, and mused a moment. 'All men are my sons,' quoth he then, very mildly; 'there is gold for thee! To him who begs once, alms are due; to him who begs twice, jails are open. Take the hint and molest me no more. Heaven bless thee!' With that he got into his coach, and drove off to the Vatican. His purse which he had left behind was well supplied. I was grateful and contented, and took my way to Terracina. I had not long passed the marshes when I saw two horsemen approach at a canter.

"'You look poor, friend,' said one of them, halting; 'yet you are strong.'

"'Poor men and strong are both serviceable and dangerous, Signor Cavalier.'

"'Well said; follow us.'

"I obeyed, and became a bandit. I rose by degrees; and as I have always been mild in my calling, and have taken purses without cutting throats, I bear an excellent character, and can eat my macaroni at Naples without any danger to life and limb. For the last two years I have settled in these parts, where I hold sway, and where I have purchased land. I am called a farmer, signor; and I myself now only rob for amusement, and to keep my hand in. I trust I have satisfied your curiosity. We are within a hundred yards of the castle."

"And how," asked the Englishman, whose interest had been much excited by his companion's narrative, — "and how came you acquainted with my host? — and by what means has he so well conciliated the goodwill of yourself and friends?"

Maestro Paolo turned his black eyes very gravely towards his questioner. "Why, signor," said he, "you must surely know more of the foreign cavalier with the hard name than I do. All I can say is, that about a fortnight ago I chanced to be standing by a booth in the Toledo at Naples, when a sober-looking gentleman touched me by the arm, and said, 'Maestro Paolo, I want to make your acquaintance; do me the favor to come into yonder tavern, and drink a flask of lacrima.' 'Willingly,' said I. So we entered the tavern. When we were seated, my new acquaintance thus accosted me: 'The Count d'O—— has offered to let me hire his old castle near B——. You know the spot?'

"'Extremely well; no one has inhabited it for a century at least; it is half in ruins, signor. A queer place to hire; I hope the rent is not heavy.'

"'Maestro Paolo,' said he, 'I am a philosopher, and don't care for luxuries. I want a quiet retreat for some scientific experiments. The castle will suit me very well, provided you will accept me as a neighbor, and place me and my friends under your special protection. I am rich; but I shall take nothing to the castle worth robbing. I will pay one rent to the count, and another to you.'

"With that we soon came to terms; and as the strange signor doubled the sum I myself proposed, he is in high favor with all his neighbors. We would guard the whole castle against an army. And now, signor, that I have been thus frank, be frank with me. Who is this singular cavalier?"

"Who? — he himself told you, a philosopher."

"Hem! searching for the Philosopher's Stone, — eh, a bit of a magician; afraid of the priests?"

"Precisely; you have hit it."

"I thought so; and you are his pupil?"

"I am."

"I wish you well through it," said the robber, seriously, and crossing himself with much devotion; "I am not much better than other people, but one's soul is one's soul. I do not mind a little honest robbery, or knocking a man on the head if need be, — but to make a bargain with the devil! Ah, take care, young gentleman, take care!"

"You need not fear," said Glyndon, smiling; "my preceptor is too wise and too good for such a compact. But here we are, I suppose. A noble ruin, — a glorious prospect!"

Glyndon paused delightedly, and surveyed the scene before and below with the eye of a painter. Insensibly, while listening to the bandit, he had wound up a considerable ascent, and now he was upon a broad ledge of rock covered with mosses and dwarf shrubs. Between this eminence and another of equal height, upon which the castle was built, there was a deep but narrow fissure, overgrown with the most profuse foliage, so that the eye could not penetrate many yards below the rugged surface of the abyss; but the profoundness might be well conjectured by the hoarse, low, monotonous roar of waters unseen that rolled below, and the subsequent course of which was visible at a distance in a perturbed and rapid stream that intersected the waste and desolate valleys.

To the left, the prospect seemed almost boundless, — the extreme clearness of the purple air serving to render distinct the features of a range of country that a conqueror of old might have deemed in itself a kingdom. Lonely and desolate as the road which Glyndon had passed that day had appeared, the landscape now seemed studded with castles, spires, and villages. Afar off, Naples gleamed whitely in the last rays of the sun, and the rose-tints of the horizon melted into the azure of her glorious bay. Yet more remote, and in another part of the prospect, might be caught, dim and shadowy, and backed by the darkest foliage, the ruined pillars of the ancient Posidonia. There, in the midst of his blackened and sterile realms, rose the dismal Mount of Fire; while on the other hand, winding through variegated plains, to which distance lent all its magic, glittered many and many a stream by which Etruscan and Sybarite, Roman and Saracen and Norman had, at intervals of ages, pitched the invading tent. All the visions of the past — the stormy and dazzling histories of Southern Italy — rushed over the artist's mind as he gazed below. And then, slowly turning to look behind, he saw the grey and moldering walls of the castle in which he sought the secrets that were to give to hope in the future a mightier empire than memory owns in the past. It was one of those baronial fortresses with which Italy was studded in the earlier middle ages, having but little of the Gothic grace or grandeur which belongs to the ecclesiastical architecture of the same time, but rude, vast, and menacing, even in decay. A wooden bridge was thrown over the chasm, wide enough to admit two horsemen abreast; and the planks trembled and gave back a hollow sound as Glyndon urged his jaded steed across.

A road which had once been broad and paved with rough flags, but which now was half-obliterated by long grass and rank weeds, conducted to the outer court of the castle hard by; the gates were open, and half the building in this part was dismantled; the ruins partially hid by ivy that was the growth of centuries. But on entering the inner court, Glyndon was not sorry to notice that there was less appearance of neglect and decay; some wild roses gave a smile to the grey walls, and in the center there was a fountain in which the waters still trickled coolly, and with a pleasing murmur, from the jaws of a gigantic Triton. Here he was met by Mejnour with a smile.

"Welcome, my friend and pupil," said he: "he who seeks for Truth can find in these solitudes an immortal Academe."

Chapter 4.II.

And Abaris, so far from esteeming Pythagoras, who taught these things, a necromancer or wizard, rather revered and admired him as something divine.

— Iamblich., "Vit. Pythag."

*T*he attendants whom Mejnour had engaged for his strange abode were such as might suit a philosopher of few wants. An old Armenian whom Glyndon recognized as in the mystic's service at Naples, a tall, hard-featured woman from the village, recommended by Maestro Paolo, and two long-haired, smooth-spoken, but fierce-visaged youths from the same place, and honored by the same sponsorship, constituted the establishment. The rooms used by the sage were commodious and weatherproof, with some remains of ancient splendor in the faded arras that clothed the walls, and the huge tables of costly marble and elaborate carving. Glyndon's sleeping apartment communicated with a kind of belvedere, or terrace, that commanded prospects of unrivalled beauty and extent, and was separated on the other side by a long gallery, and a flight of ten or a dozen stairs, from the private chambers of the mystic. There was about the whole place a somber and yet not displeasing depth of repose. It suited well with the studies to which it was now to be appropriated.

For several days Mejnour refused to confer with Glyndon on the subjects nearest to his heart.

"All without," said he, "is prepared, but not all within; your own soul must grow accustomed to the spot, and filled with the surrounding nature; for Nature is the source of all inspiration."

With these words Mejnour turned to lighter topics. He made the Englishman accompany him in long rambles through the wild scenes around, and he smiled approvingly when the young artist gave way to the enthusiasm which their fearful beauty could not have failed to rouse in a duller breast; and then Mejnour poured forth to his wondering pupil the stores of a knowledge that seemed inexhaustible and boundless. He gave accounts the most curious, graphic, and minute of the various races (their characters, habits, creeds, and manners) by which that fair land had been successively overrun. It is true that his descriptions could not be found in books, and were unsupported by learned authorities; but he possessed the true charm of the tale-teller, and spoke of all with the animated confidence of a personal witness. Sometimes, too, he would converse upon the more durable and the loftier mysteries of Nature with an eloquence and a research which invested them with all the colors rather of poetry than science. Insensibly the young artist found himself elevated and soothed by the lore of his companion; the fever of his wild desires was slaked. His mind became more and more lulled into the divine tranquility of contemplation; he felt himself a nobler being, and in the silence of his senses he imagined that he heard the voice of his soul.

It was to this state that Mejnour evidently sought to bring the neophyte, and in this elementary initiation the mystic was like every more ordinary sage. For he who seeks to *discover* must first reduce himself into a kind of abstract idealism, and be rendered up, in solemn and sweet bondage, to the faculties which *contemplate* and *imagine.*

Glyndon noticed that, in their rambles, Mejnour often paused, where the foliage was rifest, to gather some herb or flower; and this reminded him that he had seen Zanoni similarly occupied. "Can these humble children of Nature," said he one day to Mejnour, — "things that bloom and wither in a day, be serviceable to the science of the higher secrets? Is there a pharmacy for the soul as well as the body, and do the nurslings of the summer minister not only to human health but spiritual immortality?"

"If," answered Mejnour, "a stranger had visited a wandering tribe before one property of herbalism was known to them; if he had told the savages that the herbs which every day they trampled under foot were endowed with the most potent virtues; that one would restore to health a brother on the verge of death; that another would paralyze into idiocy their wisest sage; that a third would strike lifeless to the dust their most stalwart champion; that tears and laughter, vigor and disease, madness and reason, wakefulness and sleep, existence and dissolution, were coiled up in those unregarded leaves, — would they not have held him a sorcerer or a liar? To half the virtues of the vegetable world mankind are yet in the darkness of the savages I have supposed. There are faculties within us with which certain herbs have affinity, and over which they have power. The moly of the ancients is not all a fable."

The apparent character of Mejnour differed in much from that of Zanoni; and while it fascinated Glyndon less, it subdued and impressed him more. The conversation of Zanoni evinced a deep and general interest for mankind, — a feeling approaching to enthusiasm for art and beauty. The stories circulated concerning his habits elevated the mystery of his life by actions of charity and beneficence. And in all this there was something genial and humane that softened the awe he created, and tended, perhaps, to raise suspicions as to the loftier secrets that he arrogated to himself. But Mejnour seemed wholly indifferent to all the actual world. If he committed no evil, he seemed equally apathetic to good. His deeds relieved no want, his words pitied no distress. What we call the heart appeared to have merged into the intellect. He moved, thought, and lived like some regular and calm abstraction, rather than one who yet retained, with the form, the feelings and sympathies of his kind.

Glyndon once, observing the tone of supreme indifference with which he spoke of those changes on the face of earth which he asserted he had witnessed, ventured to remark to him the distinction he had noted.

"It is true," said Mejnour, coldly. "My life is the life that contemplates, — Zanoni's is the life that enjoys: when I gather the herb, I think but of its uses; Zanoni will pause to admire its beauties."

"And you deem your own the superior and the loftier existence?"

"No. His is the existence of youth, — mine of age. We have cultivated different faculties. Each has powers the other cannot aspire to. Those with whom he associates live better, — those who associate with me know more."

"I have heard, in truth," said Glyndon, "that his companions at Naples were observed to lead purer and nobler lives after intercourse with Zanoni; yet were they not strange companions, at the best, for a sage? This terrible power, too, that he exercises at will, as in the death of the Prince di ——, and that of the Count Ughelli, scarcely becomes the tranquil seeker after good."

"True," said Mejnour, with an icy smile; "such must ever be the error of those philosophers who would meddle with the active life of mankind. You cannot serve some without injuring others; you cannot protect the good without warring on the bad; and if you desire to reform the faulty, why, you must lower yourself to live with the faulty to know their faults. Even so saith Paracelsus, a great man, though often wrong.* Not mine this folly; I live but in knowledge, — I have no life in mankind!"

Another time Glyndon questioned the mystic as to the nature of that union or fraternity to which Zanoni had once referred.

"I am right, I suppose," said he, "in conjecturing that you and himself profess to be the brothers of the Rosy Cross?"

"Do you imagine," answered Mejnour, "that there were no mystic and solemn unions of men seeking the same end through the same means before the Arabians of Damus, in 1378, taught to a wandering German the secrets which founded the Institution of the Rosicrucians? I allow, however, that the Rosicrucians formed a sect descended from the greater and earlier school. They were wiser than the Alchemists, — their masters are wiser than they."

"And of this early and primary order how many still exist?"

"Zanoni and myself."

"What, two only! — and you profess the power to teach to all the secret that baffles Death?"

"Your ancestor attained that secret; he died rather than survive the only thing he loved. We have, my pupil, no arts by which we *can put death out of our option*, or out of the will of Heaven. These walls may crush me as I stand. All that we profess to do is but this, — to find out the secrets of the human frame; to know why the parts ossify and the blood stagnates, and to apply continual preventives to the effects of time. This is not magic; it is the art of medicine rightly understood. In our order we hold most noble, — first, that knowledge which elevates the intellect; secondly, that which preserves the body. But the mere art (extracted from the juices and simples) which recruits the animal vigor and arrests the progress of decay, or that more noble secret, which I will only hint to thee at present, by which *heat*, or *caloric*, as ye call it, being, as Heraclitus wisely taught, the primordial principle of life, can be made its perpetual renovator, — these I say, would not suffice for safety. It is ours also to disarm and elude the wrath of men, to turn the swords of our foes against each other, to glide (if not incorporeal) invisible to eyes over which we can throw a mist and darkness. And this some seers have professed to be the virtue of a stone of agate. Abaris placed it in his arrow. I will find you an herb in yon valley that will give a surer charm than the agate and the arrow. In one word, know this, that the humblest and meanest products of Nature are those from which the sublimest properties are to be drawn."

---

* 'It is as necessary to know evil things as good; for who can know what is good without the knowing what is evil?' etc. — Paracelsus, 'De Nat. Rer.,' lib. 3.

"But," said Glyndon, "if possessed of these great secrets, why so churlish in withholding their diffusion? Does not the false or charlatanic science differ in this from the true and indisputable, — that the last communicates to the world the process by which it attains its discoveries; the first boasts of marvelous results, and refuses to explain the causes?"

"Well said, O Logician of the Schools; but think again. Suppose we were to impart all our knowledge to all mankind indiscriminately, — alike to the vicious and the virtuous, — should we be benefactors or scourges? Imagine the tyrant, the sensualist, the evil and corrupted being possessed of these tremendous powers; would he not be a demon let loose on earth? Grant that the same privilege be accorded also to the good; and in what state would be society? Engaged in a Titan war, — the good forever on the defensive, the bad forever in assault. In the present condition of the earth, evil is a more active principle than good, and the evil would prevail. It is for these reasons that we are not only solemnly bound to administer our lore only to those who will not misuse and pervert it, but that we place our ordeal in tests that purify the passions and elevate the desires. And Nature in this controls and assists us: for it places awful guardians and insurmountable barriers between the ambition of vice and the heaven of the loftier science."

Such made a small part of the numerous conversations Mejnour held with his pupil, — conversations that, while they appeared to address themselves to the reason, inflamed yet more the fancy. It was the very disclaiming of all powers which Nature, properly investigated, did not suffice to create, that gave an air of probability to those which Mejnour asserted Nature might bestow.

Thus days and weeks rolled on; and the mind of Glyndon, gradually fitted to this sequestered and musing life, forgot at last the vanities and chimeras of the world without.

One evening he had lingered alone and late upon the ramparts, watching the stars as, one by one, they broke upon the twilight. Never had he felt so sensibly the mighty power of the heavens and the earth upon man; how much the springs of our intellectual being are moved and acted upon by the solemn influences of Nature. As a patient on whom, slowly and by degrees, the agencies of mesmerism are brought to bear, he acknowledged to his heart the growing force of that vast and universal magnetism which is the life of creation, and binds the atom to the whole. A strange and ineffable consciousness of power, of the *something great* within the perishable clay, appealed to feelings at once dim and glorious, — like the faint recognitions of a holier and former being. An impulse, that he could not resist, led him to seek the mystic. He would demand, that hour, his initiation into the worlds beyond our world, — he was prepared to breathe a diviner air. He entered the castle, and strode the shadowy and starlit gallery which conducted to Mejnour's apartment.

Chapter 4.III.

Man is the eye of things.

— Euryph, "de Vit. Hum"

... There is, therefore, a certain ecstatical or transporting power, which, if at any time it shall be excited or stirred up by an ardent desire and most strong imagination, is able to conduct the spirit of the more outward even to some absent and far-distant object.

— Von Helmont

*T*he rooms that Mejnour occupied consisted of two chambers communicating with each other, and a third in which he slept. All these rooms were placed in the huge square tower that beetled over the dark and bush-grown precipice. The first chamber which Glyndon entered was empty. With a noiseless step he passed on, and opened the door that admitted into the inner one. He drew back at the threshold, overpowered by a strong fragrance which filled the chamber: a kind of mist thickened the air rather than obscured it, for this vapor was not dark, but resembled a snow-cloud moving slowly, and in heavy undulations, wave upon wave regularly over the space. A mortal cold struck to the Englishman's heart, and his blood froze. He stood rooted to the spot; and as his eyes strained involuntarily through the vapor, he fancied (for he could not be sure that it was not the trick of his imagination) that he saw dim, specterlike, but gigantic forms floating through the mist; or was it not rather the mist itself that formed its vapors fantastically into those moving, impalpable, and bodiless apparitions? A great painter of antiquity is said, in a picture of Hades, to have represented the monsters that glide through the ghostly River of the Dead, so artfully, that the eye perceived at once that the river itself was but a specter, and the bloodless things that tenanted it had no life, their forms blending with the dead waters till, as the eye continued to gaze, it ceased to discern them from the preternatural element they were supposed to inhabit. Such were the moving outlines that coiled and floated through the mist; but before Glyndon had even drawn breath in this atmosphere — for his life itself seemed arrested or changed into a kind of horrid trance — he felt his hand seized, and he was led from that room into the outer one. He heard the door close, — his blood rushed again through his veins, and he saw Mejnour by his side. Strong convulsions then suddenly seized his whole frame, — he fell to the ground insensible. When he recovered, he found himself in the open air in a rude balcony of stone that jutted from the chamber, the stars shining serenely over the dark abyss below, and resting calmly upon the face of the mystic, who stood beside him with folded arms.

"Young man," said Mejnour, "judge by what you have just felt, how dangerous it is to seek knowledge until prepared to receive it. Another moment in the air of that chamber and you had been a corpse."

"Then of what nature was the knowledge that you, once mortal like myself, could safely have sought in that icy atmosphere, which it was death for me to breathe? Mejnour," continued Glyndon, and his wild desire, sharpened by the very danger he had passed, once more animated and nerved him, "I am prepared at least for the first steps. I come to you as of old the pupil to the Hierophant, and demand the initiation."

Mejnour passed his hand over the young man's heart, — it beat loud, regularly, and boldly. He looked at him with something almost like admiration in his passionless and frigid features, and muttered, half to himself, "Surely, in so much courage the true disciple is found at last." Then, speaking aloud, he added, "Be it so; man's first initiation is in *trance*. In dreams commences all human knowledge; in dreams hovers over measureless space the first faint bridge between spirit and spirit, — this world and the worlds beyond! Look steadfastly on yonder star!"

Glyndon obeyed, and Mejnour retired into the chamber, from which there then slowly emerged a vapor, somewhat paler and of fainter odor than that which had nearly produced so fatal an effect on his frame. This, on the contrary, as it coiled around him, and then melted in thin spires into the air, breathed a refreshing and healthful fragrance. He still kept his eyes on the star, and the star seemed gradually to fix and command his gaze. A sort of languor next seized his frame, but without, as he thought, communicating itself to the mind; and as this crept over him, he felt his temples sprinkled with some volatile and fiery essence. At the same moment a slight tremor shook his limbs and thrilled through his veins. The languor increased, still he kept his gaze upon the star, and now its luminous circumference seemed to expand and dilate. It became gradually softer and clearer in its light; spreading wider and broader, it diffused all space, — all space seemed swallowed up in it. And at last, in the midst of a silver shining atmosphere, he felt as if something burst within his brain, — as if a strong chain were broken; and at that moment a sense of heavenly liberty, of unutterable delight, of freedom from the body, of birdlike lightness, seemed to float him into the space itself. "Whom, now upon earth, dost thou wish to see?" whispered the voice of Mejnour. "Viola and Zanoni!" answered Glyndon, in his heart; but he felt that his lips moved not.

Suddenly at that thought, — through this space, in which nothing save one mellow translucent light had been discernible, — a swift succession of shadowy landscapes seemed to roll: trees, mountains, cities, seas, glided along like the changes of a phantasmagoria; and at last, settled and stationary, he saw a cave by the gradual marge of an ocean shore, — myrtles and orange trees clothing the gentle banks. On a height, at a distance, gleamed the white but shattered relics of some ruined heathen edifice; and the moon, in calm splendor, shining over all, literally bathed with its light two forms without the cave, at whose feet the blue waters crept, and he thought that he even heard them murmur. He recognized both the figures. Zanoni was seated on a fragment of stone; Viola, half-reclining by his side, was looking into his face, which was bent down to her, and in her countenance was the expression of that perfect happiness which belongs to perfect love. "Wouldst thou hear them speak?" whispered Mejnour; and again, without sound, Glyndon inly answered, "Yes!" Their voices then came to his ear, but in tones that seemed to him strange; so subdued were they, and sounding, as it were, so far off, that they were as voices heard in the visions of some holier men from a distant sphere.

"And how is it," said Viola, "that thou canst find pleasure in listening to the ignorant?"

"Because the heart is never ignorant; because the mysteries of the feelings are as full of wonder as those of the intellect. If at times thou canst not comprehend the language of my thoughts, at times also I hear sweet enigmas in that of thy emotions."

"Ah, say not so!" said Viola, winding her arm tenderly round his neck, and under that heavenly light her face seemed lovelier for its blushes. "For the enigmas are but love's common language, and love should solve them. Till I knew thee, — till I lived with thee; till I learned to watch for thy footstep when absent: yet even in absence to see thee everywhere! — I dreamed not how strong and all-pervading is the connection between nature and the human soul. . . !

"And yet," she continued, "I am now assured of what I at first believed, — that the feelings which attracted me towards thee at first were not those of love. I know *that,* by comparing the present with the past, — it was a sentiment then wholly of the mind or the spirit! I could not hear thee now say, 'Viola, be happy with another!'"

"And I could not now tell thee so! Ah, Viola, never be weary of assuring me that thou art happy!"

"Happy while thou art so. Yet at times, Zanoni, thou art so sad!"

"Because human life is so short; because we must part at last; because yon moon shines on when the nightingale sings to it no more! A little while, and thine eyes will grow dim, and thy beauty haggard, and these locks that I toy with now will be grey and loveless."

"And thou, cruel one!" said Viola, touchingly, "I shall never see the signs of age in thee! But shall we not grow old together, and our eyes be accustomed to a change which the heart shall not share!"

Zanoni sighed. He turned away, and seemed to commune with himself.

Glyndon's attention grew yet more earnest.

"But were it so," muttered Zanoni; and then looking steadfastly at Viola, he said, with a half-smile, "Hast thou no curiosity to learn more of the lover thou once couldst believe the agent of the Evil One?"

"None; all that one wishes to know of the beloved one, I know — *that thou lovest me!*"

"I have told thee that my life is apart from others. Wouldst thou not seek to share it?"

"I share it now!"

"But were it possible to be thus young and fair forever, till the world blazes round us as one funeral pyre!"

"We shall be so, when we leave the world!"

Zanoni was mute for some moments, and at length he said, —

"Canst thou recall those brilliant and aërial dreams which once visited thee, when thou didst fancy that thou wert preordained to some fate aloof and afar from the common children of the earth?"

"Zanoni, the fate is found."

"And hast thou no terror of the future?"

"The future! I forget it! Time past and present and to come reposes in thy smile. Ah, Zanoni, play not with the foolish credulities of my youth! I have been better and humbler since thy presence has dispelled the mist of the air. The future! — well, when I have cause to dread it, I will look up to heaven, and remember who guides our fate!"

As she lifted her eyes above, a dark cloud swept suddenly over the scene. It wrapped the orange trees, the azure ocean, the dense sands; but still the last images that it veiled from the charmed eyes of Glyndon were the forms of Viola and Zanoni. The face of the one rapt, serene, and radiant; the face of the other, dark, thoughtful, and locked in more than its usual rigidness of melancholy beauty and profound repose.

"Rouse thyself," said Mejnour; "thy ordeal has commenced! There are pretenders to the solemn science who could have shown thee the absent, and prated to thee, in their charlatanic jargon, of the secret electricities and the magnetic fluid of whose true properties they know but the germs and elements. I will lend thee the books of those glorious dupes, and thou wilt find, in the dark ages, how many erring steps have stumbled upon the threshold of the mighty learning, and fancied they had pierced the temple. Hermes and Albert and Paracelsus, I knew ye all; but, noble as ye were, ye were fated to be deceived. Ye had not souls of faith, and daring fitted for the destinies at which ye aimed! Yet Paracelsus — modest Paracelsus — had an arrogance that soared higher than all our knowledge. Ho, ho! — he thought he could make a race of men from chemistry; he arrogated to himself the Divine gift, — the breath of life.*

"He would have made men, and, after all, confessed that they could be but pygmies! My art is to make men above mankind. But you are impatient of my digressions. Forgive me. All these men (they were great dreamers, as you desire to be) were intimate friends of mine. But they are dead and rotten. They talked of spirits, — but they dreaded to be in other company than that of men. Like orators whom I have heard, when I stood by the Pnyx of Athens, blazing with words like comets in the assembly, and extinguishing their ardor like holiday rockets when they were in the field. Ho, ho! Demosthenes, my hero-coward, how nimble were thy heels at Chaeronea! And thou art impatient still! Boy, I could tell thee such truths of the past as would make thee the luminary of schools. But thou lustest only for the shadows of the future. Thou shalt have thy wish. But the mind must be first exercised and trained. Go to thy room, and sleep; fast austerely, read no books; meditate, imagine, dream, bewilder thyself if thou wilt. Thought shapes out its own chaos at last. Before midnight, seek me again!"

---

* Paracelsus, "De Nat. Rer.," lib. i.

Chapter 4.IV.

It is fit that we who endeavor to rise to an elevation so sublime, should study first to leave behind carnal affections, the frailty of the senses, the passions that belong to matter; secondly, to learn by what means we may ascend to the climax of pure intellect, united with the powers above, without which never can we gain the lore of secret things, nor the magic that effects true wonders.
— Tritemius "On Secret Things and Secret Spirits"

*I*t wanted still many minutes of midnight, and Glyndon was once more in the apartment of the mystic. He had rigidly observed the fast ordained to him; and in the rapt and intense reveries into which his excited fancy had plunged him, he was not only insensible to the wants of the flesh, — he felt above them.

Mejnour, seated beside his disciple, thus addressed him: —

"Man is arrogant in proportion to his ignorance. Man's natural tendency is to egotism. Man, in his infancy of knowledge, thinks that all creation was formed for him. For several ages he saw in the countless worlds that sparkle through space like the bubbles of a shoreless ocean only the petty candles, the household torches, that Providence had been pleased to light for no other purpose but to make the night more agreeable to man. Astronomy has corrected this delusion of human vanity; and man now reluctantly confesses that the stars are worlds larger and more glorious than his own, — that the earth on which he crawls is a scarce visible speck on the vast chart of creation. But in the small as in the vast, God is equally profuse of life. The traveler looks upon the tree, and fancies its boughs were formed for his shelter in the summer sun, or his fuel in the winter frosts. But in each leaf of these boughs the Creator has made a world; it swarms with innumerable races. Each drop of the water in yon moat is an orb more populous than a kingdom is of men. Everywhere, then, in this immense design, science brings new life to light. Life is the one pervading principle, and even the thing that seems to die and putrefy but engenders new life, and changes to fresh forms of matter. Reasoning, then, by evident analogy: if not a leaf, if not a drop of water, but is, no less than yonder star, a habitable and breathing world, — nay, if even man himself is a world to other lives, and millions and myriads dwell in the rivers of his blood, and inhabit man's frame as man inhabits earth, commonsense (if your schoolmen had it) would suffice to teach that the circumfluent infinite which you call space — the countless Impalpable which divides earth from the moon and stars — is filled also with its correspondent and appropriate life. Is it not a visible absurdity to suppose that being is crowded upon every leaf, and yet absent from the immensities of space? The law of the Great System forbids the waste even of an atom; it knows no spot where something of life does not breathe. In the very charnel house is the nursery of production and animation. Is that true? Well, then, can you conceive that space, which is the Infinite itself, is alone a waste, is alone lifeless, is less useful to the one design of universal being than the dead carcass of a dog, than the peopled leaf, than the swarming globule? The microscope shows you the creatures on the leaf; no mechanical tube is yet invented to discover the nobler and more gifted things that hover in the illimitable air. Yet between these last and man is a mysterious and terrible affinity. And hence, by tales and legends, not wholly false nor wholly true, have arisen from time to time, beliefs in apparitions and specters. If more common to the earlier and simpler tribes than to the men of your duller age, it is but that, with the first, the senses are more keen and quick. And as the savage can see or scent miles away the traces of a foe, invisible to the gross sense of the civilized animal, so the barrier itself between him and the creatures of the airy world is less thickened and obscured. Do you listen?"

"With my soul!"

"But first, to penetrate this barrier, the soul with which you listen must be sharpened by intense enthusiasm, purified from all earthlier desires. Not without reason have the so-styled magicians, in all lands and times, insisted on chastity and abstemious reverie as the communicants of inspiration. When thus prepared, science can be brought to aid it; the sight itself may be rendered more subtle, the nerves more acute, the spirit more alive and outward, and the element itself — the air, the space — may be made, by certain secrets of the higher chemistry, more palpable and clear. And this, too, is not magic, as the credulous call it; as I have so often said before, magic (or science that violates Nature) exists not: it is but the science by which Nature can be controlled. Now, in space there are millions of beings not literally spiritual, for they have all, like the animalculae unseen by the naked eye, certain forms of matter, though matter so delicate, air-drawn, and subtle, that it is, as it

were, but a film, a gossamer that clothes the spirit. Hence the Rosicrucian's lovely phantoms of sylph and gnome. Yet, in truth, these races
and tribes differ more widely, each from each, than the Calmuc from
the Greek, — differ in attributes and powers. In the drop of water you
see how the animalculae vary, how vast and terrible are some of those
monster mites as compared with others. Equally so with the inhabitants
of the atmosphere: some of surpassing wisdom, some of horrible malignity; some hostile as fiends to men, others gentle as messengers
between earth and heaven.

"He who would establish intercourse with these varying beings resembles the traveler who would penetrate into unknown lands. He is
exposed to strange dangers and unconjectured terrors. *That intercourse
once gained, I cannot secure thee from the chances to which thy journey is exposed.*
I cannot direct thee to paths free from the wanderings of the deadliest
foes. Thou must alone, and of thyself, face and hazard all. But if thou
art so enamored of life as to care only to live on, no matter for what
ends, recruiting the nerves and veins with the alchemist's vivifying elixir,
why seek these dangers from the intermediate tribes? Because the very
elixir that pours a more glorious life into the frame, so sharpens the
senses that those larvae of the air become to thee audible and apparent;
so that, unless trained by degrees to endure the phantoms and subdue
their malice, a life thus gifted would be the most awful doom man could
bring upon himself. Hence it is, that though the elixir be compounded
of the simplest herbs, his frame only is prepared to receive it who has
gone through the subtlest trials. Nay, some, scared and daunted into
the most intolerable horror by the sights that burst upon their eyes at
the first draft, have found the potion less powerful to save than the
agony and travail of Nature to destroy. To the unprepared the elixir is
thus but the deadliest poison. Amidst the dwellers of the threshold is
one, too, surpassing in malignity and hatred all her tribe, — one whose
eyes have paralyzed the bravest, and whose power increases over the
spirit precisely in proportion to its fear. Does thy courage falter?"

"Nay; thy words but kindle it."

"Follow me, then, and submit to the initiatory labors."

With that, Mejnour led him into the interior chamber, and proceeded
to explain to him certain chemical operations which, though extremely
simple in themselves, Glyndon soon perceived were capable of very
extraordinary results.

"In the remoter times," said Mejnour, smiling, "our brotherhood were
often compelled to recur to delusions to protect realities; and, as dexterous mechanicians or expert chemists, they obtained the name of
sorcerers. Observe how easy to construct is the Specter Lion that attended the renowned Leonardo da Vinci!"

And Glyndon beheld with delighted surprise the simple means by which the wildest cheats of the imagination can be formed. The magical landscapes in which Baptista Porta rejoiced; the apparent change of the seasons with which Albertus Magnus startled the Earl of Holland; nay, even those more dread delusions of the Ghost and Image with which the necromancers of Heraclea woke the conscience of the conqueror of Plataea*, — all these, as the showman enchants some trembling children on a Christmas Eve with his lantern and phantasmagoria, Mejnour exhibited to his pupil.

. . .

"And now laugh forever at magic! when these, the very tricks, the very sports and frivolities of science, were the very acts which men viewed with abhorrence, and inquisitors and kings rewarded with the rack and the stake."

"But the alchemist's transmutation of metals —"

"Nature herself is a laboratory in which metals, and all elements, are forever at change. Easy to make gold, — easier, more commodious, and cheaper still, to make the pearl, the diamond, and the ruby. Oh, yes; wise men found sorcery in this too; but they found no sorcery in the discovery that by the simplest combination of things of everyday use they could raise a devil that would sweep away thousands of their kind by the breath of consuming fire. Discover what will destroy life, and you are a great man! — what will prolong it, and you are an imposter! Discover some invention in machinery that will make the rich more rich and the poor more poor, and they will build you a statue! Discover some mystery in art that will equalize physical disparities, and they will pull down their own houses to stone you! Ha, ha, my pupil! such is the world Zanoni still cares for! — you and I will leave this world to itself. And now that you have seen some few of the effects of science, begin to learn its grammar."

Mejnour then set before his pupil certain tasks, in which the rest of the night wore itself away.

---

* Pausanias, — see Plutarch.

Chapter 4. V.

Great travel hath the gentle Calidore
And toyle endured. . .
There on a day, —
He chaunst to spy a sort of shepheard groomes,
Playing on pipes and caroling apace.
. . . He, there besyde
Saw a faire damzell.

Spenser, "Faerie Queene," cant. ix.

For a considerable period the pupil of Mejnour was now absorbed in labor dependent on the most vigilant attention, on the most minute and subtle calculation. Results astonishing and various rewarded his toils and stimulated his interest. Nor were these studies limited to chemical discovery, — in which it is permitted me to say that the greatest marvels upon the organization of physical life seemed wrought by experiments of the vivifying influence of heat. Mejnour professed to find a link between all intellectual beings in the existence of a certain all-pervading and invisible fluid resembling electricity, yet distinct from the known operations of that mysterious agency — a fluid that connected thought to thought with the rapidity and precision of the modern telegraph, and the influence of this fluid, according to Mejnour, extended to the remotest past, — that is to say, whenever and wheresoever man had thought. Thus, if the doctrine were true, all human knowledge became attainable through a medium established between the brain of the individual inquirer and all the farthest and obscurest regions in the universe of ideas. Glyndon was surprised to find Mejnour attached to the abstruse mysteries which the Pythagoreans ascribed to the occult science of *numbers*. In this last, new lights glimmered dimly on his eyes; and he began to perceive that even the power to predict, or rather to calculate, results, might by — *

---

* Here there is an erasure in the MS.

. . .

But he observed that the last brief process by which, in each of these experiments, the wonder was achieved, Mejnour reserved for himself, and refused to communicate the secret. The answer he obtained to his remonstrances on this head was more stern than satisfactory:

"Dost thou think," said Mejnour, "that I would give to the mere pupil, whose qualities are not yet tried, powers that might change the face of the social world? The last secrets are entrusted only to him of whose virtue the Master is convinced. Patience! It is labor itself that is the great purifier of the mind; and by degrees the secrets will grow upon thyself as thy mind becomes riper to receive them."

At last Mejnour professed himself satisfied with the progress made by his pupil. "The hour now arrives," he said, "when thou mayst pass the great but airy barrier, — when thou mayst gradually confront the terrible Dweller of the Threshold. Continue thy labors — continue to surpass thine impatience for results until thou canst fathom the causes. I leave thee for one month; if at the end of that period, when I return, the tasks set thee are completed, and thy mind prepared by contemplation and austere thought for the ordeal, I promise thee the ordeal shall commence. One caution alone I give thee: regard it as a peremptory command, enter not this chamber!"*

"Enter not this chamber till my return; or, above all, if by any search for materials necessary to thy toils thou shouldst venture hither, forbear to light the naphtha in those vessels, and to open the vases on yonder shelves. I leave the key of the room in thy keeping, in order to try thy abstinence and self-control. Young man, this very temptation is a part of thy trial."

With that, Mejnour placed the key in his hands; and at sunset he left the castle.

For several days Glyndon continued immersed in employments which strained to the utmost all the faculties of his intellect. Even the most partial success depended so entirely on the abstraction of the mind, and the minuteness of its calculations, that there was scarcely room for any other thought than those absorbed in the occupation. And doubtless this perpetual strain of the faculties was the object of Mejnour in works that did not seem exactly pertinent to the purposes in view. As the study of the elementary mathematics, for example, is not so profitable in the solving of problems, useless in our after-callings, as it is serviceable in training the intellect to the comprehension and analysis of general truths.

---

* They were then standing in the room where their experiments had been chiefly made, and in which Glyndon, on the night he had sought the solitude of the mystic, had nearly fallen a victim to his intrusion.

But in less than half the time which Mejnour had stated for the duration of his absence, all that the mystic had appointed to his toils was completed by the pupil; and then his mind, thus relieved from the drudgery and mechanism of employment, once more sought occupation in dim conjecture and restless fancies. His inquisitive and rash nature grew excited by the prohibition of Mejnour, and he found himself gazing too often, with perturbed and daring curiosity, upon the key of the forbidden chamber. He began to feel indignant at a trial of constancy which he deemed frivolous and puerile. What nursery tales of Bluebeard and his closet were revived to daunt and terrify him! How could the mere walls of a chamber, in which he had so often securely pursued his labors, start into living danger? If haunted, it could be but by those delusions which Mejnour had taught him to despise, — a shadowy lion, — a chemical phantasm! Tush! he lost half his awe of Mejnour, when he thought that by such tricks the sage could practice upon the very intellect he had awakened and instructed! Still he resisted the impulses of his curiosity and his pride, and, to escape from their dictation, he took long rambles on the hills, or amidst the valleys that surrounded the castle, — seeking by bodily fatigue to subdue the unreposing mind. One day suddenly emerging from a dark ravine, he came upon one of those Italian scenes of rural festivity and mirth in which the classic age appears to revive. It was a festival, partly agricultural, partly religious, held yearly by the peasants of that district. Assembled at the outskirts of a village, animated crowds, just returned from a procession to a neighboring chapel, were now forming themselves into groups: the old to taste the vintage, the young to dance, — all to be gay and happy. This sudden picture of easy joy and careless ignorance, contrasting so forcibly with the intense studies and that parching desire for wisdom which had so long made up his own life, and burned at his own heart, sensibly affected Glyndon. As he stood aloof and gazing on them, the young man felt once more that he was young. The memory of all he had been content to sacrifice spoke to him like the sharp voice of remorse. The flitting forms of the women in their picturesque attire, their happy laughter ringing through the cool, still air of the autumn noon, brought back to the heart, or rather perhaps to the senses, the images of his past time, the "golden shepherd hours," when to live was but to enjoy.

He approached nearer and nearer to the scene, and suddenly a noisy group swept round him; and Maestro Paolo, tapping him familiarly on the shoulder, exclaimed in a hearty voice, "Welcome, Excellency! — we are rejoiced to see you amongst us." Glyndon was about to reply to this salutation, when his eyes rested upon the face of a young girl leaning on Paolo's arm, of a beauty so attractive that his color rose and his heart beat as he encountered her gaze. Her eyes sparkled with a roguish and petulant mirth, her parted lips showed teeth like pearls; as if impatient at the pause of her companion from the revel of the rest, her little foot beat the ground to a measure that she half-hummed, half-chanted. Paolo laughed as he saw the effect the girl had produced upon the young foreigner.

"Will you not dance, Excellency? Come, lay aside your greatness, and be merry, like us poor devils. See how our pretty Fillide is longing for a partner. Take compassion on her."

Fillide pouted at this speech, and, disengaging her arm from Paolo's, turned away, but threw over her shoulder a glance half inviting, half defying. Glyndon, almost involuntarily, advanced to her, and addressed her.

Oh, yes; he addresses her! She looks down, and smiles. Paolo leaves them to themselves, sauntering off with a devil-me-carish air. Fillide speaks now, and looks up at the scholar's face with arch invitation. He shakes his head; Fillide laughs, and her laugh is silvery. She points to a gay mountaineer, who is tripping up to her merrily. Why does Glyndon feel jealous? Why, when she speaks again, does he shake his head no more? He offers his hand; Fillide blushes, and takes it with a demure coquetry. What! is it so, indeed! They whirl into the noisy circle of the revelers. Ha! ha! is not this better than distilling herbs, and breaking thy brains on Pythagorean numbers? How lightly Fillide bounds along! How her lithesome waist supples itself to thy circling arm! Tara-ra-tara, ta-tara, rara-ra! What the devil is in the measure that it makes the blood course like quicksilver through the veins? Was there ever a pair of eyes like Fillide's? Nothing of the cold stars there! Yet how they twinkle and laugh at thee! And that rosy, pursed-up mouth that will answer so sparingly to thy flatteries, as if words were a waste of time, and kisses were their proper language. Oh, pupil of Mejnour! Oh, would-be Rosicrucian, Platonist, Magian, I know not what! I am ashamed of thee! What, in the names of Averroes and Burri and Agrippa and Hermes have become of thy austere contemplations? Was it for this thou didst resign Viola? I don't think thou hast the smallest recollection of the elixir or the Cabala. Take care! What are you about, sir? Why do you clasp that small hand locked within your own? Why do you — Tara-rara tara-ra tara-rara-ra, rarara, ta-ra, a-ra! Keep your eyes off those slender ankles and that crimson bodice! Tara-rara-ra! There they go again! And now they rest under the broad trees. The revel has whirled away from them. They hear — or do they not hear — the laughter at the distance? They see — or if they have their eyes about them, they *should* see — couple after couple gliding by, love talking and love looking. But I will lay a wager, as they sit under that tree, and the round sun goes down behind the mountains, that they see or hear very little except themselves.

"Hollo, Signor Excellency! and how does your partner please you? Come and join our feast, loiterers; one dances more merrily after wine."

Down goes the round sun; up comes the autumn moon. Tara, tara, rarara, rarara, tarara-ra! Dancing again; is it a dance, or some movement gayer, noisier, wilder still? How they glance and gleam through the night shadows, those flitting forms! What confusion! — what order! Ha, that is the Tarantula dance; Maestro Paolo foots it bravely! Diavolo, what fury! the Tarantula has stung them all. Dance or die; it is fury, — the Corybantes, the Maenads, the — Ho, ho! more wine! the Sabbat of the Witches at Benevento is a joke to this! From cloud to cloud wanders the moon, — now shining, now lost. Dimness while the maiden blushes; light when the maiden smiles.

"Fillide, thou art an enchantress!"

"Buona notte, Excellency; you will see me again!"

"Ah, young man," said an old, decrepit, hollow-eyed octogenarian, leaning on his staff, "make the best of your youth. I, too, once had a Fillide! I was handsomer than you then! Alas! if we could be always young!"

"Always young!" Glyndon started, as he turned his gaze from the fresh, fair, rosy face of the girl, and saw the eyes dropping rheum, the yellow wrinkled skin, the tottering frame of the old man.

"Ha, ha!" said the decrepit creature, hobbling near to him, and with a malicious laugh. "Yet I, too, was young once! Give me a baioccho for a glass of aqua vitae!"

Tara, rara, ra-rara, tara, rara-ra! There dances Youth! Wrap thy rags round thee, and totter off, Old Age!

Chapter 4.VI.

Whilest Calidore does follow that faire mayd,
Unmindful of his vow and high beheast
Which by the Faerie Queene was on him layd.
                    Spenser, "Faerie Queene," cant. x. s. 1.

*I*t was that grey, indistinct, struggling interval between the night and the dawn, when Clarence stood once more in his chamber. The abstruse calculations lying on his table caught his eye, and filled him with a sentiment of weariness and distaste. But — "Alas, if we could be always young! Oh, thou horrid specter of the old, rheum-eyed man! What apparition can the mystic chamber shadow forth more ugly and more hateful than thou? Oh, yes, if we could be always young! But not [thinks the neophyte now] — not to labor forever at these crabbed figures and these cold compounds of herbs and drugs. No; but to enjoy, to love, to revel! What should be the companion of youth but pleasure? And the gift of eternal youth may be mine this very hour! What means this prohibition of Mejnour's? Is it not of the same complexion as his ungenerous reserve even in the minutest secrets of chemistry, or the numbers of his Cabala? — compelling me to perform all the toils, and yet withholding from me the knowledge of the crowning result? No doubt he will still, on his return, show me that the great mystery *can* be attained; but will still forbid *me* to attain it. Is it not as if he desired to keep my youth the slave to his age; to make me dependent solely on himself; to bind me to a journeyman's service by perpetual excitement to curiosity, and the sight of the fruits he places beyond my lips?" These, and many reflections still more repining, disturbed and irritated him. Heated with wine — excited by the wild revels he had left — he was unable to sleep. The image of that revolting Old Age which Time, unless defeated, must bring upon himself, quickened the eagerness of his desire for the dazzling and imperishable Youth he ascribed to Zanoni. The prohibition only served to create a spirit of defiance. The reviving day, laughing jocundly through his lattice, dispelled all the fears and superstitions that belong to night. The mystic chamber presented to his imagination nothing to differ from any other apartment in the castle. What foul or malignant apparition could harm him in the light of that blessed sun! It was the peculiar, and on the whole most unhappy, contradiction in Glyndon's nature, that while his reasonings led him to doubt, — and doubt rendered him in *Moral* conduct irresolute and unsteady; he was *Physically* brave to rashness. Nor is this uncommon: skepticism and presumption are often twins. When a man of this character determines upon any action, personal fear never deters him; and for the moral fear, any sophistry suffices to self-will. Almost without analyzing himself the mental process by which his nerves hardened themselves and his limbs moved, he traversed the corridor, gained Mejnour's apartment, and opened the forbidden door. All was as he had been accustomed to see it, save that on a table in the center of the room lay open a large volume. He approached, and gazed on the characters on the page; they were in a cipher, the study of which had made a part of his labors. With but slight difficulty he imagined that he interpreted the meaning of the first sentences, and that they ran thus: —

"To quaff the inner life, is to see the outer life: to live in defiance of time, is to live in the whole. He who discovers the elixir discovers what lies in space; for the spirit that vivifies the frame strengthens the senses. There is attraction in the elementary principle of light. In the lamps of Rosicrucius the fire is the pure elementary principle. Kindle the lamps while thou openst the vessel that contains the elixir, and the light attracts towards thee those beings whose life is that light. Beware of Fear. Fear is the deadliest enemy to Knowledge." Here the ciphers changed their character, and became incomprehensible. But had he not read enough? Did not the last sentence suffice? — "Beware of Fear!" It was as if Mejnour had purposely left the page open, — as if the trial was, in truth, the reverse of the one pretended; as if the mystic had designed to make experiment of his *courage* while affecting but that of his *forbearance.* Not Boldness, but Fear, was the deadliest enemy to Knowledge. He moved to the shelves on which the crystal vases were placed; with an untrembling hand he took from one of them the stopper, and a delicious odor suddenly diffused itself through the room. The air sparkled as if with a diamond-dust. A sense of unearthly delight, — of an existence that seemed all spirit, flashed through his whole frame; and a faint, low, but exquisite music crept, thrilling, through the chamber. At this moment he heard a voice in the corridor calling on his name; and presently there was a knock at the door without. "Are you there, signor?" said the clear tones of Maestro Paolo. Glyndon hastily reclosed and replaced the vial, and bidding Paolo await him in his own apartment, tarried till he heard the intruder's steps depart; he then reluctantly quitted the room. As he locked the door, he still heard the dying strain of that fairy music; and with a light step and a joyous heart he repaired to Paolo, inly resolving to visit again the chamber at an hour when his experiment would be safe from interruption.

As he crossed his threshold, Paolo started back, and exclaimed, "Why, Excellency! I scarcely recognize you! Amusement, I see, is a great beautifier to the young. Yesterday you looked so pale and haggard; but Fillide's merry eyes have done more for you than the Philosopher's Stone (saints forgive me for naming it) ever did for the wizards." And Glyndon, glancing at the old Venetian mirror as Paolo spoke, was scarcely less startled than Paolo himself at the change in his own mien and bearing. His form, before bent with thought, seemed to him taller by half the head, so lithesome and erect rose his slender stature; his eyes glowed, his cheeks bloomed with health and the innate and pervading pleasure. If the mere fragrance of the elixir was thus potent, well might the alchemists have ascribed life and youth to the draught!

"You must forgive me, Excellency, for disturbing you," said Paolo, producing a letter from his pouch; "but our Patron has just written to me to say that he will be here tomorrow, and desired me to lose not a moment in giving to yourself this billet, which he enclosed."

"Who brought the letter?"

"A horseman, who did not wait for any reply."

Glyndon opened the letter, and read as follows: —

"I return a week sooner than I had intended, and you will expect me tomorrow. You will then enter on the ordeal you desire, but remember that, in doing so, you must reduce Being as far as possible into Mind. The senses must be mortified and subdued, — not the whisper of one passion heard. Thou mayst be master of the Cabala and the Chemistry; but thou must be master also over the Flesh and the Blood, — over Love and Vanity, Ambition and Hate. I will trust to find thee so. Fast and meditate till we meet!"

Glyndon crumpled the letter in his hand with a smile of disdain. What! more drudgery, — more abstinence! Youth without love and pleasure! Ha, ha! baffled Mejnour, thy pupil shall gain thy secrets without thine aid!

"And Fillide! I passed her cottage in my way, — she blushed and sighed when I jested her about you, Excellency!"

"Well, Paolo! I thank thee for so charming an introduction. Thine must be a rare life."

"Ah, Excellency, while we are young, nothing like adventure, — except love, wine, and laughter!"

"Very true. Farewell, Maestro Paolo; we will talk more with each other in a few days."

All that morning Glyndon was almost overpowered with the new sentiment of happiness that had entered into him. He roamed into the woods, and he felt a pleasure that resembled his earlier life of an artist, but a pleasure yet more subtle and vivid, in the various colors of the autumn foliage. Certainly Nature seemed to be brought closer to him; he comprehended better all that Mejnour had often preached to him of the mystery of sympathies and attractions. He was about to enter into the same law as those mute children of the forests. He was to know *the renewal of life;* the seasons that chilled to winter should yet bring again the bloom and the mirth of spring. Man's common existence is as one year to the vegetable world: he has his spring, his summer, his autumn, and winter, — but only *once.* But the giant oaks round him go through a revolving series of verdure and youth, and the green of the centenarian is as vivid in the beams of May as that of the sapling by its side. "Mine shall be your spring, but not your winter!" exclaimed the aspirant.

Wrapped in these sanguine and joyous reveries, Glyndon, quitting the woods, found himself amidst cultivated fields and vineyards to which his footstep had not before wandered; and there stood, by the skirts of a green lane that reminded him of verdant England, a modest house, — half cottage, half farm. The door was open, and he saw a girl at work with her distaff. She looked up, uttered a slight cry, and, tripping gaily into the lane to his side, he recognized the dark-eyed Fillide.

"Hist!" she said, archly putting her finger to her lip; "do not speak loud, — my mother is asleep within; and I knew you would come to see me. It is kind!"

Glyndon, with a little embarrassment, accepted the compliment to his kindness, which he did not exactly deserve. "You have thought, then, of me, fair Fillide?"

"Yes," answered the girl, coloring, but with that frank, bold ingenuousness, which characterizes the females of Italy, especially of the lower class, and in the southern provinces, — "oh, yes! I have thought of little else. Paolo said he knew you would visit me."

"And what relation is Paolo to you?"

"None; but a good friend to us all. My brother is one of his band."

"One of his band! — a robber?"

"We of the mountains do not call a mountaineer 'a robber,' signor."

"I ask pardon. Do you not tremble sometimes for your brother's life? The law —"

"Law never ventures into these defiles. Tremble for him! No. My father and grandsire were of the same calling. I often wish I were a man!"

"By these lips, I am enchanted that your wish cannot be realized."

"Fie, signor! And do you really love me?"

"With my whole heart!"

"And I thee!" said the girl, with a candor that seemed innocent, as she suffered him to clasp her hand.

"But," she added, "thou wilt soon leave us; and I —" She stopped short, and the tears stood in her eyes.

There was something dangerous in this, it must be confessed. Certainly Fillide had not the seraphic loveliness of Viola; but hers was a beauty that equally at least touched the senses. Perhaps Glyndon had never really loved Viola; perhaps the feelings with which she had inspired him were not of that ardent character which deserves the name of love. However that be, he thought, as he gazed on those dark eyes, that he had never loved before.

"And couldst thou not leave thy mountains?" he whispered, as he drew yet nearer to her.

"Dost thou ask me?" she said, retreating, and looking him steadfastly in the face. "Dost thou know what we daughters of the mountains are?

You gay, smooth cavaliers of cities seldom mean what you speak. With you, love is amusement; with us, it is life. Leave these mountains! Well! I should not leave my nature."

"Keep thy nature ever, — it is a sweet one."

"Yes, sweet while thou art true; stern, if thou art faithless. Shall I tell thee what I — what the girls of this country are? Daughters of men whom you call robbers, we aspire to be the companions of our lovers or our husbands. We love ardently; we own it boldly. We stand by your side in danger; we serve you as slaves in safety: we never change, and we resent change. You may reproach, strike us, trample us as a dog, — we bear all without a murmur; betray us, and no tiger is more relentless. Be true, and our hearts reward you; be false, and our hands revenge! Dost thou love me now?"

During this speech the Italian's countenance had most eloquently aided her words, — by turns soft, frank, fierce, — and at the last question she inclined her head humbly, and stood, as in fear of his reply, before him. The stern, brave, wild spirit, in which what seemed unfeminine was yet, if I may so say, still womanly, did not recoil, it rather captivated Glyndon. He answered readily, briefly, and freely, "Fillide, — yes!"

Oh, "yes!" forsooth, Clarence Glyndon! Every light nature answers "yes" lightly to such a question from lips so rosy! Have a care, — have a care! Why the deuce, Mejnour, do you leave your pupil of four-and-twenty to the mercy of these wild cats-a-mountain! Preach fast, and abstinence, and sublime renunciation of the cheats of the senses! Very well in you, sir, Heaven knows how many ages old; but at four-and-twenty, your Hierophant would have kept you out of Fillide's way, or you would have had small taste for the Cabala.

And so they stood, and talked, and vowed, and whispered, till the girl's mother made some noise within the house, and Fillide bounded back to the distaff, her finger once more on her lip.

"There is more magic in Fillide than in Mejnour," said Glyndon to himself, walking gaily home; "yet on second thoughts, I know not if I quite so well like a character so ready for revenge. But he who has the real secret can baffle even the vengeance of a woman, and disarm all danger!"

Sirrah! dost thou even already meditate the possibility of treason? Oh, well said Zanoni, "to pour pure water into the muddy well does but disturb the mud."

Chapter 4.VII.

Cernis, custodia qualis
Vestibulo sedeat? facies quae limina servet?*

"Aeneid," lib. vi. 574.

And it is profound night. All is at rest within the old castle, — all is breathless under the melancholy stars. Now is the time. Mejnour with his austere wisdom, — Mejnour the enemy to love; Mejnour, whose eye will read thy heart, and refuse thee the promised secrets because the sunny face of Fillide disturbs the lifeless shadow that he calls repose, — Mejnour comes tomorrow! Seize the night! Beware of fear! Never, or this hour! So, brave youth, — brave despite all thy errors, — so, with a steady pulse, thy hand unlocks once more the forbidden door.

He placed his lamp on the table beside the book, which still lay there opened; he turned over the leaves, but could not decipher their meaning till he came to the following passage: —

"When, then, the pupil is thus initiated and prepared, let him open the casement, light the lamps, and bathe his temples with the elixir. He must beware how he presume yet to quaff the volatile and fiery spirit. To taste till repeated inhalations have accustomed the frame gradually to the ecstatic liquid, is to know not life, but death."

He could penetrate no farther into the instructions; the cipher again changed. He now looked steadily and earnestly round the chamber. The moonlight came quietly through the lattice as his hand opened it, and seemed, as it rested on the floor, and filled the walls, like the presence of some ghostly and mournful Power. He ranged the mystic lamps (nine in number) round the center of the room, and lighted them one by one. A flame of silvery and azure tints sprung up from each, and lighted the apartment with a calm and yet most dazzling splendor; but presently this light grew more soft and dim, as a thin, grey cloud, like a mist, gradually spread over the room; and an icy thrill shot through the heart

---

* See you what porter sits within the vestibule? — what face watches at the threshold?

of the Englishman, and quickly gathered over him like the coldness of death. Instinctively aware of his danger, he tottered, though with difficulty, for his limbs seemed rigid and stonelike, to the shelf that contained the crystal vials; hastily he inhaled the spirit, and laved his temples with the sparkling liquid. The same sensation of vigor and youth, and joy and airy lightness, that he had felt in the morning, instantaneously replaced the deadly numbness that just before had invaded the citadel of life. He stood, with his arms folded on his bosom erect and dauntless, to watch what should ensue.

The vapor had now assumed almost the thickness and seeming consistency of a snow-cloud; the lamps piercing it like stars. And now he distinctly saw shapes, somewhat resembling in outline those of the human form, gliding slowly and with regular evolutions through the cloud. They appeared bloodless; their bodies were transparent, and contracted or expanded like the folds of a serpent. As they moved in majestic order, he heard a low sound — the ghost, as it were, of voice — which each caught and echoed from the other; a low sound, but musical, which seemed the chant of some unspeakably tranquil joy. None of these apparitions heeded him. His intense longing to accost them, to be of them, to make one of this movement of aërial happiness, — for such it seemed to him, — made him stretch forth his arms and seek to cry aloud, but only an inarticulate whisper passed his lips; and the movement and the music went on the same as if the mortal were not there. Slowly they glided round and aloft, till, in the same majestic order, one after one, they floated through the casement and were lost in the moonlight; then, as his eyes followed them, the casement became darkened with some object undistinguishable at the first gaze, but which sufficed mysteriously to change into ineffable horror the delight he had before experienced. By degrees this object shaped itself to his sight. It was as that of a human head covered with a dark veil through which glared, with livid and demoniac fire, eyes that froze the marrow of his bones. Nothing else of the face was distinguishable, — nothing but those intolerable eyes; but his terror, that even at the first seemed beyond nature to endure, was increased a thousand-fold, when, after a pause, the phantom glided slowly into the chamber.

The cloud retreated from it as it advanced; the bright lamps grew wan, and flickered restlessly as at the breath of its presence. Its form was veiled as the face, but the outline was that of a female; yet it moved not as move even the ghosts that simulate the living. It seemed rather to crawl as some vast misshapen reptile; and pausing, at length it cowered beside the table which held the mystic volume, and again fixed its eyes through the filmy veil on the rash invoker. All fancies, the most grotesque, of monk or painter in the early North, would have failed to give to the visage of imp or fiend that aspect of deadly malignity which spoke to the shuddering nature in those eyes alone. All else so dark, — shrouded, veiled and larvalike. But that burning glare so intense, so livid, yet so living, had in it something that was almost *human* in its passion of hate and mockery, — something that served to show that the shadowy Horror was not all a spirit, but partook of matter enough, at least, to make it more deadly and fearful an enemy to material forms. As, clinging with the grasp of agony to the wall, — his hair erect, his eyeballs starting, he still gazed back upon that appalling gaze, — the Image spoke to him: his soul rather than his ear comprehended the words it said.

"Thou hast entered the immeasurable region. I am the Dweller of the Threshold. What wouldst thou with me? Silent? Dost thou fear me? Am I not thy beloved? Is it not for me that thou hast rendered up the delights of thy race? Wouldst thou be wise? Mine is the wisdom of the countless ages. Kiss me, my mortal lover." And the Horror crawled near and nearer to him; it crept to his side, its breath breathed upon his cheek! With a sharp cry he fell to the earth insensible, and knew no more till, far in the noon of the next day, he opened his eyes and found himself in his bed, — the glorious sun streaming through his lattice, and the bandit Paolo by his side, engaged in polishing his carbine, and whistling a Calabrian love-air.

Chapter 4.VIII.

Thus man pursues his weary calling,
And wrings the hard life from the sky,
While happiness unseen is falling
Down from God's bosom silently.

Schiller

In one of those islands whose history the imperishable literature and renown of Athens yet invest with melancholy interest, and on which

Nature, in whom "there is nothing melancholy," still bestows a glory of scenery and climate equally radiant for the freeman or the slave, — the Ionian, the Venetian, the Gaul, the Turk, or the restless Briton, — Zanoni had fixed his bridal home. There the air carries with it the perfumes of the plains for miles along the blue, translucent deep.* Seen from one of its green sloping heights, the island he had selected seemed one delicious garden. The towers and turrets of its capital gleaming amidst groves of oranges and lemons; vineyards and olive-woods filling up the valleys, and clambering along the hillsides; and villa, farm, and cottage covered with luxuriant trellises of dark-green leaves and purple fruit. For there the prodigal beauty yet seems half to justify those graceful superstitions of a creed that, too enamored of earth, rather brought the deities to man, than raised the man to their less alluring and less voluptuous Olympus.

And still to the fishermen, weaving yet their antique dances on the sand; to the maiden, adorning yet, with many a silver fibula, her glossy tresses under the tree that overshadows her tranquil cot, — the same Great Mother that watched over the wise of Samos, the democracy of Corcyra, the graceful and deep-taught loveliness of Miletus, smiles as graciously as of yore. For the North, philosophy and freedom are essentials to human happiness; in the lands which Aphrodite rose from the waves to govern, as the Seasons, hand in hand, stood to welcome her on the shores, Nature is all sufficient.†

The isle which Zanoni had selected was one of the loveliest in that divine sea. His abode, at some distance from the city, but near one of the creeks on the shore, belonged to a Venetian, and, though small, had more of elegance than the natives ordinarily cared for. On the seas, and in sight, rode his vessel. His Indians, as before, ministered in mute gravity to the service of the household. No spot could be more beautiful, — no solitude less invaded. To the mysterious knowledge of Zanoni, to the harmless ignorance of Viola, the babbling and garish world of civilized man was alike unheeded. The loving sky and the lovely earth are companions enough to Wisdom and to Ignorance while they love.

Although, as I have before said, there was nothing in the visible occupations of Zanoni that betrayed a cultivator of the occult sciences, his habits were those of a man who remembers or reflects. He loved to roam alone, chiefly at dawn, or at night, when the moon was clear (especially in each month, at its rise and full), miles and miles away over the rich inlands of the island, and to cull herbs and flowers, which he hoarded with jealous care. Sometimes, at the dead of night, Viola would wake by an instinct that told her he was not by her side, and, stretching

---

* See Dr. Holland's "Travels to the Ionian Isles," etc., page 18.
† Homeric Hymn.

out her arms, find that the instinct had not deceived her. But she early saw that he was reserved on his peculiar habits; and if at times a chill, a foreboding, a suspicious awe crept over her, she forbore to question him.

But his rambles were not always unaccompanied, — he took pleasure in excursions less solitary. Often, when the sea lay before them like a lake, the barren dreariness of the opposite coast of Cephallenia contrasting the smiling shores on which they dwelt, Viola and himself would pass days in cruising slowly around the coast, or in visits to the neighboring isles. Every spot of the Greek soil, "that fair Fable-Land," seemed to him familiar; and as he conversed of the past and its exquisite traditions, he taught Viola to love the race from which have descended the poetry and the wisdom of the world. There was much in Zanoni, as she knew him better, that deepened the fascination in which Viola was from the first enthralled. His love for herself was so tender, so vigilant, and had that best and most enduring attribute, that it seemed rather grateful for the happiness in its own cares than vain of the happiness it created. His habitual mood with all who approached him was calm and gentle, almost to apathy. An angry word never passed his lips, — an angry gleam never shot from his eyes. Once they had been exposed to the danger not uncommon in those then half-savage lands. Some pirates who infested the neighboring coasts had heard of the arrival of the strangers, and the seamen Zanoni employed had gossiped of their master's wealth. One night, after Viola had retired to rest, she was awakened by a slight noise below. Zanoni was not by her side; she listened in some alarm. Was that a groan that came upon her ear? She started up, she went to the door; all was still. A footstep now slowly approached, and Zanoni entered calm as usual, and seemed unconscious of her fears.

The next morning three men were found dead at the threshold of the principal entrance, the door of which had been forced. They were recognized in the neighborhood as the most sanguinary and terrible marauders of the coasts, — men stained with a thousand murders, and who had never hitherto failed in any attempt to which the lust of rapine had impelled them. The footsteps of many others were tracked to the seashore. It seemed that their accomplices must have fled on the death of their leaders. But when the Venetian Proveditore, or authority, of the island, came to examine into the matter, the most unaccountable mystery was the manner in which these ruffians had met their fate. Zanoni had not stirred from the apartment in which he ordinarily pursued his chemical studies. None of the servants had even been disturbed from their slumbers. No marks of human violence were on the bodies of the dead. They died, and made no sign. From that moment

Zanoni's house — nay, the whole vicinity — was sacred. The neighboring villages, rejoiced to be delivered from a scourge, regarded the stranger as one whom the Pagiana (or Virgin) held under her especial protection.

In truth, the lively Greeks around, facile to all external impressions, and struck with the singular and majestic beauty of the man who knew their language as a native, whose voice often cheered them in their humble sorrows, and whose hand was never closed to their wants, long after he had left their shore preserved his memory by grateful traditions, and still point to the lofty platanus beneath which they had often seen him seated, alone and thoughtful, in the heats of noon. But Zanoni had haunts less open to the gaze than the shade of the platanus. In that isle there are the bituminous springs which Herodotus has commemorated. Often at night, the moon, at least, beheld him emerging from the myrtle and cystus that clothe the hillocks around the marsh that imbeds the pools containing the inflammable materia, all the medical uses of which, as applied to the nerves of organic life, modern science has not yet perhaps explored. Yet more often would he pass his hours in a cavern, by the loneliest part of the beach, where the stalactites seem almost arranged by the hand of art, and which the superstition of the peasants associates, in some ancient legends, with the numerous and almost incessant earthquakes to which the island is so singularly subjected.

Whatever the pursuits that instigated these wanderings and favored these haunts, either they were linked with, or else subordinate to, one main and master desire, which every fresh day passed in the sweet human company of Viola confirmed and strengthened.

The scene that Glyndon had witnessed in his trance was faithful to truth. And some little time after the date of that night, Viola was dimly aware that an influence, she knew not of what nature, was struggling to establish itself over her happy life. Visions indistinct and beautiful, such as those she had known in her earlier days, but more constant and impressive, began to haunt her night and day when Zanoni was absent, to fade in his presence, and seem less fair than *that*. Zanoni questioned her eagerly and minutely of these visitations, but seemed dissatisfied, and at times perplexed, by her answers.

"Tell me not," he said, one day, "of those unconnected images, those evolutions of starry shapes in a choral dance, or those delicious melodies that seem to thee of the music and the language of the distant spheres. Has no *one* shape been to thee more distinct and more beautiful than the rest, — no voice uttering, or seeming to utter, thine own tongue, and whispering to thee of strange secrets and solemn knowledge?"

"No; all is confused in these dreams, whether of day or night; and when at the sound of thy footsteps I recover, my memory retains nothing but a vague impression of happiness. How different — how cold — to the rapture of hanging on thy smile, and listening to thy voice, when it says, 'I love thee!'"

"Yet, how is it that visions less fair than these once seemed to thee so alluring? How is it that they then stirred thy fancies and filled thy heart? Once thou didst desire a fairy-land, and now thou seemest so contented with common life."

"Have I not explained it to thee before? Is it common life, then, to love, and to live with the one we love? My true fairyland is won! Speak to me of no other."

And so night surprised them by the lonely beach; and Zanoni, allured from his sublimer projects, and bending over that tender face, forgot that, in the Harmonious Infinite which spread around, there were other worlds than that one human heart.

Chapter 4.IX.

There is a principle of the soul, superior to all nature, through which we are capable of surpassing the order and systems of the world. When the soul is elevated to natures better than itself, *then* it is entirely separated from subordinate natures, exchanges this for another life, and, deserting the order of things with which it was connected, links and mingles itself with another.

— Iamblichus

"Adon-Ai! Adon-Ai! — appear, appear!"

And in the lonely cave, whence once had gone forth the oracles of a heathen god, there emerged from the shadows of fantastic rocks a luminous and gigantic column, glittering and shifting. It resembled the shining but misty spray which, seen afar off, a fountain seems to send up on a starry night. The radiance lit the stalactites, the crags, the arches of the cave, and shed a pale and tremulous splendor on the features of Zanoni.

"Son of Eternal Light," said the invoker, "thou to whose knowledge, grade after grade, race after race, I attained at last, on the broad Chaldean plains; thou from whom I have drawn so largely of the unutterable knowledge that yet eternity alone can suffice to drain; thou who, congenial with myself, so far as our various beings will permit, hast been for centuries my familiar and my friend, — answer me and counsel!"

From the column there emerged a shape of unimaginable glory. Its face was that of a man in its first youth, but solemn, as with the consciousness of eternity and the tranquility of wisdom; light, like starbeams, flowed through its transparent veins; light made its limbs themselves, and undulated, in restless sparkles, through the waves of its dazzling hair. With its arms folded on its breast, it stood distant a few feet from Zanoni, and its low voice murmured gently, "My counsels were sweet to thee once; and once, night after night, thy soul could follow my wings through the untroubled splendors of the Infinite. Now thou hast bound thyself back to the earth by its strongest chains, and the attraction to the clay is more potent than the sympathies that drew to thy charms the Dweller of the Starbeam and the Air. When last thy soul hearkened to me, the senses already troubled thine intellect and obscured thy vision. Once again I come to thee; but thy power even to summon me to thy side is fading from thy spirit, as sunshine fades from the wave when the winds drive the cloud between the ocean and the sky."

"Alas, Adon-Ai!" answered the seer, mournfully, "I know too well the conditions of the being which thy presence was wont to rejoice. I know that our wisdom comes but from the indifference to the things of the world which the wisdom masters. The mirror of the soul cannot reflect both earth and heaven; and the one vanishes from the surface as the other is glassed upon its deeps. But it is not to restore me to that sublime abstraction in which the intellect, free and disembodied, rises, region after region, to the spheres, — that once again, and with the agony and travail of enfeebled power I have called thee to mine aid. I love; and in love I begin to live in the sweet humanities of another. If wise, yet in all which makes danger powerless against myself, or those on whom I can gaze from the calm height of indifferent science, I am blind as the merest mortal to the destinies of the creature that makes my heart beat with the passions which obscure my gaze."

"What matter!" answered Adon-Ai. "Thy love must be but a mockery of the name; thou canst not love as they do for whom there are death and the grave. A short time, — like a day in thy incalculable life, — and the form thou dotest on is dust! Others of the nether world go hand in hand, each with each, unto the tomb; hand in hand they ascend from the worm to new cycles of existence. For thee, below are ages; for her, but hours. And for her and thee — O poor, but mighty one! — will there be even a joint hereafter! Through what grades and heavens of spiritualized being will her soul have passed when thou, the solitary loiterer, comest from the vapors of the earth to the gates of light!"

"Son of the Starbeam, thinkest thou that this thought is not with me forever; and seest thou not that I have invoked thee to hearken and minister to my design? Readest thou not my desire and dream to raise the conditions of her being to my own? Thou, Adon-Ai, bathing the celestial joy that makes thy life in the oceans of eternal splendor, — thou, save by the sympathies of knowledge, canst conjecture not what I, the offspring of mortals, feel — debarred yet from the objects of the tremendous and sublime ambition that first winged my desires above the clay — when I see myself compelled to stand in this low world alone. I have sought amongst my tribe for comrades, and in vain. At last I have found a mate. The wild bird and the wild beast have theirs; and my mastery over the malignant tribes of terror can banish their larvae from the path that shall lead her upward, till the air of eternity fits the frame for the elixir that baffles death."

"And thou hast begun the initiation, and thou art foiled! I know it. Thou hast conjured to her sleep the fairest visions; thou hast invoked the loveliest children of the air to murmur their music to her trance, and her soul heeds them not, and, returning to the earth, escapes from their control. Blind one, wherefore? canst thou not perceive? Because in her soul all is love. There is no intermediate passion with which the things thou wouldst charm to her have association and affinities. Their attraction is but to the desires and cravings of the *Intellect*. What have they with the *Passion* that is of earth, and the *Hope* that goes direct to heaven?"

"But can there be no medium — no link — in which our souls, as our hearts, can be united, and so mine may have influence over her own?"

"Ask me not, — thou wilt not comprehend me!"

"I adjure thee! — speak!"

"When two souls are divided, knowest thou not that a third in which both meet and live is the link between them!"

"I do comprehend thee, Adon-Ai," said Zanoni, with a light of more human joy upon his face than it had ever before been seen to wear; "and if my destiny, which here is dark to mine eyes, vouchsafes to me the happy lot of the humble, — if ever there be a child that I may clasp to my bosom and call my own —"

"And is it to be man at last, that thou hast aspired to be more than man?"

"But a child, — a second Viola!" murmured Zanoni, scarcely heeding the Son of Light; "a young soul fresh from heaven, that I may rear from the first moment it touches earth, — whose wings I may train to follow mine through the glories of creation; and through whom the mother herself may be led upward over the realm of death!"

"Beware, — reflect! Knowest thou not that thy darkest enemy dwells in the Real? Thy wishes bring thee near and nearer to humanity."

"Ah, humanity is sweet!" answered Zanoni.

And as the seer spoke, on the glorious face of Adon-Ai there broke a smile.

Chapter 4.X.

Aeterna aeternus tribuit, mortalia confert
Mortalis; divina Deus, peritura caducus.*
                "Aurel. Prud. contra Symmachum," lib. ii.

Extracts from the Letters of Zanoni to Mejnour
Letter 1

Thou hast not informed me of the progress of thy pupil; and I fear that so differently does circumstance shape the minds of the generations to which we are descended, from the intense and earnest children of the earlier world, that even thy most careful and elaborate guidance would fail, with loftier and purer natures than that of the neophyte thou hast admitted within thy gates. Even that third state of being, which the Indian sage† rightly recognizes as being between the sleep and the waking, and describes imperfectly by the name of *trance*, is unknown to the children of the Northern world; and few but would recoil to indulge it, regarding its peopled calm as maya and delusion of the mind. Instead of ripening and culturing that airy soil, from which Nature, duly known,

---

* The Eternal gives eternal things, the Mortal gathers mortal things: God, that which is divine, and the perishable that which is perishable.

† The Brahmins, speaking of Brahm, say, "To the Omniscient the three modes of being — sleep, waking, and trance — are not;" distinctly recognizing trance as a third and coequal condition of being.

can evoke fruits so rich and flowers so fair, they strive but to exclude it from their gaze; they esteem that struggle of the intellect from men's narrow world to the spirit's infinite home, as a disease which the leech must extirpate with pharmacy and drugs, and know not even that it is from this condition of their being, in its most imperfect and infant form, that poetry, music, art — all that belong to an Idea of Beauty to which neither *sleeping* nor *waking* can furnish archetype and actual semblance — take their immortal birth. When we, O Mejnour in the far time, were ourselves the neophytes and aspirants, we were of a class to which the actual world was shut and barred. Our forefathers had no object in life but knowledge. From the cradle we were predestined and reared to wisdom as to a priesthood. We commenced research where modern Conjecture closes its faithless wings. And with us, those were common elements of science which the sages of today disdain as wild chimeras, or despair of as unfathomable mysteries. Even the fundamental principles, the large yet simple theories of electricity and magnetism, rest obscure and dim in the disputes of their blinded schools; yet, even in our youth, how few ever attained to the first circle of the brotherhood, and, after wearily enjoying the sublime privileges they sought, they voluntarily abandoned the light of the sun, and sunk, without effort, to the grave, like pilgrims in a trackless desert, overawed by the stillness of their solitude, and appalled by the absence of a goal. Thou, in whom nothing seems to live *but the desire to know;* thou, who, indifferent whether it leads to weal or to woe, lendest thyself to all who would tread the path of mysterious science, a human book, insensate to the precepts it enounces, — thou hast ever sought, and often made additions to our number. But to these have only been vouchsafed partial secrets; vanity and passion unfitted them for the rest; and now, without other interest than that of an experiment in science, without love, and without pity, thou exposest this new soul to the hazards of the tremendous ordeal! Thou thinkest that a zeal so inquisitive, a courage so absolute and dauntless, may suffice to conquer, where austerer intellect and purer virtue have so often failed. Thou thinkest, too, that the germ of art that lies in the painter's mind, as it comprehends in itself the entire embryo of power and beauty, may be expanded into the stately flower of the Golden Science. It is a new experiment to thee. Be gentle with thy neophyte, and if his nature disappoint thee in the first stages of the process, dismiss him back to the Real while it is yet time to enjoy the brief and outward life which dwells in the senses, and closes with the tomb. And as I thus admonish thee, O Mejnour, wilt thou smile at my inconsistent hopes? I, who have so invariably refused to initiate others into our mysteries, — I begin at last to comprehend why the great law, which binds man to his kind, even when seeking most to set himself aloof from their condition, has made thy cold and bloodless science the link between thyself and thy race; why, *thou* has sought converts and pupils; why, in seeing life after life voluntarily dropping from our starry order, thou still aspirest to renew the vanished, and repair the lost; why, amidst thy calculations, restless and unceasing as the wheels of Nature herself, thou recoilest from the *thought to be alone!* So with myself; at last I, too, seek a convert, an equal, — I, too, shudder to be alone! What thou hast warned me of has come to pass. Love reduces all things to itself. Either must I be drawn down to the nature of the beloved, or hers must be lifted to my own. As whatever belongs to true Art has always necessarily had attraction for *us*, whose very being is in the ideal whence Art descends, so in this fair creature I have learned, at last, the secret that bound me to her at the first glance. The daughter of music, — music, passing into her being, became poetry. It was not the stage that attracted her, with its hollow falsehoods; it was the land in her own fancy which the stage seemed to center and represent. There the poetry found a voice, — there it struggled into imperfect shape; and then (that land insufficient for it) it fell back upon itself. It colored her thoughts, it suffused her soul; it asked not words, it created not things; it gave birth but to emotions, and lavished itself on dreams. At last came love; and there, as a river into the sea, it poured its restless waves, to become mute and deep and still, — the everlasting mirror of the heavens.

And is it not through this poetry which lies within her that she may be led into the large poetry of the universe! Often I listen to her careless talk, and find oracles in its unconscious beauty, as we find strange virtues in some lonely flower. I see her mind ripening under my eyes; and in its fair fertility what ever-teeming novelties of thought! O Mejnour! how many of our tribe have unraveled the laws of the universe, — have solved the riddles of the exterior nature, and deduced the light from darkness! And is not the *Poet*, who studies nothing but the human heart, a greater philosopher than all? Knowledge and atheism are incompatible. To know Nature is to know that there must be a God. But does it require this to examine the method and architecture of creation? Methinks, when I look upon a pure mind, however ignorant and childlike, that I see the August and Immaterial One more clearly than in all the orbs of matter which career at His bidding through space.

Rightly is it the fundamental decree of our order, that we must impart our secrets only to the pure. The most terrible part of the ordeal is in the temptations that our power affords to the criminal. If it were possible that a malevolent being could attain to our faculties, what disorder it might introduce into the globe! Happy that it is *not* possible; the malevolence would disarm the power. It is in the purity of Viola that I rely, as thou more vainly hast relied on the courage or the genius of thy pupils. Bear me witness, Mejnour! Never since the distant day in which I pierced the Arcana of our knowledge, have I ever sought to make its mysteries subservient to unworthy objects; though, alas! the extension of our existence robs us of a country and a home; though the law that places all science, as all art, in the abstraction from the noisy passions and turbulent ambition of actual life, forbids us to influence the destinies of nations, for which Heaven selects ruder and blinder agencies; yet, wherever have been my wanderings, I have sought to soften distress, and to convert from sin. My power has been hostile only to the guilty; and yet with all our lore, how in each step we are reduced to be but the permitted instruments of the Power that vouchsafes our own, but only to direct it. How all our wisdom shrinks into naught, compared with that which gives the meanest herb its virtues, and peoples the smallest globule with its appropriate world. And while we are allowed at times to influence the happiness of others, how mysteriously the shadows thicken round our own future doom! We cannot be prophets to ourselves! With what trembling hope I nurse the thought that I may preserve to my solitude the light of a living smile!

. . .

Extracts from Letter II.

Deeming myself not pure enough to initiate so pure a heart, I invoke to her trance those fairest and most tender inhabitants of space that have furnished to poetry, which is the instinctive guess into creation, the ideas of the Glendoveer and Sylph. And these were less pure than her own thoughts, and less tender than her own love! They could not raise her above her human heart, for *that* has a heaven of its own.

. . .

I have just looked on her in sleep, — I have heard her breathe my name. Alas! that which is so sweet to others has its bitterness to me; for I think how soon the time may come when that sleep will be without a dream, — when the heart that dictates the name will be cold, and the lips that utter it be dumb. What a twofold shape there is in love! If we examine it coarsely, — if we look but on its fleshy ties, its enjoyments of a moment, its turbulent fever and its dull reaction, — how strange it seems that this passion should be the supreme mover of the world; that it is this which has dictated the greatest sacrifices, and influenced all societies and all times; that to this the loftiest and loveliest genius has ever consecrated its devotion; that, but for love, there were no civilization, no music, no poetry, no beauty, no life beyond the brute's.

But examine it in its heavenlier shape, — in its utter abnegation of self; in its intimate connection with all that is most delicate and subtle in the spirit, — its power above all that is sordid in existence; its mastery over the idols of the baser worship; its ability to create a palace of the cottage, an oasis in the desert, a summer in the Iceland, — where it breathes, and fertilizes, and glows; and the wonder rather becomes how so few regard it in its holiest nature. What the sensual call its enjoyments, are the least of its joys. True love is less a passion than a symbol. Mejnour, shall the time come when I can speak to thee of Viola as a thing that was?

. . .

Extract from Letter III.

Knowest thou that of late I have sometimes asked myself, "Is there no guilt in the knowledge that has so divided us from our race?" It is true that the higher we ascend the more hateful seem to us the vices of the short-lived creepers of the earth, — the more the sense of the goodness of the All-good penetrates and suffuses us, and the more immediately does our happiness seem to emanate from him. But, on the other hand, how many virtues must lie dead in those who live in the world of death, and refuse to die! Is not this sublime egotism, this state of abstraction and reverie, — this self-wrapped and self-dependent majesty of existence, a resignation of that nobility which incorporates our own welfare, our joys, our hopes, our fears with others? To live on in no dread of foes, undegraded by infirmity, secure through the cares, and free from the disease of flesh, is a spectacle that captivates our pride. And yet dost thou not more admire him who dies for another? Since I have loved her, Mejnour, it seems almost cowardice to elude the grave which devours the hearts that wrap us in their folds. I feel it, — the earth grows upon my spirit. Thou wert right; eternal age, serene and passionless, is a happier boon than eternal youth, with its yearnings and desires. Until we can be all spirit, the tranquility of solitude must be indifference.

. . .

Extracts from Letter IV.

I have received thy communication. What! is it so? Has thy pupil disappointed thee? Alas, poor pupil! But —

. . .

(Here follow comments on those passages in Glyndon's life already known to the reader, or about to be made so, with earnest adjurations to Mejnour to watch yet over the fate of his scholar.)

. . .

But I cherish the same desire, with a warmer heart. My pupil! how the terrors that shall encompass thine ordeal warn me from the task! Once more I will seek the Son of Light.

. . .

Yes; Adon-Ai, long deaf to my call, at last has descended to my vision, and left behind him the glory of his presence in the shape of Hope. Oh, not impossible, Viola, — not impossible, that we yet may be united, soul with soul!

Extract from Letter V. — (Many months after the last.)

Mejnour, awake from thine apathy, — rejoice! A new soul will be born to the world, — a new soul that shall call me father. Ah, if they for whom exist all the occupations and resources of human life, — if they can thrill with exquisite emotion at the thought of hailing again their own childhood in the faces of their children; if in that birth they are born once more into the holy Innocence which is the first state of existence; if they can feel that on man devolves almost an angel's duty, when he has a life to guide from the cradle, and a soul to nurture for the heaven, — what to me must be the rapture to welcome an inheritor of all the gifts which double themselves in being shared! How sweet the power to watch, and to guard, — to instill the knowledge, to avert the evil, and to guide back the river of life in a richer and broader and deeper stream to the paradise from which it flows! And beside that river our souls shall meet, sweet mother. Our child shall supply the sympathy that fails as yet; and what shape shall haunt thee, what terror shall dismay, when thy initiation is beside the cradle of thy child!

Chapter 4.XI.

They thus beguile the way
Until the blustring storme is overblowne,
When weening to returne whence they did stray
They cannot finde that path which first was showne,
But wander to and fro in waies unknowne.
                    Spenser's "Faerie Queene," book i. canto i. st. x.

Yes, Viola, thou art another being than when, by the threshold of thy Italian home, thou didst follow thy dim fancies through the Land of Shadow; or when thou didst vainly seek to give voice to an ideal beauty, on the boards where illusion counterfeits earth and heaven for an hour, till the weary sense, awaking, sees but the tinsel and the scene-shifter. Thy spirit reposes in its own happiness. Its wanderings have found a goal. In a moment there often dwells the sense of eternity; for when profoundly happy, we know that it is impossible to die. Whenever the soul *feels itself,* it feels everlasting life.

The initiation is deferred, — thy days and nights are left to no other visions than those with which a contented heart enchants a guileless fancy. Glendoveers and Sylphs, pardon me if I question whether those visions are not lovelier than yourselves.

They stand by the beach, and see the sun sinking into the sea. How long now have they dwelt on that island? What matters! — it may be months, or years — what matters! Why should I, or they, keep account of that happy time? As in the dream of a moment ages may seem to pass, so shall we measure transport or woe, — by the length of the dream, or the number of emotions that the dream involves?

The sun sinks slowly down; the air is arid and oppressive; on the sea, the stately vessel lies motionless; on the shore, no leaf trembles on the trees.

Viola drew nearer to Zanoni. A presentiment she could not define made her heart beat more quickly; and, looking into his face, she was struck with its expression: it was anxious, abstracted, perturbed. "This stillness awes me," she whispered.

Zanoni did not seem to hear her. He muttered to himself, and his eyes gazed round restlessly. She knew not why, but that gaze, which seemed to pierce into space, — that muttered voice in some foreign language — revived dimly her earlier superstitions. She was more fearful since the hour when she knew that she was to be a mother. Strange crisis in the life of woman, and in her love! Something yet unborn begins already to divide her heart with that which had been before its only monarch.

"Look on me, Zanoni," she said, pressing his hand.

He turned: "Thou art pale, Viola; thy hand trembles!"

"It is true. I feel as if some enemy were creeping near us."

"And the instinct deceives thee not. An enemy is indeed at hand. I see it through the heavy air; I hear it through the silence: the Ghostly One, — the Destroyer, the *Pestilence!* Ah, seest thou how the leaves swarm with insects, only by an effort visible to the eye. They follow the breath of the plague!" As he spoke, a bird fell from the boughs at Viola's feet; it fluttered, it writhed an instant, and was dead.

"Oh, Viola!" cried Zanoni, passionately, "that is death. Dost thou not fear to die?"

"To leave thee? Ah, yes!"

"And if I could teach thee how Death may be defied; if I could arrest for thy youth the course of time; if I could —"

He paused abruptly, for Viola's eyes spoke only terror; her cheek and lips were pale.

"Speak not thus, — look not thus," she said, recoiling from him. "You dismay me. Ah, speak not thus, or I should tremble, — no, not for myself, but for thy child."

"Thy child! But wouldst thou reject for thy child the same glorious boon?"

"Zanoni!"

"Well!"

"The sun has sunk from our eyes, but to rise on those of others. To disappear from this world is to live in the world afar. Oh, lover, — oh, husband!" she continued, with sudden energy, "tell me that thou didst but jest, — that thou didst but trifle with my folly! There is less terror in the pestilence than in thy words."

Zanoni's brow darkened; he looked at her in silence for some moments, and then said, almost severely , —

"What hast thou known of me to distrust?"

"Oh, pardon, pardon! — nothing!" cried Viola, throwing herself on his breast, and bursting into tears. "I will not believe even thine own words, if they seem to wrong thee!" He kissed the tears from her eyes, but made no answer.

"And ah!" she resumed, with an enchanting and childlike smile, "if thou wouldst give me a charm against the pestilence! see, I will take it from thee." And she laid her hand on a small, antique amulet that he wore on his breast.

"Thou knowest how often this has made me jealous of the past; surely some love-gift, Zanoni? But no, thou didst not love the giver as thou dost me. Shall I steal thine amulet?"

"Infant!" said Zanoni, tenderly; "she who placed this round my neck deemed it indeed a charm, for she had superstitions like thyself; but to me it is more than the wizard's spell, — it is the relic of a sweet vanished time when none who loved me could distrust."

He said these words in a tone of such melancholy reproach that it went to the heart of Viola; but the tone changed into a solemnity which chilled back the gush of her feelings as he resumed: "And this, Viola, one day, perhaps, I will transfer from my breast to thine; yes, whenever thou shalt comprehend me better, — *whenever the laws of our being shall be the same!*"

He moved on gently. They returned slowly home; but fear still was in the heart of Viola, though she strove to shake it off. Italian and Catholic she was, with all the superstitions of land and sect. She stole to her chamber and prayed before a little relic of San Gennaro, which the priest of her house had given to her in childhood, and which had accompanied her in all her wanderings. She had never deemed it possible to part with it before. Now, if there was a charm against the pestilence, did she fear the pestilence for herself? The next morning, when he awoke, Zanoni found the relic of the saint suspended with his mystic amulet round his neck.

"Ah! thou wilt have nothing to fear from the pestilence now," said Viola, between tears and smiles; "and when thou wouldst talk to me again as thou didst last night, the saint shall rebuke thee."

Well, Zanoni, can there ever indeed be commune of thought and spirit, except with equals?

Yes, the plague broke out, — the island home must be abandoned. Mighty Seer, *thou hast no power to save those whom thou lovest!* Farewell, thou bridal roof! — sweet resting-place from care, farewell! Climates as soft may greet ye, O lovers, — skies as serene, and waters as blue and calm; but *that time*, — can it ever more return? Who shall say that the heart does not change with the scene, — the place where we first dwelt with the beloved one? Every spot *there* has so many memories which the place only can recall. The past that haunts it seems to command such constancy in the future. If a thought less kind, less trustful, enter within us, the sight of a tree under which a vow has been exchanged, a tear has been kissed away, restores us again to the hours of the first divine illusion. But in a home where nothing speaks of the first nuptials, where there is no eloquence of association, no holy burial-places of emotions, whose ghosts are angels! — yes, who that has gone through the sad history of affection will tell us that the heart changes not with the scene! Blow fair, ye favoring winds; cheerily swell, ye sails; away from the land where death has come to snatch the scepter of Love! The shores glide by; new coasts succeed to the green hills and orange-groves of the Bridal Isle. From afar now gleam in the moonlight the columns, yet extant, of a temple which the Athenian dedicated to wisdom; and, standing on the bark that bounded on in the freshening gale, the votary who had survived the goddess murmured to himself, —

"Has the wisdom of ages brought me no happier hours than those common to the shepherd and the herdsman, with no world beyond their village, no aspiration beyond the kiss and the smile of home?"

And the moon, resting alike over the ruins of the temple of the departed creed, over the hut of the living peasant, over the immemorial mountaintop, and the perishable herbage that clothed its sides, seemed to smile back its answer of calm disdain to the being who, perchance, might have seen the temple built, and who, in his inscrutable existence, might behold the mountain shattered from its base.

BOOK V

THE EFFECTS
OF THE ELIXIR

Chapter 5.I.

Frommet's den Schleier aufzuheben,
Wo das nahe Schreckness droht?
Nur das Irrthum ist das Leben
Und das Wissen ist der Tod.*

— Schiller, Kassandro

Zwei Seelen wohnen, ach! in meiner Brust.†

. . .

Was stehst du so, und blickst erstaunt hinaus?‡

"Faust"

*I*t will be remembered that we left Master Paolo by the bedside of Glyndon; and as, waking from that profound slumber, the recollections of the past night came horribly back to his mind, the Englishman uttered a cry, and covered his face with his hands.

"Good morrow, Excellency!" said Paolo, gaily. "Corpo di Bacco, you have slept soundly!"

The sound of this man's voice, so lusty, ringing, and healthful, served to scatter before it the phantasma that yet haunted Glyndon's memory.

He rose erect in his bed. "And where did you find me? Why are you here?"

"Where did I find you!" repeated Paolo, in surprise, — "in your bed, to be sure. Why am I here! — because the Padrone bade me await your waking, and attend your commands."

"The Padrone, Mejnour! — is he arrived?"

---

* Delusion is the life we live
   And knowledge death; oh wherefore, then,
   To sight the coming evils give
   And lift the veil of Fate to Man?
† Two souls dwell, alas! in my breast.
‡ Why standest thou so, and lookest out astonished?

"Arrived and departed, signor. He has left this letter for you."

"Give it me, and wait without till I am dressed."

"At your service. I have bespoke an excellent breakfast: you must be hungry. I am a very tolerable cook; a monk's son ought to be! You will be startled at my genius in the dressing of fish. My singing, I trust, will not disturb you. I always sing while I prepare a salad; it harmonizes the ingredients." And slinging his carbine over his shoulder, Paolo sauntered from the room, and closed the door.

Glyndon was already deep in the contents of the following letter: —

"When I first received thee as my pupil, I promised Zanoni, if convinced by thy first trials that thou couldst but swell, not the number of our order, but the list of the victims who have aspired to it in vain, I would not rear thee to thine own wretchedness and doom, — I would dismiss thee back to the world. I fulfill my promise. Thine ordeal has been the easiest that neophyte ever knew. I asked for nothing but abstinence from the sensual, and a brief experiment of thy patience and thy faith. Go back to thine own world; thou hast no nature to aspire to ours!

"It was I who prepared Paolo to receive thee at the revel. It was I who instigated the old beggar to ask thee for alms. It was I who left open the book that thou couldst not read without violating my command. Well, thou hast seen what awaits thee at the threshold of knowledge. Thou hast confronted the first foe that menaces him whom the senses yet grasp and enthrall. Dost thou wonder that I close upon thee the gates forever? Dost thou not comprehend, at last, that it needs a soul tempered and purified and raised, not by external spells, but by its own sublimity and valor, to pass the threshold and disdain the foe? Wretch! all my silence avails nothing for the rash, for the sensual, — for him who desires our secrets but to pollute them to gross enjoyments and selfish vice. How have the imposters and sorcerers of the earlier times perished by their very attempt to penetrate the mysteries that should purify, and not deprave! They have boasted of the Philosopher's Stone, and died in rags; of the immortal elixir, and sunk to their grave, grey before their time. Legends tell you that the fiend rent them into fragments. Yes; the fiend of their own unholy desires and criminal designs! What they coveted, thou covetest; and if thou hadst the wings of a seraph thou couldst soar not from the slough of thy mortality. Thy desire for knowledge, but petulant presumption; thy thirst for happiness, but the diseased longing for the unclean and muddied waters of corporeal pleasure; thy very love, which usually elevates even the mean, a passion that calculates treason amidst the first glow of lust. *Thou* one of us; thou a brother of the August Order; thou an Aspirant to the Stars that shine in the Shemaia of the Chaldean lore! The eagle can raise but the eaglet to the sun. I abandon thee to thy twilight!

"But, alas for thee, disobedient and profane! thou hast inhaled the elixir; thou hast attracted to thy presence a ghastly and remorseless foe. Thou thyself must exorcise the phantom thou hast raised. Thou must return to the world; but not without punishment and strong effort canst thou regain the calm and the joy of the life thou hast left behind. This, for thy comfort, will I tell thee: he who has drawn into his frame even so little of the volatile and vital energy of the aërial juices as thyself, has awakened faculties that cannot sleep, — faculties that may yet, with patient humility, with sound faith, and the courage that is not of the body like thine, but of the resolute and virtuous mind, attain, if not to the knowledge that reigns above, to high achievement in the career of men. Thou wilt find the restless influence in all that thou wouldst undertake. Thy heart, amidst vulgar joys will aspire to something holier; thy ambition, amidst coarse excitement, to something beyond thy reach. But deem not that this of itself will suffice for glory. Equally may the craving lead thee to shame and guilt. It is but an imperfect and newborn energy which will not suffer thee to repose. As thou directest it, must thou believe it to be the emanation of thine evil genius or thy good.

"But woe to thee! insect meshed in the web in which thou hast entangled limbs and wings! Thou hast not only inhaled the elixir, thou hast conjured the specter; of all the tribes of the space, no foe is so malignant to man, — and thou hast lifted the veil from thy gaze. I cannot restore to thee the happy dimness of thy vision. Know, at least, that all of us — the highest and the wisest — who have, in sober truth, passed beyond the threshold, have had, as our first fearful task, to master and subdue its grisly and appalling guardian. Know that thou *canst* deliver thyself from those livid eyes, — know that, while they haunt, they cannot harm, if thou resistest the thoughts to which they tempt, and the horror they engender. *Dread them most when thou beholdest them not.* And thus, son of the worm, we part! All that I can tell thee to encourage, yet to warn and to guide, I have told thee in these lines. Not from me, from thyself has come the gloomy trial from which I yet trust thou wilt emerge into peace. Type of the knowledge that I serve, I withhold no lesson from the pure aspirant; I am a dark enigma to the general seeker. As man's only indestructible possession is his memory, so it is not in mine art to crumble into matter the immaterial thoughts that have sprung up within thy breast. The tyro might shatter this castle to the dust, and topple down the mountain to the plain. The master has no power to say, 'Exist no more,' to one *thought* that his knowledge has inspired. Thou mayst change the thoughts into new forms; thou mayst rarefy and sublimate it into a finer spirit, — but thou canst not annihilate that which has no home but in the memory, no substance but the idea. *Every thought is a soul!* Vainly, therefore, would I or thou undo the past, or restore to thee the gay blindness of thy youth. Thou must endure the influence of the elixir thou hast inhaled; thou must wrestle with the specter thou hast invoked!"

The letter fell from Glyndon's hand. A sort of stupor succeeded to the various emotions which had chased each other in the perusal, — a stupor resembling that which follows the sudden destruction of any ardent and long-nursed hope in the human heart, whether it be of love, of avarice, of ambition. The loftier world for which he had so thirsted, sacrificed, and toiled, was closed upon him "forever," and by his own faults of rashness and presumption. But Glyndon's was not of that nature which submits long to condemn itself. His indignation began to kindle against Mejnour, who owned he had tempted, and who now abandoned him, — abandoned him to the presence of a specter. The mystic's reproaches stung rather than humbled him. What crime had he committed to deserve language so harsh and disdainful? Was it so deep a debasement to feel pleasure in the smile and the eyes of Fillide? Had not Zanoni himself confessed love for Viola; had he not fled with her as his companion? Glyndon never paused to consider if there are no distinctions between one kind of love and another. Where, too, was the great offence of yielding to a temptation which only existed for the brave? Had not the mystic volume which Mejnour had purposely left open, bid him but "Beware of fear?" Was not, then, every willful provocative held out to the strongest influences of the human mind, in the prohibition to enter the chamber, in the possession of the key which excited his curiosity, in the volume which seemed to dictate the mode by which the curiosity was to be gratified? As rapidly these thoughts passed over him, he began to consider the whole conduct of Mejnour either as a perfidious design to entrap him to his own misery, or as the trick of an imposter, who knew that he could not realize the great professions he had made. On glancing again over the more mysterious threats and warnings in Mejnour's letter, they seemed to assume the language of mere parable and allegory, — the jargon of the Platonists and Pythagoreans. By little and little, he began to consider that the very spectra he had seen — even that one phantom so horrid in its aspect — were but the delusions which Mejnour's science had enable him to raise. The healthful sunlight, filling up every cranny in his chamber, seemed to laugh away the terrors of the past night. His pride and his resentment nerved his habitual courage; and when, having hastily dressed himself, he rejoined Paolo, it was with a flushed cheek and a haughty step.

"So, Paolo," said he, "the Padrone, as you call him, told you to expect and welcome me at your village feast?"

"He did so by a message from a wretched old cripple. This surprised me at the time, for I thought he was far distant; but these great philosophers make a joke of two or three hundred leagues."

"Why did you not tell me you had heard from Mejnour?"

"Because the old cripple forbade me."

"Did you not see the man afterwards during the dance?"

"No, Excellency."

"Humph!"

"Allow me to serve you," said Paolo, piling Glyndon's plate, and then filling his glass. "I wish, signor, now the Padrone is gone, — not," added Paolo, as he cast rather a frightened and suspicious glance round the room, "that I mean to say anything disrespectful of him, — I wish, I say, now that he is gone, that you would take pity on yourself, and ask your own heart what your youth was meant for? Not to bury yourself alive in these old ruins, and endanger body and soul by studies which I am sure no saint could approve of."

"Are the saints so partial, then, to your own occupations, Master Paolo?"

"Why," answered the bandit, a little confused, "a gentleman with plenty of pistoles in his purse need not, of necessity, make it his profession to take away the pistoles of other people! It is a different thing for us poor rogues. After all, too, I always devote a tithe of my gains to the Virgin; and I share the rest charitably with the poor. But eat, drink, enjoy yourself; be absolved by your confessor for any little peccadilloes and don't run too long scores at a time, — that's my advice. Your health, Excellency! Pshaw, signor, fasting, except on the days prescribed to a good Catholic, only engenders phantoms."

"Phantoms!"

"Yes; the devil always tempts the empty stomach. To covet, to hate, to thieve, to rob, and to murder, — these are the natural desires of a man who is famishing. With a full belly, signor, we are at peace with all the world. That's right; you like the partridge! Cospetto! when I myself have passed two or three days in the mountains, with nothing from sunset to sunrise but a black crust and an onion, I grow as fierce as a wolf. That's not the worst, too. In these times I see little imps dancing before me. Oh, yes; fasting is as full of specters as a field of battle."

Glyndon thought there was some sound philosophy in the reasoning of his companion; and certainly the more he ate and drank, the more the recollection of the past night and of Mejnour's desertion faded from his mind. The casement was open, the breeze blew, the sun shone, — all Nature was merry; and merry as Nature herself grew Maestro Paolo. He talked of adventures, of travel, of women, with a hearty gusto that had its infection. But Glyndon listened yet more complacently when Paolo turned with an arch smile to praises of the eye, the teeth, the ankles, and the shape of the handsome Fillide.

This man, indeed, seemed the very personation of animal sensual life. He would have been to Faust a more dangerous tempter than Mephistopheles. There was no sneer on *his* lip at the pleasures which animated his voice. To one awaking to a sense of the vanities in knowledge, this reckless ignorant joyousness of temper was a worse corrupter than all the icy mockeries of a learned Fiend. But when Paolo took his leave, with a promise to return the next day, the mind of the Englishman again settled back to a graver and more thoughtful mood. The elixir seemed, in truth, to have left the refining effects Mejnour had ascribed to it. As Glyndon paced to and fro the solitary corridor, or, pausing, gazed upon the extended and glorious scenery that stretched below, high thoughts of enterprise and ambition — bright visions of glory — passed in rapid succession through his soul.

"Mejnour denies me his science. Well," said the painter, proudly, "he has not robbed me of my art."

What! Clarence Glyndon, dost thou return to that from which thy career commenced? Was Zanoni right after all?

He found himself in the chamber of the mystic; not a vessel, — not an herb! the solemn volume is vanished, — the elixir shall sparkle for him no more! But still in the room itself seems to linger the atmosphere of a charm. Faster and fiercer it burns within thee, the desire to achieve, to create! Thou longest for a life beyond the sensual! — but the life that is permitted to all genius, — that which breathes through the immortal work, and endures in the imperishable name.

Where are the implements for thine art? Tush! — when did the true workman ever fail to find his tools? Thou art again in thine own chamber, — the white wall thy canvas, a fragment of charcoal for thy pencil. They suffice, at least, to give outline to the conception that may otherwise vanish with the morrow.

The idea that thus excited the imagination of the artist was unquestionably noble and august. It was derived from that Egyptian ceremonial which Diodorus has recorded, — the Judgment of the Dead by the Living*: when the corpse, duly embalmed, is placed by the margin of the Acherusian Lake; and before it may be consigned to the bark which is to bear it across the waters to its final resting-place, it is permitted to the appointed judges to hear all accusations of the past life of the deceased, and, if proved, to deprive the corpse of the rites of sepulture.

Unconsciously to himself, it was Mejnour's description of this custom, which he had illustrated by several anecdotes not to be found in books, that now suggested the design to the artist, and gave it reality and force. He supposed a powerful and guilty king whom in life scarce

---

* Diod., lib. i.

a whisper had dared to arraign, but against whom, now the breath was gone, came the slave from his fetters, the mutilated victim from his dungeon, livid and squalid as if dead themselves, invoking with parched lips the justice that outlives the grave.

Strange fervor this, O artist! breaking suddenly forth from the mists and darkness which the occult science had spread so long over thy fancies, — strange that the reaction of the night's terror and the day's disappointment should be back to thine holy art! Oh, how freely goes the bold hand over the large outline! How, despite those rude materials, speaks forth no more the pupil, but the master! Fresh yet from the glorious elixir, how thou givest to thy creatures the finer life denied to thyself! — some power not thine own writes the grand symbols on the wall. Behind rises the mighty sepulcher, on the building of which repose to the dead the lives of thousands had been consumed. There sit in a semicircle the solemn judges. Black and sluggish flows the lake. There lies the mummied and royal dead. Dost thou quail at the frown on his lifelike brow? Ha! — bravely done, O artist! — up rise the haggard forms! — pale speak the ghastly faces! Shall not Humanity after death avenge itself on Power? Thy conception, Clarence Glyndon, is a sublime truth; thy design promises renown to genius. Better this magic than the charms of the volume and the vessel. Hour after hour has gone; thou hast lighted the lamp; night sees thee yet at thy labor. Merciful Heaven! what chills the atmosphere; why does the lamp grow wan; why does thy hair bristle? There! — there! — there! at the casement! It gazes on thee, the dark, mantled, loathsome thing! There, with their devilish mockery and hateful craft, glare on thee those horrid eyes!

He stood and gazed, — it was no delusion. It spoke not, moved not, till, unable to bear longer that steady and burning look, he covered his face with his hands. With a start, with a thrill, he removed them; he felt the nearer presence of the nameless. There it cowered on the floor beside his design; and lo! the figures seemed to start from the wall! Those pale accusing figures, the shapes he himself had raised, frowned at him, and gibbered. With a violent effort that convulsed his whole being, and bathed his body in the sweat of agony, the young man mastered his horror. He strode towards the phantom; he endured its eyes; he accosted it with a steady voice; he demanded its purpose and defied its power.

And then, as a wind from a charnel, was heard its voice. What it said, what revealed, it is forbidden the lips to repeat, the hand to record. Nothing save the subtle life that yet animated the frame to which the inhalations of the elixir had given vigor and energy beyond the strength of the strongest, could have survived that awful hour. Better to wake in the catacombs and see the buried rise from their cerements, and hear the ghouls, in their horrid orgies, amongst the festering ghastliness of corruption, than to front those features when the veil was lifted, and listen to that whispered voice!

. . .

The next day Glyndon fled from the ruined castle. With what hopes of starry light had he crossed the threshold; with what memories to shudder evermore at the darkness did he look back at the frown of its timeworn towers!

Chapter 5.II.

Faust: Wohin soll es nun gehm?
Mephist: Wohin es Dir gefallt.
     Wir sehn die kleine, dann die grosse Welt.

"Faust"

(Faust: Whither go now!
Mephist: Whither it pleases thee.
     We see the small world, then the great.)

*D*raw your chair to the fireside, brush clean the hearth, and trim the lights. Oh, home of sleekness, order, substance, comfort! Oh, excellent thing art thou, Matter of Fact!

It is some time after the date of the last chapter. Here we are, not in moonlit islands or moldering castles, but in a room twenty-six feet by twenty-two, — well carpeted, well cushioned, solid armchairs and eight such bad pictures, in such fine frames, upon the walls! Thomas Mervale, Esq., merchant, of London, you are an enviable dog!

It was the easiest thing in the world for Mervale, on returning from his Continental episode of life, to settle down to his desk, — his heart had been always there. The death of his father gave him, as a birthright, a high position in a respectable though second-rate firm. To make this establishment first-rate was an honorable ambition, — it was his! He had lately married, not entirely for money, — no! he was worldly rather than mercenary. He had no romantic ideas of love; but he was too sensible a man not to know that a wife should be a companion, — not merely a speculation. He did not care for beauty and genius, but he liked health and good temper, and a certain proportion of useful understanding. He chose a wife from his reason, not his heart, and a very good choice he made. Mrs. Mervale was an excellent young woman, — bustling, managing, economical, but affectionate and good. She had a will of her own, but was no shrew. She had a great notion of the rights of a wife, and a strong perception of the qualities that insure comfort. She would never have forgiven her husband, had she found him guilty of the most passing fancy for another; but, in return, she had the most admirable sense of propriety herself. She held in abhorrence all levity, all flirtation, all coquetry, — small vices which often ruin domestic happiness, but which a giddy nature incurs without consideration. But she did not think it right to love a husband over much. She left a surplus of affection, for all her relations, all her friends, some of her acquaintances, and the possibility of a second marriage, should any accident happen to Mr. M. She kept a good table, for it suited their station; and her temper was considered even, though firm; but she could say a sharp thing or two, if Mr. Mervale was not punctual to a moment. She was very particular that he should change his shoes on coming home, — the carpets were new and expensive. She was not sulky, nor passionate, — Heaven bless her for that! — but when displeased she showed it, administered a dignified rebuke, alluded to her own virtues, to her uncle who was an admiral, and to the thirty thousand pounds which she had brought to the object of her choice. But as Mr. Mervale was a good-humored man, owned his faults, and subscribed to her excellence, the displeasure was soon over.

Every household has its little disagreements, none fewer than that of Mr. and Mrs. Mervale. Mrs. Mervale, without being improperly fond of dress, paid due attention to it. She was never seen out of her chamber with papers in her hair, nor in that worst of disillusions, — a morning wrapper. At half-past eight every morning Mrs. Mervale was dressed for the day, — that is, till she re-dressed for dinner, — her stays well laced, her cap prim, her gowns, winter and summer, of a thick, handsome silk. Ladies at that time wore very short waists; so did Mrs. Mervale. Her morning ornaments were a thick, gold chain, to which was suspended a gold watch, — none of those fragile dwarfs of mechanism that look so pretty and go so ill, but a handsome repeater which chronicled Father Time to a moment; also a mosaic brooch; also a miniature of her uncle, the admiral, set in a bracelet. For the evening she had two handsome sets, — necklace, earrings, and bracelets complete, — one of amethysts, the other topazes. With these, her costume for the most part was a gold-colored satin and a turban, in which last her picture had been taken. Mrs. Mervale had an aquiline nose, good teeth, fair hair, and light eyelashes, rather a high complexion, what is generally called a fine bust; full cheeks; large useful feet made for walking; large, white hands with filbert nails, on which not a speck of dust had, even in childhood, ever been known to a light. She looked a little older than she really was; but that might arise from a certain air of dignity and the aforesaid aquiline nose. She generally wore short mittens. She never read any poetry but Goldsmith's and Cowper's. She was not amused by novels, though she had no prejudice against them. She liked a play and a pantomime, with a slight supper afterwards. She did not like concerts nor operas. At the beginning of the winter she selected some book to read, and some piece of work to commence. The two lasted her till the spring, when, though she continued to work, she left off reading. Her favorite study was history, which she read through the medium of Dr. Goldsmith. Her favorite author in the belles lettres was, of course, Dr. Johnson. A worthier woman, or one more respected, was not to be found, except in an epitaph!

It was an autumn night. Mr. and Mrs. Mervale, lately returned from an excursion to Weymouth, are in the drawing room, — "the dame sat on this side, the man sat on that."

"Yes, I assure you, my dear, that Glyndon, with all his eccentricities, was a very engaging, amiable fellow. You would certainly have liked him, — all the women did."

"My dear Thomas, you will forgive the remark, — but that expression of yours, 'all the *women*' —"

"I beg your pardon, — you are right. I meant to say that he was a general favorite with your charming sex."

"I understand, — rather a frivolous character."

"Frivolous! no, not exactly; a little unsteady, — very odd, but certainly not frivolous; presumptuous and headstrong in character, but modest and shy in his manners, rather too much so, — just what you like. However, to return; I am seriously uneasy at the accounts I have heard of him today. He has been living, it seems, a very strange and irregular life, traveling from place to place, and must have spent already a great deal of money."

"Apropos of money," said Mrs. Mervale; "I fear we must change our butcher; he is certainly in league with the cook."

"That is a pity; his beef is remarkably fine. These London servants are as bad as the Carbonari. But, as I was saying, poor Glyndon —"

Here a knock was heard at the door. "Bless me," said Mrs. Mervale, "it is past ten! Who can that possibly be?"

"Perhaps your uncle, the admiral," said the husband, with a slight peevishness in his accent. "He generally favors us about this hour."

"I hope, my love, that none of my relations are unwelcome visitors at your house. The admiral is a most entertaining man, and his fortune is entirely at his own disposal."

"No one I respect more," said Mr. Mervale, with emphasis.

The servant threw open the door, and announced Mr. Glyndon.

"Mr. Glyndon! — what an extraordinary —" exclaimed Mrs. Mervale; but before she could conclude the sentence, Glyndon was in the room.

The two friends greeted each other with all the warmth of early recollection and long absence. An appropriate and proud presentation to Mrs. Mervale ensued; and Mrs. Mervale, with a dignified smile, and a furtive glance at his boots, bade her husband's friend welcome to England.

Glyndon was greatly altered since Mervale had seen him last. Though less than two years had elapsed since then, his fair complexion was more bronzed and manly. Deep lines of care, or thought, or dissipation, had replaced the smooth contour of happy youth. To a manner once gentle and polished had succeeded a certain recklessness of mien, tone, and bearing, which bespoke the habits of a society that cared little for the calm decorums of conventional ease. Still a kind of wild nobleness, not before apparent in him, characterized his aspect, and gave something of dignity to the freedom of his language and gestures.

"So, then, you are settled, Mervale, — I need not ask you if you are happy. Worth, sense, wealth, character, and so fair a companion deserve happiness, and command it."

"Would you like some tea, Mr. Glyndon?" asked Mrs. Mervale, kindly.

"Thank you, — no. I propose a more convivial stimulus to my old friend. Wine, Mervale, — wine, eh! — or a bowl of old English punch. Your wife will excuse us, — we will make a night of it!"

Mrs. Mervale drew back her chair, and tried not to look aghast. Glyndon did not give his friend time to reply.

"So at last I am in England," he said, looking round the room, with a slight sneer on his lips; "surely this sober air must have its influence; surely here I shall be like the rest."

"Have you been ill, Glyndon?"

"Ill, yes. Humph! you have a fine house. Does it contain a spare room for a solitary wanderer?"

Mr. Mervale glanced at his wife, and his wife looked steadily on the carpet. "Modest and shy in his manners — rather too much so!" Mrs. Mervale was in the seventh heaven of indignation and amaze!

"My dear?" said Mr. Mervale at last, meekly and interrogatingly.

"My dear!" returned Mrs. Mervale, innocently and sourly.

256   *Zanoni*

"We can make up a room for my old friend, Sarah?"

The old friend had sunk back on his chair, and, gazing intently on the fire, with his feet at ease upon the fender, seemed to have forgotten his question.

Mrs. Mervale bit her lips, looked thoughtful, and at last coldly replied, "Certainly, Mr. Mervale; your friends do right to make themselves at home."

With that she lighted a candle, and moved majestically from the room. When she returned, the two friends had vanished into Mr. Mervale's study.

Twelve o'clock struck, — one o'clock, two! Thrice had Mrs. Mervale sent into the room to know, — first, if they wanted anything; secondly, if Mr. Glyndon slept on a mattress or feather bed; thirdly, to inquire if Mr. Glyndon's trunk, which he had brought with him, should be unpacked. And to the answer to all these questions was added, in a loud voice from the visitor, — a voice that pierced from the kitchen to the attic, — "Another bowl! stronger, if you please, and be quick with it!"

At last Mr. Mervale appeared in the conjugal chamber, not penitent, nor apologetic, — no, not a bit of it. His eyes twinkled, his cheek flushed, his feet reeled; he sang, — Mr. Thomas Mervale positively sang!

"Mr. Mervale! is it possible, sir —"

"'Old King Cole was a merry old soul —'"

"Mr. Mervale! sir! — leave me alone, sir!"

"'And a merry old soul was he —'"

"What an example to the servants!"

"'And he called for his pipe, and he called for his bowl —'"

"If you don't behave yourself, sir, I shall call —"

"'Call for his fiddlers three!'"

Chapter 5.III.

In der Welt weit
Aus der Einsamkeit
Wollen sie Dich locken.*

"Faust"

*T*he next morning, at breakfast, Mrs. Mervale looked as if all the wrongs of injured woman sat upon her brow. Mr. Mervale seemed the picture of remorseful guilt and avenging bile. He said little, except to complain of headache, and to request the eggs to be removed from the table. Clarence Glyndon — impervious, unconscious, unailing, impenitent — was in noisy spirits, and talked for three.

"Poor Mervale! he has lost the habit of good-fellowship, madam. Another night or two, and he will be himself again!"

"Sir," said Mrs. Mervale, launching a premeditated sentence with more than Johnsonian dignity, "permit me to remind you that Mr. Mervale is now a married man, the destined father of a family, and the present master of a household."

"Precisely the reasons why I envy him so much. I myself have a great mind to marry. Happiness is contagious."

"Do you still take to painting?" asked Mervale, languidly, endeavoring to turn the tables on his guest.

"Oh, no; I have adopted your advice. No art, no ideal, — nothing loftier than Commonplace for me now. If I were to paint again, I positively think *you* would purchase my pictures. Make haste and finish your breakfast, man; I wish to consult you. I have come to England to see after my affairs. My ambition is to make money; your counsels and experience cannot fail to assist me here."

"Ah, you were soon disenchanted of your Philosopher's Stone! You must know, Sarah, that when I last left Glyndon, he was bent upon turning alchemist and magician."

"You are witty today, Mr. Mervale."

"Upon my honor it is true, I told you so before."

Glyndon rose abruptly.

"Why revive those recollections of folly and presumption? Have I not said that I have returned to my native land to pursue the healthful avocations of my kind! Oh, yes! what so healthful, so noble, so fitted to our nature, as what you call the Practical Life? If we have faculties, what is their use, but to sell them to advantage! Buy knowledge as we do our goods; buy it at the cheapest market, sell it at the dearest. Have you not breakfasted yet?"

The friends walked into the streets, and Mervale shrank from the irony with which Glyndon complimented him on his respectability, his station, his pursuits, his happy marriage, and his eight pictures in their

---

††In the wide world, out of the solitude, will these allure thee.

handsome frames. Formerly the sober Mervale had commanded an influence over his friend: *his* had been the sarcasm; Glyndon's the irresolute shame at his own peculiarities. Now this position was reversed. There was a fierce earnestness in Glyndon's altered temper which awed and silenced the quiet commonplace of his friend's character. He seemed to take a malignant delight in persuading himself that the sober life of the world was contemptible and base.

"Ah!" he exclaimed, "how right you were to tell me to marry respectably; to have a solid position; to live in decorous fear of the world and one's wife; and to command the envy of the poor, the good opinion of the rich. You have practiced what you preach. Delicious existence! The merchant's desk and the curtain lecture! Ha! ha! Shall we have another night of it?"

Mervale, embarrassed and irritated, turned the conversation upon Glyndon's affairs. He was surprised at the knowledge of the world which the artist seemed to have suddenly acquired, surprised still more at the acuteness and energy with which he spoke of the speculations most in vogue at the market. Yes; Glyndon was certainly in earnest: he desired to be rich and respectable, — and to make at least ten per cent for his money!

After spending some days with the merchant, during which time he contrived to disorganize all the mechanism of the house, to turn night into day, harmony into discord, to drive poor Mrs. Mervale half-distracted, and to convince her husband that he was horribly hen-pecked, the ill-omened visitor left them as suddenly as he had arrived. He took a house of his own; he sought the society of persons of substance; he devoted himself to the money market; he seemed to have become a man of business; his schemes were bold and colossal; his calculations rapid and profound. He startled Mervale by his energy, and dazzled him by his success. Mervale began to envy him, — to be discontented with his own regular and slow gains. When Glyndon bought or sold in the funds, wealth rolled upon him like the tide of a sea; what years of toil could not have done for him in art, a few months, by a succession of lucky chances, did for him in speculation. Suddenly, however, he relaxed his exertions; new objects of ambition seemed to attract him. If he heard a drum in the streets, what glory like the soldier's? If a new poem were published, what renown like the poet's? He began works in literature, which promised great excellence, to throw them aside in disgust. All at once he abandoned the decorous and formal society he had courted; he joined himself, with young and riotous associates; he plunged into the wildest excesses of the great city, where Gold reigns alike over Toil and Pleasure. Through all he carried with him a certain power and heat of soul. In all society he aspired to command, — in all pursuits to excel.

Yet whatever the passion of the moment, the reaction was terrible in its gloom. He sank, at times, into the most profound and the darkest reveries. His fever was that of a mind that would escape memory, — his repose, that of a mind which the memory seizes again, and devours as a prey. Mervale now saw little of him; they shunned each other. Glyndon had no confidant, and no friend.

Chapter 5.IV.

Ich fuhle Dich mir nahe;
Die Einsamkeit belebt;
Wie uber seinen Welten
Der Unsichtbare schwebt.*

Uhland

*F*rom this state of restlessness and agitation rather than continuous action, Glyndon was aroused by a visitor who seemed to exercise the most salutary influence over him. His sister, an orphan with himself, had resided in the country with her aunt. In the early years of hope and home he had loved this girl, much younger than himself, with all a brother's tenderness. On his return to England, he had seemed to forget her existence. She recalled herself to him on her aunt's death by a touching and melancholy letter: she had now no home but his, — no dependence save on his affection; he wept when he read it, and was impatient till Adela arrived.

This girl, then about eighteen, concerned beneath a gentle and calm exterior much of the romance or enthusiasm that had, at her own age, characterized her brother. But her enthusiasm was of a far purer order,

* I feel thee near to me,
  The loneliness takes life, —
  As over its world
  The Invisible hovers.

and was restrained within proper bounds, partly by the sweetness of a very feminine nature, and partly by a strict and methodical education. She differed from him especially in a timidity of character which exceeded that usual at her age, but which the habit of self-command concealed no less carefully than that timidity itself concealed the romance I have ascribed to her.

Adela was not handsome: she had the complexion and the form of delicate health; and too fine an organization of the nerves rendered her susceptible to every impression that could influence the health of the frame through the sympathy of the mind. But as she never complained, and as the singular serenity of her manners seemed to betoken an equanimity of temperament which, with the vulgar, might have passed for indifference, her sufferings had so long been borne unnoticed that it ceased to be an effort to disguise them. Though, as I have said, not handsome, her countenance was interesting and pleasing; and there was that caressing kindness, that winning charm about her smile, her manners, her anxiety to please, to comfort, and to soothe which went at once to the heart, and made her lovely, — because so loving.

Such was the sister whom Glyndon had so long neglected, and whom he now so cordially welcomed. Adela had passed many years a victim to the caprices, and a nurse to the maladies, of a selfish and exacting relation. The delicate and generous and respectful affection of her brother was no less new to her than delightful. He took pleasure in the happiness he created; he gradually weaned himself from other society; he felt the charm of home. It is not surprising, then, that this young creature, free and virgin from every more ardent attachment, concentrated all her grateful love on this cherished and protecting relative. Her study by day, her dream by night, was to repay him for his affection. She was proud of his talents, devoted to his welfare; the smallest trifle that could interest him swelled in her eyes to the gravest affairs of life. In short, all the long-hoarded enthusiasm, which was her perilous and only heritage, she invested in this one object of her holy tenderness, her pure ambition.

But in proportion as Glyndon shunned those excitements by which he had so long sought to occupy his time or distract his thoughts, the gloom of his calmer hours became deeper and more continuous. He ever and especially dreaded to be alone; he could not bear his new companion to be absent from his eyes: he rode with her, walked with her, and it was with visible reluctance, which almost partook of horror, that he retired to rest at an hour when even revel grows fatigued. This gloom was not that which could be called by the soft name of melancholy, — it was far more intense; it seemed rather like despair. Often after a silence as of death — so heavy, abstracted, motionless, did it appear — he would start abruptly, and cast hurried glances around him, — his limbs trembling, his lips livid, his brows bathed in dew. Convinced that some secret sorrow preyed upon his mind, and would consume his health, it was the dearest as the most natural desire of Adela to become his confidant and consoler. She observed, with the quick tact of the delicate, that he disliked her to seem affected by, or even sensible of, his darker moods. She schooled herself to suppress her fears and her feelings. She would not ask his confidence, — she sought to steal into it. By little and little she felt that she was succeeding. Too wrapped in his own strange existence to be acutely observant of the character of others, Glyndon mistook the self-content of a generous and humble affection for constitutional fortitude; and this quality pleased and soothed him. It is fortitude that the diseased mind requires in the confidant whom it selects as its physician. And how irresistible is that desire to communicate! How often the lonely man thought to himself, "My heart would be lightened of its misery, if once confessed!" He felt, too, that in the very youth, the inexperience, the poetical temperament of Adela, he could find one who would comprehend and bear with him better than any sterner and more practical nature. Mervale would have looked on his revelations as the ravings of madness, and most men, at best, as the sicklied chimeras, the optical delusions, of disease. Thus gradually preparing himself for that relief for which he yearned, the moment for his disclosure arrived thus: —

One evening, as they sat alone together, Adela, who inherited some portion of her brother's talent in art, was employed in drawing, and Glyndon, rousing himself from meditations less gloomy than usual, rose, and affectionately passing his arm round her waist, looked over her as she sat. An exclamation of dismay broke from his lips, — he snatched the drawing from her hand: "What are you about? — what portrait is this?"

"Dear Clarence, do you not remember the original? — it is a copy from that portrait of our wise ancestor which our poor mother used to say so strongly resembled you. I thought it would please you if I copied it from memory."

"Accursed was the likeness!" said Glyndon, gloomily. "Guess you not the reason why I have shunned to return to the home of my fathers! — because I dreaded to meet that portrait! — because — because — but pardon me; I alarm you!"

"Ah, no, — no, Clarence, you never alarm me when you speak: only when you are silent! Oh, if you thought me worthy of your trust; oh, if you had given me the right to reason with you in the sorrows that I yearn to share!"

Glyndon made no answer, but paced the room for some moments

with disordered strides. He stopped at last, and gazed at her earnestly. "Yes, you, too, are his descendant; you know that such men have lived and suffered; you will not mock me, — you will not disbelieve! Listen! hark! — what sound is that?"

"But the wind on the house-top, Clarence, — but the wind."

"Give me your hand; let me feel its living clasp; and when I have told you, never revert to the tale again. Conceal it from all: swear that it shall die with us, — the last of our predestined race!"

"Never will I betray your trust; I swear it, — never!" said Adela, firmly; and she drew closer to his side. Then Glyndon commenced his story. That which, perhaps, in writing, and to minds prepared to question and disbelieve, may seem cold and terrorless, became far different when told by those blanched lips, with all that truth of suffering which convinces and appalls. Much, indeed, he concealed, much he involuntarily softened; but he revealed enough to make his tale intelligible and distinct to his pale and trembling listener. "At daybreak," he said, "I left that unhallowed and abhorred abode. I had one hope still, — I would seek Mejnour through the world. I would force him to lay at rest the fiend that haunted my soul. With this intent I journeyed from city to city. I instituted the most vigilant researches through the police of Italy. I even employed the services of the Inquisition at Rome, which had lately asserted its ancient powers in the trial of the less dangerous Cagliostro. All was in vain; not a trace of him could be discovered. I was not alone, Adela." Here Glyndon paused a moment, as if embarrassed; for in his recital, I need scarcely say that he had only indistinctly alluded to Fillide, whom the reader may surmise to be his companion. "I was not alone, but the associate of my wanderings was not one in whom my soul could confide, — faithful and affectionate, but without education, without faculties to comprehend me, with natural instincts rather than cultivated reason; one in whom the heart might lean in its careless hours, but with whom the mind could have no commune, in whom the bewildered spirit could seek no guide. Yet in the society of this person the demon troubled me not. Let me explain yet more fully the dread conditions of its presence. In coarse excitement, in commonplace life, in the wild riot, in the fierce excess, in the torpid lethargy of that animal existence which we share with the brutes, its eyes were invisible, its whisper was unheard. But whenever the soul would aspire, whenever the imagination kindled to the loftier ends, whenever the consciousness of our proper destiny struggled against the unworthy life I pursued, then, Adela — then, it cowered by my side in the light of noon, or sat by my bed, — a Darkness visible through the Dark. If, in the galleries of Divine Art, the dreams of my youth woke the early emulation, — if I turned to the thoughts of sages; if the example of the great, if the converse of the wise, aroused the silenced intellect, the demon was with me as by a spell. At last, one evening, at Genoa, to which city I had traveled in pursuit of the mystic, suddenly, and when least expected, he appeared before me. It was the time of the Carnival. It was in one of those half-frantic scenes of noise and revel, call it not gayety, which establish a heathen saturnalia in the midst of a Christian festival. Wearied with the dance, I had entered a room in which several revelers were seated, drinking, singing, shouting; and in their fantastic dresses and hideous masks, their orgy seemed scarcely human. I placed myself amongst them, and in that fearful excitement of the spirits which the happy never know, I was soon the most riotous of all. The conversation fell on the Revolution of France, which had always possessed for me an absorbing fascination. The masks spoke of the millennium it was to bring on earth, not as philosophers rejoicing in the advent of light, but as ruffians exulting in the annihilation of law. I know not why it was, but their licentious language infected myself; and, always desirous to be foremost in every circle, I soon exceeded even these rioters in declamations on the nature of the liberty which was about to embrace all the families of the globe, — a liberty that should pervade not only public legislation, but domestic life; an emancipation from every fetter that men had forged for them- selves. In the midst of this tirade one of the masks whispered me, —

"'Take care. One listens to you who seems to be a spy!'

"My eyes followed those of the mask, and I observed a man who took no part in the conversation, but whose gaze was bent upon me. He was disguised like the rest, yet I found by a general whisper that none had observed him enter. His silence, his attention, had alarmed the fears of the other revelers, — they only excited me the more. Rapt in my subject, I pursued it, insensible to the signs of those about me; and, addressing myself only to the silent mask who sat alone, apart from the group, I did not even observe that, one by one, the revelers slunk off, and that I and the silent listener were left alone, until, pausing from my heated and impetuous declamations, I said, —

"'And you, signor, — what is your view of this mighty era? Opinion without persecution; brotherhood without jealousy; love without bond- age —'

"'And life without God,' added the mask as I hesitated for new images.

"The sound of that well-known voice changed the current of my thought. I sprang forward, and cried, —

"'Imposter or Fiend, we meet at last!'

"The figure rose as I advanced, and, unmasking, showed the features of Mejnour. His fixed eye, his majestic aspect, awed and repelled me. I stood rooted to the ground.

"'Yes,' he said solemnly, 'we meet, and it is this meeting that I have sought. How hast thou followed my admonitions! Are these the scenes in which the Aspirant for the Serene Science thinks to escape the Ghastly Enemy? Do the thoughts thou hast uttered — thoughts that would strike all order from the universe — express the hopes of the sage who would rise to the Harmony of the Eternal Spheres?'

"'It is thy fault, — it is thine!' I exclaimed. 'Exorcise the phantom! Take the haunting terror from my soul!'

Mejnour looked at me a moment with a cold and cynical disdain which provoked at once my fear and rage, and replied, —

"'No; fool of thine own senses! No; thou must have full and entire experience of the illusions to which the Knowledge that is without Faith climbs its Titan way. Thou pantest for this Millennium, — thou shalt behold it! Thou shalt be one of the agents of the era of Light and Reason. I see, while I speak, the Phantom thou fliest, by thy side; it marshals thy path; it has power over thee as yet, — a power that defies my own. In the last days of that Revolution which thou hailest, amidst the wrecks of the Order thou cursest as Oppression, seek the fulfillment of thy destiny, and await thy cure.'

"At that instant a troop of masks, clamorous, intoxicated, reeling, and rushing, as they reeled, poured into the room, and separated me from the mystic. I broke through them, and sought him everywhere, but in vain. All my researches the next day were equally fruitless. Weeks were consumed in the same pursuit, — not a trace of Mejnour could be discovered. Wearied with false pleasures, roused by reproaches I had deserved, recoiling from Mejnour's prophecy of the scene in which I was to seek deliverance, it occurred to me, at last, that in the sober air of my native country, and amidst its orderly and vigorous pursuits, I might work out my own emancipation from the specter. I left all whom I had before courted and clung to, — I came hither. Amidst mercenary schemes and selfish speculations, I found the same relief as in debauch and excess. The Phantom was invisible; but these pursuits soon became to me distasteful as the rest. Ever and ever I felt that I was born for something nobler than the greed of gain, — that life may be made equally worthless, and the soul equally degraded by the icy lust of avarice, as by the noisier passions. A higher ambition never ceased to torment me. But, but," continued Glyndon, with a whitening lip and a visible shudder, "at every attempt to rise into loftier existence, came that hideous form. It gloomed beside me at the easel. Before the volumes of poet and sage it stood with its burning eyes in the stillness of night, and I thought I heard its horrible whispers uttering temptations never to be divulged." He paused, and the drops stood upon his brow.

"But I," said Adela, mastering her fears and throwing her arms around him, — "but I henceforth will have no life but in thine. And in this love so pure, so holy, thy terror shall fade away."

"No, no!" exclaimed Glyndon, starting from her. "The worst revelation is to come. Since thou hast been here, since I have sternly and resolutely refrained from every haunt, every scene in which this preternatural enemy troubled me not, I — I — have — Oh, Heaven! Mercy — mercy! There it stands, — there, by thy side, — there, there!" And he fell to the ground insensible.

Chapter 5.V.

Doch wunderbar ergriff mich's diese Nacht;
Die Glieder schienen schon in Todes Macht.*

Uhland

A fever, attended with delirium, for several days deprived Glyndon of consciousness; and when, by Adela's care more than the skill of the physicians, he was restored to life and reason, he was unutterably shocked by the change in his sister's appearance; at first, he fondly imagined that her health, affected by her vigils, would recover with his own. But he soon saw, with an anguish which partook of remorse, that the malady was deep-seated, — deep, deep, beyond the reach of Aesculapius and his drugs. Her imagination, little less lively than his own, was awfully impressed by the strange confessions she had heard, — by the ravings of his delirium. Again and again had he shrieked forth, "It is there, — there, by thy side, my sister!" He had transferred to her fancy the specter, and the horror that cursed himself. He perceived this, not by her words, but her silence; by the eyes that strained into space; by the shiver that came over her frame; by the start of terror; by the look that did not dare to turn behind. Bitterly he repented his confession; bitterly he felt that between his sufferings and human sympathy there

---

* This night it fearfully seized on me; my limbs appeared already in the power of death.

could be no gentle and holy commune; vainly he sought to retract, — to undo what he had done, to declare all was but the chimera of an overheated brain!

And brave and generous was this denial of himself; for, often and often, as he thus spoke, he saw the Thing of Dread gliding to her side, and glaring at him as he disowned its being. But what chilled him, if possible, yet more than her wasting form and trembling nerves, was the change in her love for him; a natural terror had replaced it. She turned paler if he approached, — she shuddered if he took her hand. Divided from the rest of earth, the gulf of the foul remembrance yawned now between his sister and himself. He could endure no more the presence of the one whose life *his* life had embittered. He made some excuses for departure, and writhed to see that they were greeted eagerly. The first gleam of joy he had detected since that fatal night, on Adela's face, he beheld when he murmured "Farewell." He traveled for some weeks through the wildest parts of Scotland; scenery which *makes* the artist, was loveless to his haggard eyes. A letter recalled him to London on the wings of new agony and fear; he arrived to find his sister in a condition both of mind and health which exceeded his worst apprehensions.

Her vacant look, her lifeless posture, appalled him; it was as one who gazed on the Medusa's head, and felt, without a struggle, the human being gradually harden to the statue. It was not frenzy, it was not idiocy, — it was an abstraction, an apathy, a sleep in waking. Only as the night advanced towards the eleventh hour — the hour in which Glyndon had concluded his tale — she grew visibly uneasy, anxious, and perturbed. Then her lips muttered; her hands writhed; she looked round with a look of unspeakable appeal for succor, for protection, and suddenly, as the clock struck, fell with a shriek to the ground, cold and lifeless. With difficulty, and not until after the most earnest prayers, did she answer the agonized questions of Glyndon; at last she owned that at that hour, and that hour alone, wherever she was placed, however occupied, she distinctly beheld the apparition of an old hag, who, after thrice knocking at the door, entered the room, and hobbling up to her with a countenance distorted by hideous rage and menace, laid its icy fingers on her forehead: from that moment she declared that sense forsook her; and when she woke again, it was only to wait, in suspense that froze up her blood, the repetition of the ghastly visitation.

The physician who had been summoned before Glyndon's return, and whose letter had recalled him to London, was a commonplace practitioner, ignorant of the case, and honestly anxious that one more experienced should be employed. Clarence called in one of the most eminent of the faculty, and to him he recited the optical delusion of his sister. The physician listened attentively, and seemed sanguine in his hopes of cure. He came to the house two hours before the one so dreaded by the patient. He had quietly arranged that the clocks should be put forward half an hour, unknown to Adela, and even to her brother. He was a man of the most extraordinary powers of conversation, of surpassing wit, of all the faculties that interest and amuse. He first administered to the patient a harmless potion, which he pledged himself would dispel the delusion. His confident tone woke her own hopes, — he continued to excite her attention, to rouse her lethargy; he jested, he laughed away the time. The hour struck. "Joy, my brother!" she exclaimed, throwing herself in his arms; "the time is past!" And then, like one released from a spell, she suddenly assumed more than her ancient cheerfulness. "Ah, Clarence!" she whispered, "forgive me for my former desertion, — forgive me that I feared *you*. I shall live! — I shall live! in my turn to banish the specter that haunts my brother!" And Clarence smiled and wiped the tears from his burning eyes. The physician renewed his stories, his jests. In the midst of a stream of rich humor that seemed to carry away both brother and sister, Glyndon suddenly saw over Adela's face the same fearful change, the same anxious look, the same restless, straining eye, he had beheld the night before. He rose, — he approached her. Adela started up. "look — look — look!" she exclaimed. "She comes! Save me, — save me!" and she fell at his feet in strong convulsions as the clock, falsely and in vain put forward, struck the half-hour.

The physician lifted her in his arms. "My worst fears are confirmed," he said gravely; "the disease is epilepsy."*

The next night, at the same hour, Adela Glyndon died.

Chapter 5. VI.

La loi, dont le regne vous epouvante, a son glaive leve sur vous: elle vous frappera tous: le genre humain a besoin de cet exem-

---

* The most celebrated practitioner in Dublin related to the editor a story of optical delusion precisely similar in its circumstances and its physical cause to the one here narrated.

ple.*

— Couthon

"Oh, joy, joy! — thou art come again! This is thy hand — these thy lips. Say that thou didst not desert me from the love of another; say it again, — say it ever! — and I will pardon thee all the rest!"

"So thou hast mourned for me?"

"Mourned! — and thou wert cruel enough to leave me gold; there it is, — there, untouched!"

"Poor child of Nature! how, then, in this strange town of Marseilles, hast thou found bread and shelter?"

"Honestly, soul of my soul! honestly, but yet by the face thou didst once think so fair; thinkest thou *that* now?"

"Yes, Fillide, more fair than ever. But what meanest thou?"

"There is a painter here — a great man, one of their great men at Paris, I know not what they call them; but he rules over all here, — life and death; and he has paid me largely but to sit for my portrait. It is for a picture to be given to the Nation, for he paints only for glory. Think of thy Fillide's renown!" And the girl's wild eyes sparkled; her vanity was roused. "And he would have married me if I would! — divorced his wife to marry me! But I waited for thee, ungrateful!"

A knock at the door was heard, — a man entered.

"Nicot!"

"Ah, Glyndon! — hum! — welcome! What! thou art twice my rival! But Jean Nicot bears no malice. Virtue is my dream, — my country, my mistress. Serve my country, citizen; and I forgive thee the preference of beauty. Ca ira! ca ira!"

But as the painter spoke, it hymned, it rolled through the streets, — the fiery song of the Marseillaise! There was a crowd, a multitude, a people up, abroad, with colors and arms, enthusiasm and song, — with song, with enthusiasm, with colors and arms! And who could guess that that martial movement was one, not of war, but massacre, — Frenchmen against Frenchmen? For there are two parties in Marseilles, — and ample work for Jourdan Coupe-tete! But this, the Englishman, just arrived, a stranger to all factions, did not as yet comprehend. He comprehended nothing but the song, the enthusiasm, the arms, and the colors that lifted to the sun the glorious lie, "Le peuple Francais, debout contre les tyrans!"†

The dark brow of the wretched wanderer grew animated; he gazed

---

* The law, whose reign terrifies you, has its sword raised against you; it will strike you all: humanity has need of this example.

† Up, Frenchmen, against tyrants!

from the window on the throng that marched below, beneath their waving Oriflamme. They shouted as they beheld the patriot Nicot, the friend of Liberty and relentless Hebert, by the stranger's side, at the casement.

"Aye, shout again!" cried the painter, — "shout for the brave Englishman who abjures his Pitts and his Coburgs to be a citizen of Liberty and France!"

A thousand voices rent the air, and the hymn of the Marseillaise rose in majesty again.

"Well, and if it be among these high hopes and this brave people that the phantom is to vanish, and the cure to come!" muttered Glyndon; and he thought he felt again the elixir sparkling through his veins.

"Thou shalt be one of the Convention with Paine and Clootz, — I will manage it all for thee!" cried Nicot, slapping him on the shoulder: "and Paris —".

"Ah, if I could but see Paris!" cried Fillide, in her joyous voice. Joyous! the whole time, the town, the air — save where, unheard, rose the cry of agony and the yell of murder — were joy! Sleep unhaunting in thy grave, cold Adela. Joy, joy! In the Jubilee of Humanity all private griefs should cease! Behold, wild mariner, the vast whirlpool draws thee to its stormy bosom! There the individual is not. All things are of the whole! Open thy gates, fair Paris, for the stranger-citizen! Receive in your ranks, O meek Republicans, the new champion of liberty, of reason, of mankind! "Mejnour is right; it was in virtue, in valor, in glorious struggle for the human race, that the specter was to shrink to her kindred darkness."

And Nicot's shrill voice praised him; and lean Robespierre — "Flambeau, colonne, pierre angulaire de l'edifice de la Republique!"* — smiled ominously on him from his bloodshot eyes; and Fillide clasped him with passionate arms to her tender breast. And at his up rising and down sitting, at board and in bed, though he saw it not, the Nameless One guided him with the demon eyes to the sea whose waves were gore.

---

* "The light, column, and keystone of the Republic." — "Lettre du Citoyen P——; Papiers inedits trouves chez Robespierre," tom 11, page 127.

BOOK VI

SUPERSTITION
DESERTING FAITH

Why do I yield to that suggestion,
Whose horrid image doth unfix my hair.

— Shakespeare

Chapter 6.I.

Therefore the Genii were painted with a platter full of garlands
and flowers in one hand, and a whip in the other.
— Alexander Ross, "Mystag. Poet."

*A*ccording to the order of the events related in this narrative, the
departure of Zanoni and Viola from the Greek isle, in which two happy
years appear to have been passed, must have been somewhat later in
date than the arrival of Glyndon at Marseilles. It must have been in the
course of the year 1791 when Viola fled from Naples with her mysterious
lover, and when Glyndon sought Mejnour in the fatal castle. It is now
towards the close of 1793, when our story again returns to Zanoni. The
stars of winter shone down on the lagunes of Venice. The hum of the
Rialto was hushed, — the last loiterers had deserted the Place of St.
Mark's, and only at distant intervals might be heard the oars of the
rapid gondolas, bearing reveler or lover to his home. But lights still
flitted to and fro across the windows of one of the Palladian palaces,
whose shadow slept in the great canal; and within the palace watched
the twin Eumenides that never sleep for Man, — Fear and Pain.

"I will make thee the richest man in all Venice, if thou savest her."

"Signor," said the leech; "your gold cannot control death, and the
will of Heaven, signor, unless within the next hour there is some blessed
change, prepare your courage."

Ho — ho, Zanoni! man of mystery and might, who hast walked amidst
the passions of the world, with no changes on thy brow, art thou tossed
at last upon the billows of tempestuous fear? Does thy spirit reel to and
fro? — knowest thou at last the strength and the majesty of Death?

He fled, trembling, from the pale-faced man of art, — fled through
stately hall and long-drawn corridor, and gained a remote chamber in
the palace, which other step than his was not permitted to profane. Out
with thy herbs and vessels. Break from the enchanted elements, O

silvery-azure flame! Why comes he not, — the Son of the Starbeam! Why is Adon-Ai deaf to thy solemn call? It comes not, — the luminous and delightsome Presence! Cabalist! are thy charms in vain? Has thy throne vanished from the realms of space? Thou standest pale and trembling. Pale trembler! not thus didst thou look when the things of glory gathered at thy spell. Never to the pale trembler bow the things of glory: the soul, and not the herbs, nor the silvery-azure flame, nor the spells of the Cabala, commands the children of the air; and *thy* soul, by Love and Death, is made scepterless and discrowned!

At length the flame quivers, — the air grows cold as the wind in charnels. A thing not of earth is present, — a mistlike, formless thing. It cowers in the distance, — a silent Horror! it rises; it creeps; it nears thee — dark in its mantle of dusky haze; and under its veil it looks on thee with its livid, malignant eyes, — the thing of malignant eyes!

"Ha, young Chaldean! young in thy countless ages, — young as when, cold to pleasure and to beauty, thou stoodest on the old Fire-tower, and heardest the starry silence whisper to thee the last mystery that baffles Death, — fearest thou Death at length? Is thy knowledge but a circle that brings thee back whence thy wanderings began! Generations on generations have withered since we two met! Lo! thou beholdest me now!"

"But I behold thee without fear! Though beneath thine eyes thousands have perished; though, where they burn, spring up the foul poisons of the human heart, and to those whom thou canst subject to thy will, thy presence glares in the dreams of the raving maniac, or blackens the dungeon of despairing crime, thou art not my vanquisher, but my slave!"

"And as a slave will I serve thee! Command thy slave, O beautiful Chaldean! Hark, the wail of women! — hark, the sharp shriek of thy beloved one! Death is in thy palace! Adon-Ai comes not to thy call. Only where no cloud of the passion and the flesh veils the eye of the Serene Intelligence can the Sons of the Starbeam glide to man. But *I* can aid thee! — hark!" And Zanoni heard distinctly in his heart, even at that distance from the chamber, the voice of Viola calling in delirium on her beloved one.

"Oh, Viola, I can save thee not!" exclaimed the seer, passionately; "my love for thee has made me powerless!"

"Not powerless; I can gift thee with the art to save her, — I can place healing in thy hand!"

"For both? — child and mother, — for both?"

"Both!"

A convulsion shook the limbs of the seer, — a mighty struggle shook him as a child: the Humanity and the Hour conquered the repugnant spirit.

"I yield! Mother and child — save both!"

. . .

In the dark chamber lay Viola, in the sharpest agonies of travail; life seemed rending itself away in the groans and cries that spoke of pain in the midst of frenzy; and still, in groan and cry, she called on Zanoni, her beloved. The physician looked to the clock; on it beat: the Heart of Time, — regularly and slowly, — Heart that never sympathized with Life, and never flagged for Death! "The cries are fainter," said the leech; "in ten minutes more all will be past."

Fool! the minutes laugh at thee; Nature, even now, like a blue sky through a shattered temple, is smiling through the tortured frame. The breathing grows more calm and hushed; the voice of delirium is dumb, — a sweet dream has come to Viola. Is it a dream, or is it the soul that sees? She thinks suddenly that she is with Zanoni, that her burning head is pillowed on his bosom; she thinks, as he gazes on her, that his eyes dispel the tortures that prey upon her, — the touch of his hand cools the fever on her brow; she hears his voice in murmurs, — it is a music from which the fiends fly. Where is the mountain that seemed to press upon her temples? Like a vapor, it rolls away. In the frosts of the winter night, she sees the sun laughing in luxurious heaven, — she hears the whisper of green leaves; the beautiful world, valley and stream and woodland, lie before, and with a common voice speak to her, "We are not yet past for thee!" Fool of drugs and formula, look to thy dial-plate! — the hand has moved on; the minutes are with Eternity; the soul thy sentence would have dismissed, still dwells on the shores of Time. She sleeps: the fever abates; the convulsions are gone; the living rose blooms upon her cheek; the crisis is past! Husband, thy wife lives; lover, thy universe is no solitude! Heart of Time, beat on! A while, a little while, — joy! joy! joy! — father, embrace thy child!

Chapter 6.II.

Tristis Erinnys
Praetulit infaustas sanguinolenta faces.*

Ovid

And they placed the child in the father's arms! As silently he bent over it, tears — tears, how human! — fell from his eyes like rain! And the little one smiled through the tears that bathed its cheeks! Ah, with what happy tears we welcome the stranger into our sorrowing world! With what agonizing tears we dismiss the stranger back to the angels! Unselfish joy; but how selfish is the sorrow!

And now through the silent chamber a faint sweet voice is heard, — the young mother's voice.

"I am here: I am by thy side!" murmured Zanoni.

The mother smiled, and clasped his hand, and asked no more; she was contented.

. . .

Viola recovered with a rapidity that startled the physician; and the young stranger thrived as if it already loved the world to which it had descended. From that hour Zanoni seemed to live in the infant's life, and in that life the souls of mother and father met as in a new bond. Nothing more beautiful than this infant had eye ever dwelt upon. It was strange to the nurses that it came not wailing to the light, but smiled to the light as a thing familiar to it before. It never uttered one cry of childish pain. In its very repose it seemed to be listening to some happy voice within its heart: it seemed itself so happy. In its eyes you would have thought intellect already kindled, though it had not yet found a language. Already it seemed to recognize its parents; already it stretched forth its arms when Zanoni bent over the bed, in which it breathed and bloomed, — the budding flower! And from that bed he was rarely absent: gazing upon it with his serene, delighted eyes, his soul seemed to feed

---

* Erinnys, doleful and bloody, extends the unblessed torches.

its own. At night and in utter darkness he was still there; and Viola often heard him murmuring over it as she lay in a half-sleep. But the murmur was in a language strange to her; and sometimes when she heard she feared, and vague, undefined superstitions came back to her, — the superstitions of earlier youth. A mother fears everything, even the gods, for her newborn. The mortals shrieked aloud when of old they saw the great Demeter seeking to make their child immortal.

But Zanoni, wrapped in the sublime designs that animated the human love to which he was now awakened, forgot all, even all he had forfeited or incurred, in the love that blinded him.

But the dark, formless thing, though he nor invoked nor saw it, crept, often, round and round him, and often sat by the infant's couch, with its hateful eyes.

Chapter 6.III.

Fuscis tellurem amplectitur alis.*

Virgil

Letter from Zanoni to Mejnour

Mejnour, Humanity, with all its sorrows and its joys, is mine once more. Day by day, I am forging my own fetters. I live in other lives than my own, and in them I have lost more than half my empire. Not lifting them aloft, they drag me by the strong bands of the affections to their own earth. Exiled from the beings only visible to the most abstract sense, the grim Enemy that guards the Threshold has entangled me in its web. Canst thou credit me, when I tell thee that I have accepted its gifts, and endure the forfeit? Ages must pass ere the brighter beings can again obey the spirit that has bowed to the ghastly one! And —

. . .

In this hope, then, Mejnour, I triumph still; I yet have supreme power

---

* Embraces the Earth with gloomy wings.

over this young life. Insensibly and inaudibly my soul speaks to its own, and prepares it even now. Thou knowest that for the pure and unsullied infant spirit, the ordeal has no terror and no peril. Thus unceasingly I nourish it with no unholy light; and ere it yet be conscious of the gift, it will gain the privileges it has been mine to attain: the child, by slow and scarce-seen degrees, will communicate its own attributes to the mother; and content to see Youth forever radiant on the brows of the two that now suffice to fill up my whole infinity of thought, shall I regret the airier kingdom that vanishes hourly from my grasp? But thou, whose vision is still clear and serene, look into the far deeps shut from my gaze, and counsel me, or forewarn! I know that the gifts of the Being whose race is so hostile to our own are, to the common seeker, fatal and perfidious as itself. And hence, when, at the outskirts of knowledge, which in earlier ages men called Magic, they encountered the things of the hostile tribes, they believed the apparitions to be fiends, and, by fancied compacts, imagined they had signed away their souls; as if man could give for an eternity that over which he has control but while he lives! Dark, and shrouded forever from human sight, dwell the demon rebels, in their impenetrable realm; in them is no breath of the Divine One. In every human creature the Divine One breathes; and He alone can judge His own hereafter, and allot its new career and home. Could man sell himself to the fiend, man could prejudge himself, and arrogate the disposal of eternity! But these creatures, modifications as they are of matter, and some with more than the malignity of man, may well seem, to fear and unreasoning superstition, the representatives of fiends. And from the darkest and mightiest of them I have accepted a boon, — the secret that startled Death from those so dear to me. Can I not trust that enough of power yet remains to me to baffle or to daunt the Phantom, if it seek to pervert the gift? Answer me, Mejnour, for in the darkness that veils me, I see only the pure eyes of the newborn; I hear only the low beating of my heart. Answer me, thou whose wisdom is without love!

Mejnour to Zanoni

Rome

Fallen One! — I see before thee Evil and Death and Woe! Thou to have relinquished Adon-Ai for the nameless Terror, — the heavenly stars for those fearful eyes! Thou, at the last to be the victim of the Larva of the dreary Threshold, that, in thy first novitiate, fled, withered and shriveled, from thy kingly brow! When, at the primary grades of initiation, the pupil I took from thee on the shores of the changed Parthenope, fell senseless and cowering before that Phantom-Darkness, I knew that his spirit was not formed to front the worlds beyond; for *fear* is the attraction of man to earthiest earth, and while he fears, he cannot soar. But *thou*, seest thou not that to love is but to fear; seest thou not that the power of which thou boastest over the malignant one is already gone? It awes, it masters thee; it will mock thee and betray. Lose not a moment; come to me. If there can yet be sufficient sympathy between us, through *my* eyes shalt thou see, and perhaps guard against the perils that, shapeless yet, and looming through the shadow, marshal themselves around thee and those whom thy very love has doomed. Come from all the ties of thy fond humanity; they will but obscure thy vision! Come forth from thy fears and hopes, thy desires and passions. Come, as alone Mind can be the monarch and the seer, shining through the home it tenants, — a pure, impressionless, sublime intelligence!

Chapter 6.IV.

Plus que vous ne pensez ce moment est terrible.*
La Harpe, "Le Comte de Warwick," Act 3, sc. 5.

*F*or the first time since their union, Zanoni and Viola were separated, — Zanoni went to Rome on important business. "It was," he said, "but for a few days;" and he went so suddenly that there was little time either for surprise or sorrow. But first parting is always more melancholy than it need be: it seems an interruption to the existence which Love shares with Love; it makes the heart feel what a void life will be when the last parting shall succeed, as succeed it must, the first. But Viola had a new companion; she was enjoying that most delicious novelty which ever renews the youth and dazzles the eyes of woman. As the mistress — the wife — she leans on another; from another are reflected her happiness, her being, — as an orb that takes light from its sun. But now, in turn, as the mother, she is raised from dependence into power; it is another that leans on her, — a star has sprung into space, to which she herself

* The moment is more terrible than you think.

has become the sun!

A few days, — but they will be sweet through the sorrow! A few days, — every hour of which seems an era to the infant, over whom bend watchful the eyes and the heart. From its waking to its sleep, from its sleep to its waking, is a revolution in Time. Every gesture to be noted, — every smile to seem a new progress into the world it has come to bless! Zanoni has gone, — the last dash of the oar is lost, the last speck of the gondola has vanished from the ocean-streets of Venice! Her infant is sleeping in the cradle at the mother's feet; and she thinks through her tears what tales of the fairyland, that spreads far and wide, with a thousand wonders, in that narrow bed, she shall have to tell the father! Smile on, weep on, young mother! Already the fairest leaf in the wild volume is closed for thee, and the invisible finger turns the page!

. . .

By the bridge of the Rialto stood two Venetians — ardent Republicans and Democrats — looking to the Revolution of France as the earthquake which must shatter their own expiring and vicious constitution, and give equality of ranks and rights to Venice.

"Yes, Cottalto," said one; "my correspondent of Paris has promised to elude all obstacles, and baffle all danger. He will arrange with us the hour of revolt, when the legions of France shall be within hearing of our guns. One day in this week, at this hour, he is to meet me here. This is but the fourth day."

He had scarce said these words before a man, wrapped in his roquelaire, emerging from one of the narrow streets to the left, halted opposite the pair, and eying them for a few moments with an earnest scrutiny, whispered, "Salut!"

"Et fraternite," answered the speaker.

"You, then, are the brave Dandolo with whom the Comite deputed me to correspond? And this citizen —"

"Is Cottalto, whom my letters have so often mentioned."*

"Health and brotherhood to him! I have much to impart to you both. I will meet you at night, Dandolo. But in the streets we may be observed."

"And I dare not appoint my own house; tyranny makes spies of our very walls. But the place herein designated is secure;" and he slipped an address into the hand of his correspondent.

"Tonight, then, at nine! Meanwhile I have other business." The man paused, his color changed, and it was with an eager and passionate voice that he resumed, —

"Your last letter mentioned this wealthy and mysterious visitor, — this

---

* I know not if the author of the original MSS. designs, under these names, to introduce the real Cottalto and the true Dandolo, who, in 1797, distinguished themselves by their sympathy with the French, and their democratic ardor. — Ed.

Zanoni. He is still at Venice?"

"I heard that he had left this morning; but his wife is still here."

"His wife! — that is well!"

"What know you of him? Think you that he would join us? His wealth would be —"

"His house, his address, — quick!" interrupted the man.

"The Palazzo di ——, on the Grand Canal."

"I thank you, — at nine we meet."

The man hurried on through the street from which he had emerged; and, passing by the house in which he had taken up his lodging (he had arrived at Venice the night before), a woman who stood by the door caught his arm.

"Monsieur," she said in French, "I have been watching for your return. Do you understand me? I will brave all, risk all, to go back with you to France, — to stand, through life or in death, by my husband's side!"

"Citoyenne, I promised your husband that, if such your choice, I would hazard my own safety to aid it. But think again! Your husband is one of the faction which Robespierre's eyes have already marked; he cannot fly. All France is become a prison to the 'suspect.' You do not endanger yourself by return. Frankly, citoyenne, the fate you would share may be the guillotine. I speak (as you know by his letter) as your husband bade me."

"Monsieur, I will return with you," said the woman, with a smile upon her pale face.

"And yet you deserted your husband in the fair sunshine of the Revolution, to return to him amidst its storms and thunder," said the man, in a tone half of wonder, half rebuke.

"Because my father's days were doomed; because he had no safety but in flight to a foreign land; because he was old and penniless, and had none but me to work for him; because my husband was not then in danger, and my father was! *He* is dead — dead! My husband is in danger now. The daughter's duties are no more, — the wife's return!"

"Be it so, citoyenne; on the third night I depart. Before then you may retract your choice."

"Never!"

A dark smile passed over the man's face.

"O guillotine!" he said, "how many virtues hast thou brought to light! Well may they call thee 'A Holy Mother!' O gory guillotine!"

He passed on muttering to himself, hailed a gondola, and was soon amidst the crowded waters of the Grand Canal.

Chapter 6. V.

Ce que j'ignore
Est plus triste peut-etre et plus affreux encore.*
                    La Harpe, "Le Comte de Warwick," Act 5, sc. 1.

The casement stood open, and Viola was seated by it. Beneath sparkled the broad waters in the cold but cloudless sunlight; and to that fair form, that half-averted face, turned the eyes of many a gallant cavalier, as their gondolas glided by.

But at last, in the center of the canal, one of these dark vessels halted motionless, as a man fixed his gaze from its lattice upon that stately palace. He gave the word to the rowers, — the vessel approached the marge. The stranger quitted the gondola; he passed up the broad stairs; he entered the palace. Weep on, smile no more, young mother! — the last page is turned!

An attendant entered the room, and gave to Viola a card, with these words in English, "Viola, I must see you! Clarence Glyndon."

Oh, yes, how gladly Viola would see him; how gladly speak to him of her happiness, of Zanoni! — how gladly show to him her child! Poor Clarence! she had forgotten him till now, as she had all the fever of her earlier life, — its dreams, its vanities, its poor excitement, the lamps of the gaudy theater, the applause of the noisy crowd.

He entered. She started to behold him, so changed were his gloomy brow, his resolute, careworn features, from the graceful form and careless countenance of the artist-lover. His dress, though not mean, was rude, neglected, and disordered. A wild, desperate, half-savage air had supplanted that ingenuous mien, diffident in its grace, earnest in its diffidence, which had once characterized the young worshipper of Art, the dreaming aspirant after some starrier lore.

"Is it you?" she said at last. "Poor Clarence, how changed!"

"Changed!" he said abruptly, as he placed himself by her side. "And

---

* That which I know not is, perhaps, more sad and fearful still.

whom am I to thank, but the fiends — the sorcerers — who have seized upon thy existence, as upon mine? Viola, hear me. A few weeks since the news reached me that you were in Venice. Under other pretences, and through innumerable dangers, I have come hither, risking liberty, perhaps life, if my name and career are known in Venice, to warn and save you. Changed, you call me! — changed without; but what is that to the ravages within? Be warned, be warned in time!"

The voice of Glyndon, sounding hollow and sepulchral, alarmed Viola even more than his words. Pale, haggard, emaciated, he seemed almost as one risen from the dead, to appall and awe her. "What," she said, at last, in a faltering voice, — "what wild words do you utter! Can you —"

"Listen!" interrupted Glyndon, laying his hand upon her arm, and its touch was as cold as death, — "listen! You have heard of the old stories of men who have leagued themselves with devils for the attainment of preternatural powers. Those stories are not fables. Such men live. Their delight is to increase the unhallowed circle of wretches like themselves. If their proselytes fail in the ordeal, the demon seizes them, even in this life, as it hath seized me! — if they succeed, woe, yea, a more lasting woe! There is another life, where no spells can charm the evil one, or allay the torture. I have come from a scene where blood flows in rivers, — where Death stands by the side of the bravest and the highest, and the one monarch is the Guillotine; but all the mortal perils with which men can be beset, are nothing to the dreariness of the chamber where the Horror that passes death moves and stirs!"

It was then that Glyndon, with a cold and distinct precision, detailed, as he had done to Adela, the initiation through which he had gone. He described, in words that froze the blood of his listener, the appearance of that formless phantom, with the eyes that seared the brain and congealed the marrow of those who beheld. Once seen, it never was to be exorcised. It came at its own will, prompting black thoughts, — whispering strange temptations. Only in scenes of turbulent excitement was it absent! Solitude, serenity, the struggling desires after peace and virtue, — *these* were the elements it loved to haunt! Bewildered, terror-stricken, the wild account confirmed by the dim impressions that never, in the depth and confidence of affection, had been closely examined, but rather banished as soon as felt, — that the life and attributes of Zanoni were not like those of mortals, — impressions which her own love had made her hitherto censure as suspicions that wronged, and which, thus mitigated, had perhaps only served to rivet the fascinated chains in which he bound her heart and senses, but which now, as Glyndon's awful narrative filled her with contagious dread, half unbound the very spells they had woven before, — Viola started up in fear, not for *herself,* and clasped her child in her arms!

"Unhappiest one!" cried Glyndon, shuddering, "hast thou indeed given birth to a victim thou canst not save? Refuse it sustenance, — let it look to thee in vain for food! In the grave, at least, there are repose and peace!"

Then there came back to Viola's mind the remembrance of Zanoni's nightlong watches by that cradle, and the fear which even then had crept over her as she heard his murmured half-chanted words. And as the child looked at her with its clear, steadfast eye, in the strange intelligence of that look there was something that only confirmed her awe. So there both Mother and Forewarner stood in silence, — the sun smiling upon them through the casement, and dark by the cradle, though they saw it not, sat the motionless, veiled Thing!

But by degrees better and juster and more grateful memories of the past returned to the young mother. The features of the infant, as she gazed, took the aspect of the absent father. A voice seemed to break from those rosy lips, and say, mournfully, "I speak to thee in thy child. In return for all my love for thee and thine, dost thou distrust me, at the first sentence of a maniac who accuses?"

Her breast heaved, her stature rose, her eyes shone with a serene and holy light.

"Go, poor victim of thine own delusions," she said to Glyndon; "I would not believe mine own senses, if they accused *its* father! And what knowest thou of Zanoni? What relation have Mejnour and the grisly specters he invoked, with the radiant image with which thou wouldst connect them?"

"Thou wilt learn too soon," replied Glyndon, gloomily. "And the very phantom that haunts me, whispers, with its bloodless lips, that its horrors await both thine and thee! I take not thy decision yet; before I leave Venice we shall meet again."

He said, and departed.

Chapter 6.VI.

Quel est l'egarement ou ton ame se livre?*
                    La Harpe, "Le Comte de Warwick," Act 4, sc. 4.

Alas, Zanoni! the aspirer, the dark, bright one! — didst thou think that the bond between the survivor of ages and the daughter of a day could endure? Didst thou not foresee that, until the ordeal was past, there could be no equality between thy wisdom and her love? Art thou absent now seeking amidst thy solemn secrets the solemn safeguards for child and mother, and forgettest thou that the phantom that served thee hath power over its own gifts, — over the lives it taught thee to rescue from the grave? Dost thou not know that Fear and Distrust, once sown in the heart of Love, spring up from the seed into a forest that excludes the stars? Dark, bright one! the hateful eyes glare beside the mother and the child!

All that day Viola was distracted by a thousand thoughts and terrors, which fled as she examined them to settle back the darklier. She remembered that, as she had once said to Glyndon, her very childhood had been haunted with strange forebodings, that she was ordained for some preternatural doom. She remembered that, as she had told him this, sitting by the seas that slumbered in the arms of the Bay of Naples, he, too, had acknowledged the same forebodings, and a mysterious sympathy had appeared to unite their fates. She remembered, above all, that, comparing their entangled thoughts, both had then said, that with the first sight of Zanoni the foreboding, the instinct, had spoken to their hearts more audibly than before, whispering that "with *him* was connected the secret of the unconjectured life."

And now, when Glyndon and Viola met again, the haunting fears of childhood, thus referred to, woke from their enchanted sleep. With Glyndon's terror she felt a sympathy, against which her reason and her love struggled in vain. And still, when she turned her looks upon her

---

* To what delusion does thy soul abandon itself?

child, it watched her with that steady, earnest eye, and its lips moved as if it sought to speak to her, — but no sound came. The infant refused to sleep. Whenever she gazed upon its face, still those wakeful, watchful eyes! — and in their earnestness, there spoke something of pain, of upbraiding, of accusation. They chilled her as she looked. Unable to endure, of herself, this sudden and complete revulsion of all the feelings which had hitherto made up her life, she formed the resolution natural to her land and creed; she sent for the priest who had habitually attended her at Venice, and to him she confessed, with passionate sobs and intense terror, the doubts that had broken upon her. The good father, a worthy and pious man, but with little education and less sense, one who held (as many of the lower Italians do to this day) even a poet to be a sort of sorcerer, seemed to shut the gates of hope upon her heart. His remonstrances were urgent, for his horror was unfeigned. He joined with Glyndon in imploring her to fly, if she felt the smallest doubt that her husband's pursuits were of the nature which the Roman Church had benevolently burned so many scholars for adopting. And even the little that Viola could communicate seemed, to the ignorant ascetic, irrefragable proof of sorcery and witchcraft; he had, indeed, previously heard some of the strange rumors which followed the path of Zanoni, and was therefore prepared to believe the worst; the worthy Bartolomeo would have made no bones of sending Watt to the stake, had he heard him speak of the steam-engine. But Viola, as untutored as himself, was terrified by his rough and vehement eloquence, — terrified, for by that penetration which Catholic priests, however dull, generally acquire, in their vast experience of the human heart hourly exposed to their probe, Bartolomeo spoke less of danger to herself than to her child. "Sorcerers," said he, "have ever sought the most to decoy and seduce the souls of the young, — nay, the infant;" and therewith he entered into a long catalogue of legendary fables, which he quoted as historical facts. All at which an English woman would have smiled, appalled the tender but superstitious Neapolitan; and when the priest left her, with solemn rebukes and grave accusations of a dereliction of her duties to her child, if she hesitated to fly with it from an abode polluted by the darker powers and unhallowed arts, Viola, still clinging to the image of Zanoni, sank into a passive lethargy which held her very reason in suspense.

The hours passed: night came on; the house was hushed; and Viola, slowly awakened from the numbness and torpor which had usurped her faculties, tossed to and fro on her couch, restless and perturbed. The stillness became intolerable; yet more intolerable the sound that alone broke it, the voice of the clock, knelling moment after moment to its grave. The moments, at last, seemed themselves to find voice, — to gain shape. She thought she beheld them springing, wan and fairylike, from the womb of darkness; and ere they fell again, extinguished, into that womb, their grave, their low small voices murmured, "Woman, we report to eternity all that is done in time! What shall we report of thee, O guardian of a newborn soul?" She became sensible that her fancies had brought a sort of partial delirium, that she was in a state between sleep and waking, when suddenly one thought became more predominant than the rest. The chamber which, in that and every house they had inhabited, even that in the Greek isles, Zanoni had set apart to a solitude on which none might intrude, the threshold of which even Viola's step was forbid to cross, and never, hitherto, in that sweet repose of confidence which belongs to contented love, had she even felt the curious desire to disobey, — now, that chamber drew her towards it. Perhaps *there* might be found a somewhat to solve the riddle, to dispel or confirm the doubt: that thought grew and deepened in its intenseness; it fastened on her as with a palpable and irresistible grasp; it seemed to raise her limbs without her will.

And now, through the chamber, along the galleries thou glidest, O lovely shape! Sleepwalking, yet awake. The moon shines on thee as thou glidest by, casement after casement, white-robed and wandering spirit! — thine arms crossed upon thy bosom, thine eyes fixed and open, with a calm unfearing awe. Mother, it is thy child that leads thee on! The fairy moments go before thee; thou hearest still the clock-knell tolling them to their graves behind. On, gliding on, thou hast gained the door; no lock bars thee, no magic spell drives thee back. Daughter of the dust, thou standest alone with night in the chamber where, pale and numberless, the hosts of space have gathered round the seer!

Chapter 6.VII.

Des Erdenlebens
Schweres Traumbild sinkt, und sinkt, und sinkt.*
"Das Ideal und das Lebens."

---

* The Dream Shape of the heavy earthly life sinks, and sinks, and sinks.

She stood within the chamber, and gazed around her; no signs by which an inquisitor of old could have detected the scholar of the Black Art were visible. No crucibles and caldrons, no brassbound volumes and ciphered girdles, no skulls and cross-bones. Quietly streamed the broad moonlight through the desolate chamber with its bare, white walls. A few bunches of withered herbs, a few antique vessels of bronze, placed carelessly on a wooden form, were all which that curious gaze could identify with the pursuits of the absent owner. The magic, if it existed, dwelt in the artificer, and the materials, to other hands, were but herbs and bronze. So is it ever with thy works and wonders, O Genius, — Seeker of the Stars! Words themselves are the common property of all men; yet, from words themselves, Thou Architect of Immortalities, pilest up temples that shall outlive the Pyramids, and the very leaf of the Papyrus becomes a Shinar, stately with towers, round which the Deluge of Ages, shall roar in vain!

But in that solitude has the Presence that there had invoked its wonders left no enchantment of its own? It seemed so; for as Viola stood in the chamber, she became sensible that some mysterious change was at work within herself. Her blood coursed rapidly, and with a sensation of delight, through her veins, — she felt as if chains were falling from her limbs, as if cloud after cloud was rolling from her gaze. All the confused thoughts which had moved through her trance settled and centered themselves in one intense desire to see the Absent One, — to be with him. The monads that make up space and air seemed charged with a spiritual attraction, — to become a medium through which her spirit could pass from its clay, and confer with the spirit to which the unutterable desire compelled it. A faintness seized her; she tottered to the seat on which the vessels and herbs were placed, and, as she bent down, she saw in one of the vessels a small vase of crystal. By a mechanical and involuntary impulse, her hand seized the vase; she opened it, and the volatile essence it contained sparkled up, and spread through the room a powerful and delicious fragrance. She inhaled the odor, she laved her temples with the liquid, and suddenly her life seemed to spring up from the previous faintness, — to spring, to soar, to float, to dilate upon the wings of a bird. The room vanished from her eyes. Away, away, over lands and seas and space on the rushing desire flies the disprisoned mind!

Upon a stratum, not of this world, stood the world-born shapes of the sons of Science, upon an embryo world, upon a crude, wan, attenuated mass of matter, one of the Nebulae, which the suns of the myriad systems throw off as they roll round the Creator's throne*, to become

---

* "Astronomy instructs us that, in the original condition of the solar system, the sun

themselves new worlds of symmetry and glory, — planets and suns that forever and forever shall in their turn multiply their shining race, and be the fathers of suns and planets yet to come.

There, in that enormous solitude of an infant world, which thousands and thousands of years can alone ripen into form, the spirit of Viola beheld the shape of Zanoni, or rather the likeness, the simulacrum, the *Lemur* of his shape, not its human and corporeal substance, — as if, like hers, the Intelligence was parted from the Clay, — and as the sun, while it revolves and glows, had cast off into remotest space that nebular image of itself, so the thing of earth, in the action of its more luminous and enduring being, had thrown its likeness into that newborn stranger of the heavens. There stood the phantom, — a phantom Mejnour, by its side. In the gigantic chaos around raved and struggled the kindling elements; water and fire, darkness and light, at war, — vapor and cloud hardening into mountains, and the Breath of Life moving like a steadfast splendor over all.

As the dreamer looked, and shivered, she beheld that even there the two phantoms of humanity were not alone. Dim monster-forms that that disordered chaos alone could engender, the first reptile Colossal race that wreathe and crawl through the earliest stratum of a world laboring into life, coiled in the oozing matter or hovered through the meteorous vapors. But these the two seekers seemed not to heed; their gaze was fixed intent upon an object in the farthest space. With the eyes of the spirit, Viola followed theirs; with a terror far greater than the chaos and its hideous inhabitants produced, she beheld a shadowy likeness of the very room in which her form yet dwelt, its white walls, the moonshine sleeping on its floor, its open casement, with the quiet roofs and domes of Venice looming over the sea that sighed below, — and in that room the ghostlike image of herself! This double phantom — here herself a phantom, gazing there upon a phantom-self — had in it a horror which no words can tell, no length of life forego.

---

was the nucleus of a nebulosity or luminous mass which revolved on its axis, and extended far beyond the orbits of all the planets, — the planets as yet having no existence. Its temperature gradually diminished, and, becoming contracted by cooling, the rotation increased in rapidity, and zones of nebulosity were successively thrown off, in consequence of the centrifugal force overpowering the central attraction. The condensation of these separate masses constituted the planets and satellites. But this view of the conversion of gaseous matter into planetary bodies is not limited to our own system; it extends to the formation of the innumerable suns and worlds which are distributed throughout the universe. The sublime discoveries of modern astronomers have shown that every part of the realms of space abounds in large expansions of attenuated matter termed nebulae, which are irregularly reflective of light, of various figures, and in different states of condensation, from that of a diffused, luminous mass to suns and planets like our own." — From Mantell's eloquent and delightful work, entitled "The Wonders of Geology," volume i. page 22.

But presently she saw this image of herself rise slowly, leave the room with its noiseless feet: it passes the corridor, it kneels by a cradle! Heaven of Heaven! She beholds her child! — still with its wondrous, childlike beauty and its silent, wakeful eyes. But beside that cradle there sits cowering a mantled, shadowy form, — the more fearful and ghastly from its indistinct and unsubstantial gloom. The walls of that chamber seem to open as the scene of a theater. A grim dungeon; streets through which pour shadowy crowds; wrath and hatred, and the aspect of demons in their ghastly visages; a place of death; a murderous instrument; a shamble-house of human flesh; herself; her child; — all, all, rapid phantasmagoria, chased each other. Suddenly the phantom-Zanoni turned, it seemed to perceive herself, — her second self. It sprang towards her; her spirit could bear no more. She shrieked, she woke. She found that in truth she had left that dismal chamber; the cradle was before her, the child! all — all as that trance had seen it; and, vanishing into air, even that dark, formless Thing!

"My child! my child! thy mother shall save thee yet!"

Chapter 6. VIII.

Qui? Toi m'abandonner! Ou vas-tu? Non! demeure, Demeure!*
La Harpe, "Le Comte de Warwick," Act 3, sc. 5.

*L*etter from Viola to Zanoni
"It has come to this! — I am the first to part! I, the unfaithful one, bid thee farewell forever. When thine eyes fall upon this writing thou wilt know me as one of the dead. For thou that wert, and still art my life, — I am lost to thee! O lover! O husband! O still worshipped and adored! if thou hast ever loved me, if thou canst still pity, seek not to discover the steps that fly thee. If thy charms can detect and tract me, spare me, spare our child! Zanoni, I will rear it to love thee, to call thee

* Who? *Thou* abandon me! — where goest thou? No! stay, stay!

father! Zanoni, its young lips shall pray for thee! Ah, spare thy child, for infants are the saints of earth, and their mediation may be heard on high! Shall I tell thee why I part? No; thou, the wisely terrible, canst divine what the hand trembles to record; and while I shudder at thy power, — while it is thy power I fly (our child upon my bosom), — it comforts me still to think that thy power can read the heart! Thou knowest that it is the faithful mother that writes to thee, it is not the faithless wife! Is there sin in thy knowledge, Zanoni? Sin must have sorrow: and it were sweet — oh, how sweet — to be thy comforter. But the child, the infant, the soul that looks to mine for its shield! — magician, I wrest from thee that soul! Pardon, pardon, if my words wrong thee. See, I fall on my knees to write the rest!

"Why did I never recoil before from thy mysterious lore; why did the very strangeness of thine unearthly life only fascinate me with a delightful fear? Because, if thou wert sorcerer or angel-demon, there was no peril to other but myself: and none to me, for my love was my heavenliest part; and my ignorance in all things, except the art to love thee, repelled every thought that was not bright and glorious as thine image to my eyes. But *now* there is another! Look! why does it watch me thus, — why that never-sleeping, earnest, rebuking gaze? Have thy spells encompassed it already? Hast thou marked it, cruel one, for the terrors of thy unutterable art? Do not madden me, — do not madden me! — unbind the spell!

"Hark! the oars without! They come, — they come, to bear me from thee! I look round, and methinks that I see thee everywhere. Thou speakest to me from every shadow, from every star. There, by the casement, thy lips last pressed mine; there, there by that threshold didst thou turn again, and thy smile seemed so trustingly to confide in me! Zanoni — husband! — I will stay! I cannot part from thee! No, no! I will go to the room where thy dear voice, with its gentle music, assuaged the pangs of travail! — where, heard through the thrilling darkness, it first whispered to my ear, 'Viola, thou art a mother!' A mother! — yes, I rise from my knees, — I *am* a mother! They come! I am firm; farewell!"

Yes; thus suddenly, thus cruelly, whether in the delirium of blind and unreasoning superstition, or in the resolve of that conviction which springs from duty, the being for whom he had resigned so much of empire and of glory forsook Zanoni. This desertion, never foreseen, never anticipated, was yet but the constant fate that attends those who would place Mind *beyond* the earth, and yet treasure the Heart *within* it. Ignorance everlastingly shall recoil from knowledge. But never yet, from nobler and purer motives of self-sacrifice, did human love link itself to another, than did the forsaking wife now abandon the absent. For rightly had she said that it was not the faithless wife, it *was* the faithful mother that fled from all in which her earthly happiness was centered.

As long as the passion and fervor that impelled the act animated her with false fever, she clasped her infant to her breast, and was consoled, — resigned. But what bitter doubt of her own conduct, what icy pang of remorse shot through her heart, when, as they rested for a few hours on the road to Leghorn, she heard the woman who accompanied herself and Glyndon pray for safety to reach her husband's side, and strength to share the perils that would meet her there! Terrible contrast to her own desertion! She shrunk into the darkness of her own heart, — and then no voice from within consoled her.

Chapter 6.IX.

Zukunft hast du mir gegeben,
Doch du nehmst den Augenblick.*

"Kassandra."

"Mejnour, behold thy work! Out, out upon our little vanities of wisdom! — out upon our ages of lore and life! To save her from Peril I left her presence, and the Peril has seized her in its grasp!"

"Chide not thy wisdom but thy passions! Abandon thine idle hope of the love of woman. See, for those who would unite the lofty with the lowly, the inevitable curse; thy very nature uncomprehended, — thy sacrifices unguessed. The lowly one views but in the lofty a necromancer or a fiend. Titan, canst thou weep?"

"I know it now, I see it all! It *was* her spirit that stood beside our own, and escaped my airy clasp! O strong desire of motherhood and nature! unveiling all our secrets, piercing space and traversing worlds! — Mejnour, what awful learning lies hid in the ignorance of the heart that loves!"

"The heart," answered the mystic, coldly; "aye, for five thousand years

* Futurity hast thou given to me, — yet takest from me the Moment.

I have ransacked the mysteries of creation, but I have not yet discovered all the wonders in the heart of the simplest boor!"

"Yet our solemn rites deceived us not; the prophet-shadows, dark with terror and red with blood, still foretold that, even in the dungeon, and before the deathsman, I, — I had the power to save them both!"

"But at some unconjectured and most fatal sacrifice to thyself."

"To myself! Icy sage, there is no self in love! I go. Nay, alone: I want thee not. I want now no other guide but the human instincts of affection. No cave so dark, no solitude so vast, as to conceal her. Though mine art fail me; though the stars heed me not; though space, with its shining myriads, is again to me but the azure void, — I return but to love and youth and hope! When have they ever failed to triumph and to save!"

BOOK VII

THE REIGN OF TERROR

Orrida maesta nei fero aspetto
Terrore accresce, e piu superbo il rende;
Rosseggian gli occhi, e di veneno infetto
Come infausta cometa, il guardo splende,
Gil involve il mento, e sull 'irsuto petto
Ispida efoita la gran barbe scende;
E in guisa de voragine profonda
*Sapre la bocca a'atro sangue immonda.**

(Ger. Lib., Cant. iv. 7.)

---

* A horrible majesty in the fierce aspect increases it terror, and renders it more superb. Red glow the eyes, and the aspect infected, like a baleful comet, with envenomed influences, glares around. A vast beard covers the chin — and, rough and thick, descends over the shaggy breast. — And like a profound gulf expand the jaws, foul with black gore.

Chapter 7.I.

Qui suis-je, moi qu'on accuse? Un esclave de la Liberté, un martyr vivant de la Republique.*

> "Discours de Robespierre, 8 Thermidor."

*I*t roars, — The River of Hell, whose first outbreak was chanted as the gush of a channel to Elysium. How burst into blossoming hopes fair hearts that had nourished themselves on the diamond dews of the rosy dawn, when Liberty came from the dark ocean, and the arms of decrepit Thralldom — Aurora from the bed of Tithon! Hopes! ye have ripened into fruit, and the fruit is gore and ashes! Beautiful Roland, eloquent Vergniaud, visionary Condorcet, high-hearted Malesherbes! — wits, philosophers, statesmen, patriots, dreamers! behold the millennium for which ye dared and labored!

I invoke the ghosts! Saturn hath devoured his children†, and lives alone, — I his true name of Moloch!

It is the Reign of Terror, with Robespierre the king. The struggles between the boa and the lion are past: the boa has consumed the lion, and is heavy with the gorge, — Danton has fallen, and Camille Desmoulins. Danton had said before his death, "The poltroon Robespierre, — I alone could have saved him." From that hour, indeed, the blood of the dead giant clouded the craft of "Maximilien the Incorruptible," as at last, amidst the din of the roused Convention, it choked his voice.‡ If, after that last sacrifice, essential, perhaps, to his safety, Robespierre had proclaimed the close of the Reign of Terror, and acted upon the

---

* Who am I, — I whom they accuse? A slave of Liberty, — a living martyr for the Republic.

† "La Revolution est comme Saturne, elle devorera tous ses enfans." — Vergniaud.

‡ Le sang de Danton t'etouffe!" (the blood of Danton chokes thee!) said Garnier de l'Aube, when on the fatal 9th of Thermidor, Robespierre gasped feebly forth, "Pour la derniere fois, President des Assassins, je te demande la parole." (For the last time, President of Assassins, I demand to speak.)

mercy which Danton had begun to preach, he might have lived and died a monarch. But the prisons continued to reek, — the glaive to fall; and Robespierre perceived not that his mobs were glutted to satiety with death, and the strongest excitement a chief could give would be a return from devils into men.

We are transported to a room in the house of Citizen Dupleix, the menuisier, in the month of July, 1794; or, in the calendar of the Revolutionists, it was the Thermidor of the Second Year of the Republic, One and Indivisible! Though the room was small, it was furnished and decorated with a minute and careful effort at elegance and refinement. It seemed, indeed, the desire of the owner to avoid at once what was mean and rude, and what was luxurious and voluptuous. It was a trim, orderly, precise grace that shaped the classic chairs, arranged the ample draperies, sank the frameless mirrors into the wall, placed bust and bronze on their pedestals, and filled up the niches here and there with well-bound books, filed regularly in their appointed ranks. An observer would have said, "This man wishes to imply to you, — I am not rich; I am not ostentatious; I am not luxurious; I am no indolent Sybarite, with couches of down, and pictures that provoke the sense; I am no haughty noble, with spacious halls, and galleries that awe the echo. But so much the greater is my merit if I disdain these excesses of the ease or the pride, since I love the elegant, and have a taste! Others may be simple and honest, from the very coarseness of their habits; if I, with so much refinement and delicacy, am simple and honest, — reflect, and admire me!"

On the walls of this chamber hung many portraits, most of them represented but one face; on the formal pedestals were grouped many busts, most of them sculptured but one head. In that small chamber Egotism sat supreme, and made the Arts its looking glasses. Erect in a chair, before a large table spread with letters, sat the original of bust and canvas, the owner of the apartment. He was alone, yet he sat erect, formal, stiff, precise, as if in his very home he was not at ease. His dress was in harmony with his posture and his chamber; it affected a neatness of its own, — foreign both to the sumptuous fashions of the deposed nobles, and the filthy ruggedness of the sans-culottes. Frizzled and coiffe, not a hair was out of order, not a speck lodged on the sleek surface of the blue coat, not a wrinkle crumpled the snowy vest, with its under-relief of delicate pink. At the first glance, you might have seen in that face nothing but the ill-favored features of a sickly countenance; at a second glance, you would have perceived that it had a power, a character of its own. The forehead, though low and compressed, was not without that appearance of thought and intelligence which, it may be observed, that breadth between the eyebrows almost invariably gives; the lips were firm and tightly drawn together, yet ever and anon they trembled, and writhed restlessly. The eyes, sullen and gloomy, were yet piercing, and full of a concentrated vigor that did not seem supported by the thin, feeble frame, or the green lividness of the hues, which told of anxiety and disease.

Such was Maximilien Robespierre; such the chamber over the menuisier's shop, whence issued the edicts that launched armies on their career of glory, and ordained an artificial conduit to carry off the blood that deluged the metropolis of the most martial people in the globe! Such was the man who had resigned a judicial appointment (the early object of his ambition) rather than violate his philanthropical principles by subscribing to the death of a single fellow-creature; such was the virgin enemy to capital punishments; and such, Butcher-Dictator now, was the man whose pure and rigid manners, whose incorruptible honesty, whose hatred of the excesses that tempt to love and wine, would, had he died five years earlier, have left him the model for prudent fathers and careful citizens to place before their sons. Such was the man who seemed to have no vice, till circumstance, that hotbed, brought forth the two which, in ordinary times, lie ever the deepest and most latent in a man's heart, — Cowardice and Envy. To one of these sources is to be traced every murder that master-fiend committed. His cowardice was of a peculiar and strange sort; for it was accompanied with the most unscrupulous and determined *will*, — a will that Napoleon reverenced; a will of iron, and yet nerves of aspen. Mentally, he was a hero, — physically, a dastard. When the veriest shadow of danger threatened his person, the frame cowered, but the will swept the danger to the slaughterhouse. So there he sat, bolt upright, — his small, lean fingers clenched convulsively; his sullen eyes straining into space, their whites yellowed with streaks of corrupt blood; his ears literally moving to and fro, like the ignobler animals', to catch every sound, — a Dionysus in his cave; but his posture decorous and collected, and every formal hair in its frizzled place.

"Yes, yes," he said in a muttered tone, "I hear them; my good Jacobins are at their post on the stairs. Pity they swear so! I have a law against oaths, — the manners of the poor and virtuous people must be reformed. When all is safe, an example or two amongst those good Jacobins would make effect. Faithful fellows, how they love me! Hum! — what an oath was that! — they need not swear so loud, — upon the very staircase, too! It detracts from my reputation. Ha! steps!"

The soliloquist glanced at the opposite mirror, and took up a volume; he seemed absorbed in its contents, as a tall fellow, a bludgeon in his hand, a girdle adorned with pistols round his waist, opened the door, and announced two visitors. The one was a young man, said to resemble

Robespierre in person, but of a far more decided and resolute expression of countenance. He entered first, and, looking over the volume in Robespierre's hand, for the latter seemed still intent on his lecture, exclaimed, —

"What! Rousseau's Heloise? A love-tale!"

"Dear Payan, it is not the love, — it is the philosophy that charms me. What noble sentiments! — what ardor of virtue! If Jean Jacques had but lived to see this day!"

While the Dictator thus commented on his favorite author, whom in his orations he labored hard to imitate, the second visitor was wheeled into the room in a chair. This man was also in what, to most, is the prime of life, — namely, about thirty-eight; but he was literally dead in the lower limbs: crippled, paralytic, distorted, he was yet, as the time soon came to tell him, — a Hercules in Crime! But the sweetest of human smiles dwelt upon his lips; a beauty almost angelic characterized his features*; an inexpressible aspect of kindness, and the resignation of suffering but cheerful benignity, stole into the hearts of those who for the first time beheld him. With the most caressing, silver, flutelike voice, Citizen Couthon saluted the admirer of Jean Jacques.

"Nay, — do not say that it is not the *love* that attracts thee; it *is* the love! but not the gross, sensual attachment of man for woman. No! the sublime affection for the whole human race, and indeed, for all that lives!"

And Citizen Couthon, bending down, fondled the little spaniel that he invariably carried in his bosom, even to the Convention, as a vent for the exuberant sensibilities which overflowed his affectionate heart.†

"Yes, for all that lives," repeated Robespierre, tenderly. "Good Couthon, — poor Couthon! Ah, the malice of men! — how we are

---

* "Figure d'ange," says one of his contemporaries, in describing Couthon. The address, drawn up most probably by Payan (Thermidor 9), after the arrest of Robespierre, thus mentions his crippled colleague: "Couthon, ce citoyen vertueux, *qui n'a que le coeur et la tete de vivans,* mais qui les a brulants de patriotisme" (Couthon, that virtuous citizen, who has but the head and the heart of the living, yet possesses these all on flame with patriotism.)

† This tenderness for some pet animal was by no means peculiar to Couthon; it seems rather a common fashion with the gentle butchers of the Revolution. M. George Duval informs us (in "Souvenirs de la Terreur," volume iii page 183) that Chaumette had an aviary, to which he devoted his harmless leisure; the murderous Fournier carried on his shoulders a pretty little squirrel, attached by a silver chain; Panis bestowed the superfluity of his affections upon two gold pheasants; and Marat, who would not abate one of the three hundred thousand heads he demanded, *reared doves!* Apropos of the spaniel of Couthon, Duval gives us an amusing anecdote of Sergent, not one of the least relentless agents of the massacre of September. A lady came to implore his protection for one of her relations confined in the Abbaye. He scarcely deigned to speak to her. As she retired in despair, she trod by accident on the paw of his favorite spaniel. Sergent, turning round, enraged and furious, exclaimed, *"Madam, have you no humanity?"*

misrepresented! To be calumniated as the executioners of our colleagues! Ah, it is *that* which pierces the heart! To be an object of terror to the enemies of our country, — *that* is noble; but to be an object of terror to the good, the patriotic, to those one loves and reveres, — *that* is the most terrible of human tortures at least, to a susceptible and honest heart!"*

"How I love to hear him!" ejaculated Couthon.

"Hem!" said Payan, with some impatience. "But now to business!"

"Ah, to business!" said Robespierre, with a sinister glance from his bloodshot eyes.

"The time has come," said Payan, "when the safety of the Republic demands a complete concentration of its power. These brawlers of the Comite du Salut Public can only destroy; they cannot construct. They hated you, Maximilien, from the moment you attempted to replace anarchy by institutions. How they mock at the festival which proclaimed the acknowledgment of a Supreme Being: they would have no ruler, even in heaven! Your clear and vigorous intellect saw that, having wrecked an old world, it became necessary to shape a new one. The first step towards construction must be to destroy the destroyers. While we deliberate, your enemies act. Better this very night to attack the handful of gendarmes that guard them, than to confront the battalions they may raise tomorrow."

"No," said Robespierre, who recoiled before the determined spirit of Payan; "I have a better and safer plan. This is the 6th of Thermidor; on the 10th — on the 10th, the Convention go in a body to the Fete Decadaire. A mob shall form; the canonniers, the troops of Henriot, the young pupils de l'Ecole de Mars, shall mix in the crowd. Easy, then, to strike the conspirators whom we shall designate to our agents. On the same day, too, Fouquier and Dumas shall not rest; and a sufficient number of 'the suspect' to maintain salutary awe, and keep up the revolutionary excitement, shall perish by the glaive of the law. The 10th shall be the great day of action. Payan, of these last culprits, have you prepared a list?"

"It is here," returned Payan, laconically, presenting a paper.

Robespierre glanced over it rapidly. "Collot d'Herbois! — good! Barrere! — aye, it was Barrere who said, 'Let us strike: the dead alone never return.'† Vadier, the savage jester! — good — good! Vadier of the Mountain. He has called me 'Mahomet!' Scelerat! blasphemer!"

"Mahomet is coming to the Mountain," said Couthon, with his silvery accent, as he caressed his spaniel.

"But how is this? I do not see the name of Tallien? Tallien, — I hate

---

* Not to fatigue the reader with annotations, I may here observe that nearly every sentiment ascribed in the text to Robespierre is to be found expressed in his various discourses.
† "Frappons! il n'y a que les morts qui ne revient pas." — Barrere.

that man; that is," said Robespierre, correcting himself with the hypocrisy or self-deceit which those who formed the council of this phrase-monger exhibited habitually, even among themselves, — "that is, Virtue and our Country hate him! There is no man in the whole Convention who inspires me with the same horror as Tallien. Couthon, I see a thousand Dantons where Tallien sits!"

"Tallien has the only head that belongs to this deformed body," said Payan, whose ferocity and crime, like those of St. Just, were not unaccompanied by talents of no common order. "Were it not better to draw away the head, to win, to buy him, for the time, and dispose of him better when left alone? He may hate *you*, but he loves *money!*"

"No," said Robespierre, writing down the name of Jean Lambert Tallien, with a slow hand that shaped each letter with stern distinctness; "that one head *is my necessity!*"

"I have a *small* list here," said Couthon, sweetly, — "a *very* small list. You are dealing with the Mountain; it is necessary to make a few examples in the Plain. These moderates are as straws which follow the wind. They turned against us yesterday in the Convention. A little terror will correct the weathercocks. Poor creatures! I owe them no ill will; I could weep for them. But before all, la chere patrie!"

The terrible glance of Robespierre devoured the list which the man of sensibility submitted to him. "Ah, these are well chosen; men not of mark enough to be regretted, which is the best policy with the relics of that party; some foreigners too, — yes, *they* have no parents in Paris. These wives and parents are beginning to plead against us. Their complaints demoralize the guillotine!"

"Couthon is right," said Payan; "*My* list contains those whom it will be safer to dispatch en masse in the crowd assembled at the Fete. *His* list selects those whom we may prudently consign to the law. Shall it not be signed at once?"

"It *is* signed," said Robespierre, formally replacing his pen upon the inkstand. "Now to more important matters. These deaths will create no excitement; but Collot d'Herbois, Bourdon De l'Oise, Tallien," the last name Robespierre gasped as he pronounced, "*They* are the heads of parties. This is life or death to us as well as them."

"Their heads are the footstools to your curule chair," said Payan, in a half whisper. "There is no danger if we are bold. Judges, juries, all have been your selection. You seize with one hand the army, with the other, the law. Your voice yet commands the people —"

"The poor and virtuous people," murmured Robespierre.

"And even," continued Payan, "if our design at the Fete fail us, we must not shrink from the resources still at our command. Reflect! Henriot, the general of the Parisian army, furnishes you with troops to arrest; the Jacobin Club with a public to approve; inexorable Dumas with judges who never acquit. We must be bold!"

"And we *are* bold," exclaimed Robespierre, with sudden passion, and striking his hand on the table as he rose, with his crest erect, as a serpent in the act to strike. "In seeing the multitude of vices that the revolutionary torrent mingles with civic virtues, I tremble to be sullied in the eyes of posterity by the impure neighborhood of these perverse men who thrust themselves among the sincere defenders of humanity. What! — they think to divide the country like a booty! I thank them for their hatred to all that is virtuous and worthy! These men," — and he grasped the list of Payan in his hand, — "these! — not *we* — have drawn the line of demarcation between themselves and the lovers of France!"

"True, we must reign alone!" muttered Payan; "in other words, the state needs unity of will;" working, with his strong practical mind, the corollary from the logic of his word-compelling colleague.

"I will go to the Convention," continued Robespierre. "I have absented myself too long, — lest I might seem to overawe the Republic that I have created. Away with such scruples! I will prepare the people! I will blast the traitors with a look!"

He spoke with the terrible firmness of the orator that had never failed, — of the moral will that marched like a warrior on the cannon. At that instant he was interrupted; a letter was brought to him: he opened it, — his face fell, he shook from limb to limb; it was one of the anonymous warnings by which the hate and revenge of those yet left alive to threaten tortured the death-giver.

"Thou art smeared," ran the lines, "with the best blood of France. Read thy sentence! I await the hour when the people shall knell thee to the doomsman. If my hope deceive me, if deferred too long, — hearken, read! This hand, which thine eyes shall search in vain to discover, shall pierce thy heart. I see thee every day, — I am with thee every day. At each hour my arm rises against thy breast. Wretch! live yet awhile, though but for few and miserable days — live to think of me; sleep to dream of me! Thy terror and thy thought of me are the heralds of thy doom. Adieu! this day itself I go forth to riot on thy fears!"*

"Your lists are not full enough!" said the tyrant, with a hollow voice, as the paper dropped from his trembling hand. "Give them to me! — give them to me! Think again, think again! Barrere is right — right! 'Frappons! il n'y a que les morts qui ne revient pas!'"

---

* See "Papiers inedits trouves chez Robespierre," etc., volume ii. page 155. (No. lx.)

Chapter 7.II.

La haine, dans ces lieux, n'a qu'un glaive assassin.
Elle marche dans l'ombre.*
                    La Harpe, "Jeanne de Naples," Act iv. sc. 1.

While such the designs and fears of Maximilien Robespierre, common danger, common hatred, whatever was yet left of mercy or of virtue in the agents of the Revolution, served to unite strange opposites in hostility to the universal death-dealer. There was, indeed, an actual conspiracy at work against him among men little less bespattered than himself with innocent blood. But that conspiracy would have been idle of itself, despite the abilities of Tallien and Barras (the only men whom it comprised, worthy, by foresight and energy, the names of "leaders"). The sure and destroying elements that gathered round the tyrant were Time and Nature; the one, which he no longer suited; the other, which he had outraged and stirred up in the human breast. The most atrocious party of the Revolution, the followers of Hebert, gone to his last account, the butcher-atheists, who, in desecrating heaven and earth, still arrogated inviolable sanctity to themselves, were equally enraged at the execution of their filthy chief, and the proclamation of a Supreme Being. The populace, brutal as it had been, started as from a dream of blood, when their huge idol, Danton, no longer filled the stage of terror, rendering crime popular by that combination of careless frankness and eloquent energy which endears their heroes to the herd. The glaive of the guillotine had turned against *themselves*. They had yelled and shouted, and sung and danced, when the venerable age, or the gallant youth, of aristocracy or letters, passed by their streets in the dismal tumbrels; but they shut up their shops, and murmured to each other, when their own order was invaded, and tailors and cobblers, and journeymen and laborers, were huddled off to the embraces of the "Holy Mother Guil-lotine," with as little ceremony as if they had been the Montmorencies

---

* Hate, in these regions, has but the sword of the assassin. She moves in the shade.

or the La Tremouilles, the Malesherbes or the Lavoisiers. "At this time," said Couthon, justly, "Les ombres de Danton, d'Hebert, de Chaumette, se promenent parmi nous!"*

Among those who had shared the doctrines, and who now dreaded the fate of the atheist Hebert, was the painter, Jean Nicot. Mortified and enraged to find that, by the death of his patron, his career was closed; and that, in the zenith of the Revolution for which he had labored, he was lurking in caves and cellars, more poor, more obscure, more despicable than he had been at the commencement, — not daring to exercise even his art, and fearful every hour that his name would swell the lists of the condemned, — he was naturally one of the bitterest enemies of Robespierre and his government. He held secret meetings with Collot d'Herbois, who was animated by the same spirit; and with the creeping and furtive craft that characterized his abilities, he contrived, undetected, to disseminate tracts and invectives against the Dictator, and to prepare, amidst "the poor and virtuous people," the train for the grand explosion. But still so firm to the eyes, even of profounder politicians than Jean Nicot, appeared the sullen power of the incorruptible Maximilien; so timorous was the movement against him, — that Nicot, in common with many others, placed his hopes rather in the dagger of the assassin than the revolt of the multitude. But Nicot, though not actually a coward, shrunk himself from braving the fate of the martyr; he had sense enough to see that, though all parties might rejoice in the assassination, all parties would probably concur in beheading the assassin. He had not the virtue to become a Brutus. His object was to inspire a proxy-Brutus; and in the center of that inflammable population this was no improbable hope.

Amongst those loudest and sternest against the reign of blood; amongst those most disenchanted of the Revolution; amongst those most appalled by its excesses, — was, as might be expected, the Englishman, Clarence Glyndon. The wit and accomplishments, the uncertain virtues that had lighted with fitful gleams the mind of Camille Desmoulins, had fascinated Glyndon more than the qualities of any other agent in the Revolution. And when (for Camille Desmoulins had a heart, which seemed dead or dormant in most of his contemporaries) that vivid child of genius and of error, shocked at the massacre of the Girondins, and repentant of his own efforts against them, began to rouse the serpent malice of Robespierre by new doctrines of mercy and toleration, Glyndon espoused his views with his whole strength and soul. Camille Desmoulins perished, and Glyndon, hopeless at once of his own life and the cause of humanity, from that time sought only the occasion of flight from the devouring Golgotha. He had two lives to

---

* The shades of Danton, Hebert, and Chaumette walk amongst us.

heed besides his own; for them he trembled, and for them he schemed and plotted the means of escape. Though Glyndon hated the principles, the party*, and the vices of Nicot, he yet extended to the painter's penury the means of subsistence; and Jean Nicot, in return, designed to exalt Glyndon to that very immortality of a Brutus from which he modestly recoiled himself. He founded his designs on the physical courage, on the wild and unsettled fancies of the English artist, and on the vehement hate and indignant loathing with which he openly regarded the government of Maximilien.

At the same hour, on the same day in July, in which Robespierre conferred (as we have seen) with his allies, two persons were seated in a small room in one of the streets leading out of the Rue St. Honore; the one, a man, appeared listening impatiently, and with a sullen brow, to his companion, a woman of singular beauty, but with a bold and reckless expression, and her face as she spoke was animated by the passions of a half-savage and vehement nature.

"Englishman," said the woman, "beware! — you know that, whether in flight or at the place of death, I would brave all to be by your side, — you know *that!* Speak!"

"Well, Fillide; did I ever doubt your fidelity?"

"Doubt it you cannot, — betray it you may. You tell me that in flight you must have a companion besides myself, and that companion is a female. It shall not be!"

"Shall not!"

"It shall not!" repeated Fillide, firmly, and folding her arms across her breast. Before Glyndon could reply, a slight knock at the door was heard, and Nicot opened the latch and entered.

Fillide sank into her chair, and, leaning her face on her hands, appeared unheeding of the intruder and the conversation that ensued.

"I cannot bid thee good-day, Glyndon," said Nicot, as in his sans-culotte fashion he strode towards the artist, his ragged hat on his head, his hands in his pockets, and the beard of a week's growth upon his chin, — "I cannot bid thee good-day; for while the tyrant lives, evil is every sun that sheds its beams on France."

"It is true; what then? We have sown the wind, we must reap the whirlwind."

"And yet," said Nicot, apparently not heeding the reply, and as if musingly to himself, "it is strange to think that the butcher is as mortal as the butchered; that his life hangs on as slight a thread; that between

---

* None were more opposed to the Hebertists than Camille Desmoulins and his friends. It is curious and amusing to see these leaders of the mob, calling the mob "the people" one day, and the "canaille" the next, according as it suits them. "I know," says Camille, "that they (the Hebertists) have all the canaille with them." — (Ils ont toute la canaille pour eux.)

the cuticle and the heart there is as short a passage, — that, in short, one blow can free France and redeem mankind!"

Glyndon surveyed the speaker with a careless and haughty scorn, and made no answer.

"And," proceeded Nicot, "I have sometimes looked round for the man born for this destiny, and whenever I have done so, my steps have led me hither!"

"Should they not rather have led thee to the side of Maximilien Robespierre?" said Glyndon, with a sneer.

"No," returned Nicot, coldly, — "no; for I am a 'suspect:' I could not mix with his train; I could not approach within a hundred yards of his person, but I should be seized; *you*, as yet, are safe. Hear me!" — and his voice became earnest and expressive, — "hear me! There seems danger in this action; there is none. I have been with Collot d'Herbois and Bilaud-Varennes; they will hold him harmless who strikes the blow; the populace would run to thy support; the Convention would hail thee as their deliverer, the —"

"Hold, man! How darest thou couple my name with the act of an assassin? Let the tocsin sound from yonder tower, to a war between Humanity and the Tyrant, and I will not be the last in the field; but liberty never yet acknowledged a defender in a felon."

There was something so brave and noble in Glyndon's voice, mien, and manner, as he thus spoke, that Nicot at once was silenced; at once he saw that he had misjudged the man.

"No," said Fillide, lifting her face from her hands, — "no! your friend has a wiser scheme in preparation; he would leave you wolves to mangle each other. He is right; but —"

"Flight!" exclaimed Nicot; "is it possible? Flight; how? — when? — by what means? All France begirt with spies and guards! Flight! would to Heaven it were in our power!"

"Dost thou, too, desire to escape the blessed Revolution?"

"Desire! Oh!" cried Nicot, suddenly, and, falling down, he clasped Glyndon's knees, — "oh, save me with thyself! My life is a torture; every moment the guillotine frowns before me. I know that my hours are numbered; I know that the tyrant waits but his time to write my name in his inexorable list; I know that Rene Dumas, the judge who never pardons, has, from the first, resolved upon my death. Oh, Glyndon, by our old friendship, by our common art, by thy loyal English faith and good English heart, let me share thy flight!"

"If thou wilt, so be it."

"Thanks! — my whole life shall thank thee. But how hast thou prepared the means, the passports, the disguise, the —"

"I will tell thee. Thou knowest C——, of the Convention, — he has power, and he is covetous. 'Qu'on me meprise, pourvu que je dine'*, said he, when reproached for his avarice."

"Well?"

"By the help of this sturdy republican, who has friends enough in the Comite, I have obtained the means necessary for flight; I have purchased them. For a consideration I can procure thy passport also."

"Thy riches, then, are not in assignats?"

"No; I have gold enough for us all."

And here Glyndon, beckoning Nicot into the next room, first briefly and rapidly detailed to him the plan proposed, and the disguises to be assumed conformably to the passports, and then added, "In return for the service I render thee, grant me one favor, which I think is in thy power. Thou rememberest Viola Pisani?"

"Ah, — remember, yes! — and the lover with whom she fled."

"And *from* whom she is a fugitive now."

"Indeed — what! — I understand. Sacre bleu! but you are a lucky fellow, cher confrere."

"Silence, man! with thy eternal prate of brotherhood and virtue, thou seemest never to believe in one kindly action, or one virtuous thought!"

Nicot bit his lip, and replied sullenly, "Experience is a great unde-ceiver. Humph! What service can I do thee with regard to the Italian?"

"I have been accessory to her arrival in this city of snares and pitfalls. I cannot leave her alone amidst dangers from which neither innocence nor obscurity is a safeguard. In your blessed Republic, a good and unsuspected citizen, who casts a desire on any woman, maid or wife, has but to say, 'Be mine, or I denounce you!' In a word, Viola must share our flight."

"What so easy? I see your passports provide for her."

"What so easy? What so difficult? This Fillide — would that I had never seen her! — would that I had never enslaved my soul to my senses! The love of an uneducated, violent, unprincipled woman, opens with a heaven, to merge in a hell! She is jealous as all the Furies; she will not hear of a female companion; and when once she sees the beauty of Viola! — I tremble to think of it. She is capable of any excess in the storm of her passions."

"Aha, I know what such women are! My wife, Beatrice Sacchini, whom I took from Naples, when I failed with this very Viola, divorced me when my money failed, and, as the mistress of a judge, passes me in her carriage while I crawl through the streets. Plague on her! — but patience, patience! such is the lot of virtue. Would I were Robespierre for a day!"

"Cease these tirades!" exclaimed Glyndon, impatiently; "and to the

---

* Let them despise me, provided that I dine.

point. What would you advise?"

"Leave your Fillide behind."

"Leave her to her own ignorance; leave her unprotected even by the mind; leave her in the Saturnalia of Rape and Murder? No! I have sinned against her once. But come what may, I will not so basely desert one who, with all her errors, trusted her fate to my love."

"You deserted her at Marseilles."

"True; but I left her in safety, and I did not then believe her love to be so deep and faithful. I left her gold, and I imagined she would be easily consoled; but since *then we have known danger together!* And now to leave her alone to that danger which she would never have incurred but for devotion to me! — no, that is impossible. A project occurs to me. Canst thou not say that thou hast a sister, a relative, or a benefactress, whom thou wouldst save? Can we not — till we have left France — make Fillide believe that Viola is one in whom *thou* only art interested; and whom, for thy sake only, I permit to share in our escape?"

"Ha, well thought of! — certainly!"

"I will then appear to yield to Fillide's wishes, and resign the project, which she so resents, of saving the innocent object of her frantic jealousy. You, meanwhile, shall yourself entreat Fillide to intercede with me to extend the means of escape to —"

"To a lady (she knows I have no sister) who has aided me in my distress. Yes, I will manage all, never fear. One word more, — what has become of that Zanoni?"

"Talk not of him, — I know not."

"Does he love this girl still?"

"It would seem so. She is his wife, the mother of his infant, who is with her."

"Wife! — mother! He loves her. Aha! And why —"

"No questions now. I will go and prepare Viola for the flight; you, meanwhile, return to Fillide."

"But the address of the Neapolitan? It is necessary I should know, lest Fillide inquire."

"Rue M—— T——, No. 27. Adieu."

Glyndon seized his hat and hastened from the house.

Nicot, left alone, seemed for a few moments buried in thought. "Oho," he muttered to himself, "can I not turn all this to my account? Can I not avenge myself on thee, Zanoni, as I have so often sworn, — through thy wife and child? Can I not possess myself of thy gold, thy passports, and thy Fillide, hot Englishman, who wouldst humble me with thy loathed benefits, and who hast chucked me thine alms as to a beggar? And Fillide, I love her: and thy gold, I love *that* more! Puppets, I move your strings!"

He passed slowly into the chamber where Fillide yet sat, with gloomy thought on her brow and tears standing in her dark eyes. She looked up eagerly as the door opened, and turned from the rugged face of Nicot with an impatient movement of disappointment.

"Glyndon," said the painter, drawing a chair to Fillide's, "has left me to enliven your solitude, fair Italian. He is not jealous of the ugly Nicot! — ha, ha! — yet Nicot loved thee well once, when his fortunes were more fair. But enough of such past follies."

"Your friend, then, has left the house. Whither? Ah, you look away; you falter, — you cannot meet my eyes! Speak! I implore, I command thee, speak!"

"Enfant! And what dost thou fear?"

"*Fear!* — yes, alas, I fear!" said the Italian; and her whole frame seemed to shrink into itself as she fell once more back into her seat.

Then, after a pause, she tossed the long hair from her eyes, and, starting up abruptly, paced the room with disordered strides. At length she stopped opposite to Nicot, laid her hand on his arm, drew him towards an escritoire, which she unlocked, and, opening a well, pointed to the gold that lay within, and said, "Thou art poor, — thou lovest money; take what thou wilt, but undeceive me. Who is this woman whom thy friend visits, — and does he love her?"

Nicot's eyes sparkled, and his hands opened and clenched, and clenched and opened, as he gazed upon the coins. But reluctantly resisting the impulse, he said, with an affected bitterness, "Thinkest thou to bribe me? — if so, it cannot be with gold. But what if he does love a rival; what if he betrays thee; what if, wearied by thy jealousies, he designs in his flight to leave thee behind, — would such knowledge make thee happier?"

"Yes!" exclaimed the Italian, fiercely; "yes, for it would be happiness to hate and to be avenged! Oh, thou knowest not how sweet is hatred to those who have really loved!"

"But wilt thou swear, if I reveal to thee the secret, that thou wilt not betray me, — that thou wilt not fall, as women do, into weak tears and fond reproaches, when thy betrayer returns?"

"Tears, reproaches! Revenge hides itself in smiles!"

"Thou art a brave creature!" said Nicot, almost admiringly. "One condition more: thy lover designs to fly with his new love, to leave thee to thy fate; if I prove this to thee, and if I give thee revenge against thy rival, wilt thou fly with me? I love thee! — I will wed thee!"

Fillide's eyes flashed fire; she looked at him with unutterable disdain, and was silent.

Nicot felt he had gone too far; and with that knowledge of the evil part of our nature which his own heart and association with crime had taught him, he resolved to trust the rest to the passions of the Italian, when raised to the height to which he was prepared to lead them.

"Pardon me," he said; "my love made me too presumptuous; and yet it is only that love, — my sympathy for thee, beautiful and betrayed, that can induce me to wrong, with my revelations, one whom I have regarded as a brother. I can depend upon thine oath to conceal all from Glyndon?"

"On my oath and my wrongs and my mountain blood!"

"Enough! get thy hat and mantle, and follow me."

As Fillide left the room, Nicot's eyes again rested on the gold; it was much, — much more than he had dared to hope for; and as he peered into the well and opened the drawers, he perceived a packet of letters in the well-known hand of Camille Desmoulins. He seized — he opened the packet; his looks brightened as he glanced over a few sentences. "This would give fifty Glyndons to the guillotine!" he muttered, and thrust the packet into his bosom.

O artist! — O haunted one! — O erring genius! — behold the two worst foes, — the False Ideal that knows no God, and the False Love that burns from the corruption of the senses, and takes no luster from the soul!

Chapter 7.III.

Liebe sonnt das Reich der Nacht.*

"Der Triumph der Liebe."

Letter from Zanoni to Mejnour.

Paris

Dost thou remember in the old time, when the Beautiful yet dwelt in Greece, how we two, in the vast Athenian Theater, witnessed the birth of Words as undying as ourselves? Dost thou remember the thrill of terror that ran through that mighty audience, when the wild Cassandra

---

* Love illumes the realm of Night.

burst from her awful silence to shriek to her relentless god! How ghastly, at the entrance of the House of Atreus, about to become her tomb, rang out her exclamations of foreboding woe: "Dwelling abhorred of heaven! — human shamble-house and floor blood-bespattered!"* Dost thou remember how, amidst the breathless awe of those assembled thousands, I drew close to thee, and whispered, "Verily, no prophet like the poet! This scene of fabled horror comes to me as a dream, shadowing forth some likeness in my own remoter future!" As I enter this slaughterhouse that scene returns to me, and I hearken to the voice of Cassandra ringing in my ears. A solemn and warning dread gathers round me, as if I too were come to find a grave, and "the Net of Hades" had already entangled me in its web! What dark treasure houses of vicissitude and woe are our memories become! What our lives, but the chronicles of unrelenting death! It seems to me as yesterday when I stood in the streets of this city of the Gaul, as they shone with plumed chivalry, and the air rustled with silken braveries. Young Louis, the monarch and the lover, was victor of the Tournament at the Carousel; and all France felt herself splendid in the splendor of her gorgeous chief! Now there is neither throne nor altar; and what is in their stead? I see it yonder — the *guillotine!* It is dismal to stand amidst the ruins of moldering cities, to startle the serpent and the lizard amidst the wrecks of Persepolis and Thebes; but more dismal still to stand as I — the stranger from Empires that have ceased to be — stand now amidst the yet ghastlier ruins of Law and Order, the shattering of mankind themselves! Yet here, even here, Love, the Beautifier, that hath led my steps, can walk with unshrinking hope through the wilderness of Death. Strange is the passion that makes a world in itself, that individualizes the One amidst the Multitude; that, through all the changes of my solemn life, yet survives, though ambition and hate and anger are dead; the one solitary angel, hovering over a universe of tombs on its two tremulous and human wings, — Hope and Fear!

How is it, Mejnour, that, as my diviner art abandoned me, — as, in my search for Viola, I was aided but by the ordinary instincts of the merest mortal, — how is it that I have never desponded, that I have felt in every difficulty the prevailing prescience that we should meet at last? So cruelly was every vestige of her flight concealed from me, — so suddenly, so secretly had she fled, that all the spies, all the authorities of Venice, could give me no clew. All Italy I searched in vain! Her young home at Naples! — how still, in its humble chambers, there seemed to linger the fragrance of her presence! All the sublimest secrets of our lore failed me, — failed to bring her soul visible to mine; yet morning and night, thou lone and childless one, morning and night, detached from

---

* Aesch. "Agam." 1098.

myself, I can commune with my child! There in that most blessed, typical, and mysterious of all relations, Nature herself appears to supply what Science would refuse. Space cannot separate the father's watchful soul from the cradle of his first-born! I know not of its resting-place and home, — my visions picture not the land, — only the small and tender life to which all space is as yet the heritage! For to the infant, before reason dawns, — before man's bad passions can dim the essence that it takes from the element it hath left, there is no peculiar country, no native city, and no mortal language. Its soul as yet is the denizen of all airs and of every world; and in space its soul meets with mine, — the child communes with the father! Cruel and forsaking one, — thou for whom I left the wisdom of the spheres; thou whose fatal dower has been the weakness and terrors of humanity, — couldst thou think that young soul less safe on earth because I would lead it ever more up to heaven! Didst thou think that I could have wronged mine own? Didst thou not know that in its serenest eyes the life that I gave it spoke to warn, to upbraid the mother who would bind it to the darkness and pangs of the prison-house of clay? Didst thou not feel that it was I who, permitted by the Heavens, shielded it from suffering and disease? And in its wondrous beauty, I blessed the holy medium through which, at last, my spirit might confer with thine!

And how have I tracked them hither? I learned that thy pupil had been at Venice. I could not trace the young and gentle neophyte of Parthenope in the description of the haggard and savage visitor who had come to Viola before she fled; but when I would have summoned his *idea* before me, it refused to obey; and I knew then that his fate had become entwined with Viola's. I have tracked him, then, to this Lazar House. I arrived but yesterday; I have not yet discovered him.

. . .

I have just returned from their courts of justice, — dens where tigers arraign their prey. I find not whom I would seek. They are saved as yet; but I recognize in the crimes of mortals the dark wisdom of the Everlasting. Mejnour, I see here, for the first time, how majestic and beauteous a thing is death! Of what sublime virtues we robbed ourselves, when, in the thirst for virtue, we attained the art by which we can refuse to die! When in some happy clime, where to breathe is to enjoy, the charnel-house swallows up the young and fair; when in the noble pursuit of knowledge, Death comes to the student, and shuts out the enchanted land which was opening to his gaze, — how natural for us to desire to live; how natural to make perpetual life the first object of research! But here, from my tower of time, looking over the darksome past, and into the starry future, I learn how great hearts feel what sweetness and glory there is to die for the things they love! I saw a father sacrificing himself for his son; he was subjected to charges which a word of his could dispel, — he was mistaken for his boy. With what joy he seized the error, confessed the noble crimes of valor and fidelity which the son had indeed committed, and went to the doom, exulting that his death saved the life he had given, not in vain! I saw women, young, delicate, in the bloom of their beauty; they had vowed themselves to the cloister. Hands smeared with the blood of saints opened the gate that had shut them from the world, and bade them go forth, forget their vows, forswear the Divine one these demons would depose, find lovers and helpmates, and be free. And some of these young hearts had loved, and even, though in struggles, loved yet. Did they forswear the vow? Did they abandon the faith? Did even love allure them? Mejnour, with one voice, they preferred to die. And whence comes this courage? — because such *hearts live in some more abstract and holier life than their own. but to live forever upon this earth is to live in nothing diviner than ourselves.* Yes, even amidst this gory butcherdom, God, the Ever-living, vindicates to man the sanctity of His servant, Death!

. . .

Again I have seen thee in spirit; I have seen and blessed thee, my sweet child! Dost thou not know me also in thy dreams? Dost thou not feel the beating of my heart through the veil of thy rosy slumbers? Dost thou not hear the wings of the brighter beings that I yet can conjure around thee, to watch, to nourish, and to save? And when the spell fades at thy waking, when thine eyes open to the day, will they not look round for me, and ask thy mother, with their mute eloquence, "Why she has robbed thee of a father?"

Woman, dost thou not repent thee? Flying from imaginary fears, hast thou not come to the very lair of terror, where Danger sits visible and incarnate? Oh, if we could but meet, wouldst thou not fall upon the bosom thou hast so wronged, and feel, poor wanderer amidst the storms, as if thou hadst regained the shelter? Mejnour, still my researches fail me. I mingle with all men, even their judges and their spies, but I cannot yet gain the clew. I know that she is here. I know it by an instinct; the breath of my child seems warmer and more familiar.

They peer at me with venomous looks, as I pass through their streets. With a glance I disarm their malice, and fascinate the basilisks. Everywhere I see the track and scent the presence of the Ghostly One that dwells on the Threshold, and whose victims are the souls that would *aspire,* and can only *fear.* I see its dim shapelessness going before the men of blood, and marshaling their way. Robespierre passed me with his furtive step. Those eyes of horror were gnawing into his heart. I looked down upon their senate; the grim Phantom sat cowering on its floor. It hath taken up its abode in the city of Dread. And what in truth are these would-be builders of a new world? Like the students who have vainly struggled after our supreme science, they have attempted what is beyond their power; they have passed from this solid earth of usages and forms into the land of shadow, and its loathsome keeper has seized them as its prey. I looked into the tyrant's shuddering soul, as it trembled past me. There, amidst the ruins of a thousand systems which aimed at virtue, sat Crime, and shivered at its desolation. Yet this man is the only Thinker, the only Aspirant, amongst them all. He still looks for a future of peace and mercy, to begin, — aye! at what date? When he has swept away every foe. Fool! new foes spring from every drop of blood. Led by the eyes of the Unutterable, he is walking to his doom.

O Viola, thy innocence protects thee! Thou whom the sweet humanities of love shut out even from the dreams of aërial and spiritual beauty, making thy heart a universe of visions fairer than the wanderer over the rosy Hesperus can survey, — shall not the same pure affection encompass thee, even here, with a charmed atmosphere, and terror itself fall harmless on a life too innocent for wisdom?

Chapter 7.IV.

Ombra piu che di notte, in cui di luce
Raggio misto non e;
. . .
Ne piu il palagio appar, ne piu le sue
Vestigia; ne dir puossi — egli qui fue.*

"Ger. Lib., canto xvi.-lxix.

*T*he clubs are noisy with clamorous frenzy; the leaders are grim with schemes. Black Henriot flies here and there, muttering to his armed troops, "Robespierre, your beloved, is in danger!" Robespierre stalks

---

* Darkness greater than of night, in which not a ray of light is mixed; . . . The palace appears no more: not even a vestige, — nor can one say that it has been.

perturbed, his list of victims swelling every hour. Tallien, the Macduff to the doomed Macbeth, is whispering courage to his pale conspirators. Along the streets heavily roll the tumbrels. The shops are closed, — the people are gorged with gore, and will lap no more. And night after night, to the eighty theaters flock the children of the Revolution, to laugh at the quips of comedy, and weep gentle tears over imaginary woes!

In a small chamber, in the heart of the city, sits the mother, watching over her child. It is quiet, happy noon; the sunlight, broken by the tall roofs in the narrow street, comes yet through the open casement, the impartial playfellow of the air, gleesome alike in temple and prison, hall and hovel; as golden and as blithe, whether it laugh over the first hour of life, or quiver in its gay delight on the terror and agony of the last! The child, where it lay at the feet of Viola, stretched out its dimpled hands as if to clasp the dancing motes that reveled in the beam. The mother turned her eyes from the glory; it saddened her yet more. She turned and sighed.

Is this the same Viola who bloomed fairer than their own Idalia under the skies of Greece? How changed! How pale and worn! She sat listlessly, her arms dropping on her knee; the smile that was habitual to her lips was gone. A heavy, dull despondency, as if the life of life were no more, seemed to weigh down her youth, and make it weary of that happy sun! In truth, her existence had languished away since it had wandered, as some melancholy stream, from the source that fed it. The sudden enthusiasm of fear or superstition that had almost, as if still in the unconscious movements of a dream, led her to fly from Zanoni, had ceased from the day which dawned upon her in a foreign land. Then — there — she felt that in the smile she had evermore abandoned lived her life. She did not repent, — she would not have recalled the impulse that winged her flight. Though the enthusiasm was gone, the superstition yet remained; she still believed she had saved her child from that dark and guilty sorcery, concerning which the traditions of all lands are prodigal, but in none do they find such credulity, or excite such dread, as in the South of Italy. This impression was confirmed by the mysterious conversations of Glyndon, and by her own perception of the fearful change that had passed over one who represented himself as the victim of the enchanters. She did not, therefore, repent; but her very volition seemed gone.

On their arrival at Paris, Viola saw her companion — the faithful wife — no more. Ere three weeks were passed, husband and wife had ceased to live.

And now, for the first time, the drudgeries of this hard earth claimed the beautiful Neapolitan. In that profession, giving voice and shape to poetry and song, in which her first years were passed, there is, while it lasts, an excitement in the art that lifts it from the labor of a calling. Hovering between two lives, the Real and Ideal, dwells the life of music and the stage. But that life was lost evermore to the idol of the eyes and ears of Naples. Lifted to the higher realm of passionate love, it seemed as if the fictitious genius which represents the thoughts of others was merged in the genius that grows all thought itself. It had been the worst infidelity to the Lost, to have descended again to live on the applause of others. And so — for she would not accept alms from Glyndon — so, by the commonest arts, the humblest industry which the sex knows, alone and unseen, she who had slept on the breast of Zanoni found a shelter for their child. As when, in the noble verse prefixed to this chapter, Armida herself has destroyed her enchanted palace, — not a vestige of that bower, raised of old by Poetry and Love, remained to say, "It had been!"

And the child avenged the father; it bloomed, it thrived, — it waxed strong in the light of life. But still it seemed haunted and preserved by some other being than her own. In its sleep there was that slumber, so deep and rigid, which a thunderbolt could not have disturbed; and in such sleep often it moved its arms, as to embrace the air: often its lips stirred with murmured sounds of indistinct affection, — *not for her;* and all the while upon its cheeks a hue of such celestial bloom, upon its lips a smile of such mysterious joy! Then, when it waked, its eyes did not turn first to *her,* — wistful, earnest, wandering, they roved around, to fix on her pale face, at last, in mute sorrow and reproach.

Never had Viola felt before how mighty was her love for Zanoni; how thought, feeling, heart, soul, life, — all lay crushed and dormant in the icy absence to which she had doomed herself! She heard not the roar without, she felt not one amidst those stormy millions, — worlds of excitement laboring through every hour. Only when Glyndon, haggard, wan, and specterlike, glided in, day after day, to visit her, did the fair daughter of the careless South know how heavy and universal was the Death-Air that girt her round. Sublime in her passive unconsciousness, — her mechanic life, — she sat, and feared not, in the den of the Beasts of Prey.

The door of the room opened abruptly, and Glyndon entered. His manner was more agitated than usual.

"Is it you, Clarence?" she said in her soft, languid tones. "You are before the hour I expected you."

"Who can count on his hours at Paris?" returned Glyndon, with a frightful smile. "Is it not enough that I am here! Your apathy in the midst of these sorrows appalls me. You say calmly, 'Farewell;' calmly you bid me, 'Welcome!' — as if in every corner there was not a spy, and as if with every day there was not a massacre!"

"Pardon me! But in these walls lies my world. I can hardly credit all the tales you tell me. Everything here, save *that,*" and she pointed to the infant, "seems already so lifeless, that in the tomb itself one could scarcely less heed the crimes that are done without."

Glyndon paused for a few moments, and gazed with strange and mingled feelings upon that face and form, still so young, and yet so invested with that saddest of all repose, — when the heart feels old.

"O Viola," said he, at last, and in a voice of suppressed passion, "was it thus I ever thought to see you, — ever thought to feel for you, when we two first met in the gay haunts of Naples? Ah, why then did you refuse my love; or why was mine not worthy of you? Nay, shrink not! — let me touch your hand. No passion so sweet as that youthful love can return to me again. I feel for you but as a brother for some younger and lonely sister. With you, in your presence, sad though it be, I seem to breathe back the purer air of my early life. Here alone, except in scenes of turbulence and tempest, the Phantom ceases to pursue me. I forget even the Death that stalks behind, and haunts me as my shadow. But better days may be in store for us yet. Viola, I at last begin dimly to perceive how to baffle and subdue the Phantom that has cursed my life, — it is to brave, and defy it. In sin and in riot, as I have told thee, it haunts me not. But I comprehend now what Mejnour said in his dark apothegms, 'that I should dread the specter most *when unseen.*' In virtuous and calm resolution it appears, — aye, I behold it now; there, there, with its livid eyes!" — and the drops fell from his brow. "But it shall no longer daunt me from that resolution. I face it, and it gradually darkens back into the shade." He paused, and his eyes dwelt with a terrible exultation upon the sunlit space; then, with a heavy and deep-drawn breath, he resumed, "Viola, I have found the means of escape. We will leave this city. In some other land we will endeavor to comfort each other, and forget the past."

"No," said Viola, calmly; "I have no further wish to stir, till I am born hence to the last resting-place. I dreamed of him last night, Clarence! — dreamed of him for the first time since we parted; and, do not mock me, methought that he forgave the deserter, and called me 'Wife.' That dream hallows the room. Perhaps it will visit me again before I die."

"Talk not of him, — of the demifiend!" cried Glyndon, fiercely, and stamping his foot. "Thank the Heavens for any fate that hath rescued thee from him!"

"Hush!" said Viola, gravely. And as she was about to proceed, her eye fell upon the child. It was standing in the very center of that slanting column of light which the sun poured into the chamber; and the rays seemed to surround it as a halo, and settled, crownlike, on the gold of its shining hair. In its small shape, so exquisitely modeled, in its large, steady, tranquil eyes, there was something that awed, while it charmed the mother's pride. It gazed on Glyndon as he spoke, with a look which almost might have seemed disdain, and which Viola, at least, interpreted as a defense of the Absent, stronger than her own lips could frame.

Glyndon broke the pause.

"Thou wouldst stay, for what? To betray a mother's duty! If any evil happen to thee here, what becomes of thine infant? Shall it be brought up an orphan, in a country that has desecrated thy religion, and where human charity exists no more? Ah, weep, and clasp it to thy bosom; but tears do not protect and save."

"Thou hast conquered, my friend, I will fly with thee."

"Tomorrow night, then, be prepared. I will bring thee the necessary disguises."

And Glyndon then proceeded to sketch rapidly the outline of the path they were to take, and the story they were to tell. Viola listened, but scarcely comprehended; he pressed her hand to his heart and departed.

Chapter 7.V.

Van seco pur anco
Sdegno ed Amor, quasi due Veltri al fianco.*
"Ger. Lib." cant. xx. cxvii.

Glyndon did not perceive, as he hurried from the house, two forms crouching by the angle of the wall. He saw still the specter gliding by his side; but he beheld not the yet more poisonous eyes of human envy and woman's jealousy that glared on his retreating footsteps.

Nicot advanced to the house; Fillide followed him in silence. The painter, an old sans-culotte, knew well what language to assume to the

* There went with him still Disdain and Love, like two greyhounds side by side.

porter. He beckoned the latter from his lodge, "How is this, citizen? Thou harborest a 'suspect.'"

"Citizen, you terrify me! — if so, name him."

"It is not a man; a refugee, an Italian woman, lodges here."

"Yes, au troisieme, — the door to the left. But what of her? — she cannot be dangerous, poor child!"

"Citizen, beware! Dost thou dare to pity her?"

"I? No, no, indeed. But —"

"Speak the truth! Who visits her?"

"No one but an Englishman."

"That is it, — an Englishman, a spy of Pitt and Coburg."

"Just Heaven! is it possible?"

"How, citizen! dost thou speak of Heaven? Thou must be an aristocrat!"

"No, indeed; it was but an old bad habit, and escaped me unawares."

"How often does the Englishman visit her?"

"Daily."

Fillide uttered an exclamation.

"She never stirs out," said the porter. "Her sole occupations are in work, and care of her infant."

"Her infant!"

Fillide made a bound forward. Nicot in vain endeavored to arrest her. She sprang up the stairs; she paused not till she was before the door indicated by the porter; it stood ajar, she entered, she stood at the threshold, and beheld that face, still so lovely! The sight of so much beauty left her hopeless. And the child, over whom the mother bent! — she who had never been a mother! — she uttered no sound; the furies were at work within her breast. Viola turned, and saw her, and, terrified by the strange apparition, with features that expressed the deadliest hate and scorn and vengeance, uttered a cry, and snatched the child to her bosom. The Italian laughed aloud, — turned, descended, and, gaining the spot where Nicot still conversed with the frightened porter drew him from the house. When they were in the open street, she halted abruptly, and said, "Avenge me, and name thy price!"

"My price, sweet one! is but permission to love thee. Thou wilt fly with me tomorrow night; thou wilt possess thyself of the passports and the plan."

"And they —"

"Shall, before then, find their asylum in the Conciergerie. The guillotine shall requite thy wrongs."

"Do this, and I am satisfied," said Fillide, firmly.

And they spoke no more till they regained the house. But when she there, looking up to the dull building, saw the windows of the room which the belief of Glyndon's love had once made a paradise, the tiger relented at the heart; something of the woman gushed back upon her nature, dark and savage as it was. She pressed the arm on which she leaned convulsively, and exclaimed, "No, no! not him! denounce her, — let her perish; but I have slept on *his* bosom, — not *him!*"

"It shall be as thou wilt," said Nicot, with a devil's sneer; "but he must be arrested for the moment. No harm shall happen to him, for no accuser shall appear. But her, — thou wilt not relent for her?"

Fillide turned upon him her eyes, and their dark glance was sufficient answer.

Chapter 7. VI.

In poppa quella
Che guidar gli dovea, fatal Donsella.*

"Ger. Lib." cant. xv. 3.

*T*he Italian did not overrate that craft of simulation proverbial with her country and her sex. Not a word, not a look, that day revealed to Glyndon the deadly change that had converted devotion into hate. He himself, indeed, absorbed in his own schemes, and in reflections on his own strange destiny, was no nice observer. But her manner, milder and more subdued than usual, produced a softening effect upon his meditations towards the evening; and he then began to converse with her on the certain hope of escape, and on the future that would await them in less unhallowed lands.

"And thy fair friend," said Fillide, with an averted eye and a false smile, "who was to be our companion? — thou hast resigned her, Nicot tells me, in favor of one in whom he is interested. Is it so?"

"He told thee this!" returned Glyndon, evasively. "Well! does the change content thee?"

* By the prow was the fatal lady ordained to be the guide.

"Traitor!" muttered Fillide; and she rose suddenly, approached him, parted the long hair from his forehead caressingly, and pressed her lips convulsively on his brow.

"This were too fair a head for the doomsman," said she, with a slight laugh, and, turning away, appeared occupied in preparations for their departure.

The next morning, when he rose, Glyndon did not see the Italian; she was absent from the house when he left it. It was necessary that he should once more visit C—— before his final Departure, not only to arrange for Nicot's participation in the flight, but lest any suspicion should have arisen to thwart or endanger the plan he had adopted. C——, though not one of the immediate coterie of Robespierre, and indeed secretly hostile to him, had possessed the art of keeping well with each faction as it rose to power. Sprung from the dregs of the populace, he had, nevertheless, the grace and vivacity so often found impartially amongst every class in France. He had contrived to enrich himself — none knew how — in the course of his rapid career. He became, indeed, ultimately one of the wealthiest proprietors of Paris, and at that time kept a splendid and hospitable mansion. He was one of those whom, from various reasons, Robespierre deigned to favor; and he had often saved the proscribed and suspected, by procuring them passports under disguised names, and advising their method of escape. But C—— was a man who took this trouble only for the rich. "The incorruptible Maximilien," who did not want the tyrant's faculty of penetration, probably saw through all his maneuvers, and the avarice which he cloaked beneath his charity. But it was noticeable that Robespierre frequently seemed to wink at — nay, partially to encourage — such vice in men whom he meant hereafter to destroy, as would tend to lower them in the public estimation, and to contrast with his own austere and unassailable integrity and *Purism*. And, doubtless, he often grimly smiled in his sleeve at the sumptuous mansion and the griping covetousness of the worthy Citizen C——.

To this personage, then, Glyndon musingly bent his way. It was true, as he had darkly said to Viola, that in proportion as he had resisted the specter, its terrors had lost their influence. The time had come at last, when, seeing crime and vice in all their hideousness, and in so vast a theater, he had found that in vice and crime there are deadlier horrors than in the eyes of a phantom-fear. His native nobleness began to return to him. As he passed the streets, he revolved in his mind projects of future repentance and reformation. He even meditated, as a just return for Fillide's devotion, the sacrifice of all the reasonings of his birth and education. He would repair whatever errors he had committed against her, by the self-immolation of marriage with one little congenial with himself. He who had once revolted from marriage with the noble and gentle Viola! — he had learned in that world of wrong to know that right is right, and that Heaven did not make the one sex to be the victim of the other. The young visions of the Beautiful and the Good rose once more before him; and along the dark ocean of his mind lay the smile of reawakening virtue, as a path of moonlight. Never, perhaps, had the condition of his soul been so elevated and unselfish.

In the meanwhile Jean Nicot, equally absorbed in dreams of the future, and already in his own mind laying out to the best advantage the gold of the friend he was about to betray, took his way to the house honored by the residence of Robespierre. He had no intention to comply with the relenting prayer of Fillide, that the life of Glyndon should be spared. He thought with Barrere, "Il n'y a que les morts qui ne revient pas." In all men who have devoted themselves to any study, or any art, with sufficient pains to attain a certain degree of excellence, there must be a fund of energy immeasurably above that of the ordinary herd. Usually this energy is concentrated on the objects of their professional ambition, and leaves them, therefore, apathetic to the other pursuits of men. But where those objects are denied, where the stream has not its legitimate vent, the energy, irritated and aroused, possesses the whole being, and if not wasted on desultory schemes, or if not purified by conscience and principle, becomes a dangerous and destructive element in the social system, through which it wanders in riot and disorder. Hence, in all wise monarchies, — nay, in all well-constituted states, — the peculiar care with which channels are opened for every art and every science; hence the honor paid to their cultivators by subtle and thoughtful statesmen, who, perhaps, for themselves, see nothing in a picture but colored canvas, — nothing in a problem but an ingenious puzzle. No state is ever more in danger than when the talent that should be consecrated to peace has no occupation but political intrigue or personal advancement. Talent unhonored is talent at war with men. And here it is noticeable, that the class of actors having been the most degraded by the public opinion of the old regime, their very dust deprived of Christian burial, no men (with certain exceptions in the company especially favored by the Court) were more relentless and revengeful among the scourges of the Revolution. In the savage Collot d'Herbois, mauvais comedien, were embodied the wrongs and the vengeance of a class.

Now the energy of Jean Nicot had never been sufficiently directed to the art he professed. Even in his earliest youth, the political disquisitions of his master, David, had distracted him from the more tedious labors of the easel. The defects of his person had embittered his mind; the atheism of his benefactor had deadened his conscience. For one great excellence of religion — above all, the Religion of the Cross — is, that it raises *patience* first into a virtue, and next into a hope. Take away the doctrine of another life, of requital hereafter, of the smile of a Father upon our sufferings and trials in our ordeal here, and what becomes of patience? But without patience, what is man? — and what a people? Without patience, art never can be high; without patience, liberty never can be perfected. By wild throes, and impetuous, aimless struggles, Intellect seeks to soar from Penury, and a nation to struggle into Freedom. And woe, thus unfortified, guideless, and unenduring, — woe to both!

Nicot was a villain as a boy. In most criminals, however abandoned, there are touches of humanity, — relics of virtue; and the true delineator of mankind often incurs the taunt of bad hearts and dull minds, for showing that even the worst alloy has some particles of gold, and even the best that come stamped from the mint of Nature have some adulteration of the dross. But there are exceptions, though few, to the general rule, — exceptions, when the conscience lies utterly dead, and when good or bad are things indifferent but as means to some selfish end. So was it with the protégé of the atheist. Envy and hate filled up his whole being, and the consciousness of superior talent only made him curse the more all who passed him in the sunlight with a fairer form or happier fortunes. But, monster though he was, when his murderous fingers griped the throat of his benefactor, Time, and that ferment of all evil passions — the Reign of Blood — had made in the deep hell of his heart a deeper still. Unable to exercise his calling (for even had he dared to make his name prominent, revolutions are no season for painters; and no man — no! not the richest and proudest magnate of the land, has so great an interest in peace and order, has so high and essential a stake in the well being of society, as the poet and the artist), his whole intellect, ever restless and unguided, was left to ponder over the images of guilt most congenial to it. He had no future but in this life; and how in this life had the men of power around him, the great wrestlers for dominion, thriven? All that was good, pure, unselfish, — whether among Royalists or Republicans, — swept to the shambles, and the deathsmen left alone in the pomp and purple of their victims! Nobler paupers than Jean Nicot would despair; and Poverty would rise in its ghastly multitudes to cut the throat of Wealth, and then gash itself limb by limb, if Patience, the Angel of the Poor, sat not by its side, pointing with solemn finger to the life to come! And now, as Nicot neared the house of the Dictator, he began to meditate a reversal of his plans of the previous day: not that he faltered in his resolution to denounce Glyndon, and Viola would necessarily share his fate, as a companion and accomplice, — no, *there* he was resolved! for he hated both (to say nothing of his old but never-to-be-forgotten grudge against Zanoni). Viola had scorned him, Glyndon had served, and the thought of gratitude was as intolerable to him as the memory of insult. But why, now, should he fly from France? — he could possess himself of Glyndon's gold; he doubted not that he could so master Fillide by her wrath and jealousy that he could command her acquiescence in all he proposed. The papers he had purloined — Desmoulins' correspondence with Glyndon — while it insured the fate of the latter, might be eminently serviceable to Robespierre, might induce the tyrant to forget his own old liaisons with Hebert, and enlist him among the allies and tools of the King of Terror. Hopes of advancement, of wealth, of a career, again rose before him. This correspondence, dated shortly before Camille Desmoulins' death, was written with that careless and daring imprudence which characterized the spoiled child of Danton. It spoke openly of designs against Robespierre; it named confederates whom the tyrant desired only a popular pretext to crush. It was a new instrument of death in the hands of the Death-compeller. What greater gift could he bestow on Maximilien the Incorruptible?

Nursing these thoughts, he arrived at last before the door of Citizen Dupleix. Around the threshold were grouped, in admired confusion, some eight or ten sturdy Jacobins, the voluntary body-guard of Robespierre, — tall fellows, well armed, and insolent with the power that reflects power, mingled with women, young and fair, and gaily dressed, who had come, upon the rumor that Maximilien had had an attack of bile, to inquire tenderly of his health; for Robespierre, strange though it seem, was the idol of the sex!

Through this cortege stationed without the door, and reaching up the stairs to the landing-place, — for Robespierre's apartments were not spacious enough to afford sufficient antechamber for levees so numerous and miscellaneous, — Nicot forced his way; and far from friendly or flattering were the expressions that regaled his ears.

"Aha, le joli Polichinelle!" said a comely matron, whose robe his obtrusive and angular elbows cruelly discomposed. "But how could one expect gallantry from such a scarecrow!"

"Citizen, I beg to advise thee.* Take away Murder from the French Revolution and it becomes the greatest farce ever played before the angels!) that thou art treading on my feet. I beg thy pardon, but now I look at thine, I see the hall is not wide enough for them."

"Ho! Citizen Nicot," cried a Jacobin, shouldering his formidable

---

* The courteous use of the plural was proscribed at Paris. The Societies Populaires had decided that whoever used it should be prosecuted as suspect et adulateur! At the door of the public administrations and popular societies was written up, "Ici on s'honore du Citoyen, et on se tutoye!!!" ("Here they respect the title of Citizen, and they 'thee' and 'thou' one another."

bludgeon, "and what brings thee hither? — thinkest thou that Hebert's crimes are forgotten already? Off, sport of Nature! and thank the Etre Supreme that he made thee insignificant enough to be forgiven."

"A pretty face to look out of the National Window"*, said the woman whose robe the painter had ruffled.

"Citizens," said Nicot, white with passion, but constraining himself so that his words seemed to come from grinded teeth, "I have the honor to inform you that I seek the Representant upon business of the utmost importance to the public and himself; and," he added slowly and malignantly, glaring round, "I call all good citizens to be my witnesses when I shall complain to Robespierre of the reception bestowed on me by some amongst you."

There was in the man's look and his tone of voice so much of deep and concentrated malignity, that the idlers drew back, and as the remembrance of the sudden ups and downs of revolutionary life occurred to them, several voices were lifted to assure the squalid and ragged painter that nothing was farther from their thoughts than to offer affront to a citizen whose very appearance proved him to be an exemplary sans-culotte. Nicot received these apologies in sullen silence, and, folding his arms, leaned against the wall, waiting in grim patience for his admission.

The loiterers talked to each other in separate knots of two and three; and through the general hum rang the clear, loud, careless whistle of the tall Jacobin who stood guard by the stairs. Next to Nicot, an old woman and a young virgin were muttering in earnest whispers, and the atheist painter chuckled inly to overhear their discourse.

"I assure thee, my dear," said the crone, with a mysterious shake of head, "that the divine Catherine Theot, whom the impious now persecute, is really inspired. There can be no doubt that the elect, of whom Dom Gerle and the virtuous Robespierre are destined to be the two grand prophets, will enjoy eternal life here, and exterminate all their enemies. There is no doubt of it, — not the least!"

"How delightful!" said the girl; "ce cher Robespierre! — he does not look very long-lived either!"

"The greater the miracle," said the old woman. "I am just eighty-one, and I don't feel a day older since Catherine Theot promised me I should be one of the elect!"

Here the women were jostled aside by some newcomers, who talked loud and eagerly.

"Yes," cried a brawny man, whose garb denoted him to be a butcher, with bare arms, and a cap of liberty on his head; "I am come to warn Robespierre. They lay a snare for him; they offer him the Palais National.

---

* The Guillotine.

'On ne peut etre ami du peuple et habiter un palais.'"*

"No, indeed," answered a cordonnier; "I like him best in his little lodging with the menuisier: it looks like one of *us.*"

Another rush of the crowd, and a new group were thrown forward in the vicinity of Nicot. And these men gabbled and chattered faster and louder than the rest.

"But my plan is —"

"Au diable with *your* plan! I tell you *my* scheme is —"

"Nonsense!" cried a third. "When Robespierre understands *my* new method of making gunpowder, the enemies of France shall —"

"Bah! who fears foreign enemies?" interrupted a fourth; "the enemies to be feared are at home. *My* new guillotine takes off fifty heads at a time!"

"But *my* new Constitution!" exclaimed a fifth.

"*My* new Religion, citizen!" murmured, complacently, a sixth.

"Sacre mille tonnerres, silence!" roared forth one of the Jacobin guard.

And the crowd suddenly parted as a fierce-looking man, buttoned up to the chin, his sword rattling by his side, his spurs clinking at his heel, descended the stairs, — his cheeks swollen and purple with intemperance, his eyes dead and savage as a vulture's. There was a still pause, as all, with pale cheeks, made way for the relentless Henriot.† Scarce had this gruff and iron minion of the tyrant stalked through the throng, than a new movement of respect and agitation and fear swayed the increasing crowd, as there glided in, with the noiselessness of a shadow, a smiling, sober citizen, plainly but neatly clad, with a downcast humble eye. A milder, meeker face no pastoral poet could assign to Corydon or Thyrsis, — why did the crowd shrink and hold their breath? As the ferret in a burrow crept that slight form amongst the larger and rougher creatures that huddled and pressed back on each other as he passed. A wink of his stealthy eye, and the huge Jacobins left the passage clear, without sound or question. On he went to the apartment of the tyrant, and thither will we follow him.

---

* "No one can be a friend of the people, and dwell in a palace." — "Papiers inedits trouves chez Robespierre," etc., volume ii. page 132.

† Or Hanriot. It is singular how undetermined are not only the characters of the French Revolution, but even the spelling of their names. With the historians it is Vergniaud, — with the journalists of the time it is Vorgniaux. With one authority it is Robespierre, — with another Roberspierre.

Chapter 7.VII.

Constitutum est, ut quisquis eum *hominem* dixisset fuisse, capitalem penderet poenam.*
     St. Augustine, "Of the God Serapis," l. 18, "de Civ. Dei," c. 5.)

Robespierre was reclining languidly in his fauteuil, his cadaverous countenance more jaded and fatigued than usual. He to whom Catherine Theot assured immortal life, looked, indeed, like a man at death's door. On the table before him was a dish heaped with oranges, with the juice of which it is said that he could alone assuage the acrid bile that overflowed his system; and an old woman, richly dressed (she had been a Marquise in the old regime) was employed in peeling the Hesperian fruits for the sick Dragon, with delicate fingers covered with jewels. I have before said that Robespierre was the idol of the women. Strange certainly! – but then they were French women! The old Marquise, who, like Catherine Theot, called him "son," really seemed to love him piously and disinterestedly as a mother; and as she peeled the oranges, and heaped on him the most caressing and soothing expressions, the livid ghost of a smile fluttered about his meager lips. At a distance, Payan and Couthon, seated at another table, were writing rapidly, and occasionally pausing from their work to consult with each other in brief whispers.

Suddenly one of the Jacobins opened the door, and, approaching Robespierre, whispered to him the name of Guerin.† At that word the sick man started up, as if new life were in the sound.

"My kind friend," he said to the Marquise, "forgive me; I must dispense with thy tender cares. France demands me. I am never ill when I can serve my country!"

---

* It was decreed, that whoso should say that he had been a *man*, should suffer the punishment of a capital offence.
† See for the espionage on which Guerin was employed, "Les Papiers inedits," etc., volume i. page 366, No. xxviii.

The old Marquise lifted up her eyes to heaven and murmured, "Quel ange!"

Robespierre waved his hand impatiently; and the old woman, with a sigh, patted his pale cheek, kissed his forehead, and submissively withdrew. The next moment, the smiling, sober man we have before described, stood, bending low, before the tyrant. And well might Robespierre welcome one of the subtlest agents of his power, — one on whom he relied more than the clubs of his Jacobins, the tongues of his orators, the bayonets of his armies; Guerin, the most renowned of his ecouteurs, — the searching, prying, universal, omnipresent spy, who glided like a sunbeam through chink and crevice, and brought to him intelligence not only of the deeds, but the hearts of men!

"Well, citizen, well! — and what of Tallien?"

"This morning, early, two minutes after eight, he went out."

"So early? — hem!"

"He passed Rue des Quatre Fils, Rue de Temple, Rue de la Reunion, au Marais, Rue Martin; nothing observable, except that —"

"That what?"

"He amused himself at a stall in bargaining for some books."

"Bargaining for books! Aha, the charlatan! — he would cloak the intriguant under the savant! Well!"

"At last, in the Rue des Fosses Montmartre, an individual in a blue surtout (unknown) accosted him. They walked together about the street some minutes, and were joined by Legendre."

"Legendre! approach, Payan! Legendre, thou hearest!"

"I went into a fruit-stall, and hired two little girls to go and play at ball within hearing. They heard Legendre say, 'I believe his power is wearing itself out.' And Tallien answered, 'And *himself* too. I would not give three months' purchase for his life.' I do not know, citizen, if they meant *thee?*"

"Nor I, citizen," answered Robespierre, with a fell smile, succeeded by an expression of gloomy thought. "Ha!" he muttered; "I am young yet, — in the prime of life. I commit no excess. No; my constitution is sound, sound. Anything farther of Tallien?"

"Yes. The woman whom he loves — Teresa de Fontenai — who lies in prison, still continues to correspond with him; to urge him to save her by thy destruction: this my listeners overheard. His servant is the messenger between the prisoner and himself."

"So! The servant shall be seized in the open streets of Paris. The Reign of Terror is not over yet. With the letters found on him, if such their context, I will pluck Tallien from his benches in the Convention."

Robespierre rose, and after walking a few moments to and fro the room in thought, opened the door and summoned one of the Jacobins without. To him he gave his orders for the watch and arrest of Tallien's servant, and then threw himself again into his chair. As the Jacobin departed, Guerin whispered, —

"Is not that the Citizen Aristides?"

"Yes; a faithful fellow, if he would wash himself, and not swear so much."

"Didst thou not guillotine his brother?"

"But Aristides denounced him."

"Nevertheless, are such men safe about thy person?"

"Humph! that is true." And Robespierre, drawing out his pocket-book, wrote a memorandum in it, replaced it in his vest, and resumed, —

"What else of Tallien?"

"Nothing more. He and Legendre, with the unknown, walked to the Jardin Egalite, and there parted. I saw Tallien to his house. But I have other news. Thou badest me watch for those who threaten thee in secret letters."

"Guerin! hast thou detected them? Hast thou — hast thou —"

And the tyrant, as he spoke, opened and shut both his hands, as if already grasping the lives of the writers, and one of those convulsive grimaces that seemed like an epileptic affection, to which he was subject, distorted his features.

"Citizen, I think I have found one. Thou must know that amongst those most disaffected is the painter Nicot."

"Stay, stay!" said Robespierre, opening a manuscript book, bound in red morocco*, and turning to an alphabetical index, — "Nicot! — I have him, — atheist, sans-culotte†, friend of Hebert! Aha! N.B. — Rene Dumas knows of his early career and crimes. Proceed!"

"This Nicot has been suspected of diffusing tracts and pamphlets against thyself and the Comite. Yesterday evening, when he was out, his porter admitted me into his apartment, Rue Beau Repaire. With my master key I opened his desk and escritoire. I found herein a drawing of thyself at the guillotine; and underneath was written, 'Bourreau de ton pays, lis l'arret de ton chatiment!'‡ I compared the words with the fragments of the various letters thou gavest me: the handwriting tallies with one. See, I tore off the writing."

Robespierre looked, smiled, and, as if his vengeance were already satisfied, threw himself on his chair. "It is well! I feared it was a more powerful enemy. This man must be arrested at once."

"And he waits below. I brushed by him as I ascended the stairs."

"Does he so? — admit! — nay, — hold! hold! Guerin, withdraw into

---

* for Robespierre was neat and precise, even in his death-lists
† I hate slovens
‡ Executioner of thy country, read the decree of thy punishment!

the inner chamber till I summon thee again. Dear Payan, see that this Nicot conceals no weapons."

Payan, who was as brave as Robespierre was pusillanimous, repressed the smile of disdain that quivered on his lips a moment, and left the room.

Meanwhile Robespierre, with his head buried in his bosom, seemed plunged in deep thought. "Life is a melancholy thing, Couthon!" said he, suddenly.

"Begging your pardon, I think death worse," answered the philan-thropist, gently.

Robespierre made no rejoinder, but took from his portefeuille that singular letter, which was found afterwards amongst his papers, and is marked LXI. in the published collection.*

"Without doubt," it began, "you are uneasy at not having earlier received news from me. Be not alarmed; you know that I ought only to reply by our ordinary courier; and as he has been interrupted, dans sa derniere course, that is the cause of my delay. When you receive this, employ all diligence to fly a theater where you are about to appear and disappear for the last time. It were idle to recall to you all the reasons that expose you to peril. The last step that should place you sur le sopha de la presidence, but brings you to the scaffold; and the mob will spit on your face as it has spat on those whom you have judged. Since, then, you have accumulated here a sufficient treasure for existence, I await you with great impatience, to laugh with you at the part you have played in the troubles of a nation as credulous as it is avid of novelties. Take your part according to our arrangements, — all is prepared. I conclude, — our courier waits. I expect your reply."

Musingly and slowly the Dictator devoured the contents of this epistle. "No," he said to himself, — "no; he who has tasted power can no longer enjoy repose. Yet, Danton, Danton! thou wert right; better to be a poor fisherman than to govern men."

("Il vaudrait mieux," said Danton, in his dungeon, "etre un pauvre pecheur que de gouverner les hommes.")

The door opened, and Payan reappeared and whispered Robespierre, "All is safe! See the man."

The Dictator, satisfied, summoned his attendant Jacobin to conduct Nicot to his presence. The painter entered with a fearless expression in his deformed features, and stood erect before Robespierre, who scanned him with a sidelong eye.

It is remarkable that most of the principal actors of the Revolution were singularly hideous in appearance, — from the colossal ugliness of Mirabeau and Danton, or the villainous ferocity in the countenances

---

* "Papiers inedits,' etc., volume ii. page 156.

of David and Simon, to the filthy squalor of Marat, the sinister and bilious meanness of the Dictator's features. But Robespierre, who was said to resemble a cat, had also a cat's cleanness; and his prim and dainty dress, his shaven smoothness, the womanly whiteness of his lean hands, made yet more remarkable the disorderly ruffianism that characterized the attire and mien of the painter-sans-culotte.

"And so, citizen," said Robespierre, mildly, "thou wouldst speak with me? I know thy merits and civism have been overlooked too long. Thou wouldst ask some suitable provision in the state? Scruple not — say on!"

"Virtuous Robespierre, toi qui eclaires l'univers*, I come not to ask a favor, but to render service to the state. I have discovered a correspondence that lays open a conspiracy of which many of the actors are yet unsuspected." And he placed the papers on the table. Robespierre seized, and ran his eye over them rapidly and eagerly.

"Good! — good!" he muttered to himself: "this is all I wanted. Barrere, Legendre! I have them! Camille Desmoulins was but their dupe. I loved him once; I never loved them! Citizen Nicot, I thank thee. I observe these letters are addressed to an Englishman. What Frenchman but must distrust these English wolves in sheep's clothing! France wants no longer citizens of the world; that farce ended with Anarcharsis Clootz. I beg pardon, Citizen Nicot; but Clootz and Hebert were *thy* friends."

"Nay," said Nicot, apologetically, "we are all liable to be deceived. I ceased to honor them whom thou didst declare against; for I disown my own senses rather than thy justice."

"Yes, I pretend to justice; that *is* the virtue I affect," said Robespierre, meekly; and with his feline propensities he enjoyed, even in that critical hour of vast schemes, of imminent danger, of meditated revenge, the pleasure of playing with a solitary victim.† "And my justice shall no longer be blind to thy services, good Nicot. Thou knowest this Glyndon?"

"Yes, well, — intimately. He *was* my friend, but I would give up my brother if he were one of the 'indulgents.' I am not ashamed to say that I have received favors from this man."

"Aha! — and thou dost honestly hold the doctrine that where a man threatens my life all personal favors are to be forgotten?"

"All!"

"Good citizen! — kind Nicot! — oblige me by writing the address of this Glyndon."

Nicot stooped to the table; and suddenly when the pen was in his hand, a thought flashed across him, and he paused, embarrassed and

---

* Thou who enlightenest the world.

† The most detestable anecdote of this peculiar hypocrisy in Robespierre is that in which he is recorded to have tenderly pressed the hand of his old school-friend, Camille Desmoulins, the day that he signed the warrant for his arrest.

confused.

"Write on, *kind* Nicot!"

The painter slowly obeyed.

"Who are the other familiars of Glyndon?"

"It was on that point I was about to speak to thee, Representant," said Nicot. "He visits daily a woman, a foreigner, who knows all his secrets; she affects to be poor, and to support her child by industry. But she is the wife of an Italian of immense wealth, and there is no doubt that she has moneys which are spent in corrupting the citizens. She should be seized and arrested."

"Write down her name also."

"But no time is to be lost; for I know that both have a design to escape from Paris this very night."

"Our government is prompt, good Nicot, — never fear. Humph! — humph!" and Robespierre took the paper on which Nicot had written, and stooping over it — for he was near-sighted — added, smilingly, "Dost thou always write the same hand, citizen? This seems almost like a disguised character."

"I should not like them to know who denounced them, Representant."

"Good! good! Thy virtue shall be rewarded, trust me. Salut et fraternite!"

Robespierre half rose as he spoke, and Nicot withdrew.

"Ho, there! — without!" cried the Dictator, ringing his bell; and as the ready Jacobin attended the summons, "Follow that man, Jean Nicot. The instant he has cleared the house seize him. At once to the Conciergerie with him. Stay! — nothing against the law; there is thy warrant. The public accuser shall have my instruction. Away! — quick!"

The Jacobin vanished. All trace of illness, of infirmity, had gone from the valetudinarian; he stood erect on the floor, his face twitching convulsively, and his arms folded. "Ho! Guerin!" the spy reappeared — "take these addresses! Within an hour this Englishman and his woman must be in prison; their revelations will aid me against worthier foes. They shall die: they shall perish with the rest on the 10th, — the third day from this. There!" and he wrote hastily, — "there, also, is thy warrant! Off!

"And now, Couthon, Payan, we will dally no longer with Tallien and his crew. I have information that the Convention will *not* attend the Fete on the 10th. We must trust only to the sword of the law. I must compose my thoughts, — prepare my harangue. Tomorrow, I will reappear at the Convention; tomorrow, bold St. Just joins us, fresh from our victorious armies; tomorrow, from the tribune, I will dart the thunderbolt on the masked enemies of France; tomorrow, I will demand, in the face of the country, the heads of the conspirators."

Chapter 7.VIII.

Le glaive est contre toi tourne de toutes parties.*
La Harpe, "Jeanne de Naples," Act iv. sc. 4.

*I*n the meantime Glyndon, after an audience of some length with
C——, in which the final preparations were arranged, sanguine of safety,
and foreseeing no obstacle to escape, bent his way back to Fillide.
Suddenly, in the midst of his cheerful thoughts, he fancied he heard a
voice too well and too terribly recognized, hissing in his ear, "What!
thou wouldst defy and escape me! thou wouldst go back to virtue and
content. It is in vain, — it is too late. No, *I* will not haunt thee; *human*
footsteps, no less inexorable, dog thee now. Me thou shalt not see again
till in the dungeon, at midnight, before thy doom! Behold —"

And Glyndon, mechanically turning his head, saw, close behind him,
the stealthy figure of a man whom he had observed before, but with
little heed, pass and repass him, as he quitted the house of Citizen C——.
Instantly and instinctively he knew that he was watched, — that he was
pursued. The street he was in was obscure and deserted, for the day was
oppressively sultry, and it was the hour when few were abroad, either
on business or pleasure. Bold as he was, an icy chill shot through his
heart, he knew too well the tremendous system that then reigned in Paris
not to be aware of his danger. As the sight of the first plague-boil to the
victim of the pestilence, was the first sight of the shadowy spy to that
of the Revolution: the watch, the arrest, the trial, the guillotine, — these
made the regular and rapid steps of the monster that the anarchists
called Law! He breathed hard, he heard distinctly the loud beating of
his heart. And so he paused, still and motionless, gazing upon the
shadow that halted also behind him.

---

* The sword is raised against you on all sides.

Presently, the absence of all allies to the spy, the solitude of the streets, reanimated his courage; he made a step towards his pursuer, who retreated as he advanced. "Citizen, thou followest me," he said. "Thy business?"

"Surely," answered the man, with a deprecating smile, "the streets are broad enough for both? Thou art not so bad a republican as to arrogate all Paris to thyself!"

"Go on first, then. I make way for thee."

The man bowed, doffed his hat politely, and passed forward. The next moment Glyndon plunged into a winding lane, and fled fast through a labyrinth of streets, passages, and alleys. By degrees he composed himself, and, looking behind, imagined that he had baffled the pursuer; he then, by a circuitous route, bent his way once more to his home. As he emerged into one of the broader streets, a passenger, wrapped in a mantle, brushing so quickly by him that he did not observe his countenance, whispered, "Clarence Glyndon, you are dogged, — follow me!" and the stranger walked quickly before him. Clarence turned, and sickened once more to see at his heels, with the same servile smile on his face, the pursuer he fancied he had escaped. He forgot the injunction of the stranger to follow him, and perceiving a crowd gathered close at hand, round a caricature-shop, dived amidst them, and, gaining another street, altered the direction he had before taken, and, after a long and breathless course, gained without once more seeing the spy, a distant quartier of the city.

Here, indeed, all seemed so serene and fair that his artist eye, even in that imminent hour, rested with pleasure on the scene. It was a comparatively broad space, formed by one of the noble quays. The Seine flowed majestically along, with boats and craft resting on its surface. The sun gilt a thousand spires and domes, and gleamed on the white palaces of a fallen chivalry. Here fatigued and panting, he paused an instant, and a cooler air from the river fanned his brow. "Awhile, at least, I am safe here," he murmured; and as he spoke, some thirty paces behind him, he beheld the spy. He stood rooted to the spot; wearied and spent as he was, escape seemed no longer possible, — the river on one side (no bridge at hand), and the long row of mansions closing up the other. As he halted, he heard laughter and obscene songs from a house a little in his rear, between himself and the spy. It was a café fearfully known in that quarter. Hither often resorted the black troop of Henriot, — the minions and huissiers of Robespierre. The spy, then, had hunted the victim within the jaws of the hounds. The man slowly advanced, and, pausing before the open window of the café, put his head through the aperture, as to address and summon forth its armed inmates.

At that very instant, and while the spy's head was thus turned from him, standing in the half-open gateway of the house immediately before him, he perceived the stranger who had warned; the figure, scarcely distinguishable through the mantle that wrapped it, motioned to him to enter. He sprang noiselessly through the friendly opening: the door closed; breathlessly he followed the stranger up a flight of broad stairs and through a suite of empty rooms, until, having gained a small cabinet, his conductor doffed the large hat and the long mantle that had hitherto concealed his shape and features, and Glyndon beheld Zanoni!

Chapter 7.IX.

Think not my magic wonders wrought by aid
Of Stygian angels summoned up from hell;
Scorned and accursed be those who have essayed
Her gloomy Dives and Afrites to compel.
But by perception of the secret powers
Of mineral springs in Nature's inmost cell,
Of herbs in curtain of her greenest bowers,
And of the moving stars o'er mountain tops and towers.
                    Wiffen's "Translation of Tasso," cant. xiv. xliii.

"You are safe here, young Englishman!" said Zanoni, motioning Glyndon to a seat. "Fortunate for you that I come on your track at last!"

"Far happier had it been if we had never met! Yet even in these last hours of my fate, I rejoice to look once more on the face of that ominous and mysterious being to whom I can ascribe all the sufferings I have known. Here, then, thou shalt not palter with or elude me. Here, before we part, thou shalt unravel to me the dark enigma, if not of thy life, of my own!"

"Hast thou suffered? Poor neophyte!" said Zanoni, pityingly. "Yes; I see it on thy brow. But wherefore wouldst thou blame me? Did I not warn thee against the whispers of thy spirit; did I not warn thee to forbear? Did I not tell thee that the ordeal was one of awful hazard and tremendous fears, — nay, did I not offer to resign to thee the heart that was mighty enough, while mine, Glyndon, to content me? Was it not thine own daring and resolute choice to brave the initiation! Of thine own free will didst thou make Mejnour thy master, and his lore thy study!"

"But whence came the irresistible desires of that wild and unholy knowledge? I knew them not till thine evil eye fell upon me, and I was drawn into the magic atmosphere of thy being!"

"Thou errest! — the desires were in thee; and, whether in one direction or the other, would have forced their way! Man! thou askest me the enigma of thy fate and my own! Look round all being, is there not mystery everywhere? Can thine eye trace the ripening of the grain beneath the earth? In the moral and the physical world alike, lie dark portents, far more wondrous than the powers thou wouldst ascribe to me!"

"Dost thou disown those powers; dost thou confess thyself an imposter? — or wilt thou dare to tell me that thou art indeed sold to the Evil one, — a magician whose familiar has haunted me night and day?"

"It matters not what I am," returned Zanoni; "it matters only whether I can aid thee to exorcise thy dismal phantom, and return once more to the wholesome air of this common life. Something, however, will I tell thee, not to vindicate myself, but the Heaven and the Nature that thy doubts malign."

Zanoni paused a moment, and resumed with a slight smile, —

"In thy younger days thou hast doubtless read with delight the great Christian poet, whose muse, like the morning it celebrated, came to earth, 'crowned with flowers culled in Paradise.' * "No spirit was more imbued with the knightly superstitions of the time; and surely the Poet of Jerusalem hath sufficiently, to satisfy even the Inquisitor he consulted, execrated all the practitioners of the unlawful spells invoked, —

'Per isforzar Cocito o Flegetonte.'†

But in his sorrows and his wrongs, in the prison of his madhouse, know you not that Tasso himself found his solace, his escape, in the recognition of a holy and spiritual Theurgia, — of a magic that could summon the Angel, or the Good Genius, not the Fiend? And do you not remember how he, deeply versed as he was for his age, in the

---

* 'L'aurea testa Di rose colte in Paradiso infiora.' Tasso, "Ger. Lib." iv. l.
† To constrain Cocytus or Phlegethon.

mysteries of the nobler Platonism, which hints at the secrets of all the starry brotherhoods, from the Chaldean to the later Rosicrucian, discriminates in his lovely verse, between the black art of Ismeno and the glorious lore of the Enchanter who counsels and guides upon their errand the champions of the Holy Land? *His*, not the charms wrought by the aid of the Stygian Rebels* , but the perception of the secret powers of the fountain and the herb, — the Arcana of the unknown nature and the various motions of the stars. His, the holy haunts of Lebanon and Carmel, — beneath his feet he saw the clouds, the snows, the hues of Iris, the generations of the rains and dews. Did the Christian Hermit who converted that Enchanter (no fabulous being, but the type of all spirit that would aspire through Nature up to God) command him to lay aside these sublime studies, 'Le solite arte e l' uso mio'? No! but to cherish and direct them to worthy ends. And in this grand conception of the poet lies the secret of the true Theurgia, which startles your ignorance in a more learned day with puerile apprehensions, and the nightmares of a sick man's dreams."

Again Zanoni paused, and again resumed: —

"In ages far remote, — of a civilization far different from that which now merges the individual in the state, — there existed men of ardent minds, and an intense desire of knowledge. In the mighty and solemn kingdoms in which they dwelt, there were no turbulent and earthly channels to work off the fever of their minds. Set in the antique mould of casts through which no intellect could pierce, no valor could force its way, the thirst for wisdom alone reigned in the hearts of those who received its study as a heritage from sire to son. Hence, even in your imperfect records of the progress of human knowledge, you find that, in the earliest ages, Philosophy descended not to the business and homes of men. It dwelt amidst the wonders of the loftier creation; it sought to analyze the formation of matter, — the essentials of the prevailing soul; to read the mysteries of the starry orbs; to dive into those depths of Nature in which Zoroaster is said by the schoolmen first to have discovered the arts which your ignorance classes under the name of magic. In such an age, then, arose some men, who, amidst the vanities and delusions of their class, imagined that they detected gleams of a brighter and steadier lore. They fancied an affinity existing among all the works of Nature, and that in the lowliest lay the secret attraction that might conduct them upward to the loftiest.† Centuries passed, and

---

* See this remarkable passage, which does indeed not unfaithfully represent the doctrine of the Pythagorean and the Platonist, in Tasso, cant. xiv. stanzas xli. to xlvii. ("Ger. Lib.") They are beautifully translated by Wiffen.

† Agreeably, it would seem, to the notion of Iamblichus and Plotinus, that the universe is as an animal; so that there is sympathy and communication between one part and the other; in the smallest part may be the subtlest nerve. And hence the universal

lives were wasted in these discoveries; but step after step was chronicled and marked, and became the guide to the few who alone had the hereditary privilege to track their path.

At last from this dimness upon some eyes the light broke; but think not, young visionary, that to those who nursed unholy thoughts, over whom the Origin of Evil held a sway, that dawning was vouchsafed. It could be given then, as now, only to the purest ecstasies of imagination and intellect, undistracted by the cares of a vulgar life, or the appetites of the common clay. Far from descending to the assistance of a fiend, theirs was but the august ambition to approach nearer to the Fount of Good; the more they emancipated themselves from this limbo of the planets, the more they were penetrated by the splendor and beneficence of God. And if they sought, and at last discovered, how to the eye of the Spirit all the subtler modifications of being and of matter might be made apparent; if they discovered how, for the wings of the Spirit, all space might be annihilated, and while the body stood heavy and solid here, as a deserted tomb, the freed *idea* might wander from star to star, — if such discoveries became in truth their own, the sublimest luxury of their knowledge was but this, to wonder, to venerate, and adore! For, as one not unlearned in these high matters has expressed it, 'There is a principle of the soul superior to all external nature, and through this principle we are capable of surpassing the order and systems of the world, and participating the immortal life and the energy of the Sublime Celestials. When the soul is elevated to natures above itself, it deserts the order to which it is awhile compelled, and by a religious magnetism is attracted to another and a loftier, with which it blends and mingles.'* Grant, then, that such beings found at last the secret to arrest death; to fascinate danger and the foe; to walk the revolutions of the earth unharmed, — think you that this life could teach them other desire than to yearn the more for the Immortal, and to fit their intellect the better for the higher being to which they might, when Time and Death exist no longer, be transferred? Away with your gloomy fantasies of sorcerer and demon! — the soul can aspire only to the light; and even the error of our lofty knowledge was but the forgetfulness of the weakness, the passions, and the bonds which the death we so vainly conquered only can purge away!"

This address was so different from what Glyndon had anticipated, that he remained for some moments speechless, and at length faltered out, —

---

magnetism of Nature. But man contemplates the universe as an animalcule would an elephant. The animalcule, seeing scarcely the tip of the hoof, would be incapable of comprehending that the trunk belonged to the same creature, — that the effect produced upon one extremity would be felt in an instant by the other.

* From Iamblichus, "On the Mysteries," c. 7, sect. 7.

"But why, then, to me —"

"Why," added Zanoni, — "why to thee have been only the penance and the terror, — the Threshold and the Phantom? Vain man! look to the commonest elements of the common learning. Can every tyro at his mere wish and will become the master; can the student, when he has bought his Euclid, become a Newton; can the youth whom the Muses haunt, say, 'I will equal Homer;' yea, can yon pale tyrant, with all the parchment laws of a hundred system-shapers, and the pikes of his dauntless multitude, carve, at his will, a constitution not more vicious than the one which the madness of a mob could overthrow? When, in that far time to which I have referred, the student aspired to the heights to which thou wouldst have sprung at a single bound, he was trained from his very cradle to the career he was to run. The internal and the outward nature were made clear to his eyes, year after year, as they opened on the day. He was not admitted to the practical initiation till not one earthly wish chained that sublimest faculty which you call the *imagination*, one carnal desire clouded the penetrative essence that you call the *intellect*. And even then, and at the best, how few attained to the last mystery! Happier inasmuch as they attained the earlier to the holy glories for which Death is the heavenliest gate."

Zanoni paused, and a shade of thought and sorrow darkened his celestial beauty.

"And are there, indeed, others, besides thee and Mejnour, who lay claim to thine attributes, and have attained to thy secrets?"

"Others there have been before us, but we two now are alone on earth."

"Imposter, thou betrayest thyself! If they could conquer Death, why live they not yet?"*

"Child of a day!" answered Zanoni, mournfully, "have I not told thee the error of our knowledge was the forgetfulness of the desires and passions which the spirit never can wholly and permanently conquer while this matter cloaks it? Canst thou think that it is no sorrow, either to reject all human ties, all friendship, and all love, or to see, day after day, friendship and love wither from our life, as blossoms from the stem? Canst thou wonder how, with the power to live while the world shall last, ere even our ordinary date be finished we yet may prefer to die? Wonder rather that there are two who have clung so faithfully to earth! Me, I confess, that earth can enamor yet. Attaining to the last secret while youth was in its bloom, youth still colors all around me with its own luxuriant beauty; to me, yet, to breathe is to enjoy. The freshness has not faded from the face of Nature, and not an herb in

---

* Glyndon appears to forget that Mejnour had before answered the very question which his doubts here a second time suggest.

which I cannot discover a new charm, — an undetected wonder.

As with my youth, so with Mejnour's age: he will tell you that life to him is but a power to examine; and not till he has exhausted all the marvels which the Creator has sown on earth, would he desire new habitations for the renewed Spirit to explore. We are the types of the two essences of what is imperishable, — 'Art, that enjoys; and Science, that contemplates!' And now, that thou mayest be contented that the secrets are not vouchsafed to thee, learn that so utterly must the idea detach itself from what makes up the occupation and excitement of men; so must it be void of whatever would covet, or love, or hate, — that for the ambitious man, for the lover, the hater, the power avails not. And I, at last, bound and blinded by the most common of household ties; I, darkened and helpless, adjure thee, the baffled and discontented, — I adjure thee to direct, to guide me; where are they? Oh, tell me, — speak! My wife, — my child? Silent! — oh, thou knowest now that I am no sorcerer, no enemy. I cannot give thee what thy faculties deny, — I cannot achieve what the passionless Mejnour failed to accomplish; but I can give thee the next-best boon, perhaps the fairest, — I can reconcile thee to the daily world, and place peace between thy conscience and thyself."

"Wilt thou promise?"

"By their sweet lives, I promise!"

Glyndon looked and believed. He whispered the address to the house whither his fatal step already had brought woe and doom.

"Bless thee for this," exclaimed Zanoni, passionately, "and thou shalt be blessed! What! couldst thou not perceive that at the entrance to all the grander worlds dwell the race that intimidate and awe? Who in thy daily world ever left the old regions of Custom and Prescription, and felt not the first seizure of the shapeless and nameless Fear? Everywhere around thee where men aspire and labor, though they see it not, — in the closet of the sage, in the council of the demagogue, in the camp of the warrior, — everywhere cowers and darkens the Unutterable Horror. But there, where thou hast ventured, alone is the Phantom visible; and never will it cease to haunt, till thou canst pass to the Infinite, as the seraph; or return to the Familiar, as a child! But answer me this: when, seeking to adhere to some calm resolve of virtue, the Phantom hath stalked suddenly to thy side; when its voice hath whispered thee despair; when its ghastly eyes would scare thee back to those scenes of earthly craft or riotous excitement from which, as it leaves thee to worse foes to the soul, its presence is ever absent, — hast thou never bravely resisted the specter and thine own horror; hast thou never said, 'Come what may, to Virtue I will cling?'"

"Alas!" answered Glyndon, "only of late have I dared to do so."

"And thou hast felt then that the Phantom grew more dim and its power more faint?"

"It is true."

"Rejoice, then! — thou hast overcome the true terror and mystery of the ordeal. Resolve is the first success. Rejoice, for the exorcism is sure! Thou art not of those who, denying a life to come, are the victims of the Inexorable Horror. Oh, when shall men learn, at last, that if the Great Religion inculcates so rigidly the necessity of *Faith*, it is not alone that *Faith* leads to the world to be; but that without faith there is no excellence in this, — faith in something wiser, happier, diviner, than we see on earth! — the artist calls it the Ideal, — the priest, Faith. The Ideal and Faith are one and the same. Return, O wanderer, return! Feel what beauty and holiness dwell in the Customary and the Old. Back to thy gateway glide, thou Horror! and calm, on the childlike heart, smile again, O azure Heaven, with thy night and thy morning star but as one, though under its double name of Memory and Hope!"

As he thus spoke, Zanoni laid his hand gently on the burning temples of his excited and wondering listener; and presently a sort of trance came over him: he imagined that he was returned to the home of his infancy; that he was in the small chamber where, over his early slumbers, his mother had watched and prayed. There it was, — visible, palpable, solitary, unaltered. In the recess, the homely bed; on the walls, the shelves filled with holy books; the very easel on which he had first sought to call the ideal to the canvas, dust-covered, broken, in the corner. Below the window lay the old churchyard: he saw it green in the distance, the sun glancing through the yew trees; he saw the tomb where father and mother lay united, and the spire pointing up to heaven, the symbol of the hopes of those who consigned the ashes to the dust; in his ear rang the bells, pealing, as on a Sabbath day. Far fled all the visions of anxiety and awe that had haunted and convulsed; youth, boyhood, childhood came back to him with innocent desires and hopes; he thought he fell upon his knees to pray. He woke, — he woke in delicious tears, he felt that the Phantom was fled forever. He looked round, — Zanoni was gone. On the table lay these lines, the ink yet wet: —

"I will find ways and means for thy escape. At nightfall, as the clock strikes nine, a boat shall wait thee on the river before this house; the boatman will guide thee to a retreat where thou mayst rest in safety till the Reign of Terror, which nears its close, be past. Think no more of the sensual love that lured, and well-nigh lost thee. It betrayed, and would have destroyed. Thou wilt regain thy land in safety, — long years yet spared to thee to muse over the past, and to redeem it. For thy future, be thy dream thy guide, and thy tears thy baptism."

The Englishman obeyed the injunctions of the letter, and found their truth.

Chapter 7.X.

Quid mirare meas tot in uno corpore formas?*

Propert

Zanoni to Mejnour

. . .

"She is in one of their prisons, — their inexorable prisons. It is Robespierre's order, — I have tracked the cause to Glyndon. This, then, made that terrible connection between their fates which I could not unravel, but which (till severed as it now is) wrapped Glyndon himself in the same cloud that concealed her. In prison, — in prison! — it is the gate of the grave! Her trial, and the inevitable execution that follows such trial, is the third day from this. The tyrant has fixed all his schemes of slaughter for the 10th of Thermidor. While the deaths of the unoffending strike awe to the city, his satellites are to massacre his foes. There is but one hope left, — that the Power which now dooms the doomer, may render me an instrument to expedite his fall. But two days left, — two days! In all my wealth of time I see but two days; all beyond, — darkness, solitude. I may save her yet. The tyrant shall fall the day before that which he has set apart for slaughter! For the first time I mix among the broils and stratagems of men, and my mind leaps up from my despair, armed and eager for the contest."

. . .

A crowd had gathered round the Rue St. Honore; a young man was just arrested by the order of Robespierre. He was known to be in the service of Tallien, that hostile leader in the Convention, whom the tyrant had hitherto trembled to attack. This incident had therefore produced a greater excitement than a circumstance so customary as an arrest in the Reign of Terror might be supposed to create. Amongst the crowd were many friends of Tallien, many foes to the tyrant, many weary of beholding the tiger dragging victim after victim to its den. Hoarse,

---

* Why wonder that I have so many forms in a single body?

foreboding murmurs were heard; fierce eyes glared upon the officers as they seized their prisoner; and though they did not yet dare openly to resist, those in the rear pressed on those behind, and encumbered the path of the captive and his captors. The young man struggled hard for escape, and, by a violent effort, at last wrenched himself from the grasp. The crowd made way, and closed round to protect him, as he dived and darted through their ranks; but suddenly the trampling of horses was heard at hand, — the savage Henriot and his troop were bearing down upon the mob. The crowd gave way in alarm, and the prisoner was again seized by one of the partisans of the Dictator. At that moment a voice whispered the prisoner, "Thou hast a letter which, if found on thee, ruins thy last hope. Give it to me! I will bear it to Tallien." The prisoner turned in amaze, read something that encouraged him in the eyes of the stranger who thus accosted him. The troop were now on the spot; the Jacobin who had seized the prisoner released hold of him for a moment to escape the hoofs of the horses: in that moment the opportunity was found, — the stranger had disappeared.

. . .

At the house of Tallien the principal foes of the tyrant were assembled. Common danger made common fellowship. All factions laid aside their feuds for the hour to unite against the formidable man who was marching over all factions to his gory throne. There was bold Lecointre, the declared enemy; there, creeping Barrere, who would reconcile all extremes, the hero of the cowards; Barras, calm and collected; Collet d'Herbois, breathing wrath and vengeance, and seeing not that the crimes of Robespierre alone sheltered his own.

The council was agitated and irresolute. The awe which the uniform success and the prodigious energy of Robespierre excited still held the greater part under its control. Tallien, whom the tyrant most feared, and who alone could give head and substance and direction to so many contradictory passions, was too sullied by the memory of his own cruelties not to feel embarrassed by his position as the champion of mercy. "It is true," he said, after an animating harangue from Lecointre, "that the Usurper menaces us all. But he is still so beloved by his mobs, — still so supported by his Jacobins: better delay open hostilities till the hour is more ripe. To attempt and not succeed is to give us, bound hand and foot, to the guillotine. Every day his power must decline. Procrastination is our best ally —" While yet speaking, and while yet producing the effect of water on the fire, it was announced that a stranger demanded to see him instantly on business that brooked no delay.

"I am not at leisure," said the orator, impatiently. The servant placed a note on the table. Tallien opened it, and found these words in pencil, "From the prison of Teresa de Fontenai." He turned pale, started up, and hastened to the anteroom, where he beheld a face entirely strange to him.

"Hope of France!" said the visitor to him, and the very sound of his voice went straight to the heart, — "your servant is arrested in the streets. I have saved your life, and that of your wife who will be. I bring to you this letter from Teresa de Fontenai."

Tallien, with a trembling hand, opened the letter, and read, —

"Am I forever to implore you in vain? Again and again I say, 'Lose not an hour if you value my life and your own.' My trial and death are fixed the third day from this, — the 10th Thermidor. Strike while it is yet time, — strike the monster! — you have two days yet. If you fail, — if you procrastinate, — see me for the last time as I pass your windows to the guillotine!"

"Her trial will give proof against you," said the stranger. "Her death is the herald of your own. Fear not the populace, — the populace would have rescued your servant. Fear not Robespierre, — he gives himself to your hands. Tomorrow he comes to the Convention, — tomorrow you must cast the last throw for his head or your own."

"Tomorrow he comes to the Convention! And who are you that know so well what is concealed from me?"

"A man like you, who would save the woman he loves."

Before Tallien could recover his surprise, the visitor was gone.

Back went the Avenger to his conclave an altered man. "I have heard tidings, — no matter what," he cried, — "that have changed my purpose. On the 10th we are destined to the guillotine. I revoke my counsel for delay. Robespierre comes to the Convention tomorrow; *there* we must confront and crush him. From the Mountain shall frown against him the grim shade of Danton, — from the Plain shall rise, in their bloody cerements, the specters of Vergniaud and Condorcet. Frappons!"

"Frappons!" cried even Barrere, startled into energy by the new daring of his colleague, — "frappons! il n'y a que les morts qui ne reviennent pas."

It was observable* that, during that day and night†, a stranger to all the previous events of that stormy time was seen in various parts of the city, — in the cafés, the clubs, the haunts of the various factions; that, to the astonishment and dismay of his hearers, he talked aloud of the crimes of Robespierre, and predicted his coming fall; and, as he spoke, he stirred up the hearts of men, he loosed the bonds of their fear, — he inflamed them with unwonted rage and daring. But what surprised them most was, that no voice replied, no hand was lifted against him, no minion, even of the tyrant, cried, "Arrest the traitor." In that impunity

---

* and the fact may be found in one of the memoirs of the time
† the 7th Thermidor

men read, as in a book, that the populace had deserted the man of blood.

Once only a fierce, brawny Jacobin sprang up from the table at which he sat, drinking deep, and, approaching the stranger, said, "I seize thee, in the name of the Republic."

"Citizen Aristides," answered the stranger, in a whisper, "go to the lodgings of Robespierre, — he is from home; and in the left pocket of the vest which he cast off not an hour since thou wilt find a paper; when thou hast read that, return. I will await thee; and if thou wouldst then seize me, I will go without a struggle. Look round on those lowering brows; touch me *now*, and thou wilt be torn to pieces."

The Jacobin felt as if compelled to obey against his will. He went forth muttering; he returned, — the stranger was still there. "Mille tonnerres," he said to him, "I thank thee; the poltroon had my name in his list for the guillotine."

With that the Jacobin Aristides sprang upon the table and shouted, "Death to the Tyrant!"

Chapter 7.XI.

Le lendemain, 8 Thermidor, Robespierre se decida a prononcer son fameux discours.*

Thiers, "Hist. de la Revolution."

The morning rose, — the 8th of Thermidor†. Robespierre has gone to the Convention. He has gone with his labored speech; he has gone with his phrases of philanthropy and virtue; he has gone to single out his prey. All his agents are prepared for his reception; the fierce St. Just has arrived from the armies to second his courage and inflame his wrath. His ominous apparition prepares the audience for the crisis. "Citizens!"

---

* The next day, 8th Thermidor, Robespierre resolved to deliver his celebrated discourse.
† July 26

screeched the shrill voice of Robespierre "others have placed before you flattering pictures; I come to announce to you useful truths.

. . .

And they attribute to me, — to me alone! — whatever of harsh or evil is committed: it is Robespierre who wishes it; it is Robespierre who ordains it. Is there a new tax? — it is Robespierre who ruins you. They call me tyrant! — and why? Because I have acquired some influence; but how? — in speaking truth; and who pretends that truth is to be without force in the mouths of the Representatives of the French people? Doubtless, truth has its power, its rage, its despotism, its accents, touching, terrible, which resound in the pure heart as in the guilty conscience; and which Falsehood can no more imitate than Salmoneus could forge the thunderbolts of Heaven. What am I whom they accuse? A slave of liberty, — a living martyr of the Republic; the victim as the enemy of crime! All ruffianism affronts me, and actions legitimate in others are crimes in me. It is enough to know me to be calumniated. It is in my very zeal that they discover my guilt. Take from me my conscience, and I should be the most miserable of men!"

He paused; and Couthon wiped his eyes, and St. Just murmured applause as with stern looks he gazed on the rebellious Mountain; and there was a dead, mournful, and chilling silence through the audience. The touching sentiment woke no echo.

The orator cast his eyes around. Ho! he will soon arouse that apathy. He proceeds, he praises, he pities himself no more. He denounces, — he accuses. Overflooded with his venom, he vomits it forth on all. At home, abroad, finances, war, — on all! Shriller and sharper rose his voice, —

"A conspiracy exists against the public liberty. It owes its strength to a criminal coalition in the very bosom of the Convention; it has accomplices in the bosom of the Committee of Public Safety . . . What is the remedy to this evil? To punish the traitors; to purify this commit- tee; to crush all factions by the weight of the National Authority; to raise upon their ruins the power of Liberty and Justice. Such are the principles of that Reform. Must I be ambitious to profess them? — then the principles are proscribed, and Tyranny reigns amongst us! For what can you object to a man who is in the right, and has at least this knowledge, — he knows how to die for his native land! I am made to combat crime, and not to govern it. The time, alas! is not yet arrived when men of worth can serve with impunity their country. So long as the knaves rule, the defenders of liberty will be only the proscribed."

For two hours, through that cold and gloomy audience, shrilled the Death-speech. In silence it began, in silence closed. The enemies of the orator were afraid to express resentment; they knew not yet the exact balance of power. His partisans were afraid to approve; they knew not

whom of their own friends and relations the accusations were designed
to single forth. "Take care!" whispered each to each; "it is thou whom
he threatens." But silent though the audience, it was, at the first,
well-nigh subdued. There was still about this terrible man the spell of
an overmastering will. Always — though not what is called a great orator
— resolute, and sovereign in the use of words; words seemed as things
when uttered by one who with a nod moved the troops of Henriot, and
influenced the judgment of Rene Dumas, grim President of the Tribunal. Lecointre of Versailles rose, and there was an anxious movement of
attention; for Lecointre was one of the fiercest foes of the tyrant. What
was the dismay of the Tallien faction; what the complacent smile of
Couthon, — when Lecointre demanded only that the oration should be
printed! All seemed paralyzed. At length Bourdon de l'Oise, whose name
was doubly marked in the black list of the Dictator, stalked to the
tribune, and moved the bold counter-resolution, that the speech should
be referred to the two committees whom that very speech accused. Still
no applause from the conspirators; they sat torpid as frozen men. The
shrinking Barrere, ever on the prudent side, looked round before he
rose. He rises, and sides with Lecointre! Then Couthon seized the
occasion, and from his seat*†, and with his melodious voice sought to
convert the crisis into a triumph.

He demanded, not only that the harangue should be printed, but
sent to all the communes and all the armies. It was necessary to soothe
a wronged and ulcerated heart. Deputies, the most faithful, had been
accused of shedding blood. "Ah! if *he* had contributed to the death of
one innocent man, he should immolate himself with grief." Beautiful
tenderness! — and while he spoke, he fondled the spaniel in his bosom.
Bravo, Couthon! Robespierre triumphs! The reign of Terror shall endure! The old submission settles dovelike back in the assembly! They
vote the printing of the Death-speech, and its transmission to all the
municipalities. From the benches of the Mountain, Tallien, alarmed,
dismayed, impatient, and indignant, cast his gaze where sat the strangers
admitted to hear the debates; and suddenly he met the eyes of the
Unknown who had brought to him the letter from Teresa de Fontenai
the preceding day. The eyes fascinated him as he gazed. In aftertimes he
often said that their regard, fixed, earnest, half-reproachful, and yet
cheering and triumphant, filled him with new life and courage. They
spoke to his heart as the trumpet speaks to the warhorse. He moved
from his seat; he whispered with his allies: the spirit he had drawn in

---

* a privilege permitted only to the paralytic philanthropist
† M. Thiers in his History, volume iv. page 79, makes a curious blunder: he says,
"Couthon s'elance a la tribune.' (Couthon darted towards the tribune.) Poor
Couthon! whose half body was dead, and who was always wheeled in his chair into
the Convention, and spoke sitting.

was contagious; the men whom Robespierre especially had denounced, and who saw the sword over their heads, woke from their torpid trance. Vadier, Cambon, Billaud-Varennes, Panis, Amar, rose at once, — all at once demanded speech. Vadier is first heard, the rest succeed. It burst forth, the Mountain, with its fires and consuming lava; flood upon flood they rush, a legion of Ciceros upon the startled Catiline! Robespierre falters, hesitates, — would qualify, retract. They gather new courage from his new fears; they interrupt him; they drown his voice; they demand the reversal of the motion. Amar moves again that the speech be referred to the Committees, to the Committees, — to his enemies! Confusion and noise and clamor! Robespierre wraps himself in silent and superb disdain. Pale, defeated, but not yet destroyed, he stands, — a storm in the midst of storm!

The motion is carried. All men foresee in that defeat the Dictator's downfall. A solitary cry rose from the galleries; it was caught up; it circled through the hall, the audience: "A bas le tyrant! Vive la republique!"*

Chapter 7.XII.

Aupres d'un corps aussi avili que la Convention, il restait des chances pour que Robespierre sortit vainqueur de cette lutte.†
Lacretelle, volume xii.

*A*s Robespierre left the hall, there was a dead and ominous silence in the crowd without. The herd, in every country, side with success; and the rats run from the falling tower. But Robespierre, who wanted courage, never wanted pride, and the last often supplied the place of the first; thoughtfully, and with an impenetrable brow, he passed through the throng, leaning on St. Just, Payan and his brother following him.

* Down with the tyrant! Hurrah for the republic!
† Amongst a body so debased as the Convention, there still remained some chances that Robespierre would come off victor in the struggle.

As they got into the open space, Robespierre abruptly broke the silence.

"How many heads were to fall upon the tenth?"

"Eighty," replied Payan.

"Ah, we must not tarry so long; a day may lose an empire: terrorism must serve us yet!"

He was silent a few moments, and his eyes roved suspiciously through the street.

"St. Just," he said abruptly, "they have not found this Englishman whose revelations, or whose trial, would have crushed the Amars and the Talliens. No, no! my Jacobins themselves are growing dull and blind. But they have seized a woman, — only a woman!"

"A woman's hand stabbed Marat," said St. Just. Robespierre stopped short, and breathed hard.

"St. Just," said he, "when this peril is past, we will found the Reign of Peace. There shall be homes and gardens set apart for the old. David is already designing the porticos. Virtuous men shall be appointed to instruct the young. All vice and disorder shall be *not* exterminated — no, no! only banished! We must not die yet. Posterity cannot judge us till our work is done. We have recalled L'Etre Supreme; we must now remodel this corrupted world. All shall be love and brotherhood; and — ho! Simon! Simon! — hold! Your pencil, St. Just!" And Robespierre wrote hastily. "This to Citizen President Dumas. Go with it quick, Simon. These eighty heads must fall *tomorrow*, — *tomorrow*, Simon. Dumas will advance their trial a day. I will write to Fouquier-Tinville, the public accuser. We meet at the Jacobins tonight, Simon; there we will denounce the Convention itself; there we will rally round us the last friends of liberty and France."

A shout was heard in the distance behind, "Vive la republique!"

The tyrant's eye shot a vindictive gleam. "The republic! — faugh! We did not destroy the throne of a thousand years for that canaille!"

The trial, the execution, of the victims is advanced a day! By the aid of the mysterious intelligence that had guided and animated him hitherto, Zanoni learned that his arts had been in vain. He knew that Viola was safe, if she could but survive an hour the life of the tyrant. He knew that Robespierre's hours were numbered; that the 10th of Thermidor, on which he had originally designed the execution of his last victims, would see himself at the scaffold. Zanoni had toiled, had schemed for the fall of the Butcher and his reign. To what end? A single word from the tyrant had baffled the result of all. The execution of Viola is advanced a day. Vain seer, who wouldst make thyself the instrument of the Eternal, the very dangers that now beset the tyrant but expedite the doom of his victims! Tomorrow, eighty heads, and hers whose pillow has been thy heart! Tomorrow! and Maximilien is safe tonight!

Chapter 7.XIII.

Erde mag zuruck in Erde stauben;
Fliegt der Geist doch aus dem morschen Haus.
Seine Asche mag der Sturmwind treiben,
Sein Leben dauert ewig aus!*

Elegie

*T*omorrow! — and it is already twilight. One after one, the gentle stars come smiling through the heaven. The Seine, in its slow waters, yet trembles with the last kiss of the rosy day; and still in the blue sky gleams the spire of Notre Dame; and still in the blue sky looms the guillotine by the Barriere du Trone. Turn to that timeworn building, once the church and the convent of the Freres-Precheurs, known by the then holy name of Jacobins; there the new Jacobins hold their club. There, in that oblong hall, once the library of the peaceful monks, assemble the idolaters of St. Robespierre. Two immense tribunes, raised at either end, contain the lees and dregs of the atrocious populace, — the majority of that audience consisting of the furies of the guillotine†. In the midst of the hall are the bureau and chair of the president, — the chair long preserved by the piety of the monks as the relic of St. Thomas Aquinas! Above this seat scowls the harsh bust of Brutus. An iron lamp and two branches scatter over the vast room a murky, fuliginous ray, beneath the light of which the fierce faces of that Pandemonium seem more grim and haggard. There, from the orator's tribune, shrieks the shrill wrath of Robespierre!

Meanwhile all is chaos, disorder, half daring and half cowardice, in

---

* Earth may crumble back into earth; the Spirit will still escape from its frail tenement. The wind of the storm may scatter his ashes; his being endures forever.
† furies de guillotine

the Committee of his foes. Rumors fly from street to street, from haunt to haunt, from house to house. The swallows flit low, and the cattle group together before the storm. And above this roar of the lives and things of the little hour, alone in his chamber stood he on whose starry youth — symbol of the imperishable bloom of the calm Ideal amidst the moldering Actual — the clouds of ages had rolled in vain.

All those exertions which ordinary wit and courage could suggest had been tried in vain. All such exertions *were* in vain, where, in that Saturnalia of death, a life was the object. Nothing but the fall of Robespierre could have saved his victims; now, too late, that fall would only serve to avenge.

Once more, in that last agony of excitement and despair, the seer had plunged into solitude, to invoke again the aid or counsel of those mysterious intermediates between earth and heaven who had renounced the intercourse of the spirit when subjected to the common bondage of the mortal. In the intense desire and anguish of his heart, perhaps, lay a power not yet called forth; for who has not felt that the sharpness of extreme grief cuts and grinds away many of those strongest bonds of infirmity and doubt which bind down the souls of men to the cabined darkness of the hour; and that from the cloud and thunderstorm often swoops the Olympian eagle that can ravish us aloft!

And the invocation was heard, — the bondage of sense was rent away from the visual mind. He looked, and saw, — no, not the being he had called, with its limbs of light and unutterably tranquil smile — not his familiar, Adon-Ai, the Son of Glory and the Star, but the Evil Omen, the dark Chimera, the implacable Foe, with exultation and malice burning in its hell-lit eyes. The Specter, no longer cowering and retreating into shadow, rose before him, gigantic and erect; the face, whose veil no mortal hand had ever raised, was still concealed, but the form was more distinct, corporeal, and cast from it, as an atmosphere, horror and rage and awe. As an iceberg, the breath of that presence froze the air; as a cloud, it filled the chamber and blackened the stars from heaven.

"Lo!" said its voice, "I am here once more. Thou hast robbed me of a meaner prey. Now exorcise *thyself* from my power! Thy life has left thee, to live in the heart of a daughter of the charnel and the worm. In that life I come to thee with my inexorable tread. Thou art returned to the Threshold, — thou, whose steps have trodden the verges of the Infinite! And as the goblin of its fantasy seizes on a child in the dark, — mighty one, who wouldst conquer Death, — I seize on thee!"

"Back to thy thralldom, slave! If thou art come to the voice that called thee not, it is again not to command, but to obey! Thou, from whose whisper I gained the boons of the lives lovelier and dearer than my own; thou — I command thee, not by spell and charm, but by the force of a soul mightier than the malice of thy being, — thou serve me yet, and speak again the secret that can rescue the lives thou hast, by permission of the Universal Master, permitted me to retain awhile in the temple of the clay!"

Brighter and more devouringly burned the glare from those lurid eyes; more visible and colossal yet rose the dilating shape; a yet fiercer and more disdainful hate spoke in the voice that answered, "Didst thou think that my boon would be other than thy curse? Happy for thee hadst thou mourned over the deaths which come by the gentle hand of Nature, — hadst thou never known how the name of mother consecrates the face of Beauty, and never, bending over thy first-born, felt the imperishable sweetness of a father's love! They are saved, for what? — the mother, for the death of violence and shame and blood, for the doomsman's hand to put aside that shining hair which has entangled thy bridegroom kisses; the child, first and last of thine offspring, in whom thou didst hope to found a race that should hear with thee the music of celestial harps, and float, by the side of thy familiar, Adon-Ai, through the azure rivers of joy, — the child, to live on a few days as a fungus in a burial-vault, a thing of the loathsome dungeon, dying of cruelty and neglect and famine. Ha! ha! thou who wouldst baffle Death, learn how the deathless die if they dare to love the mortal. Now, Chaldean, behold my boons! Now I seize and wrap thee with the pestilence of my presence; now, evermore, till thy long race is run, mine eyes shall glow into thy brain, and mine arms shall clasp thee, when thou wouldst take the wings of the Morning and flee from the embrace of Night!"

"I tell thee, no! And again I compel thee, speak and answer to the lord who can command his slave. I know, though my lore fails me, and the reeds on which I leaned pierce my side, — I know yet that it is written that the life of which I question can be saved from the headsman. Thou wrappest her future in the darkness of thy shadow, but thou canst not shape it. Thou mayest foreshow the antidote; thou canst not effect the bane. From thee I wring the secret, though it torture thee to name it. I approach thee, — I look dauntless into thine eyes. The soul that loves can dare all things. Shadow, I defy thee, and compel!"

The specter waned and recoiled. Like a vapor that lessens as the sun pierces and pervades it, the form shrank cowering and dwarfed in the dimmer distance, and through the casement again rushed the stars.

"Yes," said the Voice, with a faint and hollow accent, "thou *canst* save her from the headsman; for it is written, that sacrifice can save. Ha! ha!" And the shape again suddenly dilated into the gloom of its giant stature, and its ghastly laugh exulted, as if the Foe, a moment baffled, had regained its might. "Ha! ha! — thou canst save her life, if thou wilt sacrifice thine own! Is it for this thou hast lived on through crumbling empires and countless generations of thy race? At last shall Death reclaim thee? Wouldst thou save her? — *die for her!* Fall, O stately column, over which stars yet unformed may gleam, — fall, that the herb at thy base may drink a few hours longer the sunlight and the dews! Silent! Art thou ready for the sacrifice? See, the moon moves up through heaven. Beautiful and wise one, wilt thou bid her smile tomorrow on thy headless clay?"

"Back! for my soul, in answering thee from depths where thou canst not hear it, has regained its glory; and I hear the wings of Adon-Ai gliding musical through the air."

He spoke; and, with a low shriek of baffled rage and hate, the Thing was gone, and through the room rushed, luminous and sudden, the Presence of silvery light.

As the heavenly visitor stood in the atmosphere of his own luster, and looked upon the face of the Theurgist with an aspect of ineffable tenderness and love, all space seemed lighted from his smile. Along the blue air without, from that chamber in which his wings had halted, to the farthest star in the azure distance, it seemed as if the track of his flight were visible, by a lengthened splendor in the air, like the column of moonlight on the sea. Like the flower that diffuses perfume as the very breath of its life, so the emanation of that presence was joy. Over the world, as a million times swifter than light, than electricity, the Son of Glory had sped his way to the side of love, his wings had scattered delight as the morning scatters dew. For that brief moment, Poverty had ceased to mourn, Disease fled from its prey, and Hope breathed a dream of Heaven into the darkness of Despair.

"Thou art right," said the melodious Voice. "Thy courage has restored thy power. Once more, in the haunts of earth, thy soul charms me to thy side. Wiser now, in the moment when thou comprehendest Death, than when thy unfettered spirit learned the solemn mystery of Life; the human affections that thralled and humbled thee awhile bring to thee, in these last hours of thy mortality, the sublimest heritage of thy race, — the eternity that commences from the grave."

"O Adon-Ai," said the Chaldean, as, circumfused in the splendor of the visitant, a glory more radiant than human beauty settled round his form, and seemed already to belong to the eternity of which the Bright One spoke, "as men, before they die, see and comprehend the enigmas hidden from them before*, so in this hour, when the sacrifice of self to another brings the course of ages to its goal, I see the littleness of Life,

---

* The greatest poet, and one of the noblest thinkers, of the last age, said, on his deathbed, "Many things obscure to me before, now clear up, and become visible." — See the "Life of Schiller."

compared to the majesty of Death; but oh, Divine Consoler, even here, even in thy presence, the affections that inspire me, sadden. To leave behind me in this bad world, unaided, unprotected, those for whom I die! the wife! the child! — oh, speak comfort to me in this!"

"And what," said the visitor, with a slight accent of reproof in the tone of celestial pity, — "what, with all thy wisdom and thy starry secrets, with all thy empire of the past, and thy visions of the future; what art thou to the All-Directing and Omniscient? Canst thou yet imagine that thy presence on earth can give to the hearts thou lovest the shelter which the humblest take from the wings of the Presence that lives in heaven? Fear not thou for their future. Whether thou live or die, their future is the care of the Most High! In the dungeon and on the scaffold looks everlasting the Eye of *Him*, tenderer than thou to love, wiser than thou to guide, mightier than thou to save!"

Zanoni bowed his head; and when he looked up again, the last shadow had left his brow. The visitor was gone; but still the glory of his presence seemed to shine upon the spot, still the solitary air seemed to murmur with tremulous delight. And thus ever shall it be with those who have once, detaching themselves utterly from life, received the visit of the Angel *Faith*. Solitude and space retain the splendor, and it settles like a halo round their graves.

Chapter 7.XIV.

Dann zur Blumenflor der Sterne
Aufgeschauet liebewarm,
Fass' ihn freundlich Arm in Arm
Trag' ihn in die blaue Ferne.

Uhland, "An den Tod."

Then towards the Garden of the Star
Lift up thine aspect warm with love,
And, friendlike link'd through space afar,
Mount with him, arm in arm, above.

*H*e stood upon the lofty balcony that overlooked the quiet city. Though afar, the fiercest passions of men were at work on the web of strife and doom, all that gave itself to his view was calm and still in the rays of the summer moon, for his soul was wrapped from man and man's narrow sphere, and only the serener glories of creation were present to the vision of the seer. There he stood, alone and thoughtful, to take the last farewell of the wondrous life that he had known.

Coursing through the fields of space, he beheld the gossamer shapes, whose choral joys his spirit had so often shared. There, group upon group, they circled in the starry silence multiform in the unimaginable beauty of a being fed by ambrosial dews and serenest light. In his trance, all the universe stretched visible beyond; in the green valleys afar, he saw the dances of the fairies; in the bowels of the mountains, he beheld the race that breathe the lurid air of the volcanoes, and hide from the light of heaven; on every leaf in the numberless forests, in every drop of the unmeasured seas, he surveyed its separate and swarming world; far up, in the farthest blue, he saw orb upon orb ripening into shape, and planets starting from the central fire, to run their day of ten thousand years. For everywhere in creation is the breath of the Creator, and in every spot where the breath breathes is life! And alone, in the distance, the lonely man beheld his Magian brother. There, at work with his numbers and his Cabala, amidst the wrecks of Rome, passionless and calm, sat in his cell the mystic Mejnour, — living on, living ever while the world lasts, indifferent whether his knowledge produces weal or woe; a mechanical agent of a more tender and a wiser will, that guides every spring to its inscrutable designs. Living on, — living ever, — as science that cares alone for knowledge, and halts not to consider how knowledge advances happiness; how Human Improvement, rushing through civilization, crushes in its march all who cannot grapple to its wheels*; ever, with its Cabala and its number, lives on to change, in its bloodless movements, the face of the habitable world!

And, "Oh, farewell to life!" murmured the glorious dreamer. "Sweet, O life! hast thou been to me. How fathomless thy joys, — how raptur-

---

* "You colonize the lands of the savage with the Anglo-Saxon, — you civilize that portion of *the earth*; but is the *savage* civilized? He is exterminated! You accumulate machinery, — you increase the total of wealth; but what becomes of the labor you displace? One generation is sacrificed to the next. You diffuse knowledge, — and the world seems to grow brighter; but Discontent at Poverty replaces Ignorance, happy with its crust. Every improvement, every advancement in civilization, injures some, to benefit others, and either cherishes the want of today, or prepares the revolution of tomorrow." — Stephen Montague.

ously has my soul bounded forth upon the upward paths! To him who forever renews his youth in the clear fount of Nature, how exquisite is the mere happiness *to be!* Farewell, ye lamps of heaven, and ye million tribes, the Populace of Air. Not a mote in the beam, not an herb on the mountain, not a pebble on the shore, not a seed far-blown into the wilderness, but contributed to the lore that sought in all the true principle of life, the Beautiful, the Joyous, the Immortal. To others, a land, a city, a hearth, has been a home; *my* home has been wherever the intellect could pierce, or the spirit could breathe the air."

He paused, and through the immeasurable space his eyes and his heart, penetrating the dismal dungeon, rested on his child. He saw it slumbering in the arms of the pale mother, and *his* soul spoke to the sleeping soul. "Forgive me, if my desire was sin; I dreamed to have reared and nurtured thee to the divinest destinies my visions could foresee. Betimes, as the mortal part was strengthened against disease, to have purified the spiritual from every sin; to have led thee, heaven upon heaven, through the holy ecstasies which make up the existence of the orders that dwell on high; to have formed, from thy sublime affections, the pure and ever-living communication between thy mother and myself. The dream was but a dream — it is no more! In sight myself of the grave, I feel, at last, that through the portals of the grave lies the true initiation into the holy and the wise. Beyond those portals I await ye both, beloved pilgrims!"

From his numbers and his Cabala, in his cell, amidst the wrecks of Rome, Mejnour, startled, looked up, and through the spirit, felt that the spirit of his distant friend addressed him.

"Fare thee well forever upon this earth! Thy last companion forsakes thy side. Thine age survives the youth of all; and the Final Day shall find thee still the contemplator of our tombs. I go with my free will into the land of darkness; but new suns and systems blaze around us from the grave. I go where the souls of those for whom I resign the clay shall be my co-mates through eternal youth. At last I recognize the true ordeal and the real victory. Mejnour, cast down thy elixir; lay by thy load of years! Wherever the soul can wander, the Eternal Soul of all things protects it still!"

Chapter 7.XV.

Il ne veulent plus perdre un moment d'une nuit si precieuse.*

Lacretelle, tom. xii.

*I*t was late that night, and Rene-Francois Dumas, President of the Revolutionary Tribunal, had reentered his cabinet, on his return from the Jacobin Club. With him were two men who might be said to represent, the one the moral, the other the physical force of the Reign of Terror: Fouquier-Tinville, the Public Accuser, and Francois Henriot, the General of the Parisian National Guard. This formidable triumvirate were assembled to debate on the proceedings of the next day; and the three sister-witches over their hellish caldron were scarcely animated by a more fiendlike spirit, or engaged in more execrable designs, than these three heroes of the Revolution in their premeditated massacre of the morrow.

Dumas was but little altered in appearance since, in the earlier part of this narrative, he was presented to the reader, except that his manner was somewhat more short and severe, and his eye yet more restless. But he seemed almost a superior being by the side of his associates. Rene Dumas, born of respectable parents, and well educated, despite his ferocity, was not without a certain refinement, which perhaps rendered him the more acceptable to the precise and formal Robespierre.† But Henriot had been a lackey, a thief, a spy of the police; he had drunk the blood of Madame de Lamballe, and had risen to his present rank for no quality but his ruffianism; and Fouquier-Tinville, the son of a provincial agriculturist, and afterwards a clerk at the Bureau of the Police, was little less base in his manners, and yet more, from a certain loathsome buffoonery, revolting in his speech, — bull-headed, with black, sleek hair, with a narrow and livid forehead, with small eyes, that

---

* They would not lose another moment of so precious a night.

† Dumas was a beau in his way. His gala-dress was a *blood-red coat*, with the finest ruffles.

twinkled with a sinister malice; strongly and coarsely built, he looked what he was, the audacious bully of a lawless and relentless Bar.

Dumas trimmed the candles, and bent over the list of the victims for the morrow.

"It is a long catalogue," said the president; "eighty trials for one day! And Robespierre's orders to dispatch the whole fournee are unequivocal."

"Pooh!" said Fouquier, with a coarse, loud laugh; "we must try them en masse. I know how to deal with our jury. 'Je pense, citoyens, que vous etes convaincus du crime des accuses?'* Ha! ha! — the longer the list, the shorter the work."

"Oh, yes," growled out Henriot, with an oath, — as usual, half-drunk, and lolling on his chair, with his spurred heels on the table, — "little Tinville is the man for dispatch."

"Citizen Henriot," said Dumas, gravely, "permit me to request thee to select another footstool; and for the rest, let me warn thee that tomorrow is a critical and important day; one that will decide the fate of France."

"A fig for little France! Vive le Vertueux Robespierre, la Colonne de la Republique!† Plague on this talking; it is dry work. Hast thou no eau de vie in that little cupboard?"

Dumas and Fouquier exchanged looks of disgust. Dumas shrugged his shoulders, and replied, —

"It is to guard thee against eau de vie, Citizen General Henriot, that I have requested thee to meet me here. Listen if thou canst!"

"Oh, talk away! thy metier is to talk, mine to fight and to drink."

"Tomorrow, I tell thee then, the populace will be abroad; all factions will be astir. It is probable enough that they will even seek to arrest our tumbrels on their way to the guillotine. Have thy men armed and ready; keep the streets clear; cut down without mercy whomsoever may obstruct the ways."

"I understand," said Henriot, striking his sword so loudly that Dumas half-started at the clank, — "Black Henriot is no 'Indulgent.'"

"Look to it, then, citizen, — look to it! And hark thee," he added, with a grave and somber brow, "if thou wouldst keep thine own head on thy shoulders, beware of the eau de vie."

"My own head! — sacre mille tonnerres! Dost thou threaten the general of the Parisian army?"

Dumas, like Robespierre, a precise atrabilious, and arrogant man, was about to retort, when the craftier Tinville laid his hand on his arm, and, turning to the general, said, "My dear Henriot, thy dauntless republi-

---

* I think, citizens, that you are convinced of the crime of the accused.
† Long life to the virtuous Robespierre, the pillar of the Republic!

canism, which is too ready to give offence, must learn to take a reprimand from the representative of Republican Law. Seriously, mon cher, thou must be sober for the next three or four days; after the crisis is over, thou and I will drink a bottle together. Come, Dumas relax thine austerity, and shake hands with our friend. No quarrels amongst ourselves!"

Dumas hesitated, and extended his hand, which the ruffian clasped; and, maudlin tears succeeding his ferocity, he half-sobbed, half-hiccoughed forth his protestations of civism and his promises of sobriety.

"Well, we depend on thee, mon general," said Dumas; "and now, since we shall all have need of vigor for tomorrow, go home and sleep soundly."

"Yes, I forgive thee, Dumas, — I forgive thee. I am not vindictive, — I! but still, if a man threatens me; if a man insults me —" and, with the quick changes of intoxication, again his eyes gleamed fire through their foul tears. With some difficulty Fouquier succeeded at last in soothing the brute, and leading him from the chamber. But still, as some wild beast disappointed of a prey, he growled and snarled as his heavy tread descended the stairs. A tall trooper, mounted, was leading Henriot's horse to and fro the streets; and as the general waited at the porch till his attendant turned, a stranger stationed by the wall accosted him:

"General Henriot, I have desired to speak with thee. Next to Robespierre, thou art, or shouldst be, the most powerful man in France."

"Hem! — yes, I ought to be. What then? — every man has not his deserts!"

"Hist!" said the stranger; "thy pay is scarcely suitable to thy rank and thy wants."

"That is true."

"Even in a revolution, a man takes care of his fortunes!"

"Diable! speak out, citizen."

"I have a thousand pieces of gold with me, — they are thine, if thou wilt grant me one small favor."

"Citizen, I grant it!" said Henriot, waving his hand majestically. "Is it to denounce some rascal who has offended thee?"

"No; it is simply this: write these words to President Dumas, 'Admit the bearer to thy presence; and, if thou canst, grant him the request he will make to thee, it will be an inestimable obligation to Francois Henriot.'" The stranger, as he spoke, placed pencil and tablets in the shaking hands of the soldier.

"And where is the gold?"

"Here."

With some difficulty, Henriot scrawled the words dictated to him, clutched the gold, mounted his horse, and was gone.

Meanwhile Fouquier, when he had closed the door upon Henriot, said sharply, "How canst thou be so mad as to incense that brigand? Knowest thou not that our laws are nothing without the physical force of the National Guard, and that he is their leader?"

"I know this, that Robespierre must have been mad to place that drunkard at their head; and mark my words, Fouquier, if the struggle come, it is that man's incapacity and cowardice that will destroy us. Yes, thou mayst live thyself to accuse thy beloved Robespierre, and to perish in his fall."

"For all that, we must keep well with Henriot till we can find the occasion to seize and behead him. To be safe, we must fawn on those who are still in power; and fawn the more, the more we would depose them. Do not think this Henriot, when he wakes tomorrow, will forget thy threats. He is the most revengeful of human beings. Thou must send and soothe him in the morning!"

"Right," said Dumas, convinced. "I was too hasty; and now I think we have nothing further to do, since we have arranged to make short work with our fournee of tomorrow. I see in the list a knave I have long marked out, though his crime once procured me a legacy, — Nicot, the Hebertist."

"And young Andre Chenier, the poet? Ah, I forgot; we be headed *him* today! Revolutionary virtue is at its acme. His own brother abandoned him."[*]

"There is a foreigner, — an Italian woman in the list; but I can find no charge made out against her."

"All the same we must execute her for the sake of the round number; eighty sounds better than seventy-nine!"

Here a huissier brought a paper on which was written the request of Henriot.

"Ah! this is fortunate," said Tinville, to whom Dumas chucked the scroll, — "grant the prayer by all means; so at least that it does not lessen our bead-roll. But I will do Henriot the justice to say that he never asks to let off, but to put on. Good-night! I am worn out — my escort waits below. Only on such an occasion would I venture forth in the streets at night."[†] And Fouquier, with a long yawn, quitted the room.

---

[*] His brother is said, indeed, to have contributed to the condemnation of this virtuous and illustrious person. He was heard to cry aloud, "Si mon frere est coupable, qu'il perisse" (If my brother be culpable, let him die). This brother, Marie-Joseph, also a poet, and the author of "Charles IX.," so celebrated in the earlier days of the Revolution, enjoyed, of course, according to the wonted justice of the world, a triumphant career, and was proclaimed in the Champ de Mars "le premier de poetes Francais," a title due to his murdered brother.

[†] During the latter part of the Reign of Terror, Fouquier rarely stirred out at night, and never without an escort. In the Reign of Terror those most terrified were its kings.

"Admit the bearer!" said Dumas, who, withered and dried, as lawyers in practice mostly are, seemed to require as little sleep as his parchments.

The stranger entered.

"Rene-Francois Dumas," said he, seating himself opposite to the president, and markedly adopting the plural, as if in contempt of the revolutionary jargon, "amidst the excitement and occupations of your later life, I know not if you can remember that we have met before?"

The judge scanned the features of his visitor, and a pale blush settled on his sallow cheeks, "Yes, citizen, I remember!"

"And you recall the words I then uttered! You spoke tenderly and philanthropically of your horror of capital executions; you exulted in the approaching Revolution as the termination of all sanguinary punishments; you quoted reverently the saying of Maximilien Robespierre, the rising statesman, 'The executioner is the invention of the tyrant:' and I replied, that while you spoke, a foreboding seized me that we should meet again when your ideas of death and the philosophy of revolutions might be changed! Was I right, Citizen Rene-Francois Dumas, President of the Revolutionary Tribunal?"

"Pooh!" said Dumas, with some confusion on his brazen brow, "I spoke then as men speak who have not acted. Revolutions are not made with rose-water! But truce to the gossip of the long-ago. I remember, also, that thou didst then save the life of my relation, and it will please thee to learn that his intended murderer will be guillotined tomorrow."

"That concerns yourself, — your justice or your revenge. Permit me the egotism to remind you that you then promised that if ever a day should come when you could serve me, your life — yes, the phrase was, 'your heart's blood' — was at my bidding. Think not, austere judge, that I come to ask a boon that can affect yourself, — I come but to ask a day's respite for another!"

"Citizen, it is impossible! I have the order of Robespierre that not one less than the total on my list must undergo their trial for tomorrow. As for the verdict, that rests with the jury!"

"I do not ask you to diminish the catalogue. Listen still! In your death-roll there is the name of an Italian woman whose youth, whose beauty, and whose freedom not only from every crime, but every tangible charge, will excite only compassion, and not terror. Even *you* would tremble to pronounce her sentence. It will be dangerous on a day when the populace will be excited, when your tumbrels may be arrested, to expose youth and innocence and beauty to the pity and courage of a revolted crowd."

Dumas looked up and shrunk from the eye of the stranger.

"I do not deny, citizen, that there is reason in what thou urgest. But my orders are positive."

"Positive only as to the number of the victims. I offer you a substitute for this one. I offer you the head of a man who knows all of the very conspiracy which now threatens Robespierre and yourself, and compared with one clew to which, you would think even eighty ordinary lives a cheap purchase."

"That alters the case," said Dumas, eagerly; "if thou canst do this, on my own responsibility I will postpone the trial of the Italian. Now name the proxy!"

"You behold him!"

"Thou!" exclaimed Dumas, while a fear he could not conceal betrayed itself through his surprise. "Thou! — and thou comest to me alone at night, to offer thyself to justice. Ha! — this is a snare. Tremble, fool! — thou art in my power, and I can have *both!*"

"You can," said the stranger, with a calm smile of disdain; "but my life is valueless without my revelations. Sit still, I command you, — hear me!" and the light in those dauntless eyes spellbound and awed the judge. "You will remove me to the Conciergerie, — you will fix my trial, under the name of Zanoni, amidst your fournee of tomorrow. If I do not satisfy you by my speech, you hold the woman I die to save as your hostage. It is but the reprieve for her of a single day that I demand. The day following the morrow I shall be dust, and you may wreak your vengeance on the life that remains. Tush! judge and condemner of thousands, do you hesitate, — do you imagine that the man who voluntarily offers himself to death will be daunted into uttering one syllable at your Bar against his will? Have you not had experience enough of the inflexibility of pride and courage? President, I place before you the ink and implements! Write to the jailer a reprieve of one day for the woman whose life can avail you nothing, and I will bear the order to my own prison: I, who can now tell this much as an earnest of what I can communicate, — while I speak, your own name, judge, is in a list of death. I can tell you by whose hand it is written down; I can tell you in what quarter to look for danger; I can tell you from what cloud, in this lurid atmosphere, hangs the storm that shall burst on Robespierre and his reign!"

Dumas grew pale; and his eyes vainly sought to escape the magnetic gaze that overpowered and mastered him. Mechanically, and as if under an agency not his own, he wrote while the stranger dictated.

"Well," he said then, forcing a smile to his lips, "I promised I would serve you; see, I am faithful to my word. I suppose that you are one of those fools of feeling, — those professors of anti-revolutionary virtue, of whom I have seen not a few before my Bar. Faugh! it sickens me to see those who make a merit of incivism, and perish to save some bad patriot, because it is a son, or a father, or a wife, or a daughter, who is saved."

"*I am* one of those fools of feeling," said the stranger, rising. "You have divined aright."

"And wilt thou not, in return for my mercy, utter tonight the revelations thou wouldst proclaim tomorrow? Come; and perhaps thou too — nay, the woman also — may receive, not reprieve, but pardon."

"Before your tribunal, and there alone! Nor will I deceive you, president. My information may avail you not; and even while I show the cloud, the bolt may fall."

"Tush! prophet, look to thyself! Go, madman, go. I know too well the contumacious obstinacy of the class to which I suspect thou belongest, to waste further words. Diable! but ye grow so accustomed to look on death, that ye forget the respect ye owe to it. Since thou offerest me thy head, I accept it. Tomorrow thou mayst repent; it will be too late."

"Aye, too late, president!" echoed the calm visitor.

"But, remember, it is not pardon, it is but a day's reprieve, I have promised to this woman. According as thou dost satisfy me tomorrow, she lives or dies. I am frank, citizen; thy ghost shall not haunt me for want of faith."

"It is but a day that I have asked; the rest I leave to justice and to Heaven. Your huissiers wait below."

Chapter 7.XVI.

Und den Mordstahl seh' ich blinken;
Und das Morderauge gluhn!*

"Kassandra"

Viola was in the prison that opened not but for those already condemned before adjudged. Since her exile from Zanoni, her very intellect had seemed paralyzed. All that beautiful exuberance of fancy

---

* And I see the steel of Murder glitter,
  And the eye of Murder glow.

which, if not the fruit of genius, seemed its blossoms; all that gush of exquisite thought which Zanoni had justly told her flowed with mysteries and subtleties ever new to him, the wise one, — all were gone, annihilated; the blossom withered, the fount dried up. From something almost above womanhood, she seemed listlessly to sink into something below childhood. With the inspirer the inspirations had ceased; and, in deserting love, genius also was left behind.

She scarcely comprehended why she had been thus torn from her home and the mechanism of her dull tasks. She scarcely knew what meant those kindly groups, that, struck with her exceeding loveliness, had gathered round her in the prison, with mournful looks, but with words of comfort. She, who had hitherto been taught to abhor those whom Law condemns for crime, was amazed to hear that beings thus compassionate and tender, with cloudless and lofty brows, with gallant and gentle mien, were criminals for whom Law had no punishment short of death. But they, the savages, gaunt and menacing, who had dragged her from her home, who had attempted to snatch from her the infant while she clasped it in her arms, and laughed fierce scorn at her mute, quivering lips, — *they* were the chosen citizens, the men of virtue, the favorites of Power, the ministers of Law! Such thy black caprices, O thou, the ever-shifting and calumnious, — Human Judgment!

A squalid, and yet a gay world, did the prison-houses of that day present. There, as in the sepulcher to which they led, all ranks were cast with an even-handed scorn. And yet there, the reverence that comes from great emotions restored Nature's first and imperishable, and most lovely, and most noble Law, — *The inequality between man and man!* There, place was given by the prisoners, whether royalists or sans-culottes, to Age, to Learning, to Renown, to Beauty; and Strength, with its own inborn chivalry, raised into rank the helpless and the weak. The iron sinews and the Herculean shoulders made way for the woman and the child; and the graces of Humanity, lost elsewhere, sought their refuge in the abode of Terror.

"And wherefore, my child, do they bring thee hither?" asked an old, grey-haired priest.

"I cannot guess."

"Ah, if you know not your offence, fear the worst!"

"And my child?" — for the infant was still suffered to rest upon her bosom.

"Alas, young mother, they will suffer thy child to live.'

"And for this, — an orphan in the dungeon!" murmured the accusing heart of Viola, — "have I reserved his offspring! Zanoni, even in thought, ask not — ask not what I have done with the child I bore thee!"

Night came; the crowd rushed to the grate to hear the muster-roll.*

Her name was with the doomed. And the old priest, better prepared to die, but reserved from the death-list, laid his hands on her head, and blessed her while he wept. She heard, and wondered; but she did not weep. With downcast eyes, with arms folded on her bosom, she bent submissively to the call. But now another name was uttered; and a man, who had pushed rudely past her to gaze or to listen, shrieked out a howl of despair and rage. She turned, and their eyes met. Through the distance of time she recognized that hideous aspect. Nicot's face settled back into its devilish sneer. "At least, gentle Neapolitan, the guillotine will unite us. Oh, we shall sleep well our wedding-night!" And, with a laugh, he strode away through the crowd, and vanished into his lair.

. . .

She was placed in her gloomy cell, to await the morrow. But the child was still spared her; and she thought it seemed as if conscious of the awful present. In their way to the prison it had not moaned or wept. It had looked with its clear eyes, unshrinking, on the gleaming pikes and savage brows of the huissiers. And now, alone in the dungeon, it put its arms round her neck, and murmured its indistinct sounds, low and sweet as some unknown language of consolation and of heaven. And of heaven it was! — for, at the murmur, the terror melted from her soul; upward, from the dungeon and the death, — upward, where the happy cherubim chant the mercy of the All-loving, whispered that cherub's voice. She fell upon her knees and prayed. The despoilers of all that beautifies and hallows life had desecrated the altar, and denied the God! — they had removed from the last hour of their victims the Priest, the Scripture, and the Cross! But Faith builds in the dungeon and the lazar-house its sublimest shrines; and up, through roofs of stone, that shut out the eye of Heaven, ascends the ladder where the angels glide to and fro, — *Prayer.*

And there, in the very cell beside her own, the atheist Nicot sits stolid amidst the darkness, and hugs the thought of Danton, that death is nothingness.* His, no spectacle of an appalled and perturbed conscience! Remorse is the echo of a lost virtue, and virtue he never knew. Had he to live again, he would live the same. But more terrible than the deathbed of a believing and despairing sinner that blank gloom of apathy, — that contemplation of the worm and the rat of the charnel-house; that grim and loathsome *nothingness* which, for his eye, falls like a pall over the universe of life. Still, staring into space, gnawing his livid lip, he looks upon the darkness, convinced that darkness is forever and forever!

---

‡‡Called, in the mocking jargon of the day, *The Evening Gazette.*
* "Ma demeure sera bientot *Le Neant*" (My abode will soon be nothingness), said Danton before his judges.)

. . .

Place, there! place! Room yet in your crowded cells. Another has come
to the slaughterhouse.

As the jailer, lamp in hand, ushered in the stranger, the latter touched
him and whispered. The stranger drew a jewel from his finger. Diantre,
how the diamond flashed in the ray of the lamp! Value each head of
your eighty at a thousand francs, and the jewel is more worth than all!
The jailer paused, and the diamond laughed in his dazzled eyes. O thou
Cerberus, thou hast mastered all else that seems human in that fell
employ! Thou hast no pity, no love, and no remorse. But Avarice
survives the rest, and the foul heart's master-serpent swallows up the
tribe. Ha! ha! crafty stranger, thou hast conquered! They tread the
gloomy corridor; they arrive at the door where the jailer has placed the
fatal mark, now to be erased, for the prisoner within is to be reprieved
a day. The key grates in the lock; the door yawns, — the stranger takes
the lamp and enters.

Chapter 7.XVII.

The Seventeenth and Last

Cosi vince Goffredo!*

"Ger. Lib." cant. xx.-xliv.

*A*nd Viola was in prayer. She heard not the opening of the door;
she saw not the dark shadow that fell along the floor. *His* power, *his* arts
were gone; but the mystery and the spell known to *her* simple heart did
not desert her in the hours of trial and despair. When Science falls as a

* Thus conquered Godfrey.

firework from the sky it would invade; when Genius withers as a flower in the breath of the icy charnel, — the hope of a childlike soul wraps the air in light, and the innocence of unquestioning Belief covers the grave with blossoms.

In the farthest corner of the cell she knelt; and the infant, as if to imitate what it could not comprehend, bent its little limbs, and bowed its smiling face, and knelt with her also, by her side.

He stood and gazed upon them as the light of the lamp fell calmly on their forms. It fell over those clouds of golden hair, disheveled, parted, thrown back from the rapt, candid brow; the dark eyes raised on high, where, through the human tears, a light as from above was mirrored; the hands clasped, the lips apart, the form all animate and holy with the sad serenity of innocence and the touching humility of woman. And he heard her voice, though it scarcely left her lips: the low voice that the heart speaks, — loud enough for God to hear!

"And if never more to see him, O Father! Canst Thou not make the love that will not die, minister, even beyond the grave, to his earthly fate? Canst Thou not yet permit it, as a living spirit, to hover over him, — a spirit fairer than all his science can conjure? Oh, whatever lot be ordained to either, grant — even though a thousand ages may roll between us — grant, when at last purified and regenerate, and fitted for the transport of such reunion — grant that we may meet once more! And for his child, — it kneels to Thee from the dungeon floor! Tomorrow, and whose breast shall cradle it; whose hand shall feed; whose lips shall pray for its weal below and its soul hereafter!" She paused, — her voice choked with sobs.

"Thou Viola! — thou, thyself. He whom thou hast deserted is here to preserve the mother to the child!"

She started! — those accents, tremulous as her own! She started to her feet! — he was there, — in all the pride of his unwaning youth and superhuman beauty; there, in the house of dread, and in the hour of travail; there, image and personation of the love that can pierce the Valley of the Shadow, and can glide, the unscathed wanderer from the heaven, through the roaring abyss of hell!

With a cry never, perhaps, heard before in that gloomy vault, — a cry of delight and rapture, she sprang forward, and fell at his feet.

He bent down to raise her; but she slid from his arms. He called her by the familiar epithets of the old endearment, and she only answered him by sobs. Wildly, passionately, she kissed his hands, the hem of his garment, but voice was gone.

"Look up, look up! — I am here, — I am here to save thee! Wilt thou deny to me thy sweet face? Truant, wouldst thou fly me still?"

"Fly thee!" she said, at last, and in a broken voice; "oh, if my thoughts wronged thee, — oh, if my dream, that awful dream, deceived, — kneel down with me, and pray for our child!" Then springing to her feet with a sudden impulse, she caught up the infant, and, placing it in his arms, sobbed forth, with deprecating and humble tones, "Not for my sake, — not for mine, did I abandon thee, but —"

"Hush!" said Zanoni; "I know all the thoughts that thy confused and struggling senses can scarcely analyze themselves. And see how, with a look, thy child answers them!"

And in truth the face of that strange infant seemed radiant with its silent and unfathomable joy. It seemed as if it recognized the father; it clung — it forced itself to his breast, and there, nestling, turned its bright, clear eyes upon Viola, and smiled.

"Pray for my child!" said Zanoni, mournfully. "The thoughts of souls that would aspire as mine are All *prayer!*" And, seating himself by her side, he began to reveal to her some of the holier secrets of his lofty being. He spoke of the sublime and intense faith from which alone the diviner knowledge can arise, — the faith which, seeing the immortal everywhere, purifies and exalts the mortal that beholds, the glorious ambition that dwells not in the cabals and crimes of earth, but amidst those solemn wonders that speak not of men, but of God; of that power to abstract the soul from the clay which gives to the eye of the soul its subtle vision, and to the soul's wing the unlimited realm; of that pure, severe, and daring initiation from which the mind emerges, as from death, into clear perceptions of its kindred with the Father-Principles of life and light, so that in its own sense of the Beautiful it finds its joy; in the serenity of its will, its power; in its sympathy with the youthfulness of the Infinite Creation, of which itself is an essence and a part, the secrets that embalm the very clay which they consecrate, and renew the strength of life with the ambrosia of mysterious and celestial sleep. And while he spoke, Viola listened, breathless. If she could not comprehend, she no longer dared to distrust. She felt that in that enthusiasm, self-deceiving or not, no fiend could lurk; and by an intuition, rather than an effort of the reason, she saw before her, like a starry ocean, the depth and mysterious beauty of the soul which her fears had wronged. Yet, when he said (concluding his strange confessions) that to this life *within* life and *above* life he had dreamed to raise her own, the fear of humanity crept over her, and he read in her silence how vain, with all his science, would the dream have been.

But now, as he closed, and, leaning on his breast, she felt the clasp of his protecting arms, — when, in one holy kiss, the past was forgiven and the present lost, — then there returned to her the sweet and warm hopes of the natural life, of the loving woman. He was come to save her! She asked not how, — she believed it without a question. They

should be at last again united. They would fly far from those scenes of
violence and blood. Their happy Ionian isle, their fearless solitudes,
would once more receive them. She laughed, with a child's joy, as this
picture rose up amidst the gloom of the dungeon. Her mind, faithful
to its sweet, simple instincts, refused to receive the lofty images that
flitted confusedly by it, and settled back to its human visions, yet more
baseless, of the earthly happiness and the tranquil home.

"Talk not now to me, beloved, — talk not more now to me of the
past! Thou art here, — thou wilt save me; we shall live yet the common
happy life, that life with thee is happiness and glory enough to me.
Traverse, if thou wilt, in thy pride of soul, the universe; thy heart again
is the universe to mine. I thought but now that I was prepared to die; I
see thee, touch thee, and again I know how beautiful a thing is life! See
through the grate the stars are fading from the sky; the morrow will
soon be here, — The *morrow* which will open the prison doors! Thou
sayest thou canst save me, — I will not doubt it now. Oh, let us dwell
no more in cities! I never doubted thee in our lovely isle; no dreams
haunted me there, except dreams of joy and beauty; and thine eyes made
yet more beautiful and joyous the world in waking. Tomorrow! — why
do you not smile? Tomorrow, love! is not *tomorrow* a blessed word! Cruel!
you would punish me still, that you will not share my joy. Aha! see our
little one, how it laughs to my eyes! I will talk to *that*. Child, thy father
is come back!"

And taking the infant in her arms, and seating herself at a little
distance, she rocked it to and fro on her bosom, and prattled to it, and
kissed it between every word, and laughed and wept by fits, as ever and
anon she cast over her shoulder her playful, mirthful glance upon the
father to whom those fading stars smiled sadly their last farewell. How
beautiful she seemed as she thus sat, unconscious of the future! Still half
a child herself, her child laughing to her laughter, — two soft triflers on
the brink of the grave! Over her throat, as she bent, fell, like a golden
cloud, her redundant hair; it covered her treasure like a veil of light, and
the child's little hands put it aside from time to time, to smile through
the parted tresses, and then to cover its face and peep and smile again.
It were cruel to damp that joy, more cruel still to share it.

"Viola," said Zanoni, at last, "dost thou remember that, seated by the
cave on the moonlit beach, in our bridal isle, thou once didst ask me
for this amulet? — the charm of a superstition long vanished from the
world, with the creed to which it belonged. It is the last relic of my
native land, and my mother, on her deathbed, placed it round my neck.
I told thee then I would give it thee on that day *when the laws of our being
should become the same.*"

"I remember it well."

"Tomorrow it shall be thine!"

"Ah, that dear tomorrow!" And, gently laying down her child, — for it slept now, — she threw herself on his breast, and pointed to the dawn that began greyly to creep along the skies.

There, in those horror-breathing walls, the day-star looked through the dismal bars upon those three beings, in whom were concentrated whatever is most tender in human ties; whatever is most mysterious in the combinations of the human mind; the sleeping Innocence; the trustful Affection, that, contented with a touch, a breath, can foresee no sorrow; the weary Science that, traversing all the secrets of creation, comes at last to Death for their solution, and still clings, as it nears the threshold, to the breast of Love. Thus, within, *the within,* — a dungeon; without, the *without,* — stately with marts and halls, with palaces and temples; Revenge and Terror, at their dark schemes and counter-schemes; to and fro, upon the tide of the shifting passions, reeled the destinies of men and nations; and hard at hand that day-star, waning into space, looked with impartial eye on the church tower and the guillotine. Up springs the blithesome morn. In yon gardens the birds renew their familiar song. The fishes are sporting through the freshening waters of the Seine. The gladness of divine nature, the roar and dissonance of mortal life, awake again: the trader unbars his windows; the flower-girls troop gaily to their haunts; busy feet are tramping to the daily drudgeries that revolutions which strike down kings and kaisers, leave the same Cain's heritage to the boor; the wagons groan and reel to the mart; Tyranny, up betimes, holds its pallid levee; Conspiracy, that hath not slept, hears the clock, and whispers to its own heart, "The hour draws near." A group gather, eager-eyed, round the purlieus of the Convention Hall; today decides the sovereignty of France, — about the courts of the Tribunal their customary hum and stir. No matter what the hazard of the die, or who the ruler, this day eighty heads shall fall!

. . .

And she slept so sweetly. Wearied out with joy, secure in the presence of the eyes regained, she had laughed and wept herself to sleep; and still in that slumber there seemed a happy consciousness that the loved was by, — the lost was found. For she smiled and murmured to herself, and breathed his name often, and stretched out her arms, and sighed if they touched him not. He gazed upon her as he stood apart, — with what emotions it were vain to say. She would wake no more to him; she could not know how dearly the safety of that sleep was purchased. That morrow she had so yearned for, — it had come at last. *How would she greet the eve?* Amidst all the exquisite hopes with which love and youth contemplate the future, her eyes had closed. Those hopes still lent their iris-colors to her dreams. She would wake to live! Tomorrow, and the

Reign of Terror was no more; the prison gates would be opened, — she would go forth, with their child, into that summer-world of light. And *he?* — he turned, and his eye fell upon the child; it was broad awake, and that clear, serious, thoughtful look which it mostly wore, watched him with a solemn steadiness. He bent over and kissed its lips.

"Never more," he murmured, "O heritor of love and grief, — never more wilt thou see me in thy visions; never more will the light of those eyes be fed by celestial commune; never more can my soul guard from thy pillow the trouble and the disease. Not such as I would have vainly shaped it, must be thy lot. In common with thy race, it must be thine to suffer, to struggle, and to err. But mild be thy human trials, and strong be thy spirit to love and to believe! And thus, as I gaze upon thee, — thus may my nature breathe into thine its last and most intense desire; may my love for thy mother pass to thee, and in thy looks may she hear my spirit comfort and console her. Hark! they come! Yes! I await ye both beyond the grave!"

The door slowly opened; the jailer appeared, and through the aperture rushed, at the same instant, a ray of sunlight: it streamed over the fair, hushed face of the happy sleeper, — it played like a smile upon the lips of the child that, still, mute, and steadfast, watched the movements of its father. At that moment Viola muttered in her sleep, "The day is come, — the gates are open! Give me thy hand; we will go forth! To sea, to sea! How the sunshine plays upon the waters! — to home, beloved one, to home again!"

"Citizen, thine hour is come!"

"Hist! she sleeps! A moment! There, it is done! thank Heaven! — and *still* she sleeps!" He would not kiss, lest he should awaken her, but gently placed round her neck the amulet that would speak to her, hereafter, the farewell, — and promise, in that farewell, reunion! He is at the threshold, — he turns again, and again. The door closes! He is gone forever!

She woke at last, — she gazed round. "Zanoni, it is day!" No answer but the low wail of her child. Merciful Heaven! was it then all a dream? She tossed back the long tresses that must veil her sight; she felt the amulet on her bosom, — it was *no* dream! "O God! and he is gone!" She sprang to the door, — she shrieked aloud. The jailer comes. "My husband, my child's father?"

"He is gone before thee, woman!"

"Whither? Speak — speak!"

"To the guillotine!" — and the black door closed again.

It closed upon the senseless! As a lightning-flash, Zanoni's words, his sadness, the true meaning of his mystic gift, the very sacrifice he made for her, all became distinct for a moment to her mind, — and then darkness swept on it like a storm, yet darkness which had its light. And while she sat there, mute, rigid, voiceless, as congealed to stone, *A Vision*, like a wind, glided over the deeps within, — the grim court, the judge, the jury, the accuser; and amidst the victims the one dauntless and radiant form.

"Thou knowest the danger to the State, — confess!"

"I know; and I keep my promise. Judge, I reveal thy doom! I know that the Anarchy thou callest a State expires with the setting of this sun. Hark, to the tramp without; hark to the roar of voices! Room there, ye dead! — room in hell for Robespierre and his crew!"

They hurry into the court, — the hasty and pale messengers; there is confusion and fear and dismay! "Off with the conspirator, and tomorrow the woman thou wouldst have saved shall die!"

"Tomorrow, president, the steel falls on *thee!*"

On, through the crowded and roaring streets, on moves the Procession of Death. Ha, brave people! thou art aroused at last. They shall not die! Death is dethroned! — Robespierre has fallen! — they rush to the rescue! Hideous in the tumbrel, by the side of Zanoni, raved and gesticulated that form which, in his prophetic dreams, he had seen his companion at the place of death. "Save us! — save us!" howled the atheist Nicot. "On, brave populace! we *shall* be saved!" And through the crowd, her dark hair streaming wild, her eyes flashing fire, pressed a female form, "My Clarence!" she shrieked, in the soft Southern language native to the ears of Viola; "butcher! what hast thou done with Clarence?" Her eyes roved over the eager faces of the prisoners; she saw not the one she sought. "Thank Heaven! — thank Heaven! I am not thy murderess!"

Nearer and nearer press the populace, — another moment, and the deathsman is defrauded. O Zanoni! why still upon *thy* brow the resignation that speaks no hope? Tramp! tramp! through the streets dash the armed troop; faithful to his orders, Black Henriot leads them on. Tramp! tramp! over the craven and scattered crowd! Here, flying in disorder, — there, trampled in the mire, the shrieking rescuers! And amidst them, stricken by the sabers of the guard, her long hair blood-bedabbled, lies the Italian woman; and still upon her writhing lips sits joy, as they murmur, "Clarence! I have not destroyed thee!"

On to the Barriere du Trone. It frowns dark in the air, — the giant instrument of murder! One after one to the glaive, — another and another and another! Mercy! O mercy! Is the bridge between the sun and the shades so brief, — brief as a sigh? There, there, — *his* turn has come. "Die not yet; leave me not behind; hear me — hear me!" shrieked the inspired sleeper. "What! and thou smilest still!" They smiled, — those pale lips, — and *with* the smile, the place of doom, the headsman, the horror vanished. With that smile, all space seemed suffused in eternal sunshine. Up from the earth he rose; he hovered over her, — a thing not of matter, an *idea* of joy and light! Behind, Heaven opened, deep after deep; and the Hosts of Beauty were seen, rank upon rank, afar; and "Welcome!" in a myriad melodies, broke from your choral multitude, ye People of the Skies, — "welcome! O purified by sacrifice, and immortal only through the grave, — this it is to die." And radiant amidst the radiant, the *Image* stretched forth its arms, and murmured to the sleeper: "Companion of Eternity! — *This* it is to die!"

. . .

"Ho! wherefore do they make us signs from the house-tops? Wherefore gather the crowds through the street? Why sounds the bell? Why shrieks the tocsin? Hark to the guns! — the armed clash! Fellow-captives, is there hope for us at last?"

So gasp out the prisoners, each to each. Day wanes — evening closes; still they press their white faces to the bars, and still from window and from house-top they see the smiles of friends, — the waving signals! "Hurrah!" at last, — "Hurrah! Robespierre is fallen! The Reign of Terror is no more! God hath permitted us to live!"

Yes; cast thine eyes into the hall where the tyrant and his conclave hearkened to the roar without! Fulfilling the prophecy of Dumas, Henriot, drunk with blood and alcohol, reels within, and chucks his gory saber on the floor. "All is lost!"

"Wretch! thy cowardice hath destroyed us!" yelled the fierce Coffinhal, as he hurled the coward from the window.

Calm as despair stands the stern St. Just; the palsied Couthon crawls, groveling, beneath table; a shot, — an explosion! Robespierre would destroy himself! The trembling hand has mangled, and failed to kill! The clock of the Hotel de Ville strikes the third hour. Through the battered door, along the gloomy passages, into the Death-hall, burst the crowd. Mangled, livid, blood-stained, speechless but not unconscious, sits haughty yet, in his seat erect, the Master-Murderer! Around him they throng; they hoot, — they execrate, their faces gleaming in the tossing torches! *He*, and not the starry Magian, the *real* Sorcerer! And round *his* last hours gather the Fiends he raised!

They drag him forth! Open thy gates, inexorable prison! The Conciergerie receives its prey! Never a word again on earth spoke Maximilien Robespierre! Pour forth thy thousands, and tens of thousands, emancipated Paris! To the Place de la Revolution rolls the tumbrel of the King of Terror, — St. Just, Dumas, Couthon, his companions to the grave! A woman — a childless woman, with hoary hair — springs to his side, "Thy death makes me drunk with joy!" He opened his bloodshot eyes, — "Descend to hell with the curses of wives and mothers!"

The headsmen wrench the rag from the shattered jaw; a shriek, and the crowd laugh, and the axe descends amidst the shout of the countless thousands, and blackness rushes on thy soul, Maximilien Robespierre! So ended the Reign of Terror.

. . .

Daylight in the prison. From cell to cell they hurry with the news, — crowd upon crowd; the joyous captives mingled with the very jailers, who, for fear, would fain seem joyous too; they stream through the dens and alleys of the grim house they will shortly leave. They burst into a cell, forgotten since the previous morning. They found there a young female, sitting upon her wretched bed; her arms crossed upon her bosom, her face raised upward; the eyes unclosed, and a smile of more than serenity — of bliss — upon her lips. Even in the riot of their joy, they drew back in astonishment and awe. Never had they seen life so beautiful; and as they crept nearer, and with noiseless feet, they saw that the lips breathed not, that the repose was of marble, that the beauty and the ecstasy were of death. They gathered round in silence; and lo! at her feet there was a young infant, who, wakened by their tread, looked at them steadfastly, and with its rosy fingers played with its dead mother's robe. An orphan there in a dungeon vault!

"Poor one!" said a female (herself a parent), "and they say the father fell yesterday; and now the mother! Alone in the world, what can be its fate?"

The infant smiled fearlessly on the crowd, as the woman spoke thus. And the old priest, who stood amongst them, said gently, "Woman, see! the orphan smiles! *The fatherless are the care of God!*"

Note

The curiosity which Zanoni has excited among those who think it worth while to dive into the subtler meanings they believe it intended to convey, may excuse me in adding a few words, not in explanation of its mysteries, but upon the principles which permit them. Zanoni is not, as some have supposed, an allegory; but beneath the narrative it relates, *typical* meanings are concealed. It is to be regarded in two characters, distinct yet harmonious, — 1st, that of the simple and objective fiction, in which* the reader judges the writer by the usual canons, — namely, by the consistency of his characters under such admitted circumstances, the interest of his story, and the coherence of his plot; of the work regarded in this view, it is not my intention to say anything, whether in exposition of the design, or in defense of the execution. No typical meanings (which, in plain terms are but moral suggestions, more or less numerous, more or less subtle) can afford just excuse to a writer of fiction, for the errors he should avoid in the most ordinary novel. We have no right to expect the most ingenious reader to search for the inner meaning, if the obvious course of the narrative be tedious and displeasing. It is, on the contrary, in proportion as we are satisfied with the objective sense of a work of imagination, that we are inclined to search into its depths for the more secret intentions of the author. Were we not so divinely charmed with "Faust," and "Hamlet," and "Prometheus," so ardently carried on by the interest of the story told to the common understanding, we should trouble ourselves little with the types in each which all of us can detect, — none of us can elucidate; none elucidate, for the essence of type is mystery. We behold the figure, we cannot lift the veil. The author himself is not called upon to explain what he designed. An allegory is a personation of distinct and definite things, — virtues or qualities, — and the key can be given easily; but a writer who conveys typical meanings, may express them in myriads. He cannot disentangle all the hues which commingle into the

---

* once granting the license of the author to select a subject which is, or appears to be, preternatural

light he seeks to cast upon truth; and therefore the great masters of this enchanted soil, — Fairyland of Fairyland, Poetry imbedded beneath Poetry, — wisely leave to each mind to guess at such truths as best please or instruct it. To have asked Goethe to explain the "Faust" would have entailed as complex and puzzling an answer as to have asked Mephistopheles to explain what is beneath the earth we tread on. The stores beneath may differ for every passenger; each step may require a new description; and what is treasure to the geologist may be rubbish to the miner. Six worlds may lie under a sod, but to the common eye they are but six layers of stone.

Art in itself, if not necessarily typical, is essentially a suggester of something subtler than that which it embodies to the sense. What Pliny tells us of a great painter of old, is true of most great painters; "their works express something beyond the works," — "more felt than understood." This belongs to the concentration of intellect which high art demands, and which, of all the arts, sculpture best illustrates. Take Thorwaldsen's Statue of Mercury, — it is but a single figure, yet it tells to those conversant with mythology a whole legend. The god has removed the pipe from his lips, because he has already lulled to sleep the Argus, whom you do not see. He is pressing his heel against his sword, because the moment is come when he may slay his victim. Apply the principle of this noble concentration of art to the moral writer: he, too, gives to your eye but a single figure; yet each attitude, each expression, may refer to events and truths you must have the learning to remember, the acuteness to penetrate, or the imagination to conjecture. But to a classical judge of sculpture, would not the exquisite pleasure of discovering the all not told in Thorwaldsen's masterpiece be destroyed if the artist had engraved in detail his meaning at the base of the statue? Is it not the same with the typical sense which the artist in words conveys? The pleasure of divining art in each is the noble exercise of all by whom art is worthily regarded.

We of the humbler race not unreasonably shelter ourselves under the authority of the masters, on whom the world's judgment is pronounced; and great names are cited, not with the arrogance of equals, but with the humility of inferiors.

The author of Zanoni gives, then, no key to mysteries, be they trivial or important, which may be found in the secret chambers by those who lift the tapestry from the wall; but out of the many solutions of the main enigma — if enigma, indeed, there be — which have been sent to him, he ventures to select the one which he subjoins, from the ingenuity and thought which it displays, and from respect for the distinguished writer (one of the most eminent our time has produced) who deemed him worthy of an honor he is proud to display. He leaves it to the reader to agree with, or dissent from the explanation. "A hundred men," says the old Platonist, "may read the book by the help of the same lamp, yet all may differ on the text, for the lamp only lights the characters, — the mind must divine the meaning." The object of a parable is not that of a problem; it does not seek to convince, but to suggest. It takes the thought below the surface of the understanding to the deeper intelligence which the world rarely tasks. It is not sunlight on the water; it is a hymn chanted to the nymph who hearkens and awakes below.

. . .

"Zanoni Explained.
by ——."

Mejnour: — Contemplation of the Actual, — *Science.* Always old, and must last as long as the Actual. Less fallible than Idealism, but less practically potent, from its ignorance of the human heart.

Zanoni: — Contemplation of the Ideal, — *Idealism.* Always necessarily sympathetic: lives by enjoyment; and is therefore typified by eternal youth. ("I do not understand the making Idealism less undying (on this scene of existence) than Science." — Commentator. Because, granting the above premises, Idealism is more subjected than Science to the Affections, or to Instinct, because the Affections, sooner or later, force Idealism into the Actual, and in the Actual its immortality departs. The only absolutely Actual portion of the work is found in the concluding scenes that depict the Reign of Terror. The introduction of this part was objected to by some as out of keeping with the fanciful portions that preceded it. But if the writer of the solution has rightly shown or suggested the intention of the author, the most strongly and rudely actual scene of the age in which the story is cast was the necessary and harmonious completion of the whole. The excesses and crimes of Humanity are the grave of the Ideal. — Author.) Idealism is the potent Interpreter and Prophet of the Real; but its powers are impaired in proportion to their exposure to human passion.

Viola: — Human *Instinct.* (Hardly worthy to be called *Love,* as Love would not forsake its object at the bidding of Superstition.) Resorts, first in its aspiration after the Ideal, to tinsel shows; then relinquishes these for a higher love; but is still, from the conditions of its nature, inadequate to this, and liable to suspicion and mistrust. Its greatest force (Maternal Instinct) has power to penetrate some secrets, to trace some movements of the Ideal, but, too feeble to command them, yields to Superstition, sees sin where there is none, while committing sin, under a false guidance; weakly seeking refuge amidst the very tumults of the warring passions of the Actual, while deserting the serene Ideal, — pining, nevertheless, in the absence of the Ideal, and expiring (not perishing, but becoming transmuted) in the aspiration after having the laws of the two natures reconciled.

(It might best suit popular apprehension to call these three the Understanding, the Imagination, and the Heart.)

Child: − *Newborn Instinct,* while trained and informed by Idealism, promises a preter-human result by its early, incommunicable vigilance and intelligence, but is compelled, by inevitable orphanhood, and the one-half of the laws of its existence, to lapse into ordinary conditions.

Aidon-Ai: − *Faith,* which manifests its splendor, and delivers its oracles, and imparts its marvels, only to the higher moods of the soul, and whose directed antagonism is with Fear; so that those who employ the resources of Fear must dispense with those of Faith. Yet aspiration holds open a way of restoration, and may summon Faith, even when the cry issues from beneath the yoke of fear.

Dweller of the Threshold: − *Fear (or Horror),* from whose ghastliness men are protected by the opacity of the region of Prescription and Custom. The moment this protection is relinquished, and the human spirit pierces the cloud, and enters alone on the unexplored regions of Nature, this Natural Horror haunts it, and is to be successfully encountered only by defiance, − by aspiration towards, and reliance on, the Former and Director of Nature, whose Messenger and Instrument of reassurance is Faith.

Mervale: − *Conventionalism.*

Nicot: − Base, groveling, malignant *Passion.*

Glyndon: − *Unsustained Aspiration*: Would follow Instinct, but is deterred by Conventionalism, is overawed by Idealism, yet attracted, and transiently inspired, but has not steadiness for the initiatory contemplation of the Actual. He conjoins its snatched privileges with a besetting sensualism, and suffers at once from the horror of the one and the disgust of the other, involving the innocent in the fatal conflict of his spirit. When on the point of perishing, he is rescued by Idealism, and, unable to rise to that species of existence, is grateful to be replunged into the region of the Familiar, and takes up his rest henceforth in Custom. (Mirror of Young Manhood.)

. . .

Argument.

Human Existence subject to, and exempt from, ordinary conditions (Sickness, Poverty, Ignorance, Death).

Science is ever striving to carry the most gifted beyond ordinary conditions, − the result being as many victims as efforts, and the striver being finally left a solitary, − for his object is unsuitable to the natures he has to deal with.

The pursuit of the Ideal involves so much emotion as to render the

Idealist vulnerable by human passion, however long and well guarded, still vulnerable, — liable, at last, to a union with Instinct. Passion obscures both Insight and Forecast. All effort to elevate Instinct to Idealism is abortive, the laws of their being not coinciding (in the early stage of the existence of the one). Instinct is either alarmed, and takes refuge in Superstition or Custom, or is left helpless to human charity, or given over to providential care.

Idealism, stripped of in sight and forecast, loses its serenity, becomes subject once more to the horror from which it had escaped, and by accepting its aids, forfeits the higher help of Faith; aspiration, however, remaining still possible, and, thereby, slow restoration; and also, *something better.*

Summoned by aspiration, Faith extorts from Fear itself the saving truth to which Science continues blind, and which Idealism itself hails as its crowning acquisition, — the inestimable *proof* wrought out by all labors and all conflicts.

Pending the elaboration of this proof,

Conventionalism plods on, safe and complacent;

Selfish passion perishes, groveling and hopeless;

Instinct sleeps, in order to a loftier waking; and

Idealism learns, as its ultimate lesson, that self-sacrifice is true redemption; that the region beyond the grave is the fitting one for exemption from mortal conditions; and that Death is the everlasting portal, indicated by the finger of God, — the broad avenue through which man does not issue solitary and stealthy into the region of Free Existence, but enters triumphant, hailed by a hierarchy of immortal natures.

The result is (in other words), *that the universal human lot is, after all, that of the highest privilege.*

Printed in the United Kingdom
by Lightning Source UK Ltd.
101380UKS00004B/184